WHITE-JACKET

HERMAN MELVILLE was born in New York City in 1819, a descendant of English and Dutch colonial families. His father died bankrupt in 1832, leaving his widow and eight children in penury. Melville left school at the age of 15 and after taking various jobs he sailed on a trading ship to Liverpool in the summer of 1839, a trip that was to form the basis for *Redburn* (1849). In 1841 he joined the whaling ship *Acushnet*, bound for the South Seas, abandoning it with a companion in the Marquesas Islands. This and other voyages on whaling boats were to provide the material for *Moby-Dick* (1851). The South Seas became the setting and subject for his novels *Typee* (1846) and *Omoo* (1847). After a period in Honolulu, he returned to the USA in 1843–4 as an ordinary seaman aboard the frigate *United States*, the model for the *Neversink* in *White-Jacket* (1850). In 1850 Melville moved with his wife and son to a farm near Pittsfield, Massachusetts, and became a close friend of his neighbour, Nathaniel Hawthorne, to whom *Moby-Dick* is dedicated. His *Piazza Tales* appeared in 1856, and a year later *The Confidence-Man* was published. The increasingly metaphysical and exploratory cast of his writing meant that his popularity had begun to wane long before, however, and by 1866 he was forced to make a living as an inspector of customs at the port of New York. He died in obscurity in 1891, leaving a number of poems and *Billy Budd, Sailor* in manuscript.

TONY TANNER is a Fellow of King's College, Cambridge. His books on American literature include *The Reign of Wonder*, *City of Words*, and *Scenes of Nature, Signs of Men*. For the World's Classics he has edited Melville's *Moby-Dick* and *The Confidence-Man* (also with John Dugdale).

JOHN DUGDALE is the author of a forthcoming study of the novelist Thomas Pynchon.

THE WORLD'S CLASSICS

HERMAN MELVILLE

White-Jacket
or
The World in a
Man-of-War

With an Introduction by
TONY TANNER

and Explanatory Notes by
JOHN DUGDALE

Oxford   New York

OXFORD UNIVERSITY PRESS

Oxford University Press, Walton Street, Oxford OX2 6DP

Oxford New York Toronto
Delhi Bombay Calcutta Madras Karachi
Petaling Jaya Singapore Hong Kong Tokyo
Nairobi Dar es Salaam Cape Town
Melbourne Auckland

and associated companies in
Berlin Ibadan

Oxford is a trade mark of Oxford University Press

First published as a World's Classics paperback 1990
Reprinted 1992

British Library Cataloguing in Publication Data

Melville, Herman, 1819–1891
White-Jacket, or, The world in a man-of-war.
I. Title
813.3

ISBN 0-19-281828-7

Library of Congress Cataloging in Publication Data

Melville, Herman, 1819–1891.
White-Jacket, or, The world in a man-of-war/Herman Melville; with an
introduction by Tony Tanner; and explanatory notes by John Dugdale.
p. cm.—(The World's classics)
Includes bibliographical references.
1. United States—History, Naval—19th century—Fiction.
I. Dugdale, John. II. Title. III. Title: World in a man-of-war.
IV. Series.
[PS2384.W5 1990]   813'.3—dc20   89–70906

ISBN 0-19-281828-7

Printed in Great Britain by
BPCC Hazells Ltd
Aylesbury, Bucks

CONTENTS

CONTENTS

CONTENTS

INTRODUCTION

'This man-of-war book, My Dear Sir, is in some parts rather man-of-warish in style—rather aggressive I fear.—But you, who like myself, have experienced in person the usages to which a sailor is subjected, will not wonder, perhaps, at any thing in the book. Would to God, that every man who shall read it, had been before the mast in an armed ship, that he might know something himself of what he shall only read of.' (Melville to Richard Henry Dana, 6 October 1849.)

'Can't a man ask a question here without being flogged?'
'No,' shouted the captain; 'nobody shall open his mouth aboard this vessel but myself;' and began laying the blows upon his back, swinging half round between each blow to give it full effect. As he went on his passion increased, and he danced about the deck, calling out as he swung the rope, 'If you want to know what I flog you for, I'll tell you. It's because I like to do it!—because I like to do it!—It suits me! That's what I do it for!'

The man writhed under the pain, until he could endure it no longer, when he called out, with an exclamation more common among foreigners than with us—'Oh, Jesus Christ! Oh, Jesus Christ!'

'Don't call on Jesus Christ,' shouted the captain; *'he can't help you. Call on Captain T*—he's the man. He can help you! Jesus Christ can't help you now!' . . . 'You see your condition! You see where I've got you all, and you know what to expect! You've been mistaken in me—you didn't know what I was! Now you know what I am! I'll make you toe the mark, every soul of you, or I'll flog you all, fore and aft, from the boy up!—You've got a driver over you! Yes, a *slave-driver—a negro-driver!*'

THIS is from the most famous—or sensational—scene in Dana's *Two Years Before the Mast* and perhaps the best-known, even notorious scene in nineteenth-century American fiction. The whipping to death of Tom in *Uncle Tom's Cabin* would subsequently arouse a more widespread public horror, but, appearing in 1840, Dana's scene seemed uniquely shocking. Not that flogging in the navy was news: the two 'institutions' had been for too long infamously inseparable. What Dana's account inscribes is an intolerable contradiction at the heart of the newly emerged—recently invented—republic of America itself. This new country, as much a conceptual construct as a land, as much an abstraction as a terrain, was founded on proclaimed ideas and ideals of liberty and equality, yet it was economically quite substantially grounded in slavery. Whereas the axe—the instrument of land-clearance, agriculture, settlement, and thus culture—was the symbol of its public triumph and the ever-advancing frontier; the whip was the mark of its secret shame, the cancer of a slavery always seeking to spread. The shock of Dana's scene is the spectacle of a white American seaman being flogged like a slave, and of a white American captain glorying in his blasphemous tyranny and sadistically identifying with a slave-driver with unashamed pleasure. Of that flogged sailor it could be said, as Melville was to write in *White-Jacket*: 'For him our Revolution was in vain; to him our Declaration of Independence is a lie.' This dread possibility was a nerve which Dana's scene electrically touched on. Melville's work probes relentlessly deeper.

Melville certainly had Dana's book well in mind when he wrote *White-Jacket*. In a letter to Dana of 1 May 1850, he refers to 'those strange, congenial feelings, with which after my first voyage, I for the first time read "Two Years Before the Mast", and while so engaged was, as it were, tied and welded to you by a sort of Siamese link of affectionate sympathy'. Dana, a Harvard student of law who embarked on his adventure 'before the mast' (that is, with the common sailors of the forecastle) partly for health reasons and for a strictly limited period ('two years') never forgets in his book that he is a gentleman-sailor—an oxymoron for the time. A large part of his satisfaction derives from the discovery that 'I—home-bred, gentleman-bred, college-bred—could stand it as well as the roughest of them', but while he is indeed initiated into the seaman's life, achieves (or proves) his manhood, and is accepted as a genuine member of the crew, he never forgets and never wants to forget his 'difference'. This is not simply snobbery or élitism. It has more to do with wishing both to share in immediate common experience—the sailor—and to retain the reflective privilege of detachment and commentary—the lawyer-writer. It is also related to the more general problem felt with especial urgency by many American writers (among others): how to hold on to some individualizing specialness or distinctness without seeming to support un-American notions of hierarchy, class, privilege, and rank. How to be a Gentleman and a Democrat? All these considerations, barring some modifications, apply to Melville as well. He gives a very direct nod to Dana at the start of *Moby-Dick*: 'When I go to sea, I go as a simple sailor, right before the mast' says Ishmael; but when Melville goes to write, he goes as a complex writer, to some lonely space of his own. (Other writers would use Dana's phrase as a metaphor to gesture towards direct experience unmediated by tradition or convention, as for example Thoreau at the end of *Walden*: 'I did not wish to take a cabin passage, but rather to go before the mast and on the deck of the world, for there I could best see the moonlight amid the mountains.') And these words from *White-Jacket*: 'Virtue must come down from aloft, even as our blessed Redeemer came down to redeem our whole man-of-war world; to that end, mixing with its sailors and sinners as equals', might be compared to Dana's assertion: 'We must come down from our heights . . . if we would learn truths by strong contrasts.'

There are a number of similarities, and revealing differences, between Dana's book and Melville's. Dana, seeking both to learn and control a whole new experiential world, limits himself as far as possible to information—facts and figures, 'the life of a common sailor as it really is'. The weather, the sails, the different jobs, the shipboard routine, the longitude and latitude, the wages, the quantities of goods—all these—and more—are matters for almost itemizing report. The surfaces of things are, as it were, meticulously inventoried. Melville engages in a lot of this as well, but invariably with some Melvillian twist or elaboration. We cannot imagine Dana writing, as Melville does, of 'serenely concocting information into wisdom'. When Melville writes about rounding Cape Horn he pays specific tribute to Dana's own account ('But if you want the best idea of Cape Horn, get my friend Dana's unmatchable *Two Years Before the Mast*. . . . His chapters describing Cape Horn must have been written with an icicle.'); but we cannot imagine Dana adding after his account, as

Melville does: 'But, sailor or landsman, there is some sort of a Cape Horn for all.' Some of Dana's characters almost seem to prefigure some of Melville's—for instance Bill Jackson, 'the best specimen of a thoroughbred English sailor that I ever saw', seems to anticipate the figure of Jack Chase. Again, just as Captain Thomas threatens to turn Dana's ship, the *Pilgrim*, into 'hell afloat' so Melville tells us that men-of-war are known among sailors as 'Floating Hells'. Dana is interested in 'manliness' as it is defined or determined at sea, just as Melville has an eye for the 'manhood-testing conjuncture', though here again Melville's speculations range more widely. One final similarity involving a yet greater difference: near the end of his voyage Dana describes a 'narrow escape' when he is almost 'thrown violently from the height of ninety or a hundred feet overboard, or, what is worse, upon the deck'. He regains his footing and this effectively ends the voyage, for there are only two incident-free chapters to follow. Melville makes the final climax of his voyage a terrifying account of a tremendous fall which never happened to him but is instead his own amplification of a more prosaic account of a somewhat less tremendous fall which he found in Nathaniel Ames's *Mariner's Sketches*. Following which there are, indeed, two incident-free chapters to conclude before—like Dana—he is back in home harbour.

That Melville was well aware of the crucial difference between his writing and Dana's—in spite of the many similarities and 'congenialities'—is clear from another passage from the letter last quoted:

About the 'whaling voyage'—I am half-way in the work, and am very glad that your suggestion so jumps with mine. It will be a strange sort of book, tho', I fear; blubber is blubber you know; tho' you may get oil out of it, the poetry runs as hard as sap from a frozen maple tree;—and to cook the thing up, one must needs throw in a little fancy, which from the nature of the thing, must be ungainly as the gambols of the whales themselves. Yet I mean to give the truth of the thing, spite of this.

Throwing in fancy to cook things up and indulging in ungainly gambolling in pursuit of poetry was just exactly what Dana would never do: he stayed squarely—and powerfully—within the known and knowable longitudes and latitudes of experience. He was, after all, a lawyer and he kept scrupulously to the brief he had set himself. Melville was a writer and in 1849—when he wrote *Redburn* in two months and then, incredibly, *White-Jacket* in two more—he was a writer at odds with himself, or with what he imagined was his public, and in trouble. While he was writing *Mardi* in 1848, Melville wrote to John Murray: 'Proceeding in my narrative of *facts* I began to feel an incurable distaste for the same; and a longing to plume my pinions for a flight, and felt irked, cramped and fettered by plodding along with dull common places,—So suddenly standing [abandoning?] the thing alltogether, I went to work heart and soul at a romance which is now in fair progress.' (25 March.) *Mardi* came out on 14 April 1849 and was what might be called an instant unsuccess. With a young family Melville now needed money badly and immediately turned to a different mode of writing. As he explained to Richard Bentley:

I have now in preparation a thing of a widely different cast from *Mardi*:—a plain, straightforward, amusing narrative of personal experience—the son of a gentleman on his first voyage to sea as a sailor—no metaphysics, no conic-sections, nothing but cakes and ale. I have shifted my ground from the South Seas to a different quarter of the globe—nearer home—and what I write I have almost wholly picked up by my own observations under comical circumstances. (5 June.)

This 'widely different' type of writing resulted in *Redburn* and *White-Jacket*, and, if we are to believe a letter he wrote after their publication to his stepfather Lemuel Shaw, it was writing against the grain:

They are two *jobs*, which I have done for money—being forced to it, as other men are to sawing wood. And while I have felt obliged to refrain from writing the kind of book I would wish to; yet, in writing these two books, I have not repressed myself much—so far as *they* are concerned; but have spoken pretty much as I feel.—Being books, then, written in this way, my only desire for their 'success' (as it is called) springs from my pocket, and not from my heart. So far as I am individually concerned, and independent of my pocket, it is my

earnest desire to write those sort of books which are said to 'fail'.—
Pardon this egotism.'

By Melville's relatively modest standards, these two '*jobs*' were
quite successful; and we need not decide that his turn to a more
'cakes and ale' sort of writing was wholly uncongenial to him,
nor a complete, cynical–financial perversion of his instincts as a
writer. As we have seen in his letter to Dana, he was fully
resolved to add poetry to blubber in his next book—*Moby-Dick*
of course; but in a letter to Evert Duyckinck of 12 February
1851, in the course of some unstinting praise for the work of
Hawthorne, he adds a slight reservation which indicates that he
sensed that writing which aimed too directly for the 'deeper
meanings' might suffer from its own kind of impoverishments
and attenuations. 'Some of those sketches are wonderfully
subtle. Their deeper meanings are worthy of a Brahmin. Still
there is something lacking—a good deal lacking—to the plump
sphericity of the man. What is that?—He doesn't patronise the
butcher—he needs roast-beef, done rare.' In *White-Jacket*, in
more ways, I am sure, than he intended by his use of the image,
Melville did indeed 'patronise the butcher'. But the butcher
turned out to be the American Navy.

The biographical facts are as follows. Herman Melville first
went to sea in June 1839 when he was 19. He joined a trans-
Atlantic packet sailing between New York and Liverpool (see
Redburn). He subsequently joined the whaling ship *Acushnet* on
31 December 1840 at Fairhaven, and deserted in the Marquesas
(see *Typee*). He joined another whaling ship and again
deserted, this time in Tahiti (see *Omoo*). He made his way to
the Hawaiian Islands in May 1843, and worked in a store in
Honolulu until August, when he signed on in a United States
frigate called, indeed, *United States*. There followed fourteen
months of naval service before he reached Boston on 14
October 1844. It was his last voyage and is, of course, the one
described—along with a number of invented or interpolated
episodes—in *White-Jacket*. In June 1851 he wrote to Hawthorne:
'Until I was twenty-five, I had no development at all. From my
twenty-fifth year I date my life.' That twenty-fifth birthday
occurred shortly before the end of his voyage on the *United*

States. During that voyage 163 floggings are reported as having taken place—all hands always summoned to witness punishment—and, as in Dana's book, the horrific flogging scene provides the explosive emotional centre of *White-Jacket*. But this final similarity between the two books serves to bring into focus their most important difference. Dana's first reaction to the flogging is a mixture of sickness, anger, and excitement. 'A man—a human being, made in God's likeness—fastened up and flogged like a beast! The first and almost uncontrollable impulse was resistance. But what was to be done?' And gradually the lawyer in him, we might say, becomes uppermost. 'But beside the numbers, what is there for sailors to do? If they resist, it is mutiny; and if they succeed, and take the vessel, it is piracy. Bad as it was it must be borne. It is what a sailor ships for.' Elsewhere he supports and justifies the captain's absolute authority and the necessity for corporal punishment. As a gentleman he averts his eyes from the scene of the flogging: 'Disgusted, sick, and horror-struck, I turned away and leaned over the rail and looked down into the water.' As a lawyer he 'vows' that 'if God should ever give me the means, I would do something to redress the grievances and relieve the sufferings of that poor class of beings, of whom I then was one'. And he seems to think that more intelligence and efficiency in running ships will gradually make flogging obsolete.

Melville's reaction is different by 180 degrees, as it were. He attacks man-made law on all sides. He attacks the 'arbitrary laws' by which a human being can be 'scourged worse than a hound . . . for things not essentially criminal'. He attacks the laws—or legalism—of the land which serves to legitimate and support that so-called naval law, which is in fact a 'tyranny' that is permitted to 'convert into slaves some of the citizens of a nation of free-men', and he invokes the 'Law of Nature' with a supporting quotation from Blackstone. This law is 'coeval with mankind, dictated by God himself, superior in obligation to any other, and no human laws are of any validity if contrary to this'. Dana exhibits the spirit of functionalism which was coming to mark American law. He respects the law already in place and considers how it might be modified and its codifications adjusted. Melville cuts through these constructs and appeals to a quite different order or level of reality. The Founding Fathers—Jefferson certainly—believed in Natural Law, and indeed that what they were doing (writing 'America') was grounded in it. But during the first half of the nineteenth century the discourse of law in America was becoming more instrumental and local, and less given to general statements and ideal claims. In his excellent book *Law and Letters* Robert Ferguson has considered some of the implications of this and comments very illuminatingly on the difference between Dana and Melville:

The narrowing professionalism of the mid-century lawyer is the visible side of a curious reversal in American literature. For even as leaders of the bar reject natural law in the name of a more technical expertise, a new breed of literary intellectual arises to seize the abandoned legacy. Few have noticed how frequently the writers of the American Renaissance resort to higher law as a mode of explanation, and no one has appreciated the continuities involved. Melville, Emerson, Thoreau, and Hawthorne are reacting against the past, against the civic tones and themes of early republican literature; nonetheless, it is Melville, the romantic novelist, who reaches back to natural law to condemn flogging, and not Dana, the student of law.[1]

The difference—it is the difference between two Americas and two American discourses—is nicely illustrated, as Ferguson points out, by the fact that one year after *Two Years Before the Mast*, Dana published what he called 'purely a business book', namely *The Seaman's Friend: Containing a Treatise of Practical Seamanship with Plates; A Dictionary of Sea Terms; Customs and Usages of the Merchant Services; Laws Relating to the Practical Duties of Master and Mariners*; while one year after *White-Jacket* Melville published—*Moby-Dick*.

But the treatment of flogging in *White-Jacket* is not quite as uncomplicated a matter as might at first appear. When Melville intimated to Dana that his book was 'man-of-*warish*' and

[1] Robert A. Ferguson, *Law and Letters in American Culture* (Cambridge, Mass., 1984), 266.

'aggressive' he probably had in mind his ringing denunciations of the practice of flogging in the American Navy—passages such as this:

Irrespective of incidental considerations, we assert that flogging in the Navy is opposed to the essential dignity of man, which no legislator has a right to violate; that it is oppressive, and glaringly unequal in its operations; that it is utterly repugnant to the spirit of our democratic institutions; indeed, that it involves a lingering trait of the worst times of a barbarous feudal aristocracy; in a word, we denounce it as religiously, morally, and immutably *wrong*.

However impeccable the sentiments expressed in them, these somewhat stilted and sonorous declamations hardly show Melville's style at its most imaginative or forceful. Melville is happier undermining—or at least problematizing—than uni-vocally advancing a cause, and some of these propagandist passages ring curiously hollow in spite of—or more likely because of—their strident rhetoric. *White-Jacket* has acquired the vague reputation of having brought about the abolition of flogging in the American Navy, but this is both entirely unsubstantiated and highly unlikely. Flogging in the United States Navy had been debated in Congress throughout the 1840s and an act to abolish it was finally passed on 28 September 1850. ('I am offering up devout jubilations for the abolition of the flogging law' wrote Melville to Evert Duyckinck on 6 October, 1850.) But it should be noted that *White-Jacket* was not even mentioned in the congressional debate, and indeed its publication only preceded the conclusion of the long debate by a few months. The fact is, not to put too fine a point upon it, that Melville was on fairly safe ground when he vociferated so loudly, and with such righteous indignation, about an indisputable barbarism that was about to disappear. This is in no way to question the sincerity of Melville's outrage, nor the depths of his outraged repugnance. Rather, it is to raise the question of whether this apparently fearless and principled rhetoric, so loud and clear in its support of a cause that had almost ceased to be contentious, against an abuse about to be eradicated, might not be some kind of compensation for an uneasy silence elsewhere: a strategy to deflect attention from another abuse that was growing yearly *more* contentious, an abuse that, far from being eradicated, seemed to be trying to consolidate itself in the Union to the point of threatening the union of that Union—namely, slavery. Melville is clear enough that it is entirely abhorrent that white men should be flogged like black slaves. He is not quite so clear that it is equally abhorrent for blacks to be whipped—or to be slaves either for that matter. Again, this is not to suggest that within Melville's rightly famous democratic and humane heart there lingered traces of a toxic racism, but rather that this work of 1849 contains within it some of the crucial tensions, ambivalences, and contradictions that were to tear the nation to pieces little more than a decade later. Far from pointing out black spots in Melville, I am suggesting that this work is most interesting in the way that works of great writers often are—that is, seemingly in spite of themselves. Let me just consider briefly the way the book touches on three phenomena, which were inseparably and constitutively involved in the origin of the United States: revolution (or rebellion), slavery, and egalitarianism.

Because the arbitrariness of the martial law that operated at sea was so utterly at variance with American institutions which 'claim to be based upon broad principles of political liberty and equality', Melville feels that—according to the Natural Law he invoked—'every man-of-war's-man would be morally justified in resisting the scourge to the uttermost; and, in so resisting, would be religiously justified in what would be judicially styled "the act of mutiny" itself'. This is quite in line with the justification of America's act of mutiny or rebellion against the oppressive tyranny of its parent country, or 'captain'. Melville was consistently a supporter of great political revolutions of the past, from the Greeks against the Thirty Tyrants, to the Puritans against the English king, to the French Revolution, and of course to America's own throwing off of the feudal yoke. He is also sympathetic to more specifically naval mutinies, as for example those of Spithead and Nore.[2] Given this spirited

[2] There is also a familial aspect to this sympathy with mutineers. In Ch. LXX he refers in passing to 'three sailors on board an American armed vessel . . . who

sympathy with cases and instincts of justified mutiny it is curious that two of the fabricated incidents in the book (that is, with *no* basis in Melville's own experience) start with the provoking and arousing of mutinous feelings, but end in incredible appeasement and limp dispersal. The first is Melville's fantasy about nearly being flogged when he imagines White-Jacket unjustly condemned to the cat. This enables him to imagine how he might have felt if about to be whipped: 'I cannot analyse my heart, though it then stood still within me. . . . I felt my man's manhood so bottomless within me, that no word, no blow, no scourge of Captain Claret could cut me deep enough for that. I but swung to an instinct in me—the instinct diffused through all animated nature, the same that prompts even a worm to turn under the heel' (Ch. LXVII). And he resolves to clasp the Captain and drag him overboard in a combined murder-suicide. Then a 'gentlemanly corporal of marines', Colbrook mildly speaks up on White-Jacket's behalf, and Jack Chase—that model of prudence and circumspection— seeing that the Captain takes no action against Colbrook, ventures also to put in a good word for White-Jacket 'in a manly but carefully respectful manner'. The Captain listens, then strolls away telling White-Jacket '*you may go*'. White-Jacket, understandably, nearly bursts 'into tears of thankfulness'. Now this is all very incredible. In Dana's scene when a man mildly questions the reason for the flogging he is instantly

once were alive, but now are dead', which is an allusion to three seamen who were executed without trial for suspected mutinous intentions on board the brig-of-war *Somers*. Melville heard of this while he was sailing on the *United States*. The officer who presided over the court which sentenced the men was Melville's cousin, Guert Gansevoort. Melville himself had been taking part, fairly marginally, in a somewhat less serious mutiny on the *Lucy Ann* at about the time the other men were hanged (see *Omoo* in which Melville generously promotes himself to being the ringleader of the untragic mutiny). Melville's family was a distinguished one and his ancestors included Scottish nobles, Dutch patricians, and heroes of the American Revolution. His cousin represented the kind of filocidal autocratic exercise of power against which Melville was rebelling. He was, as it were, the self-styled mutineer within the family. For the rich story of Melville's deeply ambivalent relationship to his illustrious family—and the way that relationship feeds and informs his fiction— see the excellent book by M. P. Rogin, *Subversive Genealogy: The Politics and Art of Herman Melville* (New York, 1983).

put in irons and then flogged himself, and it would have been infinitely more plausible if the fairly sadistic, and completely autocratic, Captain Claret had done the same. Yet Melville's scene transforms the bloody decks of the man-of-war into a site of almost courtly decorum with good manners, mild speaking and mutually attentive respect all round. Even stranger is the fact that Melville almost certainly took this episode from a story by William Leggett entitled 'Brought to the Gangway', in which a seaman is also unjustly condemned to be flogged but does indeed carry his despotic persecutor to death with him in a way which White-Jacket only fantasizes about.[3] Melville's episode is the emasculating fiction of a fiction, quite against the grain of the book—or at least much of the book. But we may consider it together with another failed or aborted mutiny— 'The Great Massacre of the Beards'.

Again this has no basis in anything that Melville experienced (though there had been an order sent out from Washington in 1841 to similar effect), which means that Melville was under no constraints of historical accuracy or verisimilitude to make it into what in effect it is—the climactic event of the voyage. Indeed, quite the contrary. Once again we have a strange, imagined interpolation, and one which finds Melville as tonally adrift as he is ever likely to get. The men decide to let their beards grow. A 'cruel thought entered into the heart of our captain' and he orders them to have their beards cut (that technically he has the naval law on his side is made secondary; it is presented as yet another example of the cruel caprice and arbitrary edicts of the tyrannous captain). Melville first pretends to feelings of inexpressible melancholy prompted by the memory of what happened: 'Such a heartless massacre of hair! Such a Bartholomew's Day and Sicilian Vespers of assassinated beards! Ah! who would believe it!' This sort of mock-epic inflation (possibly a burlesque of Carlyle, as Priscilla Zirker[4] has suggested) would seem to preclude any high

---

[3] See P. S. Proctor, 'A Source for the Flogging Incident in *White-Jacket*', *American Literature*, 22 (May 1950).

[4] In 'Evidence of the Slavery Dilemma in *White-Jacket*', *American Quarterly*, 18 (Fall 1966).

seriousness in what follows. And yet the indubitably serious language of mutiny soon begins to stir.

Train your guns inboard [my italics], let the marines fix their bayonets, let the officers draw their swords; we *will not* let our beards be reaped—the last insult inflicted upon a vanquished foe in the East! Where are you, sheet-anchor men! captains of the tops! gunners mates! mariners, all! Muster round the capstan your venerable beards, and while you braid them together in token of brotherhood, cross hands and swear that we will enact over again the mutiny of the Nore, and sooner perish than yield up a hair!

The mutiny has really begun to look potentially serious when it is effortlessly scattered and defused by a few words from Mad Jack—for which Melville admires him: 'Therefore, Mad Jack! you did right . . . you perhaps quelled a very serious affair in the bud, and prevented the disgrace to the American Navy of a tragical mutiny, growing out of whiskers, soap-suds, and razors.' It is hard to see what has happened to Melville's credentials as a principled mutineer at this point (remember it is all his invention: Mad Jack's effortless and even contemptuous mastery over the would-be mutineers is Melville's own). And the crew—save one—all submit to have their beards cut. Under some sort of protest, to be sure: 'Captain Claret . . . I yielded to your tyranny—by this manly beard, I swear it was barbarous.'

Now there is a certain kind of word play of which Melville is particularly fond and it is quite possible that one reason for the interpolation of this episode was the opportunity it offered him to juggle with the barbarous/barber-ous treatment of men who are symbolically castrated by the whim of a tyrant. (The incident starts in a chapter entitled 'Man-of-War Barbers' and many details of barbering are given.) The etymologies of the two homonymous words are of course quite distinct—*barba* (beard) having nothing to do with the 'bar-bar' noises which the Greeks thought that non-Greeks made. But Melville was seriously interested in what exactly was 'barbarous', and throughout his work it is clear that he recognized that barbarities could issue from the heart of the United States— just as they are to be found at the centre of *United States* with its barbarous floggings—which could equal if not surpass in savagery the barbarities of so-called primitive peoples. So the barbarous/barber-ous edict of the Captain could have become a serious matter. But Melville lets, or makes, it all turn silly and even sentimental with the barber being absolved and, in turn, treating the shorn beard of Jack Chase (who had of course 'deemed it but wisdom to succumb') almost as a sacred relic.

Then it all turns most unpleasantly serious. Old Ushant, the 'sea-Socrates', refuses to comply with the order and the Captain orders him to be flogged, showing again a sadistic fury which hardly conceals its pleasure. There is the tiniest ripple and murmur of incipient protest and resistance, which is stilled and silenced even as it indulges in its carefully *sotto voce* expression. ' "By heaven!" thrillingly whispered Jack Chase who stood by, "it's only a halter; I'll strike him!" "Better not" said a top-mate, "it's death or worse punishment, remember." ' And that is the full extent of the protest. Jack Chase instead turns away 'with moist eyes'. It is impossible to estimate how much irony Melville intended by the phrase 'thrillingly whispered' but as far as the 'matchless and unmatchable Jack Chase' and his pretentions to any kind of heroic status are concerned, it is effectively the *coup de grâce*. And it cannot be a coincidence that the words he uses as he forces his way away from the flogging, 'I can't stand it', are exactly echoed by the cowardly slave Guinea, who also pushes away from the sight of a flogging with the words 'I can't 'tand it'. As Melville shows, Jack Chase can only be a 'hero' in the amateur theatricals, in which he plays the 'chivalric' character of Percy Royal-Mast and rescues 'fifteen oppressed sailors' to great applause (Chapter XXIII). It is impossible even to sense how far the mockery of handsome Jack Chase's empty theatrical posturing and actual faint-hearted circumspection is meant to go. But looked at closely, he is, in Melville's larger vocabulary, as much a 'slave' as anyone on the ship.

Meanwhile, old Ushant takes his dozen lashes and is standing 'as the Dying Gladiator lies'. Still refusing to shave his beard, he spends five more days in irons. He becomes the one figure on the ship who has held fast to his principled refusal to comply with the arbitrary dictates of a tyrannous captain or to succumb to his brutality. In this sense he is the only hero: the one true mutineer-martyr to stand out and stand firm. At this point, almost madly one might feel, Melville seems to offer a kind of defence of Captain Claret: 'Let it not be supposed that it is here sought to impale him before the world as a cruel, black-hearted man. Such he was not.' Certainly not, says Melville; why 'it has been related what privileges he accorded to the seamen respecting the free playing of checkers. . . .' By which time it is becoming impossible to have any sure sense of what Melville might be trying to do with the whole episode. At the end of it all he seems to return to a firm conviction that the men were right in the first place to make it a matter of principle, and thus potentially a matter for mutiny. 'And that our man-of-war's-men were right in desiring to perpetuate their beards, as martial appurtenances, must seem very plain, when it is considered that, as the beard is the token of manhood, so, in some shape or other, has it ever been held the true badge of the warrior.' Which would seem to lend honour and vindication to the figure of Ushant, sea-Socrates and Dying Gladiator. But then Melville's tone changes yet again as he veers off into his own kind of inscrutable jocularity: 'Most all fighting creatures sport either whiskers or beards; it seems a law of Dame Nature. Witness the boar, the tiger, the cougar, man, the leopard, the ram, the cat—all warriors, and all whiskerandos. Whereas, the peace-loving tribes have mostly enamelled chins.' Ushant as just another of Dame Nature's 'whiskerandos' is a much reduced figure.

I will return to these failed, or stylistically subverted and tonally betrayed, mutinies shortly. But first I want to draw attention to the sequence of chapters and subjects with which Melville proceeds to conclude his book after that final episode. In his next chapter he returns to flogging in its most horrific form—'Flogging through the Fleet'—which is indeed a 'Golgotha' of a chapter. This leads him on to extending the 'catalogue of evil' to be found in 'The Social State in a Man-of-War', and here we move from Golgotha to Gomorrah: 'The sins for which the cities of the plain were overthrown still linger in some of these wooden-walled Gomarrahs of the Deep. More than once complaints were made at the mast in the *Neversink*, from which the deck officer would turn away with loathing, refuse to hear them, and command the complainant out of his sight. There are evils in men-of-war which . . . will neither bear representing, nor reading, and will hardly bear thinking of.' Whether Melville himself questioned the arguable perversity of conventions of representation which allow him to describe sadistic floggings at detailed length while preventing him from even writing the word 'homosexuality' is not here clear. But the proximity of the two things in his text gives some weight to those who detect a suggestion of incipient sexual excitement in the flogging scenes; 'sodomy and the lash', as Winston Churchill used to say, always going closely together in the Navy. Melville's apparent horror at the very idea or word 'homosexual', feigned or real, is a far cry from the at times almost outrageous homo-erotic playfulness to be found in *Moby-Dick*. But at this point Melville is following a line of evil. In 'The Manning of Navies' we are among the 'many moral monsters' to be found in the 'Floating Hells' at sea. The chapter concludes with the sketch of Landless, a man who has, as it were, been flogged into a state of 'invincible indifference' during ten years in the Navy. Apparently happy-go-lucky and popular with the officers, he represents for Melville a kind of ultimate degradation: 'A fellow without shame, without a soul, so dead to the least dignity of manhood that he could hardly be called a man.' The following chapter aspires to be more cheerful but can only conclude that a man-of-war is but a microcosm of the world's badness—'though boasting some fine fellows here and there, yet, upon the whole, charged to the combings of her hatchways with the spirit of Belial and all unrighteousness.' After the chapter describing his 'imagined' fall we soon move on to the concluding words of the book: 'For the rest, whatever befall us, *let us never train our murderous guns inboard* [my italics]; let us not mutiny with bloody pikes in our hands. Our Lord High Admiral will yet interpose; and though long ages should elapse, and leave our wrongs unredressed, yet, shipmates and worldmates! let us never forget, that,

Whoever afflict us, whatever surround,
Life is a voyage that's homeward bound.'

This, by any other name, is quietism, and a comparison of the italicized words with those italicized earlier marks the inversion of the discourse of mutiny into the discourse of pacifism. (Melville is hardly known for his belief in the beneficent supervision of a 'Lord High Admiral', or indeed in His existence.) Guns turned inboard were often crucial in mutiny, and of course—given Melville's use of the ship as microcosm—could easily signify a state of civil war. Priscilla Zirker, to whose crucial article ('Evidence of the Slavery Dilemma in *White-Jacket*', *American Quarterly*, 18, Fall 1966) I owe this and other points, shows that the fear of the possibility of national disunity and the sense of impending crisis, if not worse, was growing throughout the 1840s and was 'probably at its height in 1849' when Melville was writing his book (the fear intensified, of course, by the revolutions in Europe during 1848).[5] It was that fear, it would seem, that led Melville to radically muffle his mutineering instincts in such strange, dissonant ways.

The fear of national disunity was of course precipitated by the problem of slavery. It has to be remembered that many of the liberals who were against slavery and opposed its extension—including Lincoln himself—had little respect for negroes as men and no doubt at all about white superiority. The Democrats—and Melville was a Democrat at this time—regarded themselves as the 'Party of Equality'. They thought, as did many others, that it should be possible to reconcile their proclaimed political ideals of freedom and equality with at least a tolerance—in the name of national unity—of the 'peculiar institution' of the South. Priscilla Zirker comments:

But the conciliatory gesture, upholding the sacred rights of property in slaves and denying the Negroes status as men, which began with the Compromise of 1850 and continued with the Fugitive Slave Act, the Kansas–Nebraska Act and the Dred Scott decision, only forced the opponents of conciliation into new and irrevocable paths or into

[5] 'Evidence of the Slavery Dilemma in *White-Jacket*', pp. 480–1.

underground activity . . . the Democratic Party transformed itself from the 'party of Equality' into the party of slavery. And even then the Union could not be saved except through war and the conquering of one section by another.[6]

In the event, nothing finally could stop the training of the murderous guns inboard. And there was another issue that was making it increasingly difficult to keep the question of slavery somehow separate from the central political problems facing the United States: the debate concerning flogging in the navy. Inevitably, since to all but the most benightedly racist eye the flogging of a black man must seem mighty similar to the flogging of a white one, the connection between the issues of flogging and slavery become obvious and irreversible. Priscilla Zirker again: 'The alignment of congressmen on the issues of flogging and slavery was clear in the 1840s; it would have taken no prescience of the final severing of these members into opposing parties and then into opposing nations, as was to happen, to see that the abolition of flogging and slavery were related, that egalitarianism must inevitably proceed like water, to cover the lowest depths.'[7]

Priscilla Zirker is right, I think, to say that Melville was frightened by the whole matter and problem of slavery; meaning not a general metaphysical or ontological condition ('who aint a slave?' asks Ishmael, cheerfully enough, in *Moby-Dick*), but the black slaves, rapidly increasing in numbers—and volatility—in mid-century America. When, apropos the gunpowder kept in the depths of the ship, Melvile characteristically generalizes the fact into a trope and says 'it is pretty certain that the whole earth is a vast hogshead, full of inflammable materials, and which we are always bestriding', we may take it for some of his off-the-cuff metaphysics; but it is also in line with a recurring image which can be found in other writing of the period which suggests that America is a volcano waiting to erupt, and that the 'inflammable material' is slavery. When Melville wants to convey a sense of the difference between a 'sham fight' which is used for training the men, and

---

[6] 'Evidence of the Slavery Dilemma in *White-Jacket*', p. 483.
[7] Ibid.

a 'real cannonading' he suggests that '*then* our bulwarks might look like the walls of the houses in West Broadway in New York, after being broken into and burned out by the negro mob'. '*The* negro mob': Melville is being specific, and there was indeed a slave revolt in 1741 in which fires were started in New York. But Melville suppresses the history and instead offers an apocalyptic scenario of hideous butchery, rivers of blood, and terrifying destruction. He hardly needed to reach back to 'the negro mob' for such a scene of generalized carnage (there was after all the French Revolution—but of course he approved of that), but it came to him. In *Benito Cereno* he would subsequently offer an incomparable study of the myopic, self-deceiving and cruel complacencies of a white, American, racist, imperialist consciousness—but the slave revolt is still frightening. White-Jacket feels some sympathy with the black Rose-Water when he is flogged, and pities him as 'one of an oppressed race', which prompts the unashamed exclamation 'Thank God! I am white'. However, being white is no protection against being flogged in the Navy, and immediately after this White-Jacket is himself sentenced to be flogged. Clearly his expressed relief at being white is meant to be ironically undercut. But this does not lead to a sense of *identification* with the black. And the negroes on board hardly enjoy the full reach of Melville's humanism. They are given minstrel names—Sunshine, May-Day, Old Coffee, Rose-Water—and if Melville does not degrade them like the Captain, who makes them engage in head-bumping contests for his amusement, he does rather ridicule them. About Guinea, the one slave on board who paradoxically enjoys an ease and freedom denied the sailors, White-Jacket is positively resentful. And when Melville writes 'the lieutenants from the Southern States, the descendants of the old Virginians, are much less severe, and much more gentle and gentlemanly in command, than the Northern officers, as a class' he sounds almost like an apologist for the old South and its peculiar institution. He was, of course, nothing of the kind; but at this point the figure of the black slave (or freed slave) provokes ambivalent feelings which confuse him.

This is one reason, I think, why Melville felt much easier making sweeping general statements about the Rights of Man: when a writer engages in universals he absolves himself from having to confront local, historical, and political problems— like the status of the black slave in the America of 1849. Elsewhere in the book Melville displays the kind of enlightened cultural relativism which is a consistent feature of his writing. Thus when the Polynesian figure, Wooloo, confronted by western and ship-board phenomena which are quite new to him, makes all sorts of amusing mistakes, Melville comments: 'In our man-of-war, this semi-savage, wandering about the gun-deck in his barbaric robe, seemed a being from some other sphere. His tastes were our abominations: ours his. Our creed he rejected: his we. We thought him a loon: he fancied us fools. *Had the case been reversed* [my italics]; had we been Polynesians and he an American, our mutual opinion of each other would still have remained the same. A fact proving that neither was wrong, but both right.' It is a quintessentially Melvillian observation, and indeed 'reversibility'—of function, category, culture, belief—becomes a major motif in his later work, at times threatening to obliterate 'difference' altogether. That is another story. In terms of this book it must be said that the figure of the black American slave worries Melville a good deal more than that of the Polynesian servant. (It should perhaps be noted here that later in his life Melville spoke unambiguously of the evil of slavery; but I am trying to identify some of the tensions which are present in *White-Jacket*.) Quite apart from anything else, the presence of slaves in America placed an added strain on his not always unequivocal egalitarian principles and beliefs. According to those principles, of course, the American slave should have been an impossible contradiction in terms. Yet there he was, staring him, and countless other worried white liberals, frighteningly in the face.

Melville's proclaimed and doubtless sincere egalitarianism is the third problematical area of this book I wish to touch on, and it is of course intimately involved with the previous two. In 1851 he wrote to Hawthorne: 'When you see or hear of my ruthless democracy on all sides, you may possibly feel a touch of a shrink, or something of that sort. It is but nature to be shy of a mortal who boldly declares that a thief in jail is as honorable a personage as Gen. George Washington.' At an abstract or idealistic level Melville's democracy is fervent and ruthless enough. But the account of his voyage on the *United States* seethes with matters of rank, class distinction, and hierarchy. The arbitrary tyranny of the captain prompts Melville to make comparative references to feudalism, sultanism, Czars, emperors, Caesar, Charles the Fifth, and so on— understandably, since one of Melville's constant questions and concerns is 'by what monstrous grafting of tyranny upon freedom' did the *American* Navy acquire such a barbaric and despotic code while sailing in protection of the nation which had produced the Declaration of Independence. At the other extreme there are recurrent references to '*the people*', that generically classless class of common humanity for which Melville the democrat regards himself as the spokesman. But there are other terms for the common people—such as 'mob', 'desperadoes', 'gang', 'miscellaneous rabble', and so on. This is absolutely in line with a common ambivalence to be found in republics in which 'the people' are the honoured abstraction, 'the masses' the ambiguous unadmired reality, and 'the mob' the dreaded nightmare. In Chapter XLV there is a revealing exchange between Lemsford (who like Melville is both a 'gentleman' and a writer) and Jack Chase. Lemsford is a notably unsuccessful writer who despises the 'mob and rabble' who ignored his book: 'What they call the public is a monster, like the idol we saw in Owhyhee, with the head of a jackass, the body of a baboon, and the tail of a scorpion'. Jack demurs, pointing out that on shore he is, inevitably, part of that public. Not so, says Lemsford: 'You are then part of the people, just as you are aboard the frigate here. The public is one thing, Jack, and the people another.' Jack instantly approves of the distinction: 'Ay, ay, my lads, let us hate the one, and cleave to the other.' Whether these are exactly Melville's own sentiments we may hardly ponder, but it seems likely; and on board ship White-Jacket shows himself to be keen to mark himself off from the common crew ('the people').

He is very aware of a kind of 'aristocracy' among the sailors—one based on an appreciation of literature, good manners, sensitivity, and a certain nonchalant elegance of style, epitomized of course by Jack Chase—with which he identifies and to which he soon belongs. For the official insignia of rank and its attendant ceremonies he has little time, and indeed he talks of the need for 'levelling downward' and getting rid of the differentiating pomp of official hierarchy: 'To gain the true level, in some things, we must *cut* downward; for how can you make every sailor a commodore? . . . by bringing down naval officers . . . without affecting their legitimate dignity and authority, we shall correspondingly elevate the common sailor.' But White-Jacket's aspirations are distinctly upward, and when he is accepted into the élite of the topmen, he regards himself as being both literally and figuratively at the top of the unofficial hierarchy among the crew. 'We accounted ourselves the best seamen in the ship; and from our airy perch, literally looked down upon the land-lopers below, sneaking about the deck, among the guns.' There is always a touch of humour in White-Jacket's account; but there is no doubt that he enjoys his promotion, his being accepted into the best 'club', his 'elevation' and the feeling of 'aboveness' it affords him. When he is in fact 'blackballed' from an earlier and much less prestigious 'club' his comment is: 'I was shocked. Such a want of tact and delicacy'; and he shows his highly developed fastidiousness early on when he realizes the dangers of 'indiscriminate intimacy'. He admires those who somehow retain an aura of distinction and difference while still being part of the crew—like Nord: 'How he managed to preserve his dignity, as he did, among such a rabble rout was . . . a mystery.' By the end of the voyage one certainly has the sense of the crew as being more a rabble—lazy, coarse, even depraved—than 'the people'.

Perhaps the most significant lexical symptom is the frequent occurrence of the word 'gentlemen'. The history of that word is a large piece of social history in itself. Suffice it here to note that by the Victorian period it had become both crucial and undefinable as a word. In an increasingly secular and democratic society it was used to signify some sort of human distinction, style, and worth. Yet just what made someone a gentleman was not easy to say. Trollope, for whom the figure and the concept is absolutely central, confessed that he had no idea what a gentleman really was. One advantage of this vagueness was that the word was not tied to social rank or status (or, by this time, to birth or wealth) so that any one might turn out to have those mysterious qualities which made him a gentleman wherever he might find himself. (The disadvantage was the possible dilution, diffusion, and general distribution of the term to the point of meaninglessness—as is arguably the case today.) Melville takes advantage of the relatively free-floating status of the word (in his vocabulary it would be a 'loose fish') to make it clear that while many of the officers were quite decidedly *not* gentlemen, a rare and precious few among the crew (conspicuously Jack Chase of course) most definitely were. To what extent being a gentleman might militate against one's being a democrat—or indeed vice versa—might be said to be another problem which vexes the book.[8]

Finally, the title merits some comment. Not the subtitle: 'The World in a Man-of-War' is self-explanatory and after Melville's extraordinarily rich and varied evocation, analysis, and probing, not only of the men and activities of the ship, but also of their possible emblematic significance and figurative suggestiveness, we readily recognize that when he writes at the end: 'Outwardly regarded, our craft is a lie; for all that is outwardly seen of it is the clean-swept deck, and oft-painted planks comprised above the water-line; whereas, the vast mass of our fabric, with all its store-rooms of secrets, forever slides along the water far under the surface,' he is referring not only to the ship, but to the individual, to society, and perhaps to the cosmos itself. But why *White-Jacket*? Melville's father imported fine clothes and accessories for a possible American aristocracy (his business failed) and Melville was always peculiarly aware of the varying extents (laughable or appalling) to which social,

---

[8] Apropos Melville's problematical attitude to egalitarianism, see Larry J. Reynolds, 'Anti-Democratic Emphasis in *White-Jacket*', *American Literature*, 48/1 (March 1976).

if not human, identity was a sartorial construction (Carlyle's *Sartor Resartus* was a favourite book). In *White-Jacket* he satirizes dandyish officers and overdressed monarchs with rich Melvillian humour. But what sort of garment is that white jacket, and what might it be suggesting, over and above the possible fact that it was, as Melville claimed to Dana, an actual garment he had? It has been seen variously as the sign of his alienation or estrangement or proud isolation or aristocratic pretensions or egotistical self-absorption; thus the final episode, when he rips himself out of it after his fall into the water and 'bursts . . . free', can be seen as a self-procured rebirth into society, 'the people', communality, maturity, or some other new lease of life now that he has freed himself from his self-imposed, self-isolating incubus. Clearly Melville does intend it to do some special work since, apart from the title, he starts the book describing how he made this 'outlandish garment of my own devising' and ends it by describing his desperate liberation from a garment which threatens to become his shroud. The jacket sinks from sight as the sailors harpoon it, mistaking it for a shark. It figures in nine chapters in all and is responsible for involving him in various, usually unpleasant, incidents. It tends to turn the crew against him. He is humiliated when no one even bids for it when he tries to auction it off. He often berates and regrets his 'horrible jacket' and indeed 'had it not once jeopardized my very existence?' It does inevitably serve to 'individualize' him in the 'mob of incognitos' and while that means he is often singled out for a task, one comes to feel that being 'individualized' from the 'mob', no matter what pains and penalties it may incur or prejudices it might arouse, is something that White-Jacket greatly desires. The fact that, with all its secret places and private pockets, it is on one occasion likened to both an 'old castle' and 'a confidential writing desk' must give it some sort of special token value for Melville, with his aristocratic heritage and his writer's vocation. An ambiguous garment of his own making which marks him as an odd-man-out with frequently socially unpleasant results—this is surely no very unapt vestment for sailor-writer Melville on his last voyage. That it finally becomes a hampering garment from which he must break free may indeed be interpreted in many ways. But it certainly does not initiate him into any new-found solidarity with the crew or 'the people'. We last see him where he has always been most comfortable—above, with his élite: 'We maintop-men are all aloft in the top; and round our mast we circle, a brother-band, hand in hand, all spliced together.' What he breaks out to is life on the land, and commitment to a full-time career as a writer.

White-Jacket was well received and reviewed on the whole. Melville's friend Evert Dyckinck set the favourable tone by pointing to the 'union of culture and experience, of thought and observation, the sharp breeze of the forecastle alternating with the mellow stillness of the library, books and work imparting to each other mutual life', though this makes the book sound a more serene performance than in fact it is. Indeed, it is possible to sympathize with the reviewer who found a 'want of continuity of interest', a 'want of motive', and 'a want of composition' (*Britannia*, 2 February 1850) in the book, and it is even possible to understand, if not actually to share, the impatience of Charles Gordon Brown for what he felt bound to designate as the 'autobiographical twaddle' to which Melville has recourse (Boston *Post*, 10 April 1850). It is a rich book written with self-amplifying energy, but deeply uncertain of its direction, apart from the minimal linearity of the voyage being 'homeward bound'. At times Melville seeks to pull his intentions together with bursts of what might fairly be called 'Manifest Destiny' rhetoric, such as:

The Past is dead, and has no resurrection; but the Future is endowed with such a life, that it lives to us even in anticipation. . . . Let us leave the Past, then, to dictate laws to immovable China. . . . There are occasions when it is for America to make precedents, and not to obey them . . . we Americans are the peculiar, chosen people—the Israel of our time; we bear the ark of the liberties of the world. . . . We are the pioneers of the world; the advance-guard, sent on through the wilderness of untried things, to break a new path in the New World that is ours (Ch. XXXVI).

But to some extent this sort of thing reads rather like those clean-swept decks and oft-painted planks which made, so he said, 'our craft . . . a lie'. This is the official, outward-looking rhetoric of American triumphalist optimism. But Melville is always better in seeking out those 'store-rooms of secrets' which slide along 'far under the surface' and it is in the exposure and exhibition of some of those secret and secreted evils—the corruptions and degradations, the amputations and flagellations—that *White-Jacket* tears itself free from any hampering orthodoxy and achieves a true Melvillian unsettling power. For clearly Melville's experiences on the *United States* took him to the heart of some of the most profound problems, which were troubling, not only Melville himself, but the unity, stability, and indeed the meaning of America itself.

NOTE ON THE TEXT

This edition is based on the London text of February 1850 as corrected by the New York text of March, which was set up from it but shows a good many alterations. Many of these are clearly authoritative; others have consequently been accepted here even when it is not clear why they were made, provided they are not evident or probable errors in transmission. Readings which, though identical in both texts, are or seem to be wrong are indicated in the notes. A list of variants is given on page 405.

The early punctuation has generally been kept, since it suggests characteristic phrasal rhythms, except when it would lead to clumsiness or obscurity; where the first editions differ, the London one has been taken as the primary authority in this respect, as it has in general for spellings. Some words occur in variant spellings ('canvas/canvass', 'trousers/trowsers', 'mizen/ mizzen', 'canister/cannister', and so on); the spelling which occurs the more frequently has been adopted throughout.

Errors or variants in proper names have generally been left as in the first editions, but corrections, if at all significant, are provided in the notes. Ship names and book and song titles have been italicized. Capitalization has been brought into line with modern practice except when to do so would have destroyed some effect Melville was intending.

SELECT BIBLIOGRAPHY

BIOGRAPHY, LETTERS

Howard, Leon, *Herman Melville: A Biography* (Berkeley, Calif., 1951).

Leyda, Jan, *The Melville Log: A Documentary Life of Herman Melville, 1819–91* (New York, 1951).

Davis, Merrell R., and Gilman, William H., eds., *The Letters of Herman Melville* (New Haven, Conn., 1960).

Metcalf, Eleanor Melville, *Herman Melville: Cycle and Epicycle* (Cambridge, Mass., 1953).

GENERAL CRITICISM

Bloom, Harold, ed., *Herman Melville* (New York, 1986).

Branch, Watson G., ed., *Melville: The Critical Heritage* (London, 1974).

Chase, Richard, *Melville: A Collection of Critical Essays* (Englewood Cliffs, NJ, 1962).

Duban, James, *Melville's Major Fiction: Politics, Theology, and Imagination* (Dekalb, Ill., 1983).

Feidelson, Charles, Jr., *Symbolism and American Literature* (Chicago, 1953).

Franklin, H. Bruce, *The Wake of the Gods: Melville's Mythology* (Stanford, Calif., 1963).

Fussell, Edwin, *Frontier: American Literature and the American West* (Princeton, NJ, 1965).

Lee, A. Robert, ed., *Herman Melville: Reassessments* (London, 1984).

Mathiessen, F. O., *American Renaissance* (New York, 1941).

Parker, Hershel, *The Recognition of Herman Melville* (Ann Arbor, Mich., 1967).

Pullin, Faith, ed., *New Perspectives on Melville* (Edinburgh, 1978).

Rogin, Michael Paul, *Subversive Genealogy: The Politics and Art of Herman Melville* (New York, 1983).

Rosenberry, Edward H., *Melville* (London, 1979).

Seelye, John, *Melville: The Ironic Diagram* (Evanston, Ill., 1970).

Sherrill, Rowland, *The Prophetic Melville: Experience, Transcendence, and Tragedy* (Athens, Ga., 1979).

CRITICISM OF WHITE-JACKET

Anderson, Charles Roberts, *Melville in the South Seas* (New York, 1939).

Dillingham, William, *An Artist in the Rigging: The Early Works of Herman Melville* (Athens, Ga., 1972).

Dimok, Wai-Chee, '*White-Jacket*: Authors and Audiences', *Nineteenth-Century Fiction*, 36 (Dec. 1981).

Gerlach, John, 'Messianic Nationalism in the Early Works of Herman Melville: Against Perry Miller', *Arizona Quarterly*, 27 (Spring 1972).

James, C. L. R., *Mariners, Renegades and Castaways* (1953; rev. repr. London, 1985).

Proctor, Page S., 'A Source for the Flogging Incident in *White-Jacket*', *American Literature*, 22 (May 1950).

Reynolds, Larry J., 'Anti-Democratic Emphasis in *White-Jacket*', *American Literature*, 48 (March 1976).

Vincent, Howard P., *The Tailoring of Melville's* White-Jacket (Evanston, Ill., 1970).

—— '*White-Jacket*: An Essay in Interpretation', *New England Quarterly*, 22 (Sept. 1949).

Zirker, Priscilla Allen, 'Evidence of the Slavery Dilemma in *White-Jacket*', *American Quarterly*, 18 (Fall 1966).

There are relevant chapters in the studies listed above by Duban, Rogin, Rosenberry, and Seelye. For the sources of *White-Jacket*, see the study by Anderson, Vincent's *The Tailoring of Melville's* White-Jacket (listed above), and Melville's *Journal of a Cruise to the Pacific Ocean, 1842–1844, in the Frigate 'United States'*, ed. and introd. Charles R. Anderson (Durham, NC, 1937).

BIBLIOGRAPHIES

Important nineteenth-century criticism is collected in Hershel Parker, ed., *The Recognition of Herman Melville* (Ann Arbor, Mich., 1967), and in Watson G. Branch, ed., *Melville: The Critical Heritage* (London, 1974). Jeanetta Boswell's *Herman Melville and the Critics: A Checklist of Criticism 1900–78* (Metuchen, NJ, 1981) covers twentieth-century books and articles on Melville. For recent criticism, see the annual MLA Bibliographies.

A CHRONOLOGY OF
HERMAN MELVILLE

1819   Born in New York City (1 August), son of Allan Melvill, a merchant, and Maria Gansevoort.

1830   Father declared bankrupt.

1832   Father dies, leaving mother with family of eight children and large debts.

1832–8   Employed in various short-lived jobs: in a bank, on a farm, in a store, teaching in an elementary school. Later takes engineering and surveying course.

1839   Signs on as merchant seaman on the *St Lawrence*; makes the round trip to Liverpool described in *Redburn*. Teaches in school in New York State on return.

1840   Visits uncle in Galena, Illinois, then travels down Mississippi to Cairo, returning via Ohio River.

1841   Ships aboard the whaler *Acushnet*, bound for Cape Horn and the Pacific.

1842   Jumps ship with shipmate in the Marquesas Islands, and lives with cannibal tribe as recounted in *Typee*. Rescued by Australian whaler, but leaves the ship after a mutiny, and spends time in Tahiti, as described in *Omoo*.

1843–4   After period in Honolulu, returns to the USA as ordinary seaman in the frigate *United States*, the model for the *Neversink* in *White-Jacket*.

1846   *Typee*.

1847   *Omoo*. Marries Elizabeth Shaw, daughter of Chief Justice of Massachusetts, and settles in New York.

1849   *Mardi* and *Redburn*. Birth of first son, and second voyage to Europe.

1850   *White-Jacket*. Buys estate near Pittsfield, Massachusetts, close to home of Nathaniel Hawthorne.

1851   *Moby-Dick, or, The Whale*. Second son born.

1852   *Pierre, or, The Ambiguities*.

1853   Fire at publishers destroys remaining copies of his works. Fails to obtain post as US Consul. First daughter born.

1855   *Israel Potter*. Second daughter born.

1856   *The Piazza Tales*, a collection of his magazine stories. Travels to Europe and Holy Land for his health after completion of *The Confidence-Man: His Masquerade* in summer.

1857   *The Confidence-Man: His Masquerade*.

1858–65 Turns to verse, and makes fitful attempts to earn a living by means other than writing.

1866   *Battle-Pieces*, poems. Becomes Customs Inspector, for the next twenty years, in the port of New York.

1876   *Clarel: A Poem and Pilgrimage in the Holy Land*.

1888   *John Marr and Other Sailors*, poems.

1891   *Timoleon*, poems. Dies, 28 September.

1924   *Billy Budd, Sailor* published.

White-Jacket

or

The World in a Man-of-War

PREFACE
TO THE FIRST ENGLISH EDITION

THE object of this work is to give some idea of the interior life in a man-of-war. In the year 1843, the author shipped as a common sailor on board of a United States frigate, then lying in a harbour of the Pacific Ocean. After serving on board of this frigate for more than a year, he was discharged, with the rest of the crew, upon the vessel's arrival home. His man-of-war experiences and observations have been incorporated into the present volumes. But these volumes are not presented as a journal of the cruise.

As the object of this work is not to portray the particular man-of-war in which the author sailed, and its officers and crew, but, by illustrative scenes, to paint general life in the Navy, the true name of the frigate is not given. Nor is it here asserted that any of the persons introduced in the following chapters are real individuals. Wherever statements are made in any way concerning the established laws and usages of the Navy, facts have been strictly adhered to. Allusion is sometimes made to events or facts in the past history of navies. In these cases, no statement is presented unless supported by the best authorities. For the hitherto unrecorded by-play of circumstances in one or two well-known naval actions referred to, the writer is indebted to the seamen into whose mouths these things are put.

The work opens at the frigate's last harbour in the Pacific, just previous to weighing her anchor for the homeward-bound passage, by the way of Cape Horn.

New York
October 1849

*In the first American edition the following Note took the place
of the Preface:*

NOTE

IN the year 1843 I shipped as 'ordinary seaman' on board
of a United States frigate, then lying in a harbor of the
Pacific Ocean. After remaining in this frigate for more than
a year, I was discharged from the service upon the vessel's
arrival home. My man-of-war experiences and observations
are incorporated in the present volume.

*New York
March 1850*

2

I

The Jacket

IT was not a *very* white jacket, but white enough, in all conscience, as the sequel will show.

The way I came by it was this.

When our frigate lay in Callao, on the coast of Peru—her last harbour in the Pacific—I found myself without a *grego*, or sailor's surtout; and as, toward the end of a three years' cruise, no pea-jackets could be had from the purser's steward; and being bound for Cape Horn, some sort of a substitute was indispensable; I employed myself, for several days, in manufacturing an outlandish garment of my own devising, to shelter me from the boisterous weather we were so soon to encounter.

It was nothing more than a white duck frock, or rather shirt; which, laying on deck, I folded double at the bosom, and by then making a continuation of the slit there, opened it lengthwise—much as you would cut a leaf in the last new novel. The gash being made, a metamorphosis took place, transcending any related by Ovid.*For, presto! the shirt was a coat!—a strange-looking coat, to be sure; of a Quakerish amplitude about the skirts; with an infirm, tumble-down collar; and a clumsy fullness about the wristbands; and white, yea, white as a shroud. And my shroud it afterward came very near proving, as he who reads further will find.

But, bless me, my friend, what sort of a summer jacket is this, in which to weather Cape Horn? A very tasty and beautiful white linen garment it may have seemed; but then, people almost universally sport their linen next to their skin.

Very true; and that thought very early occurred to me; for no idea had I of scudding round Cape Horn in my shirt; for *that* would have been almost scudding under bare poles* indeed.

3

So, with many odds and ends of patches—old socks, old trowser-legs, and the like—I bedarned and bequilted the inside of my jacket, till it became, all over, stiff and padded, as King James's cotton-stuffed and dagger-proof doublet; and no buckram or steel hauberk stood up more stoutly.

So far, very good; but pray, tell me, White-Jacket, how do you propose keeping out the rain and the wet in this quilted *grego* of yours? You don't call this wad of old patches a mackintosh, do you?—You don't pretend to say that worsted is water-proof?

No, my dear friend; and that was the deuce of it. Water-proof it was not, no more than a sponge. Indeed, with such recklessness had I bequilted my jacket, that in a rainstorm I became a universal absorber; swabbing bone-dry the very bulwarks I leaned against. Of a damp day, my heartless ship-mates even used to stand up against me, so powerful was the capillary attraction between this luckless jacket of mine and all drops of moisture. I dripped like a turkey a-roasting; and long after the rainstorms were over, and the sun showed his face, I still stalked a Scotch mist; and when it was fair weather with others, alas! it was foul weather with me.

Me? Ah me! Soaked and heavy, what a burden was that jacket to carry about, especially when I was sent up aloft; dragging myself up, step by step, as if I were weighing the anchor. Small time then, to strip, and wring it out in a rain, when no hanging back or delay was permitted. No, no; up you go: fat or lean: Lambert or Edson:* never mind how much avoirdupois you might weigh. And thus, in my own proper person, did many showers of rain reascend toward the skies, in accordance with the natural laws.

But here be it known, that I had been terribly disappointed in carrying out my original plan concerning this jacket. It had been my intention to make it thoroughly impervious, by giving it a coating of paint. But bitter fate ever overtakes us unfortunates. So much paint had been stolen by the sailors, in daubing their overhaul trowsers and tarpaulins, that by the time I—an honest man—had completed my quiltings, the paint-pots were banned, and put under strict lock and key.

4

Said old Brush, the captain of the *paint-room*—'Look ye, White-Jacket,' said he, 'ye can't have any paint.'

Such, then, was my jacket: a well-patched, padded, and porous one; and in a dark night, gleaming white, as the White Lady of Avenel!*

II

Homeward Bound

'ALL hands up anchor! Man the capstan!'

'High die! my lads, we're homeward bound!'

Homeward bound!—harmonious sound! Were you ever homeward bound?—No?—Quick! take the wings of the morning, or the sails of a ship, and fly to the uttermost parts of the earth. There, tarry a year or two; and then let the gruffest of boatswains, his lungs all goose-skin, shout forth those magical words, and you'll swear 'the harp of Orpheus* were not more enchanting.'

All was ready; boats hoisted in, stun'-sail gear rove, messenger passed, capstan-bars in their places, accommodation-ladder below; and in glorious spirits, we sat down to dinner. In the ward-room, the lieutenants were passing round their oldest port, and pledging their friends; in the steerage, the *middies**were busy raising loans to liquidate the demands of their laundress, or else—in the Navy phrase—preparing to pay their creditors *with a flying fore-topsail*. On the poop, the captain was looking to windward; and in his grand, inaccessible cabin, the high and mighty commodore sat silent and stately, as the statue of Jupiter in Dodona.*

We were all arrayed in our best and our bravest; like strips of blue sky lay the pure blue collars of our frocks upon our shoulders; and our pumps were so springy and playful, that we danced up and down as we dined.

It was on the gun-deck that our dinners were spread; all along between the guns; and there, as we cross-legged sat, you would have thought a hundred farmyards and meadows were nigh. Such a cackling of ducks, chickens, and ganders; such a lowing of oxen, and bleating of lambkins, penned up here and there along the deck, to provide sea-repasts for the officers. More rural than naval were the sounds; continually reminding each mother's son of the old paternal homestead in the green old clime; the old arching elms; the hill where we gambolled; and down by the barley banks of the stream where we bathed.

'All hands up anchor!'

When that order was given, how we sprang to the bars, and heaved round that capstan; every man a Goliath, every tendon a hawser!—round and round—round, round it spun like a sphere, keeping time with our feet to the time of the fifer, till the cable was straight up and down, and the ship with her nose in the water.

'Heave and pall! unship your bars, and make sail!'

It was done:—bar-men, nipper-men,* tierers, veerers, idlers and all, scrambled up the ladder to the braces and halyards; while, like monkeys in palm-trees, the sail-loosers ran out on those broad boughs, our yards; and down fell the sails like white clouds from the ether—topsails, topgallants, and royals; and away we ran with the halyards, till every sheet was distended.

'Once more to the bars!'

'Heave, my hearties, heave hard!'

With a jerk and a yerk, we broke ground; and up to our bows came several thousand pounds of old iron, in the shape of our ponderous anchor.

Where was White-Jacket then?

White-Jacket was where he belonged. It was White-Jacket that loosed that main-royal, so far up aloft there, it looks like a white albatross' wing. It was White-Jacket that was taken for an albatross himself, as he flew out on the giddy yard-arm!

6

III

A Glance at the principal Divisions into which a Man-of-war's Crew is divided

HAVING just designated the place where White-Jacket belonged, it must needs be related how White-Jacket came to belong there.

Everyone knows that in merchantmen the seamen are divided into watches—starboard and larboard—taking their turn at the ship's duty by night. This plan is followed in all men-of-war. But in all men-of-war, besides this division, there are others, rendered indispensable from the great number of men, and the necessity of precision and discipline. Not only are particular bands assigned to the three *tops*, but in getting under weigh, or any other proceeding requiring all hands, particular men of these bands are assigned to each yard of the tops. Thus, when the order is given to loose the main-royal, White-Jacket flies to obey it; and no one but he.

And not only are particular bands stationed on the three decks of the ship at such times, but particular men of those bands are also assigned to particular duties. Also, in tacking ship, reefing topsails, or 'coming to', every man of a frigate's five-hundred-strong knows his own special place, and is infallibly found there. He sees nothing else, attends to nothing else, and will stay there till grim death or an epaulet orders him away. Yet there are times when, through the negligence of the officers, some exceptions are found to this rule. A rather serious circumstance growing out of such a case will be related in some future chapter.

Were it not for these regulations a man-of-war's crew would be nothing but a mob, more ungovernable stripping the canvass in a gale than Lord George Gordon's tearing down the lofty house of Lord Mansfield.*

But this is not all. Besides White-Jacket's office as looser of the main-royal, when all hands were called to make sail; and besides his special offices, in tacking ship, coming to anchor, &c.; he permanently belonged to the starboard watch, one of the two primary, grand divisions of the ship's company. And in this watch he was a maintop-man, that is, was stationed in the maintop, with a number of other seamen, always in readiness to execute any orders pertaining to the mainmast, from above the main-yard. For, including the main-yard, and below it to the deck, the mainmast belongs to another detachment.

Now the fore, main, and mizzentop* men of each watch— starboard and larboard—are at sea respectively subdivided into quarter-watches; which regularly relieve each other in the tops to which they may belong; while, collectively, they relieve the whole larboard watch of top-men.

Besides these top-men, who are always made up of active sailors, there are sheet-anchor-men—old veterans all— whose place is on the forecastle; the fore-yard, anchors, and all the sails on the bowsprit being under their care.

They are an old weather-beaten set, culled from the most experienced seamen on board. These are the fellows that sing you *The Bay of Biscay Oh!* and *Here a sheer hulk lies poor Tom Bowling!*, *Cease, rude Boreas, blustering railer!* who, when ashore, at an eating-house, call for a bowl of tar* and a biscuit. These are the fellows who spin interminable yarns about Decatur, Hull, and Bainbridge;* and carry about their persons bits of '*Old Ironsides*', as Catholics do the wood of the true cross. These are the fellows that some officers never pretend to damn, however much they may anathematize others. These are the fellows that it does your soul good to look at;—hearty old members of the Old Guard; grim sea-grenadiers, who, in tempest time, have lost many a tarpaulin overboard. These are the fellows whose society some of the youngster midshipmen much affect; from whom they learn their best seamanship; and to whom they look up as veterans; if so be that they have any reverence in their souls, which is not the case with all midshipmen.

Then, there is the *after-guard*, stationed on the quarter-deck; who, under the quarter-masters and quarter-gunners, attend to the mainsail and spanker, and help haul the main-brace,* and other ropes in the stern of the vessel.

The duties assigned to the after-guard's-men being comparatively light and easy, and but little seamanship being expected from them, they are composed chiefly of landsmen; the least robust, least hardy, and least sailor-like of the crew; and being stationed on the quarter-deck, they are generally selected with some eye to their personal appearance. Hence, they are mostly slender young fellows, of a genteel figure and gentlemanly address; not weighing much on a rope, but weighing considerably in the estimation of all foreign ladies who may chance to visit the ship. They lounge away the most part of their time, in reading novels and romances; talking over their lover affairs ashore; and comparing notes concerning the melancholy and sentimental career which drove them—poor young gentlemen—into the hard-hearted Navy. Indeed, many of them show tokens of having moved in very respectable society. They always maintain a tidy exterior; and express an abhorrence of the tar-bucket, into which they are seldom or never called to dip their digits. And pluming themselves upon the cut of their trowsers, and the glossiness of their tarpaulins, from the rest of the ship's company they acquire the name of 'sea-dandies' and 'silk-sock-gentry'.

Then, there are the waisters, always stationed on the gun-deck. These haul aft the fore- and main-sheets, besides being subject to ignoble duties; attending to the drainage and sewerage below hatches. These fellows are all Jimmy Duxes —sorry chaps, who never put foot in ratlin,* or venture above the bulwarks. Inveterate 'sons of farmers', with the hay-seed yet in their hair, they are consigned to the congenial superintendence of the chicken-coops, pig-pens, and potato-lockers. These are generally placed amidships, on the gun-deck of a frigate, between the fore and main hatches; and comprise so extensive an area, that it much resembles the market-place of a small town. The melodious sounds thence issuing continually draw tears from the eyes of the waisters; reminding them of their old paternal pig-pens and potato-patches. They are the tag-rag and bob-tail of the crew; and he who is good for nothing else is good enough for a waister.

Three decks down—spar-deck, gun-deck, and berth-deck —and we come to a parcel of troglodites* or holders, who burrow, like rabbits in warrens, among the water-tanks, casks, and cables. Like Cornwall miners, wash off the soot from their skins, and they are all pale as ghosts. Unless upon rare occasions, they seldom come on deck to sun themselves. They may circumnavigate the world fifty times, and they see about as much of it as Jonah did in the whale's belly. They are a lazy, lumpish, torpid set; and when going ashore after a long cruise, come out into the day like terrapins from their caves, or bears in the spring, from tree trunks. No one ever knows the names of these fellows; after a three years' voyage, they still remain strangers to you. In time of tempests, when all hands are called to save ship, they issue forth into the gale, like the mysterious old men of Paris, during the massacre of the Three Days of September;* everyone marvels who they are, and whence they come; they disappear as mysteriously, and are seen no more, until another general commotion.

Such are the principal divisions into which a man-of-war's crew is divided; but the inferior allotments of duties are endless, and would require a German commentator to chronicle.

We say nothing here of boatswain's mates, gunner's mates, carpenter's mates, sail-maker's mates, armourer's mates, master-at-arms, ship's corporals, cockswains, quartermasters, quarter-gunners, captains of the forecastle, captains of the foretop, captains of the maintop, captains of the mizzentop, captains of the after-guard, captains of the main-hold, captains of the fore-hold, captains of the head, coopers, painters, tinkers, commodore's steward, captain's steward, ward-room steward, steerage steward, commodore's cook, captain's cook, officers' cook, cooks of the range, mess-cooks, hammock-boys, messenger-boys, cot-boys, loblolly-boys, and numberless others, whose functions are fixed and peculiar.

It is from this endless subdivision of duties in a man-of-war, that, upon first entering one, a sailor has need of a good memory, and the more of an arithmetician he is, the better. White-Jacket, for one, was a long time rapt in calculations, concerning the various 'numbers' allotted him by the *first luff*, otherwise known as the first lieutenant. In the first place, White-Jacket was given the *number of his mess*; then, his *ship's number*, or the number to which he must answer when the watch-roll is called; then, the number of his hammock; then, the number of the gun to which he was assigned; besides a variety of other numbers; all of which would have taken Jedediah Buxton* himself some time to arrange in battalions, previous to adding up. All these numbers, moreover, must be well remembered, or woe betide you.

Consider, now, a sailor altogether unused to the tumult of a man-of-war, for the first time stepping on board, and given all these numbers to recollect. Already, before hearing them, his head is half stunned with the unaccustomed sounds ringing in his ears; which ears seem to him like belfries full of tocsins. On the gun-deck, a thousand scythed chariots seem passing; he hears the tread of armed marines; the clash of cutlasses and curses. The boatswain's mates whistle round him, like hawks screaming in a gale, and the strange noises under decks are like volcanic rumblings in a mountain. He dodges sudden sounds, as a raw recruit falling bombs.

Well-nigh useless to him, now, all previous circumnavigations of this terraqueous globe; of no account his arctic, antarctic, or equinoctial experiences; his gales off Beachy Head, or his dismastings off Hatteras.* He must begin anew; he knows nothing; Greek and Hebrew could not help him, for the language he must learn has neither grammar nor lexicon.

Mark him, as he advances along the files of old ocean-warriors; mark his debased attitude, his deprecating gestures, his Sawney* stare, like a Scotchman in London; his—'*cry your mercy, noble seignors!*' He is wholly nonplussed, and confounded. And when, to crown all, the first lieutenant, whose business it is to welcome all new-comers, and assign them their quarters; when this officer—none of the most bland or amiable either—gives him number after number to recollect—246—139—478—351—the poor fellow feels like decamping.

Study, then, your mathematics, and cultivate all your memories, oh ye! who think of cruising in men-of-war!

IV

Jack Chase

THE first night out of port was a clear, moonlight one; the frigate gliding through the water, with all her batteries.

It was my quarter-watch in the top, and there I reclined on the best possible terms with my top-mates. Whatever the other seamen might have been, these were a noble set of tars, and well worthy an introduction to the reader.

First and foremost was Jack Chase, our noble first captain of the top. He was a Briton, and a true-blue; tall and well-knit, with a clear open eye, a fine broad brow, and an abounding nut-brown beard. No man ever had a better heart or a bolder. He was loved by the seamen, and admired by the officers; and even when the captain spoke to him, it was with a slight air of respect. Jack was a frank and charming man.

No one could be better company in forecastle or saloon; no man told such stories, sang such songs, or with greater alacrity sprang to his duty. Indeed, there was only one thing wanting about him, and that was a finger of his left hand, which finger he had lost at the great Battle of Navarino.*

He had a high conceit of his profession as a seaman; and being deeply versed in all things pertaining to a man-of-war, was universally regarded as an oracle. The maintop, over which he presided, was a sort of Delphi, to which many pilgrims ascended, to have their perplexities or differences settled.

There was such an abounding air of good sense and good feeling about the man, that he who could not love him would thereby pronounce himself a knave. I thanked my sweet stars that kind fortune had placed me near him, though under him, in the frigate; and from the outset Jack and I were fast friends.

Wherever you may be now rolling over the blue billows, dear Jack! take my best love along with you; and God bless you, wherever you go!

Jack was a gentleman. What though his hand was hard, so was not his heart, too often the case with soft palms. His manners were easy and free; none of the boisterousness so common to tars; and he had a polite, courteous way of saluting you, if it were only to borrow your knife. Jack had read all the verses of Byron, and all the romances of Scott. He talked of Rob Roy, Don Juan, and Pelham;* Macbeth and Ulysses; but, above all things, was an ardent admirer of Camoens.* Parts of *The Lusiad* he could recite in the original. Where he had obtained his wonderful accomplishments, it is not for me, his humble subordinate, to say. Enough, that those accomplishments were so various; the languages he could converse in, so numerous; that he more than furnished an example of that saying of Charles the Fifth—*he who speaks five languages is as good as five men*. But Jack, he was better than a hundred common mortals; Jack was a whole phalanx, an entire army; Jack was a thousand strong; Jack would have done honour to the Queen of England's drawing-room; Jack must have been a by-blow of some British Admiral of the Blue. A finer specimen of the island race of Englishmen could not have been picked out of Westminster Abbey of a coronation day.

His whole demeanour was in strong contrast to that of one of the captains of the foretop. This man, though a good seaman, furnished an example of those insufferable Britons, who, while preferring other countries to their own as places of residence, still overflow with all the pompousness of national and individual vanity combined. 'When I was on board the *Audacious*—' for a long time was almost the invariable exordium to the foretop captain's most cursory remarks. It is often the custom of men-of-war's-men, when they deem anything to be going on wrong aboard ship, to refer to *last cruise*, when of course everything was done *ship-shape and Bristol fashion*. And by referring to the *Audacious*—

an expressive name, by the way—the foretop captain meant a ship in the English Navy, in which he had had the honour of serving. So continual were his allusions to this craft with the amiable name, that at last, the *Audacious* was voted a bore by his shipmates. And one hot afternoon, during a calm, when the foretop captain, like many others, was standing still and yawning on the spar-deck, Jack Chase, his own countryman, came up to him, and pointing at his open mouth, politely inquired, whether that was the way they caught *flies* in Her Britannic Majesty's ship the *Audacious*? After that, we heard no more of the craft.

Now, the tops of a frigate are quite spacious and cosy. They are railed in behind so as to form a kind of balcony, very pleasant of a tropical night. From twenty to thirty loungers may agreeably recline there, cushioning themselves on old sails and jackets. We had rare times in that top. We accounted ourselves the best seamen in the ship; and from our airy perch, literally looked down upon the land-lopers below, sneaking about the deck, among the guns. In a large degree we nourished that feeling of *esprit de corps*, always pervading, more or less, the various sections of a man-of-war's crew. We maintop-men were brothers, one and all; and we loaned ourselves to each other with all the freedom in the world.

Nevertheless, I had not long been a member of this fraternity of fine fellows, ere I discovered that Jack Chase, our captain, was—like all prime favourites and oracles among men—a little bit of a dictator; not peremptorily, or annoyingly so, but amusingly intent on egotistically mending our manners and improving our taste, so that we might reflect credit upon our tutor.

He made us all wear our hats at a particular angle; instructed us in the tie of our neck handkerchiefs; and protested against our wearing vulgar *dungeree**trowsers; besides giving us lessons in seamanship, and solemnly conjuring us forever to eschew the company of any sailor we suspected of having served in a whaler. Against all whalers, indeed, he cherished the unmitigated detestation of a true man-of-war's-man. Poor Tubbs can testify to that.

Tubbs was in the after-guard; a long, lank Vineyarder,* eternally talking of line-tubs, Nantucket, sperm-oil, stove boats, and Japan. Nothing could silence him; and his comparisons were ever invidious.

Now, with all his soul, Jack abominated this Tubbs. He said he was vulgar, an upstart—Devil take him, he's been in a whaler. But, like many men who have been where *you* haven't been, or seen what *you* haven't seen, Tubbs, on account of his whaling experiences, absolutely affected to look down upon Jack, even as Jack did upon him; and this it was that so enraged our noble captain.

One night, with a peculiar meaning in his eye, he sent me down on deck to invite Tubbs up aloft for a chat. Flattered by so marked an honour—for we were somewhat fastidious, and did not extend such invitations to everybody—Tubbs quickly mounted the rigging, looking rather abashed at finding himself in the august presence of the assembled quarter-watch of maintop-men. Jack's courteous manner, however, very soon relieved his embarrassment; but it is no use to be courteous to *some* men in this world. Tubbs belonged to that category. No sooner did the bumpkin feel himself at ease, than he launched out, as usual, into tremendous laudations of whalemen; declaring that whalemen alone deserved the name of sailors. Jack stood it some time; but when Tubbs came down upon men-of-war, and particularly upon maintop-men, his sense of propriety was so outraged, that he launched into Tubbs like a forty-two-pounder.

'Why, you limb of Nantucket! you train-oil man! you sea-tallow strainer! you bobber after carrion! do *you* pretend to vilify a man-of-war? Why, you lean rogue you, a man-of-war is to whalemen as a metropolis to shire towns and sequestered hamlets. *Here's* the place for life and commotion; *here's* the place to be gentlemanly and jolly. And what did you know, you bumpkin! before you came on board this *Andrew Miller*? What knew you of gun-deck, or orlop, mustering round the capstan, beating to quarters, and piping to dinner? Did you ever roll to *grog* on board your greasy ballyhoo of blazes? Did you ever winter at Mahon?* Did you ever '*lash and carry*'? Why, what are even a merchant-seaman's sorry yarns of voyages to China after tea-caddies, and voyages to the West Indies after sugar puncheons,* and voyages to the Shetlands after seal-skins—what are even these yarns, you Tubbs you! to high life in a man-of-war? Why, you dead-eye! I have sailed with lords and marquises for captains; and the King of the Two Sicilies has passed me, as I here stood up at my gun. Bah! you are full of the fore-peak and the forecastle; you are only familiar with Burtons and Billy-tackles; your ambition never mounted above pig-killing! which, in my poor opinion, is the proper phrase for whaling! Top-mates! has not this Tubbs here been but a misuser of good oak planks, and a vile desecrator of the thrice-holy sea? turning his ship, my hearties! into a fat-kettle, and the ocean into a whale-pen? Begone, you graceless, godless knave! pitch him over the top there, White-Jacket!'

But there was no necessity for my exertions. Poor Tubbs, astounded at these fulminations, was already rapidly descending by the rigging.

This outburst on the part of my noble friend, Jack, made me shake all over, spite of my padded surtout; and caused me to offer up devout thanksgivings, that in no evil hour had I divulged the fact of having myself served in a whaler; for having previously marked the prevailing prejudice of man-of-war's-men to that much-maligned class of mariners, I had wisely held my peace concerning stove boats on the coast of Japan.

V

Jack Chase on a Spanish Quarter-deck

HERE, I must frankly tell a story about Jack, which, as touching his honour and integrity, I am sure, will not work against him in any charitable man's estimation. On this present cruise of the frigate *Neversink*, Jack had deserted; and after a certain interval, had been captured.

But with what purpose had he deserted? To avoid naval discipline? to riot in some abandoned seaport? for love of some worthless signorita? Not at all. He abandoned the frigate from far higher and nobler, nay, glorious motives. Though bowing to naval discipline afloat, yet ashore, he was a stickler for the Rights of Man,* and the liberties of the world. He went to draw a partisan blade in the civil commotions of Peru,* and befriend, heart and soul, what he deemed the cause of the Right.

At the time, his disappearance excited the utmost astonishment among the officers, who had little suspected him of any such conduct as deserting.

'What? Jack, my great man of the maintop, gone!' cried the captain: 'I'll not believe it.'

'Jack Chase cut and run!' cried a sentimental middy. 'It must have been all for love, then; the signoritas have turned his head.'

'Jack Chase not to be found?' cried a growling old sheet-anchor-man, one of your malicious prophets of past events: 'I thought so; I know'd it; I could have sworn it—just the chap to make sail on the sly. I always s'pected him.'

Months passed away, and nothing was heard of Jack; till at last the frigate came to anchor on the coast, alongside of a Peruvian sloop of war.

Bravely clad in the Peruvian uniform, and with a fine, mixed martial and naval step, a tall, striking figure of a long-bearded officer was descried, promenading the quarter-deck of the stranger, and superintending the salutes, which are exchanged between national vessels on these occasions.

This fine officer touched his laced hat most courteously to our captain, who, after returning the compliment, stared at him, rather impolitely, through his spyglass.

'By heaven!' he cried at last—'it is he—he can't disguise his walk—that's his beard; I'd know him in Cochin China. Man the first cutter there! Lieutenant Blink, go on board that sloop of war, and fetch me yon officer.'

All hands were aghast.—What? when a piping-hot peace was between the United States and Peru, to send an armed body on board a Peruvian sloop of war, and seize one of its officers, in broad daylight?—Monstrous infraction of the Law of Nations! What would Vattel*say?

But Captain Claret must be obeyed. So off went the cutter, every man armed to the teeth, the lieutenant commanding having secret instructions, and the midshipmen attending looking ominously wise, though, in truth, they could not tell what was coming.

Gaining the sloop of war, the lieutenant was received with the customary honours; but by this time the tall, bearded officer had disappeared from the quarter-deck. The lieutenant now inquired for the Peruvian captain; and being shown into the cabin, made known to him, that on board his vessel was a person belonging to the United States Ship *Neversink*; and his orders were, to have that person delivered up instanter.

The foreign captain curled his moustache in astonishment and indignation; he hinted something about beating to quarters, and chastising this piece of Yankee insolence.

But resting one gloved hand upon the table, and playing with his sword-knot, the lieutenant, with a bland firmness, repeated his demand. At last, the whole case being so plainly made out, and the person in question being so accurately described, even to a mole on his cheek, there remained nothing but immediate compliance.

So the fine-looking, bearded officer, who had so courteously doffed his chapeau to our captain, but disappeared upon the arrival of the lieutenant, was summoned into the cabin, before his superior, who addressed him thus:—

'Don John, this gentleman declares, that of right you belong to the frigate *Neversink*. Is it so?'

'It is even so, Don Sereno,' said Jack Chase, proudly folding his gold-laced coat-sleeves across his chest—'and as there is no resisting the frigate, I comply.—Lieutenant Blink, I am ready. Adieu! Don Sereno, and Madre de Dios protect you! You have been a most gentlemanly friend and captain to me. I hope you will yet thrash your beggarly foes.'

With that he turned; and entering the cutter, was pulled back to the frigate, and stepped up to Captain Claret, where that gentleman stood on the quarter-deck.

'Your servant, my fine Don,' said the captain, ironically lifting his chapeau, but regarding Jack at the same time with a look of intense displeasure.

'Your most devoted and penitent captain of the maintop, sir; and one who, in his very humility of contrition, is yet proud to call Captain Claret his commander,' said Jack, making a glorious bow, and then tragically flinging overboard his Peruvian sword.

'Reinstate him at once,' shouted Captain Claret—'and now, sir, to your duty; and discharge that well to the end of the cruise, and you will hear no more of your having run away.'

So Jack went forward among crowds of admiring tars, who swore by his nut-brown beard, which had amazingly lengthened and spread during his absence. They divided his laced hat and coat among them, and on their shoulders carried him in triumph along the gun-deck.

VI

The Quarter-deck Officers, Warrant Officers, and Berth-deck Underlings of a Man-of-war; where they live in the Ship; how they live; their social Standing on Shipboard; and what sort of Gentlemen they are

SOME account has been given of the various divisions into which our crew was divided; so it may be well to say something of the officers; who they are, and what are their functions.

Our ship, be it known, was the flagship; that is, we sported a *broad pennant*, or *bougee*, at the main, in token that we carried a commodore—the highest rank of officers recognized in the American Navy. The bougee is not to be confounded with the *long pennant* or *coach-whip*, a tapering, serpentine streamer worn by all men-of-war.

Owing to certain vague, republican scruples, about creating great officers of the Navy, America has thus far had no admirals; though, as her ships of war increase, they may become indispensable. This will assuredly be the case, should she ever have occasion to employ large fleets; when she must adopt something like the English plan, and introduce three or four grades of flag-officers, above a commodore —admirals, vice-admirals, and rear-admirals of squadrons; distinguished by the colours of their flags—red, white, and blue, corresponding to the centre, van, and rear. These rank respectively with generals, lieutenant-generals, and major-generals in the Army; just as a commodore takes rank with a brigadier-general. So that the same prejudice which prevents the American government from creating admirals should have precluded the creation of all Army officers above a brigadier.

An American commodore, like an English commodore, or the French *chef d'escadre*, is but a senior captain, temporarily commanding a small number of ships, detached for any special purpose. He has no permanent rank, recognized by government, above his captaincy; though once employed as a commodore, usage and courtesy unite in continuing the title.

Our commodore was a gallant old man, who had seen service in his time. When a lieutenant, he served in the late war with England;*and in the gun-boat actions on the Lakes near New Orleans, just previous to the grand land engagements, received a musket-ball in his shoulder; which, with the two balls in his eyes, he carries about with him to this day.

Often, when I looked at the venerable old warrior, doubled up from the effect of his wound, I thought what a curious as well as painful sensation it must be, to have one's shoulder a lead-mine; though, sooth to say, so many of us civilized mortals convert our mouths into Golcondas.*

On account of this wound in his shoulder, our commodore had a body-servant's pay allowed him, in addition to his regular salary. I cannot say a great deal, personally, of the commodore; he never sought my company at all; never extended any gentlemanly courtesies.

But though I cannot say much of him personally, I can mention something of him in his general character, as a flag-officer. In the first place, then, I have serious doubts, whether, for the most part, he was not dumb; for, in my hearing, he seldom or never uttered a word. And not only did he seem dumb himself, but his presence possessed the strange power of making other people dumb for the time. His appearance on the quarter-deck seemed to give every officer the lockjaw.

Another phenomenon about him was the strange manner in which everyone shunned him. At the first sign of those epaulets of his on the weather side of the poop, the officers there congregated invariably shrunk over to leeward, and left him alone. Perhaps he had an evil eye; maybe he was the Wandering Jew*afloat. The real reason probably was, that, like all high functionaries, he deemed it indispensable religiously to sustain his dignity; one of the most troublesome things in the world, and one calling for the greatest self-denial. And the constant watch, and many-sided guardedness, which this sustaining of a commodore's dignity requires, plainly enough shows that, apart from the common dignity of manhood, commodores, in general, possess no real dignity at all. True, it is expedient for crowned heads, general-issimos, lord high admirals, and commodores, to carry themselves straight, and beware of the spinal complaint; but it is not the less veritable, that it is a piece of assumption, exceedingly uncomfortable to themselves, and ridiculous to an enlightened generation.

Now, how many rare good fellows there were among us maintop-men, who, invited into his cabin over a social bottle or two, would have rejoiced our old commodore's heart, and caused that ancient wound of his to heal up at once.

Come, come, commodore, don't look so sour, old boy; step up aloft here into the *top*, and we'll spin you a sociable yarn.

Truly, I thought myself much happier in that white jacket of mine, than our old commodore in his dignified epaulets.

One thing, perhaps, that more than anything else helped to make our commodore so melancholy and forlorn, was the fact of his having so little to do. For as the frigate had a captain, of course, so far as *she* was concerned, our commodore was a supernumerary. What abundance of leisure he must have had, during a three years' cruise! how indefinitely he might have been improving his mind!

But as everyone knows that idleness is the hardest work in the world, so our commodore was specially provided with a gentleman to assist him. This gentleman was called the *commodore's secretary*. He was a remarkably urbane and polished man, with a very graceful exterior, and looked much like an ambassador extraordinary from Versailles. He messed with the lieutenants in the ward-room, where he had a state-room, elegantly furnished as the private cabinet of Pelham. His cot-boy used to entertain the sailors with all manner of stories about the silver-keyed flutes and flageolets,* fine oil-paintings, morocco-bound volumes, Chinese chess-men, gold shirt-buttons, enamelled pencil-cases, extraordinary fine French boots with soles no thicker than a sheet of scented notepaper, embroidered vests, incense-burning sealing-wax, alabaster statuettes of Venus and Adonis, tortoise-shell snuff-boxes, inlaid toilet-cases, ivory-handled hair-brushes and mother-of-pearl combs, and a hundred other luxurious appendages scattered about this magnificent secretary's state-room.

I was a long time in finding out what this secretary's duties comprised. But it seemed, he wrote the commodore's dispatches for Washington, and also was his general amanuensis. Nor was this a very light duty, at times; for some commodores, though they do not *say* a great deal on board ship, yet they have a vast deal to write. Very often, the regimental orderly, stationed at our commodore's cabin-door, would touch his hat to the first lieutenant, and with a mysterious air hand him a note. I always thought these notes must contain most important matters of state; until one day, seeing a slip of wet, torn paper in a scupper-hole, I read the following:—

'Sir, you will give the people pickles to-day with their fresh meat.

'To Lieutenant Bridewell.

'By command of the Commodore.

'ADOLPHUS DASHMAN, Priv. Sec.'

This was a new revelation; for, from his almost immutable reserve, I had supposed that the commodore never meddled immediately with the concerns of the ship, but left all that to the captain. But the longer we live, the more we learn of commodores.

Turn we now to the second officer in rank, almost supreme, however, in the internal affairs of his ship. Captain Claret was a large, portly man, a Harry the Eighth afloat, bluff and hearty; and as kingly in his cabin as Harry on his throne. For a ship is a bit of terra firma cut off from the main; it is a state in itself; and the captain is its king.

It is no limited monarchy, where the sturdy Commons have a right to petition, and snarl if they please; but almost a despotism, like the Grand Turk's. The captain's word is law; he never speaks but in the imperative mood. When he stands on his quarter-deck at sea, he absolutely commands as far as eye can reach. Only the moon and stars are beyond his jurisdiction. He is lord and master of the sun.

It is not twelve o'clock till he says so. For when the sailing-master, whose duty it is to take the regular observation at noon, touches his hat, and reports twelve o'clock to the officer of the deck, that functionary orders a midshipman to repair to the captain's cabin, and humbly inform him of the respectful suggestion of the sailing-master.

'Twelve o'clock reported, sir,' says the middy.

'*Make* it so,' replies the captain.

And the bell is struck eight by the messenger-boy, and twelve o'clock it is.

As in the case of the commodore, when the captain visits the deck, his subordinate officers generally beat a retreat to the other side; and, as a general rule, would no more think of addressing him, except concerning the ship, than a lackey would think of hailing the Czar of Russia on his throne, and inviting him to tea. Perhaps no mortal man has more reason to feel such an intense sense of his own personal conse-quence, as the captain of a man-of-war at sea.

Next in rank comes the first or senior lieutenant, the chief executive officer. I have no reason to love the particular gentleman who filled that post aboard of our frigate, for it was he who refused my petition for as much black paint as would render water-proof that white jacket of mine. All my soakings and drenchings lie at his state-room door. I hardly think I shall ever forgive him; every twinge of the rheu-matism, which I still occasionally feel, is directly referable to him. The Immortals have a reputation for clemency, and *they* may pardon him; but he must not dun me to be merci-ful. But my personal feelings toward the man shall not pre-vent me from here doing him justice. In most things, he was an excellent seaman; prompt, loud, and to the point; and as such, was well fitted for his station. The first lieutenancy of a frigate demands a good disciplinarian, and, every way, an energetic man. By the captain he is held responsible for everything; by that magnate, indeed, he is supposed to be omnipresent; down in the hold, and up aloft, at one and the same time.

He presides at the head of the ward-room officers' table, who are so called from their messing together in a part of the ship thus designated. In a frigate it comprises the after part of the berth-deck. Sometimes it goes by the name of the gun-room, but oftener is called the ward-room. Within, this ward-room much resembles a long, wide corridor in a large hotel; numerous doors opening on both hands to the private apartments of the officers. I never had a good interior look at it but once; and then the chaplain was seated at the table in the centre, playing chess with the lieutenant of marines. It was mid-day, but the place was lighted by lamps.

Besides the first lieutenant, the ward-room officers include the junior lieutenants, in a frigate six or seven in number, the sailing-master, purser, chaplain, surgeon, marine officers, and midshipmen's schoolmaster, or 'the professor'. They generally form a very agreeable club of good fellows; from their diversity of character, admirably calculated to form an agreeable social whole. The lieutenants discuss sea-fights, and tell anecdotes of Lord Nelson and Lady Hamilton;*the marine officers talk of storming fortresses, and the siege of Gibraltar;* the purser steadies this wild conversation by occasional allusions to the rule of three; the professor is always charged with a scholarly reflection, or an apt line from the classics, generally Ovid; the surgeon's stories of the amputation-table judiciously serve to suggest the mortality of the whole party as men; while the good chaplain stands ready at all times to give them pious counsel and con-solation.

Of course these gentlemen all associate on a footing of perfect social equality.

Next in order come the warrant or forward officers, con-sisting of the boatswain, gunner, carpenter, and sail-maker. Though these worthies sport long coats, and wear the anchor-button, yet, in the estimation of the ward-room officers, they are not, technically speaking, rated gentlemen. The first lieutenant, chaplain, or surgeon, for example, would never dream of inviting them to dinner. In sea parlance, 'they come in at the hawse-holes'; they have hard hands; and the carpenter and sail-maker practically understand the duties which they are called upon to superintend. They mess by themselves. Invariably four in number, they never have need to play whist with a dummy.

In this part of the category now come the 'reefers', otherwise 'middies', or midshipmen. These boys are sent to sea, for the purpose of making commodores; and in order to become commodores, many of them deem it indispensable forthwith to commence chewing tobacco, drinking brandy and water, and swearing at the sailors. As they are only placed on board a sea-going ship to go to school and learn the duty of a lieutenant; and until qualified to act as such have few or no special functions to attend to; they are little more, while midshipmen, than supernumeraries on board. Hence, in a crowded frigate, they are so everlastingly crossing the path of both men and officers, that in the Navy it has become a proverb, that a useless fellow is 'as much in the way as a reefer'.

In a gale of wind, when all hands are called, and the deck swarms with men, the little 'middies' running about distracted, and having nothing particular to do, make it up in vociferous swearing; exploding all about under foot like torpedoes. Some of them are terrible little boys, cocking their caps at alarming angles, and looking fierce as young roosters. They are generally great consumers of Macassar Oil and the Balm of Columbia; they thirst and rage after whiskers; and sometimes, applying their ointments, lay themselves out in the sun, to promote the fertility of their chins.

As the only way to learn to command is to learn to obey, the usage of a ship of war is such that the midshipmen are constantly being ordered about by the lieutenants; though, without having assigned them their particular destinations, they are always going somewhere, and never arriving. In some things they almost have a harder time of it than the seamen themselves. They are messengers and errand-boys to their superiors.

'Mr. Pert,' cries an officer of the deck, hailing a young gentleman forward. Mr. Pert advances, touches his hat, and remains in an attitude of deferential suspense. 'Go and tell the boatswain I want him.' And with this perilous errand the middy hurries away, looking proud as a king.

The middies live by themselves in the steerage, where, nowadays, they dine off a table spread with a cloth. They have a castor*at dinner; they have some other little boys (selected from the ship's company) to wait upon them; they sometimes drink coffee out of china. But for all these, their modern refinements, in some instances the affairs of their club go sadly to rack and ruin. The china is broken; the japanned*coffee-pot dented like a pewter mug in an ale-house; the pronged forks resemble toothpicks (for which they are sometimes used); the table-knives are hacked into hand-saws; and the cloth goes to the sail-maker to be patched. Indeed, they are something like collegiate fresh-men and sophomores, living in the college buildings, especially so far as the noise they make in their quarters is concerned. The steerage buzzes, hums, and swarms like a hive; or like an infant-school of a hot day, when the school-mistress falls asleep with a fly on her nose.

In frigates, the ward-room—the retreat of the lieutenants—immediately adjoining the steerage, is on the same deck with it. Frequently, when the middies, waking early of a morning, as most youngsters do, would be kicking up their heels in their hammocks, or running about in double-reefed night-gowns, playing *tag* among the 'clews', the senior lieutenant would burst among them with a—'Young gentle-men, I am astonished. You must stop this sky-larking. Mr. Pert, what are you doing at the table there, without your pantaloons? To your hammock, sir. Let me see no more of this. If you disturb the ward-room again, young gentlemen, you shall hear of it.' And so saying, this hoary-headed senior lieutenant would retire to his cot in his state-room, like the father of a numerous family after getting up in his dressing-gown and slippers, to quiet a daybreak tumult in his populous nursery.

Having now descended from commodore to middy, we come lastly to a set of nondescripts, forming also a 'mess' by themselves, apart from the seamen. Into this mess the usage of a man-of-war thrusts various subordinates—including the master-at-arms, purser's steward, ship's corporals, marine sergeants, and ship's yeoman, forming the first aristocracy above the sailors.

The master-at-arms is a sort of high constable and school-master, wearing citizen's clothes, and known by his official rattan.* He it is whom all sailors hate. His is the universal duty of a universal informer and hunter-up of delinquents. On the berth-deck he reigns supreme; spying out all grease-spots made by the various cooks of the seamen's messes, and driving the laggards up the hatches, when all hands are called. It is indispensable that he should be a very Vidocq in vigilance.* But as it is a heartless, so is it a thankless office. Of dark nights, most masters-at-arms keep themselves in readiness to dodge forty-two-pound balls, dropped down the hatchways near them.

The ship's corporals are this worthy's deputies and ushers.

The marine sergeants are generally tall fellows with unyielding spines and stiff upper lips, and very exclusive in their tastes and predilections.

The ship's yeoman is a gentleman who has a sort of counting-room in a tar-cellar down in the fore hold. More will be said of him anon.

Except the officers above enumerated, there are none who mess apart from the seamen. The 'petty officers', so called, that is, the boatswain's, gunner's, carpenter's, and sail-maker's mates, the captains of the tops, of the forecastle, and of the after-guard, and of the fore and main holds, and the quarter-masters, all mess in common with the crew, and in the American Navy are only distinguished from the common seamen by their slightly additional pay.

But in the English Navy they wear crowns and anchors worked on the sleeves of their jackets, by way of badges of office. In the French Navy they are known by strips of worsted worn in the same place, like those designating the sergeants and corporals in the Army.

Thus it will be seen, that the dinner-table is the criterion of rank in our man-of-war world. The commodore dines alone, because he is the only man of his rank in the ship. So too with the captain; and the ward-room officers, warrant officers, midshipmen, the master-at-arms' mess, and the common seamen;—all of them, respectively, dine together, because they are respectively on a footing of equality.

VII

Breakfast, Dinner, and Supper

NOT only is the dinner-table a criterion of rank on board a man-of-war, but also the dinner-hour. He who dines latest is the greatest man; and he who dines earliest is accounted the least. In a flagship, the commodore generally dines about four or five o'clock; the captain about three; the lieutenants about two; while *the people* (by which phrase the common seamen are specially designated in the nomenclature of the quarter-deck) sit down to their salt beef exactly at noon.

Thus it will be seen, that while the two estates of sea-kings and sea-lords dine at rather patrician hours—and thereby, in the long run, impair their digestive functions—the sea-commoners, or *the people*, keep up their constitutions, by keeping up the good old-fashioned, Elizabethan, Franklin-warranted*dinner-hour of twelve.

Twelve o'clock! It is the natural centre, keystone, and very heart of the day. At that hour, the sun has arrived at the top of his hill; and as he seems to hang poised there awhile, before coming down on the other side, it is but reasonable to suppose that he is then stopping to dine; setting an eminent example to all mankind. The rest of the day is called *afternoon*; the very sound of which fine old Saxon word conveys a feeling of the lee bulwarks and a nap; a summer sea—soft breezes creeping over it; dreamy dolphins gliding in the distance. *Afternoon!* the word implies that it is an after-piece, coming after the grand drama of the day; something to be taken leisurely and lazily. But how can this be, if you dine at five? For, after all, though *Paradise Lost* be a noble poem, and we man-of-war's-men, no doubt, largely partake in the immortality of the immortals; yet, let us candidly confess it, shipmates, that, upon the whole, our dinners are the most momentous affairs of these lives we lead beneath the moon. What were a day without a dinner? a dinnerless day! such a day had better be a night.

Again: twelve o'clock is the natural hour for us man-of-war's-men to dine, because at that hour the very time-pieces we have invented arrive at their terminus; they can get no further than twelve; when straightway they continue their old rounds again. Doubtless, Adam and Eve dined at twelve; and the patriarch Abraham in the midst of his cattle; and old Job with his noon mowers and reapers, in that grand plantation of Uz; and old Noah himself, in the Ark, must have gone to dinner at precisely *eight bells* (noon), with all his floating families and farmyards.

But though this antediluvian dinner-hour is rejected by modern commodores and captains, it still lingers among *the people* under their command. Many sensible things banished from high life find an asylum among the mob.

Some commodores are very particular in seeing to it, that no man on board the ship dare to dine after his (the commodore's) own dessert is cleared away.—Not even the captain. It is said, on good authority, that a captain once ventured to dine at five, when the commodore's hour was four. Next day, as the story goes, that captain received a private note; and in consequence of that note, dined for the future at half-past three.

Though, in respect of the dinner-hour on board a man-of-war, *the people* have no reason to complain; yet they have just cause, almost for mutiny, in the outrageous hours assigned for their breakfast and supper.

Eight o'clock for breakfast; twelve for dinner; four for supper; and no meals but these; no lunches and no cold snacks. Owing to this arrangement (and partly to one watch going to their meals before the other, at sea), all the meals of the twenty-four hours are crowded into a space of less than eight! Sixteen mortal hours elapse between supper and breakfast; including, to one watch, eight hours on deck! This is barbarous; any physician will tell you so. Think of it! Before the commodore has dined, you have supped. And in high latitudes, in summer-time, you have taken your last meal for the day, and five hours, or more, daylight to spare!

Mr. Secretary of the Navy, in the name of *the people*, you should interpose in this matter. Many a time have I, a main-top-man, found myself actually faint of a tempestuous morning watch, when all my energies were demanded—owing to this miserable, unphilosophical mode of allotting the government meals at sea. We beg of you, Mr. Secretary, not to be swayed in this matter by the Honourable Board of Commodores, who will no doubt tell you that eight, twelve, and four are the proper hours for *the people* to take their meals; inasmuch, as at these hours the watches are relieved. For, though this arrangement makes a neater and cleaner thing of it for the officers, and looks very nice and superfine on paper, yet it is plainly detrimental to health, and in time of war is attended with still more serious consequences to the whole nation at large. If the necessary researches were made, it would perhaps be found that in those instances where men-of-war adopting the above-mentioned hours for meals have encountered an enemy at night, they have pretty generally been beaten; that is, in those cases where the enemies' meal-times were reasonable; which is only to be accounted for by the fact, that *the people* of the beaten vessels were fighting on an empty stomach instead of a full one.

VIII

Selvagee contrasted with Mad. Jack

HAVING glanced at the grand divisions of a man-of-war, let us now descend to specialities; and, particularly, to two of the junior lieutenants; lords and noblemen; members of that House of Peers, the gun-room. There were several young lieutenants on board; but from these two—representing the extremes of character to be found in their department—the nature of the other officers of their grade in the *Neversink* must be derived.

One of these two quarter-deck lords went among the sailors by a name of their own devising—Selvagee. Of course, it was intended to be characteristic; and even so it was.

In frigates, and all large ships of war, when getting under weigh, a large rope, called a *messenger*, is used to carry the strain of the cable to the capstan; so that the anchor may be weighed, without the muddy, ponderous cable itself going round the capstan. As the cable enters the hawse-hole, therefore, something must be constantly used to keep this travelling chain attached to this travelling *messenger*; something that may be rapidly wound round both, so as to bind them together. The article used is called a *selvagee*. And what could be better adapted to the purpose? It is a slender, tapering, unstranded piece of rope; prepared with much solicitude; peculiarly flexible; and wreathes and serpentines round the cable and messenger like an elegantly modelled garter-snake round the twisted stalks of a vine. Indeed, *Selvagee* is the exact type and symbol of a tall, genteel, limber, spiralizing exquisite. So much for the derivation of the name which the sailors applied to the lieutenant.

From what sea-alcove, from what mermaid's milliner's shop, hast thou emerged, Selvagee! with that dainty waist and languid cheek? What heartless step-dame drove thee forth, to waste thy fragrance on the salt sea air?

Was it *you*, Selvagee! that, outward-bound, off Cape Horn, looked at Hermit Island through an opera-glass? Was it *you*, who thought of proposing to the captain, that when the sails were furled in a gale, a few drops of lavender should be dropped in their 'bunts', so that when the canvass was set again, your nostrils might not be offended by its musty smell? I do not *say* it was you, Selvagee; I but deferentially inquire.

In plain prose, Selvagee was one of those officers whom the sight of a trim-fitting naval coat had captivated in the days of his youth. He fancied, that if a sea-officer dressed well, and conversed genteelly, he would abundantly uphold the honour of his flag, and immortalize the tailor that made him. On that rock many young gentlemen split. For upon a frigate's quarter-deck, it is not enough to sport a coat fashioned by a Stultz;* it is not enough to be well braced with straps and suspenders; it is not enough to have sweet reminiscences of Lauras and Matildas. It is a right down life of hard wear and tear, and the man who is not, in a good degree, fitted to become a common sailor will never make an officer. Take that to heart, all ye naval aspirants. Thrust your arms up to the elbow in pitch, and see how you like it, ere you solicit a warrant. Prepare for white squalls, living gales and typhoons; read accounts of shipwrecks and horrible disasters; peruse the narratives of Byron and Bligh;* familiarize yourselves with the story of the English frigate *Alceste*, and the French frigate *Medusa*.* Though you may go ashore, now and then, at Cadiz and Palermo; for every day so spent among oranges and ladies, you will have whole months of rains and gales.

And even thus did Selvagee prove it. But with all the intrepid effeminacy of your true dandy, he still continued his Cologne-water baths, and sported his lace-bordered handkerchiefs in the very teeth of a tempest. Alas, Selvagee! there was no getting the lavender out of you.

But Selvagee was no fool. Theoretically he understood his profession; but the mere theory of seamanship forms but the thousandth part of what makes a seaman. You cannot save a ship by working out a problem in the cabin; the deck is the field of action.

Well aware of his deficiency in some things, Selvagee never

33

took the trumpet—which is the badge of the deck officer for the time—without a tremulous movement of the lip, and an earnest, inquiring eye to the windward. He encouraged those old Tritons, the quarter-masters, to discourse with him concerning the likelihood of a squall; and often followed their advice as to taking in, or making sail. The smallest favours in that way were thankfully received. Sometimes, when all the north looked unusually lowering, by many conversational blandishments he would endeavour to prolong his predecessor's stay on deck, after that officer's watch had expired. But in fine, steady weather, when the captain would emerge from his cabin, Selvagee might be seen, pacing the poop with long, bold, indefatigable strides, and casting his eye up aloft with the most ostentatious fidelity.

But vain these pretences; he could not deceive. Selvagee! you know very well, that if it comes on to blow pretty hard, the first lieutenant will be sure to interfere with his paternal authority. Every man and every boy in the frigate knows, Selvagee, that you are no Neptune.

How unenviable his situation! His brother officers do not insult him, to be sure; but sometimes their looks are as daggers. The sailors do not laugh at him outright; but of dark nights they jeer, when they hearken to that mantua-maker's voice ordering '*a strong pull at the main-brace*', or '*hands by the halyards!*' Sometimes, by way of being terrific, and making the men jump, Selvagee raps out an oath; but the soft bomb stuffed with confectioner's kisses seems to burst like a crushed rose-bud diffusing its odours. Selvagee! Selvagee! take a maintop-man's advice; and this cruise over, never more tempt the sea.

With this gentleman of cravats and curling-irons, how strongly contrasts the man who was born in a gale! For in some time of tempest—off Cape Horn or Hatteras—*Mad Jack* must have entered the world—such things have been—not with a silver spoon, but with a speaking-trumpet in his mouth; wrapped up in a caul, as in a mainsail—for a charmed life against shipwrecks he bears—and crying, '*Luff! luff, you may!—steady!—port! World ho!—here I am!*'

Mad Jack is in his saddle on the sea. *That* is his home; he would not care much, if another Flood came and overflowed the dry land; for what would it do but float his good ship higher and higher, and carry his proud nation's flag round the globe, over the very capitals of all hostile states! Then would masts surmount spires; and all mankind, like the Chinese boatmen in Canton River, live in flotillas and fleets, and find their food in the sea.

Mad Jack was expressly created and labelled for a tar. Five feet nine is his mark, in his socks; and not weighing over eleven stone before dinner. Like so many ship's shrouds, his muscles and tendons are all set true, trim, and taut; he is braced up fore and aft, like a ship on the wind. His broad chest is a bulkhead, that dams off the gale; and his nose is an aquiline, that divides it in two, like a keel. His loud, lusty lungs are two belfries, full of all manner of chimes; but you only hear his deepest bray in the height of some tempest— like the great bell of St. Paul's, which only sounds when the King or the Devil is dead.

Look at him there, where he stands on the poop—one foot on the rail, and one hand on a shroud—his head thrown back, and his trumpet like an elephant's trunk thrown up in the air. Is he going to shoot dead with sound those fellows on the main-topsail-yard?

Mad Jack was a bit of a tyrant—they *say* all good officers are—but the sailors loved him all round; and would much rather stand fifty watches with him, than one with a rose-water sailor.

But Mad Jack, alas! has one fearful failing. He drinks. And so do we all. But Mad Jack, *he* only drinks brandy. The vice was inveterate; surely, like Ferdinand, Count Fathom,* he must have been suckled at a puncheon. Very often, this bad habit got him into very serious scrapes. Twice was he put off duty by the commodore; and once he came near being broken for his frolics. So far as his efficiency as a sea-officer was concerned, on shore at least Jack might *bouse away* as much as he pleased; but afloat it will not do at all.

Now, if he only followed the wise example set by those

35

ships of the desert, the camels; and while in port, drank for the thirst past, the thirst present, and the thirst to come—so that he might cross the ocean sober; Mad Jack would get along pretty well. Still better, if he would but eschew brandy altogether, and only drink of the limpid white-wine of the rills and the brooks.

IX

Of the Pockets that were in the Jacket

I MUST make some further mention of that white jacket of mine.

And here be it known—by way of introduction to what is to follow—that to a common sailor the living on board a man-of-war is like living in a market; where you dress on the door-steps, and sleep in the cellar. No privacy can you have; hardly one moment's seclusion. It is almost a physical impossibility that you can ever be alone. You dine at a vast *table d'hôte*; sleep in commons, and make your toilet where and when you can. There is no calling for a mutton-chop and a pint of claret by yourself; no selecting of chambers for the night; no hanging of pantaloons over the back of a chair; no ringing your bell of a rainy morning, to take your coffee in bed. It is something like life in a large manufactory.* The bell strikes to dinner, and hungry or not, you must dine.

Your clothes are stowed in a large canvass bag, generally painted black, which you can get out of the 'rack' only once in the twenty-four hours; and then during a time of the utmost confusion; among five hundred other bags, with five hundred other sailors diving into each, in the midst of the twilight of the berth-deck. In some measure to obviate this inconvenience, many sailors divide their wardrobes between their hammocks and their bags; stowing a few frocks and trowsers in the former; so that they can shift at night, if they wish, when the hammocks are piped down. But they gain very little by this.

You have no place whatever but your bag or hammock, in which to put anything in a man-of-war. If you lay anything down, and turn your back for a moment, ten to one it is gone.

Now, in sketching the preliminary plan, and laying out the foundation of that memorable white jacket of mine, I had had an earnest eye to all these inconveniences, and resolved to avoid them. I proposed, that not only should my jacket keep me warm, but that it should also be so constructed as to contain a shirt or two, a pair of trowsers, and divers knick-knacks—sewing utensils, books, biscuits, and the like. With this object, I had accordingly provided it with a great variety of pockets, pantries, clothes-presses, and cupboards.

The principal apartments, two in number, were placed in the skirts, with a wide, hospitable entrance from the inside; two more, of smaller capacity, were planted in each breast, with folding-doors communicating, so that in case of emergency, to accommodate any bulky articles, the two pockets in each breast could be thrown into one. There were, also, several unseen recesses behind the arras; insomuch, that my jacket, like an old castle, was full of winding stairs, and mysterious closets, crypts, and cabinets; and like a confidential writing-desk, abounded in snug little out-of-the-way lairs and hiding-places, for the storage of valuables.

Superadded to these, were four capacious pockets on the outside; one pair to slip books into when suddenly started from my studies to the main-royal-yard; and the other pair for permanent mittens, to thrust my hands into of a cold night-watch. This last contrivance was regarded as needless by one of my top-mates, who showed me a pattern for sea-mittens, which he said was much better than mine.

It must be known, that sailors, even in the bleakest weather, only cover hands when unemployed; they never wear mittens aloft; since aloft, they literally carry their lives in their hands, and want nothing between their grasp of the hemp and the hemp itself.—Therefore, it is desirable that whatever things they cover their hands with should be capable of being slipped on and off in a moment. Nay, it is desirable that they should be of such a nature that in a dark night, when you are in a great hurry—say, going to the helm—they may be jumped into, indiscriminately; and not be like a pair of right-and-left kids;* neither of which will admit any hand but the particular one meant for it.

My top-mate's contrivance was this—he ought to have got out a patent for it—each of his mittens was provided with two thumbs, one on each side; the convenience of which needs no comment. But though for clumsy seamen, whose fingers are all thumbs, this description of mitten might do very well, White-Jacket did not so much fancy it. For when your hand was once in the bag of the mitten, the empty thumb-hole sometimes dangled at your palm, confounding your ideas of where your real thumb might be; or else, being carefully grasped in the hand, was continually suggesting the insane notion, that you were all the while having hold of someone else's thumb.

No; I told my good top-mate to go away with his four thumbs, I would have nothing to do with them; two thumbs were enough for any man.

For some time after completing my jacket, and getting the furniture and household stores in it, I thought that nothing could exceed it for convenience. Seldom now did I have occasion to go to my bag, and be jostled by the crowd who were making their wardrobe in a heap. If I wanted anything in the way of clothing, thread, needles, or literature, the chances were that my invaluable jacket contained it. Yes: I fairly hugged myself, and revelled in my jacket; till alas! a long rain put me out of conceit of it. I, and all my pockets and their contents, were soaked through and through, and my pocket edition of Shakspeare was reduced to an omelet.

However, availing myself of a fine sunny day that followed, I emptied myself out in the maintop, and spread all my goods and chattels to dry. But spite of the bright sun, that day proved a black one. The scoundrels on deck detected me in the act of discharging my saturated cargo; they now knew that the white jacket was used for a store-house. The consequence was, that my goods being well dried and again stored away in my pockets; the very next night, when it was my quarter-watch on deck, and not in the top (where they were all honest men), I noticed a parcel of fellows skulking about after me wherever I went. To a man, they were pickpockets, and bent upon pillaging me. In vain I kept clapping my pockets like nervous old gentlemen in a crowd; that same night I found myself minus several valuable articles. So, in the end, I masoned up my lockers and pantries;*and save the two used for mittens, the white jacket ever after was pocketless.

X

From Pockets to Pickpockets

As the latter part of the preceding chapter may seem strange to those landsmen who have been habituated to indulge in high-raised, romantic notions of the man-of-war's-man's character, it may not be amiss to set down here certain facts on this head, which may serve to place the thing in its true light.

From the wild life they lead, and various other causes (needless to mention), sailors, as a class, entertain the most liberal notions concerning morality and the Decalogue; or, rather, they take their own views of such matters, caring little for the theological or ethical definitions of others concerning what may be criminal, or wrong.

Their ideas are much swayed by circumstances. They will covertly abstract a thing from one whom they dislike; and insist upon it, that, in such a case, stealing is no robbing. Or, where the theft involves something funny, as in the case of the white jacket, they only steal for the sake of the joke; but this much is to be observed nevertheless, i.e., that they never spoil the joke by returning the stolen article.

It is a good joke, for instance, and one often perpetrated on board ship, to stand talking to a man in a dark night-watch, and all the while be cutting the buttons from his coat.

But once off, those buttons never grow on again. There is no spontaneous vegetation in buttons.

Perhaps it is a thing unavoidable, but the truth is, that among the crew of a man-of-war, scores of desperadoes are too often found, who stop not at the largest enormities. A species of highway robbery is not unknown to them. A *gang* will be informed, that such a fellow has three or four gold pieces in the monkey-bag, so called, or purse, which many tars wear round their necks, tucked out of sight. Upon this, they deliberately lay their plans, and in due time proceed to carry them into execution. The man they have marked is perhaps strolling along the benighted berth-deck to his mess-chest; when, of a sudden, the footpads dash out from their hiding-place, throw him down, and while two or three gag him and hold him fast, another cuts the bag from his neck, and makes away with it, followed by his comrades. This was more than once done in the *Neversink*.

At other times, hearing that a sailor has something valuable secreted in his hammock, they will rip it open from underneath while he sleeps, and reduce the conjecture to a certainty.

To enumerate all the minor pilferings on board a man-of-war would be endless. With some highly commendable exceptions, they rob from one another, and rob back again, till, in the matter of small things, a community of goods seems almost established; and at last, as a whole, they become relatively honest, by nearly every man becoming the reverse. It is in vain that the officers, by threats of condign punishment, endeavour to instil more virtuous principles into their crew; so thick is the mob, that not one thief in a thousand is detected.

XI

The Pursuit of Poetry under Difficulties

THE feeling of insecurity concerning one's possessions in the *Neversink*, which the things just narrated begat in the minds of honest men, was curiously exemplified in the case of my poor friend Lemsford, a gentlemanly young member of the after-guard. I had very early made the acquaintance of Lemsford. It is curious, how unerringly a man pitches upon a spirit any way akin to his own, even in the most miscellaneous mob.

Lemsford was a poet; so thoroughly inspired with the divine afflatus, that not even all the tar and tumult of a man-of-war could drive it out of him.

As may readily be imagined, the business of writing verse is a very different thing on the gun-deck of a frigate, from what the gentle and sequestered Wordsworth found it at placid Rydal Mount,* in Westmoreland. In a frigate, you cannot sit down and meander off your sonnets, when the full heart prompts; but only when more important duties permit: such as bracing round the yards, or reefing topsails fore and aft. Nevertheless, every fragment of time at his command was religiously devoted by Lemsford to the Nine. At the most unseasonable hours, you would behold him, seated apart, in some corner among the guns—a shot-box before him, pen in hand, and eyes *'in a fine frenzy rolling'*.*

'What's that 'ere born nat'ral about?'—'He's got a fit, hain't he?' were exclamations often made by the less learned of his shipmates. Some deemed him a conjurer; others a lunatic; and the knowing ones said, that he must be a crazy Methodist. But well knowing by experience the truth of the saying, that *poetry is its own exceeding great reward*, Lemsford wrote on; dashing off whole epics, sonnets, ballads, and acrostics, with a facility which, under the circumstances, amazed me. Often he read over his effusions to me; and well worth the hearing they were. He had wit, imagination, feeling, and humour in abundance; and out of the very ridicule

41

with which some persons regarded him he made rare metrical sport, which we two together enjoyed by ourselves, or shared with certain select friends.

Still, the taunts and jeers so often levelled at my fine friend the poet would now and then rouse him into rage; and at such times the haughty scorn he would hurl on his foes was proof positive of his possession of that one attribute, irritability, almost universally ascribed to the votaries of Parnassus and the Nine.*

My noble captain, Jack Chase, rather patronized Lemsford, and he would stoutly take his part against scores of adversaries. Frequently, inviting him up aloft into his top, he would beg him to recite some of his verses; to which he would pay the most heedful attention, like Mæcenas*listening to Virgil, with a book of the *Æneid* in his hand. Taking the liberty of a well-wisher, he would sometimes gently criticise the piece, suggesting a few immaterial alterations. And upon my word, noble Jack, with his native-born good sense, taste, and humanity, was not ill qualified to play the true part of a *Quarterly Review;*—which is, to give quarter at last, however severe the critique.

Now Lemsford's great care, anxiety, and endless source of tribulation was the preservation of his manuscripts. He had a little box, about the size of a small dressing-case, and secured with a lock, in which he kept his papers and stationery. This box, of course, he could not keep in his bag or hammock, for, in either case, he would only be able to get at it once in the twenty-four hours. It was necessary to have it accessible at all times. So, when not using it, he was obliged to hide it out of sight, where he could. And of all places in the world, a ship of war, above her *hold*, least abounds in secret nooks. Almost every inch is occupied; almost every inch is in plain sight; and almost every inch is continually being visited and explored. Added to all this, was the deadly hostility of the whole tribe of ship-underlings—master-at-arms, ship's corporals, and boatswain's mates—both to the poet and his casket. They hated his box, as if it had been Pandora's, crammed to the very lid with hurricanes and gales. They hunted out his hiding-places like pointers, and gave him no peace night or day.

Still, the long twenty-four-pounders on the main-deck offered some promise of a hiding-place to the box; and, accordingly, it was often tucked away behind the carriages, among the side tackles; its black colour blending with the ebon hue of the guns.

But Quoin, one of the quarter-gunners, had eyes like a ferret. Quoin was a little old man-of-war's-man, hardly five feet high, with a complexion like a gun-shot wound after it is healed. He was indefatigable in attending to his duties, which consisted in taking care of one division of the guns, embracing ten of the aforesaid twenty-four-pounders. Ranged up against the ship's side at regular intervals, they resembled not a little a stud of sable chargers in their stalls. Among this iron stud little Quoin was continually running in and out, currying them down, now and then, with an old rag, or keeping the flies off with a brush. To Quoin, the honour and dignity of the United States of America seemed indissolubly linked with the keeping his guns unspotted and glossy. He himself was black as a chimney-sweep with continually tending them, and rubbing them down with black paint. He would sometimes get outside of the port-holes and peer into their muzzles, as a monkey into a bottle. Or, like a dentist, he seemed intent upon examining their teeth. Quite as often, he would be brushing out their touch-holes with a little wisp of oakum, like a Chinese barber in Canton, cleaning a patient's ear.

Such was his solicitude, that it was a thousand pities he was not able to dwarf himself still more, so as to creep in at the touch-hole, and, examining the whole interior of the tube, emerge at last from the muzzle. Quoin swore by his guns, and slept by their side. Woe betide the man whom he found leaning against them, or in any way soiling them. He seemed seized with the crazy fancy, that his darling twenty-four-pounders were fragile, and might break, like glass retorts.

Now, from this Quoin's vigilance, how could my poor friend the poet hope to escape with his box? Twenty times a week it was pounced upon, with a 'Here's that d——d pill-box again!' and a loud threat, to pitch it overboard the next time, without a moment's warning, or benefit of clergy. Like many poets, Lemsford was nervous, and upon these occasions he trembled like a leaf. Once, with an inconsolable countenance, he came to me, saying that his casket was no-where to be found; he had sought for it in his hiding-place, and it was not there.

I asked him where he had hidden it.

'Among the guns,' he replied.

'Then depend upon it, Lemsford, that Quoin has been the death of it.'

Straight to Quoin went the poet. But Quoin knew nothing about it. For ten mortal days the poet was not to be comforted; dividing his leisure time between cursing Quoin and lamenting his loss. The world is undone, he must have thought; no such calamity has befallen it since the Deluge;—my verses are perished.

But though Quoin, as it afterward turned out, had indeed found the box, it so happened that he had not destroyed it; which no doubt led Lemsford to infer that a superintending Providence had interposed to preserve to posterity his invaluable casket. It was found at last, lying exposed near the galley.

Lemsford was not the only literary man on board the *Neversink*. There were three or four persons who kept journals of the cruise. One of these journalists embellished his work—which was written in a large blank account-book—with various coloured illustrations of the harbours and bays at which the frigate had touched; and also, with small crayon sketches of comical incidents on board the frigate itself. He would frequently read passages of his book to an admiring circle of the more refined sailors, between the guns. They pronounced the whole performance a miracle of art. As the author declared to them that it was all to be printed and published so soon as the vessel reached home, they vied with each other in procuring interesting items, to be incorporated into additional chapters. But it having been rumoured abroad that this journal was to be ominously entitled *The Cruise of the Neversink, or a Paixhan Shot into Naval Abuses*; and it having also reached the ears of the ward-room that the work contained reflections somewhat derogatory to the dignity of the officers, the volume was seized by the master-at-arms, armed with a warrant from the captain. A few days after, a large nail was driven straight through the two covers, and clinched on the other side, and, thus everlastingly sealed, the book was committed to the deep. The ground taken by the authorities on this occasion was, perhaps, that the book was obnoxious to a certain clause in the Articles of War, forbidding any person in the Navy to bring any other person in the Navy into contempt, which the suppressed volume undoubtedly did.

XII

The good or bad Temper of Man-of-war's-men in a great degree attributable to their particular Stations and Duties aboard Ship

QUOIN, the quarter-gunner, was the representative of a class on board the *Neversink*, altogether too remarkable to be left astern, without further notice, in the rapid wake of these chapters.

As has been seen, Quoin was full of unaccountable whimsies; he was, withal, a very cross, bitter, ill-natured, inflammable little old man. So, too, were all the members of the gunner's gang, including the two gunner's mates, and all the quarter-gunners. Every one of them had the same dark brown complexion; all their faces looked like smoked hams. They were continually grumbling and growling about the batteries; running in and out among the guns; driving the sailors away from them; and cursing and swearing as if all their consciences had been powder-singed and made callous by their calling. Indeed they were a most unpleasant set of men, especially Priming, the nasal-voiced gunner's mate, with the hare-lip; and Cylinder, his stuttering co-adjutor, with the clubbed foot. But you will always observe, that the gunner's gang of every man-of-war are invariably ill-tempered, ugly-featured, and quarrelsome. Once when I visited an English line-of-battle ship, the gunner's gang were at work fore and aft, polishing up the batteries, which, according to the admiral's fancy, had been painted white as snow. Fidgeting round the great thirty-two-pounders, and making stinging remarks at the sailors and each other, they reminded one of a swarm of black wasps, buzzing about rows of white head-stones in a churchyard.

Now, there can be little doubt that their being so much among the guns is the very thing that makes a gunner's gang so cross and quarrelsome. Indeed, this was once proved to the satisfaction of our whole company of maintop-men. A fine top-mate of ours, a most merry and companionable fellow, chanced to be promoted to a quarter-gunner's berth. A few days afterward, some of us maintop-men, his old comrades, went to pay him a visit, while he was going his regular rounds through the division of guns allotted to his care. But instead of greeting us with his usual heartiness, and cracking his pleasant jokes, to our amazement he did little else but scowl; and at last, when we rallied him upon his ill-temper, he seized a long black rammer from overhead, and drove us on deck, threatening to report us if we ever dared to be familiar with him again.

My top-mates thought that this remarkable meta-morphose was the effect produced upon a weak, vain character, suddenly elevated from the level of a mere seaman to the dignified position of a *petty officer*. But though, in similar cases, I had seen such effects produced upon some of the crew, yet, in the present instance, I knew better than that;—it was solely brought about by his consorting with those villainous, irritable, ill-tempered cannon; more especially from his being subject to the orders of those deformed blunderbusses, Priming and Cylinder.

The truth seems to be, indeed, that all people should be very careful in selecting their callings and vocations; very careful in seeing to it, that they surround themselves by good-humoured, pleasant-looking objects, and agreeable, temper-soothing sounds. Many an angelic disposition has had its even edge turned, and hacked like a saw; and many a sweet draught of piety has soured on the heart, from people's choosing ill-natured employments, and omitting to gather round them good-natured landscapes. Gardeners are almost always pleasant, affable people to converse with; but beware of quarter-gunners, keepers of arsenals, and lonely lighthouse men. And though you will generally observe that people living in arsenals and lighthouses endeavour to cultivate a few flowers in pots, and perhaps a few cabbages in patches, by way of keeping up, if possible, some gaiety of spirits; yet, it will not do; their going among great guns and muskets everlastingly mildews the blossoms of the one, and how can even cabbages thrive in a soil whereunto the mouldering keels of shipwrecked vessels have imparted the loam?

It would be advisable for any man, who from an unlucky choice of a profession, which it is too late to change for another, should find his temper souring, to endeavour to counteract that misfortune, by filling his private chamber with amiable, pleasurable sights and sounds. In summer time an Æolian harp*can be placed in your window at a very trifling expense; a conch-shell might stand on your mantel, to be taken up and held to the ear, that you may be soothed by its continual lulling sound, when you feel the blue fit stealing over you. For sights, a gay-painted punch-bowl, or Dutch tankard—never mind about filling it—might be recommended. It should be placed on a bracket in the pier. Nor is an old-fashioned silver ladle, nor a chased dinner-castor, nor a fine portly demijohn,*nor anything, indeed, that savours of eating and drinking, bad to drive off the spleen. But perhaps the best of all is a shelf of merrily-bound books, containing comedies, farces, songs, and humorous novels. You need never open them; only have the titles in plain sight. For this purpose, *Peregrine Pickle* is a good book; so is *Gil Blas*; so is Goldsmith.*

But of all chamber furniture in the world, best calculated to cure a bad temper, and breed a pleasant one, is the sight of a lovely wife. If you have children, however, that are teething, the nursery should be a good way upstairs; at sea, it ought to be in the mizzentop. Indeed, teething children play the very deuce with a husband's temper. I have known three promising young husbands completely spoil on their wives' hands, by reason of a teething child, whose worrisomeness happened to be aggravated at the time by the summer complaint. With a breaking heart, and my handkerchief to my eyes, I followed those three hapless young husbands, one after the other, to their premature graves.

Gossiping scenes breed gossips. Who so chatty as hotel-clerks, market-women, auctioneers, bar-keepers, apothecaries, newspaper reporters, monthly nurses, and all those who live in bustling crowds, or are present at scenes of chatty interest?

Solitude breeds taciturnity; *that* everybody knows; who so taciturn as authors, taken as a race?

A forced, interior quietude, in the midst of great outward commotion, breeds moody people. Who so moody as rail-road brakemen, steam-boat engineers, helmsmen, and tenders of power-looms in cotton factories? For all these must hold their peace while employed, and let the machinery do the chatting; they cannot even edge in a single syllable.

Now, this theory about the wondrous influence of habitual sights and sounds upon the human temper was suggested by my experiences on board our frigate. And although I regard the example furnished by our quarter-gunners—especially him who had once been our top-mate—as by far the strongest argument in favour of the general theory; yet the entire ship abounded with illustrations of its truth. Who were more liberal-hearted, lofty-minded, gayer, more jocund, elastic, adventurous, given to fun and frolic, than the top-men of the fore, main, and mizzen masts? The reason of their liberal-heartedness was, that they were daily called upon to expatiate themselves all over the rigging; the reason of their lofty-mindedness was, that they were high lifted above the petty

48

tumults, carping cares, and paltrinesses of the decks below.

And I feel persuaded in my inmost soul, that it is to the fact of my having been a maintop-man, and especially my particular post being on the loftiest yard of the frigate, the main-royal-yard, that I am now enabled to give such a free, broad, off-hand, bird's-eye, and, more than all, impartial account of our man-of-war world; withholding nothing; inventing nothing; nor flattering, nor scandalizing any; but meting out to all—commodore and messenger-boy alike— their precise descriptions and deserts.

The reason of the mirthfulness of these top-men was, that they always looked out upon the blue, boundless, dimpled, laughing, sunny sea. Nor do I hold that it militates against this theory, that of a stormy day, when the face of the ocean was black and overcast, some of them would grow moody, and chose to sit apart. On the contrary, it only proves the thing which I maintain. For even on shore there are many people, naturally gay and light-hearted, who, whenever the autumnal wind begins to bluster round the corners, and roar along the chimney-stacks, straight become cross, petulant, and irritable. What is more mellow than fine old ale? Yet thunder will sour the best nut-brown ever brewed.

The *holders* of our frigate, the troglodytes, who lived down in the tarry cellars and caves below the berth-deck, were, nearly all of them, men of gloomy dispositions, taking sour views of things; one of them was a blue-light* Calvinist. Whereas the old sheet-anchor-men, who spent their time in the bracing sea air and broadcast sunshine of the fore-castle, were free, generous-hearted, charitable, and full of good will to all hands; though some of them, to tell the truth, proved sad exceptions; but exceptions only prove the rule.

The 'steady-cooks' on the berth-deck, the 'steady-sweepers', and 'steady-spit-box-musterers', in all divisions of the frigate, fore and aft, were a narrow-minded set; with contracted souls; imputable, no doubt, to their grovelling duties. More especially was this evinced in the case of those odious ditchers and night scavengers, the ignoble 'waisters'.

The members of the band, some ten or twelve in number,

who had nothing to do but keep their instruments polished, and play a lively air now and then, to stir the stagnant current in our poor old commodore's torpid veins, were the most gleeful set of fellows you ever saw. They were Portuguese, who had been shipped at the Cape de Verd Islands, on the passage out. They messed by themselves; forming a dinner-party, not to be exceeded in mirthfulness by a club of young bridegrooms, three months after marriage, completely satisfied with their bargains, after testing them.

But what made them, now, so full of fun? What indeed but their merry, martial, mellow calling. Who could be a churl, and play a flageolet? who mean and spiritless, braying forth the souls of thousand heroes from his brazen trump? But still more efficacious, perhaps, in ministering to the light spirits of the band, was the consoling thought, that should the ship ever go into action, they would be exempted from the perils of battle. In ships of war, the members of the 'music', as the band is called, are generally non-combatants; and mostly ship with the express understanding, that as soon as the vessel comes within long-gun shot of an enemy, they shall have the privilege of burrowing down in the cable-tiers, or sea coal-hole. Which shows that they are inglorious, but uncommonly sensible fellows.

Look at the barons of the gun-room—lieutenants, purser, marine officers, sailing-master—all of them gentlemen with stiff upper lips, and aristocratic cut noses. Why was this? Will anyone deny, that from their living so long in high military life, served by a crowd of menial stewards and cot-boys, and always accustomed to command right and left; will anyone deny, I say, that by reason of this, their very noses had become thin, peaked, aquiline, and aristocratically cartilaginous? Even old Cuticle, the surgeon, had a Roman nose.

But I never could account how it came to be, that our grey-headed first lieutenant was a little lop-sided; that is, one of his shoulders disproportionately drooped. And when I observed, that nearly all the first lieutenants I saw in other men-of-war, besides many second and third lieutenants, were similarly lop-sided, I knew that there must be some general law which induced the phenomenon; and I put myself to studying it out, as an interesting problem. At last, I came to the conclusion—to which I still adhere—that their so long wearing only one epaulet (for to only one does their rank entitle them) was the infallible clue to this mystery. And when anyone reflects upon so well-known a fact, that many sea-lieutenants grow decrepit from age, without attaining a captaincy and wearing *two* epaulets, which would strike the balance between their shoulders, the above reason assigned will not appear unwarrantable.

XIII
A Man-of-war Hermit in a Mob

THE allusion to the poet Lemsford, in a previous chapter, leads me to speak of our mutual friends, Nord and Williams, who with Lemsford himself, Jack Chase, and my comrades of the maintop, comprised almost the only persons with whom I unreservedly consorted while on board the frigate; for I had not been long on board ere I found that it would not do to be intimate with everybody. An indiscrimate intimacy with all hands leads to sundry annoyances and scrapes, too often ending with a dozen at the gangway. Though I was above a year in the frigate, there were scores of men who to the last remained perfect strangers to me, whose very names I did not know, and whom I would hardly be able to recognize now should I happen to meet them in the streets.

In the dog-watches at sea, during the early part of the evening, the main-deck is generally filled with crowds of pedestrians, promenading up and down past the guns, like people taking the air in Broadway. At such times, it is curious to see the men nodding to each other's recognitions (they might not have seen each other for a week); exchanging a pleasant word with a friend; making a hurried appointment to meet him somewhere aloft on the morrow, or passing group after group without deigning the slightest salutation. Indeed, I was not at all singular in having but comparatively few acquaintances on board, though certainly carrying my fastidiousness to an unusual extent.

My friend Nord was a somewhat remarkable character; and if mystery includes romance, he certainly was a very romantic one. Before seeking an introduction to him through Lemsford, I had often marked his tall, spare, upright figure stalking like Don Quixote among the pigmies of the after-guard, to which he belonged. At first I found him exceed-ingly reserved and taciturn; his saturnine brow wore a scowl; he was almost repelling in his demeanour. In a word, he seemed desirous of hinting, that his list of man-of-war friends was already made up, complete, and full; and there was no room for more. But observing that the only man he ever consorted with was Lemsford, I had too much magna-nimity, by going off in a pique at his coldness, to let him lose forever the chance of making so capital an acquaintance as myself. Besides, I saw it in his eye, that the man had been a reader of good books; I would have staked my life on it, that he seized the right meaning of Montaigne.* I saw that he was an earnest thinker; I more than suspected that he had been bolted in the mill of adversity. For all these things my heart yearned toward him; I determined to know him.

At last I succeeded; it was during a profoundly quiet mid-night watch, when I perceived him walking alone in the waist, while most of the men were dozing on the carronade-slides.

That night we scoured all the prairies of reading; dived into the bosoms of authors, and tore out their hearts; and that night White-Jacket learned more than he has ever done in any single night since.

The man was a marvel. He amazed me, as much as Coleridge did the troopers among whom he enlisted.* What could have induced such a man to enter a man-of-war, all my sapience cannot fathom. And how he managed to pre-serve his dignity, as he did, among such a rabble rout was equally a mystery. For he was no sailor; as ignorant of a ship, indeed, as a man from the sources of the Niger. Yet the officers respected him; and the men were afraid of him. This much was observable, however, that he faithfully discharged whatever special duties devolved upon him; and was so fortunate as never to render himself liable to a reprimand. Doubtless he took the same view of the thing that another of the crew did; and had early resolved, so to conduct himself as never to run the risk of the scourge. And this it must have been—added to whatever incommunicable grief which might have been his—that made this Nord such a wandering recluse, even among our man-of-war mob. Nor could he have long swung his hammock on board, ere he must have found that, to ensure his exemption from that thing which alone affrighted him, he must be content for the most part to turn a man-hater, and socially expatriate himself from many things which might have rendered his situation more tolerable. Still more, several events that took place must have horrified him, at times, with the thought that, however he might isolate and entomb himself, yet for all this, the improbability of his being overtaken by what he most dreaded never advanced to the infallibility of the impossible.

In my intercourse with Nord, he never made allusion to his past career—a subject upon which most high-bred castaways in a man-of-war are very diffuse; relating their adventures at the gaming-table; the recklessness with which they have run through the amplest fortunes in a single season; their alms-givings, and gratuities to porters and poor relations; and above all, their youthful indiscretions, and the broken-hearted ladies they have left behind. No such tales had Nord to tell. Concerning the past, he was barred and locked up like the specie-vaults of the Bank of England. For anything that dropped from him, none of us could be sure that he had ever existed till now. Altogether he was a remarkable man.

My other friend, Williams, was a thorough-going Yankee from Maine, who had been both a peddler and a pedagogue in his day. He had all manner of stories to tell about nice little country frolics, and would run over an endless list of his sweethearts. He was honest, acute, witty, full of mirth and good humour—a laughing philosopher. He was invaluable as a pill against the spleen; and, with the view of extending the advantages of his society to the saturnine Nord, I introduced them to each other; but Nord cut him dead the very same evening, when we sallied out from between the guns for a walk on the main-deck.

XIV

A Drought in a Man-of-war

WE were not many days out of port, when a rumour was set afloat that dreadfully alarmed many tars. It was this: that, owing to some unprecedented oversight in the purser, or some equally unprecedented remissness in the naval store-keeper at Callao, the frigate's supply of that delectable beverage called 'grog' was well-nigh expended.

In the American Navy, the law allows one gill of spirits per day to every seaman. In two portions, it is served out just previous to breakfast and dinner. At the roll of the drum, the sailors assemble round a large tub, or cask, filled with the liquid; and, as their names are called off by a midshipman, they step up and regale themselves from a little tin measure called a 'tot'. No high-liver helping himself to Tokay*off a well-polished sideboard smacks his lips with more mighty satisfaction than the sailor does over this *tot*. To many of them, indeed, the thought of their daily *tots* forms a perpetual perspective of ravishing landscapes, indefinitely receding in the distance. It is their great 'prospect in life'. Take away their grog, and life possesses no further charms for them. It is hardly to be doubted, that the controlling inducement which keeps many men in the Navy is the unbounded confidence they have in the ability of the United States government to supply them, regularly and unfailingly, with their daily allowance of this beverage. I have known several forlorn individuals, shipping as landsmen, who have confessed to me, that having contracted a love for ardent spirits, which they could not renounce, and having by their foolish courses been brought into the most abject poverty—insomuch that they could no longer gratify their thirst ashore—they incontinently entered the Navy; regarding it as the asylum for all drunkards, who might there prolong their lives by regular hours and exercise, and twice every day quench their thirst by moderate and undeviating doses.

When I once remonstrated with an old toper of a top-man about his daily dram-drinking; when I told him it was ruining him, and advised him to *stop his grog* and receive the money for it, in addition to his wages, as provided by law, he turned about on me, with an irresistibly waggish look, and said, 'Give up my grog? And why? Because it is ruining me? No, no; I am a good Christian, White-Jacket, and love my enemy too much to drop his acquaintance.'

It may be readily imagined, therefore, what consternation and dismay pervaded the gun-deck at the first announcement of the tidings that the grog was expended.

'The grog gone!' roared an old sheet-anchor-man.

'Oh Lord! what a pain in my stomach!' cried a maintop-man.

'It's worse than the cholera!' cried a man of the afterguard.

'I'd sooner the water-casks would give out!' said a captain of the hold.

'Are we ganders and geese, that we can live without grog?' asked a corporal of marines.

'Ay, we must now drink with the ducks!' cried a quartermaster.

'Not a tot left?' groaned a waister.

'Not a toothful!' sighed a holder, from the bottom of his boots.

Yes, the fatal intelligence proved true. The drum was no longer heard rolling the men to the tub, and deep gloom and dejection fell like a cloud. The ship was like a great city, when some terrible calamity has overtaken it. The men stood apart, in groups, discussing their woes, and mutually condoling. No longer, of still moonlight nights, was the song heard from the giddy tops; and few and far between were the stories that were told.

It was during this interval, so dismal to many, that, to the amazement of all hands, ten men were reported by the master-at-arms to be intoxicated. They were brought up to the mast, and at their appearance the doubts of the most sceptical were dissipated; but whence they had obtained their liquor no one could tell. It was observed, however, at the time, that the tarry knaves all smelled of lavender, like so many dandies.

After their examination they were ordered into the 'brig', a jail-house between two guns on the main-deck, where prisoners are kept. Here they laid for some time, stretched out stark and stiff, with their arms folded over their breasts, like so many effigies of the Black Prince*on his monument in Canterbury Cathedral.

Their first slumbers over, the marine sentry who stood guard over them had as much as he could do to keep off the crowd, who were all eagerness to find out how, in such a time of want, the prisoners had managed to drink themselves into oblivion. In due time they were liberated, and the secret simultaneously leaked out.

It seemed that an enterprising man of their number, who had suffered severely from the common deprivation, had all at once been struck by a brilliant idea. It had come to his knowledge that the purser's steward was supplied with a large quantity of *Eau-de-Cologne*, clandestinely brought out in the ship, for the purpose of selling it, on his own account, to the people of the coast; but the supply proving larger than the demand, and having no customers on board the frigate but Lieutenant Selvagee, he was now carrying home more than a third of his original stock. To make a short story of it, this functionary, being called upon in secret, was readily prevailed upon to part with a dozen bottles, with whose contents the intoxicated party had regaled themselves.

The news spread far and wide among the men, being only kept secret from the officers and underlings, and that night the long, crane-necked Cologne bottles jingled in out-of-the-way corners and by-places, and, being emptied, were sent flying out of the ports. With brown sugar, taken from the mess-chests, and hot water begged from the galley-cooks, the men made all manner of punches, toddies, and cocktails, letting fall therein a small drop of tar, like a bit of brown toast, by way of imparting a flavour. Of course, the thing was managed with the utmost secrecy; and as a whole dark night elapsed after their orgies, the revellers were, in a good measure, secure from detection; and those who indulged too freely had twelve long hours to get sober before daylight obtruded.

Next day, fore and aft, the whole frigate smelled like a lady's toilet; the very tar-buckets were fragrant; and from the mouth of many a grim, grizzled old quarter-gunner came the most fragrant of breaths. The amazed lieutenants went about snuffing up the gale; and, for once, Selvagee had no further need to flourish his perfumed handkerchief. It was as if we were sailing by some odoriferous shore, in the vernal season of violets. Sabaean odours!*

> For many a league,
> Cheer'd with the grateful smell, old Ocean smiled.*

But, alas! all this perfume could not be wasted for nothing; and the master-at-arms and ship's corporals, putting this and that together, very soon burrowed into the secret. The purser's steward was called to account, and no more lavender punches and Cologne toddies were drank on board the *Neversink*.

XV

A Salt-Junk Club in a Man-of-war, with a Notice to quit*

I T was about the period of the Cologne-water excitement that my self-conceit was not a little wounded, and my sense of delicacy altogether shocked, by a polite hint received from the cook of the mess to which I happened to belong. To understand the matter, it is needful to enter into preliminaries.

The common seamen in a large frigate are divided into some thirty or forty messes, put down on the purser's books as *Mess No.* 1, *Mess No.* 2, *Mess No.* 3, &c. The members of each mess club their rations of provisions, and breakfast, dine, and sup together in allotted intervals between the guns on the main-deck. In undeviating rotation, the members of each mess (excepting the petty officers) take their turn in performing the functions of cook and steward. And for the time being, all the affairs of the club are subject to their inspection and control.

It is the cook's business, also, to have an eye to the general interests of his mess; to see that, when the aggregated allowances of beef, bread, &c., are served out by one of the master's mates, the mess over which he presides receives its full share, without stint or subtraction. Upon the berth-deck he has a chest, in which to keep his pots, pans, spoons, and small stores of sugar, molasses, tea, and flour.

But though entitled a cook, strictly speaking the head of the mess is no cook at all; for the cooking for the crew is all done by a high and mighty functionary, officially called the *ship's cook*, assisted by several deputies. In our frigate, this personage was a dignified coloured gentleman, whom the men dubbed *Old Coffee*; and his assistants, negroes also, went by the poetical appellations of *Sunshine*, *Rose-Water*, and *May-Day*.

Now, the *ship's cooking* required very little science, though Old Coffee often assured us that he had graduated at the New York Astor House, under the immediate eye of the celebrated Coleman and Stetson.* All he had to do was, in the first place, to keep bright and clean the three huge coppers, or cauldrons, in which many hundred pounds of beef were daily boiled. To this end, Rose-Water, Sunshine, and May-Day every morning sprang into their respective apartments, stripped to the waist, and well-provided with bits of soap-stone and sand. By exercising these in a very vigorous manner, they threw themselves into a violent perspiration, and put a fine polish upon the interior of the coppers.

Sunshine was the bard of the trio; and while all three would be busily employed clattering their soap-stones against the metal, he would exhilarate them with some remarkable St. Domingo* melodies, one of which was the following:

> Oh! I los' my shoe in an old canoe,
>   Johnio! come Winum so!
> Oh! I los' my boot in a pilot-boat,
>   Johnio! come Winum so!
> Den rub-a-dub de copper, oh!
> Oh! copper rub-a-dub-a-oh!

When I listened to these jolly Africans, thus making gleeful their toil by their cheering songs, I could not help murmuring against that immemorial rule of men-of-war, which forbids the sailors to sing out, as in merchant-vessels, when pulling ropes, or occupied at any other ship's duty. Your only music, at such times, is the shrill pipe of the boatswain's mate, which is almost worse than no music at all. And if the boatswain's mate is not by, you must pull the ropes, like convicts, in profound silence; or else endeavour to impart unity to the exertions of all hands, by singing out mechanically, *one*, *two*, *three*, and then pulling all together.

Now, when Sunshine, Rose-Water, and May-Day have so polished the ship's coppers, that a white kid glove might be drawn along the inside and show no stain, they leap out of their holes, and the water is poured in for the coffee. And the coffee being boiled, and decanted off in bucketsful, the cooks of the messes march up with their salt beef for dinner, strung upon strings and tallied with labels; all of which are plunged together into the self-same coppers, and there boiled. When, upon the beef being fished out with a huge pitch-fork, the water for the evening's tea is poured in; which, consequently, possesses a flavour not unlike that of shank-soup.

From this it will be seen, that, so far as cooking is concerned, a *cook of the mess* has very little to do; merely carrying his provisions to and from the grand democratic cookery. Still, in some things, his office involves many annoyances. Twice a week butter and cheese are served out—so much to each man—and the mess-cook has the sole charge of these delicacies. The great difficulty consists in so catering for the mess, touching these luxuries, as to satisfy all. Some guzzlers are for devouring the butter at a meal, and finishing off with the cheese the same day; others contend for saving it up against *Banyan Day*, when there is nothing but beef and bread; and others, again, are for taking a very small bit of butter and cheese, by way of dessert, to each and every meal through the week. All this gives rise to endless disputes, debates, and altercations.

Sometimes, with his mess-cloth—a square of painted canvass—set out on deck between the guns, garnished with pots, and pans, and *kids*, you see the mess-cook seated on a match-tub at its head, his trowser-legs rolled up and arms bared, presiding over the convivial party.

'Now, men, you can't have any butter to-day. I'm saving it up for to-morrow. You don't know the value of butter, men. You, Jim, take your hoof off the cloth! Devil take me, if some of you chaps haven't no more manners than so many swines! Quick, men, quick; bear a hand, and *scoff* (eat) away.—I've got my to-morrow's *duff* to make yet, and some of you fellows keep *scoffing* as if I had nothing to do but sit still here on this here tub here, and look on. There, there, men, you've all had enough; so sail away out of this, and let me clear up the wreck.'

In this strain would one of the periodical cooks of Mess No. 15 talk to us. He was a tall, resolute fellow, who had once been a brakeman on a railroad, and he kept us all pretty straight; from his fiat there was no appeal.

But it was not thus when the turn came to others among us. Then it was, *look out for squalls*. The business of dining became a bore, and digestion was seriously impaired by the unamiable discourse we had over our *salt horse*.

I sometimes thought that the junks of lean pork—which were boiled in their own bristles, and looked gaunt and grim, like pickled chins of half-famished, unwashed Cossacks—had something to do with creating the bristling bitterness at times prevailing in our mess. The men tore off the tough hide from their pork, as if they were Indians scalping Christians.

Some cursed the cook for a rogue, who kept from us our butter and cheese, in order to make away with it himself in an underhand manner; selling it at a premium to other messes, and thus accumulating a princely fortune at our expense. Others anathematized him for his slovenliness, casting hypercritical glances into their pots and pans, and scraping them with their knives. Then he would be railed at for his miserable 'duffs', and other short-coming preparations.

Marking all this from the beginning, I, White-Jacket, was sorely troubled with the idea, that, in the course of time, my own turn would come round to undergo the same objurgations.* How to escape, I knew not. However, when the dreaded period arrived, I received the keys of office (the keys of the mess-chest) with a resigned temper, and offered up a devout ejaculation for fortitude under the trial. I resolved, please Heaven, to approve myself an unexceptionable caterer, and the most impartial of stewards.

The first day there was *duff* to make—a business which devolved upon the mess-cooks, though the boiling of it pertained to Old Coffee and his deputies. I made up my mind to lay myself out on that *duff*; to centre all my energies upon it; to put the very soul of art into it, and achieve an unrivalled *duff*—a *duff* that should put out of conceit all other *duffs*, and forever make my administration memorable.

From the proper functionary the flour was obtained, and the raisins; the beef-fat, or *slush*, from Old Coffee; and the requisite supply of water from the scuttle-butt. I then went among the various cooks, to compare their receipts for making 'duffs'; and having well weighed them all, and gathered from each a choice item to make an original receipt of my own, with due deliberation and solemnity I proceeded to business. Placing the component parts in a tin pan, I kneaded them together for an hour, entirely reckless as to pulmonary considerations, touching the ruinous expenditure of breath; and having decanted the semi-liquid dough into a canvass bag, secured the muzzle, tied on the tally, and delivered it to Rose-Water, who dropped the precious bag into the coppers, along with a score or two of others.

Eight bells had struck. The boatswain and his mates had piped the hands to dinner; my mess-cloth was set out, and my messmates were assembled, knife in hand, all ready to precipitate themselves upon the devoted *duff*. Waiting at the grand cookery till my turn came, I received the bag of pudding, and gallanting it into the mess, proceeded to loosen the string.

It was an anxious, I may say, a fearful moment. My hands trembled; every eye was upon me; my reputation and credit were at stake. Slowly I undressed the *duff*, dandling it upon my knee, much as a nurse does a baby about bed-time. The excitement increased, as I curled down the bag from the pudding; it became intense, when at last I plumped it into the pan, held up to receive it by an eager hand. Bim! it fell like a man shot down in a riot. Distraction! It was harder than a sinner's heart; yea, tough as the cock that crowed on the morn that Peter told a lie.*

'Gentlemen of the mess, for heaven's sake! permit me one word. I have done my duty by that duff—I have——'

But they beat down my excuses with a storm of criminations. One present proposed that the fatal pudding should be tied round my neck, like a millstone, and myself pushed overboard. No use, no use; I had failed; ever after, that duff lay heavy at my stomach and my heart.

After this, I grew desperate; despised popularity; returned scorn for scorn; till at length my week expired, and in the duff-bag I transferred the keys of office to the next man on the roll.

Somehow, there had never been a very cordial feeling between this mess and me; all along they had nourished a prejudice against my white jacket. They must have harboured the silly fancy that in it I gave myself airs, and wore it in order to look consequential; perhaps, as a cloak to cover pilferings of tit-bits from the mess. But to out with the plain truth, they themselves were not a very irreproachable set. Considering the sequel I am coming to, this avowal may be deemed sheer malice; but for all that, I cannot avoid speaking my mind.

After my week of office, the mess gradually changed their behaviour to me; they cut me to the heart; they became cold and reserved; seldom or never addressed me at meal-times without invidious allusions to my *duff*, and also to my jacket, and its dripping in wet weather upon the mess-cloth. However, I had no idea that anything serious, on their part, was brewing; but alas! so it turned out.

We were assembled at supper one evening, when I noticed certain winks and silent hints tipped to the cook, who presided. He was a little, oily fellow, who had once kept an oyster-cellar ashore; he bore me a grudge. Looking down on the mess-cloth, he observed that some fellows never knew when their room was better than their company. This being a maxim of indiscriminate application, of course I silently assented to it, as any other reasonable man would have done. But this remark was followed up by another, to the effect that not only did some fellows never know when their room was better than their company, but they persisted in staying when their company wasn't wanted, and by so doing disturbed the serenity of society at large. But this, also, was a general observation that could not be gainsaid. A long and ominous pause ensued; during which I perceived every eye upon me, and my white jacket; while the cook went on to enlarge upon the disagreeableness of a perpetually damp garment in the mess, especially when that garment was white. This was coming nearer home.

Yes, they were going to blackball me; but I resolved to sit it out a little longer; never dreaming that my moralist would proceed to extremities while all hands were present. But bethinking him that by going this roundabout way he would never get at his object, he went off on another tack; apprising me, in substance, that he was instructed by the whole mess, then and there assembled, to give me warning to seek out another club, as they did not longer fancy the society either of myself or my jacket.

I was shocked. Such a want of tact and delicacy! Common propriety suggested that a point-blank intimation of that nature should be conveyed in a private interview; or, still better, by note. I immediately rose, tucked my jacket about me, bowed, and departed.

And now, to do myself justice, I must add that, the next day, I was received with open arms by a glorious set of fellows—Mess No. 1!—numbering, among the rest, my noble captain, Jack Chase.

This mess was principally composed of the headmost men of the gun-deck; and, out of a pardonable self-conceit, they called themselves the *Forty-two-pounder Club*; meaning that they were, one and all, fellows of large intellectual and corporeal calibre. Their mess-cloth was well located. On their starboard hand was *Mess No.* 2, embracing sundry rare jokers and high livers, who waxed gay and epicurean over their salt fare, and were known as the *Society for the Destruction of Beef and Pork*. On the larboard hand was *Mess No.* 31, made up entirely of foretop-men, a dashing, blaze-away set of man-of-war's-men, who called themselves the *Cape Horn Snorters and Neversink Invincibles*. Opposite, was one of the marine messes, mustering the aristocracy of the marine corps—the two corporals, the drummer and fifer, and some six or eight rather gentlemanly privates, native-born Americans, who had served in the Seminole campaigns* of Florida; and they now enlivened their salt fare with stories of wild ambushes in the everglades; and one of them related a surprising tale of his hand-to-hand encounter with Osceola, the Indian chief, whom he fought one morning from day-break till breakfast-time. This slashing private also boasted that he could take a chip from between your teeth at twenty paces; he offered to bet any amount on it; and as he could get no one to hold the chip, his boast remained forever good.

Besides many other attractions which the *Forty-two-pounder Club* furnished, it had this one special advantage, that, owing to there being so many *petty officers* in it, all the members of the mess were exempt from doing duty as cooks and stewards. A fellow called a *steady-cook* attended to that business during the entire cruise. He was a long, lank, pallid varlet, going by the name of Shanks. In very warm weather this Shanks would sit at the foot of the mess-cloth, fanning himself with the front flap of his frock or shirt, which he inelegantly wore over his trowsers. Jack Chase, the President of the Club, frequently remonstrated against this breach of good manners; but the *steady-cook* had somehow contracted the habit, and it proved incurable. For a time, Jack Chase, out of a polite nervousness touching myself, as a newly-elected member of the club, would frequently endeavour to excuse to me the vulgarity of Shanks. One day he wound up his remarks by the philosophic reflection—'But White-Jacket, my dear fellow, what can you expect of him? Our real misfortune is, that our noble club should be obliged to dine with its cook.'

There were several of these *steady-cooks* on board; men of no mark or consideration whatever in the ship; lost to all noble promptings; sighing for no worlds to conquer, and perfectly contented with mixing their *duffs*, and spreading their mess-cloths, and mustering their pots and pans together three times every day for a three years' cruise. They were very seldom to be seen on the spar-deck, but kept below out of sight.

XVI

General Training in a Man-of-war

To a quiet, contemplative character, averse to uproar, undue exercise of his bodily members, and all kind of useless confusion, nothing can be more distressing than a proceeding in all men-of-war called *general quarters*. And well may it be so called, since it amounts to a general drawing and quartering of all the parties concerned.

As the specific object for which a man-of-war is built and put into commission is to fight and fire off cannon, it is, of course, deemed indispensable that the crew should be duly instructed in the art and mystery involved. Hence these 'general quarters', which is a mustering of all hands to their stations at the guns on the several decks, and a sort of sham-fight with an imaginary foe.

The summons is given by the ship's drummer, who strikes a peculiar beat—short, broken, rolling, shuffling—like the sound made by the march into battle of iron-heeled grenadiers. It is a regular tune, with a fine song composed to it; the words of the chorus, being most artistically arranged, may give some idea of the air:—

> Hearts of oak are our ships, jolly tars are our men,
> We always are ready, steady, boys, steady,
> To fight and to conquer, again and again.*

In warm weather this pastime at the guns is exceedingly unpleasant, to say the least, and throws a quiet man into a violent passion and perspiration. For one, I ever abominated it.

I have a heart like Julius Caesar, and upon occasion would fight like Caius Marcius Coriolanus. If my beloved and forever glorious country should be ever in jeopardy from invaders, let Congress put me on a war-horse, in the vanguard, and *then* see how I will acquit myself. But to toil and sweat in a fictitious encounter; to squander the precious breath of my precious body in a ridiculous fight of shams and pretensions; to hurry about the decks, pretending to carry the killed and wounded below; to be told that I must consider the ship blowing up, in order to exercise myself in presence of mind, and prepare for a real explosion; all this I despise, as beneath a true tar and man of valour.

These were my sentiments at the time, and these remain my sentiments still; but as, while on board the frigate, my liberty of thought did not extend to liberty of expression, I was obliged to keep these sentiments to myself; though, indeed, I had some thoughts of addressing a letter, marked *Private and Confidential*, to his Honour the Commodore, on the subject.

My station at the batteries was at one of the thirty-two-pound carronades, on the starboard side of the quarter-deck.*

I did not fancy this station at all; for it is well known on shipboard that, in time of action, the quarter-deck is one of the most dangerous posts of a man-of-war. The reason is, that the officers of the highest rank are there stationed, and the enemy have an ungentlemanly way of target-shooting at their buttons. If we should chance to engage a ship, then, who could tell but some bungling small-arm marksman in

---

* For the benefit of a Quaker reader here and there, a word or two in explanation of a carronade may not be amiss. The carronade is a gun comparatively short and light for its calibre. A carronade throwing a thirty-two-pound shot weighs considerably less than a long-gun only throwing a twenty-four-pound shot. It further differs from a long-gun, in working with a joint and bolt underneath, instead of the short arms or *trunnions* at the sides. Its *carriage*, likewise, is quite different from that of a long-gun, having a sort of sliding apparatus, something like an extension dining-table; the goose on it, however, is a tough one, and villainously stuffed with most indigestible dumplings. Point-blank, the range of a carronade does not exceed one hundred and fifty yards, much less than the range of a long-gun. When of large calibre, however, it throws within that limit Paixhan shot, all manner of shells and combustibles, with great effect, being a very destructive engine at close quarters. This piece is now very generally found mounted in the batteries of the English and American navies. The quarter-deck armaments of most modern frigates wholly consist of carronades. The name is derived from the village of Carron, in Scotland, at whose celebrated foundries this iron Attila was first cast.

the enemy's tops might put a bullet through *me* instead of the commodore? If they hit *him*, no doubt he would not feel it much, for he was used to that sort of thing, and, indeed, had a bullet in him already; whereas, *I* was altogether unaccustomed to having blue pills playing round my head in such an indiscriminate way. Besides, ours was a flagship; and everyone knows what a peculiarly dangerous predicament the quarter-deck of Nelson's flagship was in at the Battle of Trafalgar;* how the lofty tops of the enemy were full of soldiers, peppering away at the English admiral and his officers. Many a poor sailor, at the guns of that quarter-deck, must have received a bullet intended for some wearer of an epaulet.

By candidly confessing my feelings on this subject, I do by no means invalidate my claims to being held a man of prodigious valour. I merely state my invincible repugnance to being shot for somebody else. If I am shot, be it with the express understanding in the shooter that I am the identical person intended so to be served. That Thracian who, with his compliments, sent an arrow into the King of Macedon,* superscribed 'For Philip's right eye', set a fine example to all warriors. The hurried, hasty, indiscriminate, reckless, abandoned manner in which both sailors and soldiers nowadays fight is really painful to any serious-minded, methodical old gentleman, especially if he chance to have systematized his mind as an accountant. There is little or no skill and bravery about it. Two parties, armed with lead and old iron, envelop themselves in a cloud of smoke, and pitch their lead and old iron about in all directions. If you happen to be in the way, you are hit; possibly killed; if not, you escape. In sea-actions, if by good or bad luck, as the case may be, a round shot fired at random through the smoke happens to send overboard your foremast, another to unship your rudder, there you lie crippled, pretty much at the mercy of your foe; who, accordingly, pronounces himself victor, though that honour properly belongs to the law of gravitation operating on the enemy's balls in the smoke. Instead of tossing this old lead and iron into the air, therefore, it would be much better amicably to toss up a copper and let heads win.

The carronade at which I was stationed was known as 'Gun No. 5', on the first lieutenant's quarter-bill. Among our gun's crew, however, it was known as *Black Bet*. This name was bestowed by the captain of the gun—a fine negro—in honour of his sweetheart, a coloured lady of Philadelphia. Of Black Bet I was rammer and sponger; and ram and sponge I did, like a good fellow. I have no doubt that, had I and my gun been at the Battle of the Nile,* we would mutually have immortalized ourselves; the ramming-pole would have been hung up in Westminster Abbey; and I, ennobled by the King, besides receiving the illustrious honour of an autograph letter from His Majesty through the perfumed right hand of his private secretary.

But it was terrible work to help run in and out of the porthole that amazing mass of metal, especially as the thing must be done in a trice. Then, at the summons of a horrid, rasping rattle swayed by the captain in person, we were made to rush from our guns, seize pikes and pistols, and repel an imaginary army of boarders, who, by a fiction of the officers, were supposed to be assailing all sides of the ship at once. After cutting and slashing at them awhile, we jumped back to our guns, and again went to jerking our elbows.

Meantime, a loud cry is heard of 'Fire! fire! fire!' in the foretop; and a regular engine, worked by a set of Bowery-boy tars, is forthwith set to playing streams of water aloft. And now it is 'Fire! fire! fire!' on the main-deck; and the entire ship is in as great a commotion as if a whole city ward were in a blaze.

Are our officers of the Navy utterly unacquainted with the laws of good health? Do they not know that this violent exercise, taking place just after a hearty dinner, as it generally does, is eminently calculated to breed the dyspepsia? There was no satisfaction in dining; the flavour of every mouthful was destroyed by the thought that the next moment the cannonading drum might be beating to quarters.

Such a sea-martinet was our captain, that sometimes we

were roused from our hammocks at night; when a scene would ensue that it is not in the power of pen and ink to describe. Five hundred men spring to their feet, dress themselves, take up their bedding, and run to the nettings and stow it; then hie to their stations—each man jostling his neighbour—some alow, some aloft; some this way, some that; and in less than five minutes the frigate is ready for action, and still as the grave; almost every man precisely where he would be were an enemy actually about to be engaged. The gunner, like a Cornwall miner in a cave, is burrowing down in the magazine under the ward-room, which is lighted by battle-lanterns, placed behind glazed glass bull's-eyes inserted in the bulkhead. The *powder-monkeys*, or boys who fetch and carry cartridges, are scampering to and fro among the guns; and the *first and second loaders* stand ready to receive their supplies.

These *powder-monkeys*, as they are called, enact a curious part in time of action. The entrance to the magazine on the berth-deck, where they procure their food for the guns, is guarded by a woollen* screen; and a gunner's mate, standing behind it, thrusts out the cartridges through a small arm-hole in this screen. The enemy's shot (perhaps red hot) are flying in all directions; and to protect their cartridges, the powder-monkeys hurriedly wrap them up in their jackets; and with all haste scramble up the ladders to their respective guns, like eating-house waiters hurrying along with hot cakes for breakfast.

At *general quarters* the shot-boxes are uncovered; showing the grape-shot—aptly so called, for they precisely resemble bunches of the fruit; though, to receive a bunch of iron grapes in the abdomen would be but a sorry dessert; and also showing the cannister-shot—old iron of various sorts, packed in a tin case, like a tea-caddy.

Imagine some midnight craft sailing down on her enemy thus; twenty-four-pounders levelled, matches lighted, and each captain of his gun at his post!

But if verily going into action, then would the *Neversink* have made still further preparations; for however alike in some things, there is always a vast difference—if you sound them—between a reality and a sham. Not to speak of the pale sternness of the men at their guns at such a juncture, and the choked thoughts at their hearts, the ship itself would here and there present a far different appearance; something like that of an extensive mansion preparing for a grand entertainment, when folding-doors are withdrawn, chambers converted into drawing-rooms, and every inch of available space thrown into one continuous whole. For previous to an action, every bulkhead of a man-of-war is knocked down; great guns are run out of the commodore's parlour windows; nothing separates the ward-room officers' quarters from those of the men, but an ensign used for a curtain. The sailors' mess-chests are tumbled down into the hold; and the hospital cots—of which all men-of-war carry a large supply—are dragged forth from the sail-room, and piled near at hand to receive the wounded; amputation-tables are ranged in the *cock-pit* or in the *tiers*, whereon to carve the bodies of the maimed. The yards are slung in chains; fire-screens distributed here and there; hillocks of cannon-balls piled between the guns; shot-plugs suspended within easy reach from the beams; and solid masses of wads, big as Dutch cheeses, braced to the cheeks of the gun-carriages.

No small difference, also, would be visible in the wardrobe of both officers and men. The officers generally fight as dandies dance, namely, in silk stockings; inasmuch as, in case of being wounded in the leg, the silk hose can be more easily drawn off by the surgeon; cotton sticks, and works into the wound. An economical captain, while taking care to case his legs in silk, might yet see fit to save his best suit, and fight in his old clothes. For, besides that an old garment might much better be cut to pieces than a new one, it must be a mighty disagreeable thing to die in a stiff, tight-breasted coat, not yet worked easy under the armpits. At such times, a man should feel free, unencumbered, and perfectly at ease in point of straps and suspenders. No ill-will concerning his tailor should intrude upon his thoughts of eternity. Seneca* understood this, when he chose to die naked in a bath. And

71

man-of-war's-men understand it also; for most of them, in battle, strip to the waist-bands; wearing nothing but a pair of duck trowsers, and a handkerchief round their head.

A captain combining a heedful patriotism with economy, would probably 'bend' his old topsails before going into battle, instead of exposing his best canvass to be riddled to pieces; for it is generally the case that the enemy's shot flies high. Unless allowance is made for it in pointing the tube, at long-gun distance, the slightest roll of the ship, at the time of firing, would send a shot, meant for the hull, high over the topgallant-yards.

But besides these differences between a sham fight at *general quarters* and a real cannonading, the aspect of the ship, at the beating of the retreat, would, in the latter case, be very dissimilar to the neatness and uniformity in the former.

Then our bulwarks might look like the walls of the houses in West Broadway in New York, after being broken into and burned out by the negro mob. Our stout masts and yards might be lying about decks, like tree-boughs after a tornado in a piece of woodland; our dangling ropes, cut and sundered in all directions, would be bleeding tar at every yarn; and strewn with jagged splinters from our wounded planks, the gun-deck might resemble a carpenter's shop. *Then*, when all was over, and all hands would be piped to take down the hammocks from the exposed nettings (where they play the part of the cotton bales at New Orleans), we might find bits of broken shot, iron bolts, and bullets in our blankets. And, while smeared with blood like butchers, the surgeon and his mates would be amputating arms and legs on the berth-deck, an underling of the carpenter's gang would be new-legging and arming the broken chairs and tables in the commodore's cabin, while the rest of his *squad* would be *splicing* and *fishing* the shattered masts and yards. The scupper-holes having discharged the last rivulet of blood, the decks would be washed down; and the galley-cooks would be going fore and aft, sprinkling them with hot vinegar, to take out the shambles smell from the planks; which, unless some such means are employed, often create a highly offensive effluvia for weeks after a fight.

Then, upon mustering the men, and calling the quarter-bills by the light of a battle-lantern, many a wounded seaman, with his arm in a sling, would answer for some poor shipmate who could never more make answer for himself:—

'Tom Brown?'

'Killed, sir.'

'Jack Jewel?'

'Killed, sir.'

'Joe Hardy?'

'Killed, sir.'

And opposite all these poor fellows' names, down would go on the quarter-bills the bloody marks of red ink—a murderer's fluid, fitly used on these occasions.

XVII

Away! Second, Third, and Fourth Cutters, Away!

I T was the morning succeeding one of these *general quarters* that we picked up a life-buoy, descried floating by.

It was a circular mass of cork, about eight inches thick and four feet in diameter, covered with tarred canvass. All round its circumference there trailed a number of knotted rope's-ends, terminating in fanciful Turk's-heads. These were the life-lines, for the drowning to clutch. Inserted into the middle of the cork was an upright, carved pole, somewhat shorter than a pike-staff. The whole buoy was embossed with barnacles, and its sides festooned with seaweed. Dolphins were sporting and flashing around it, and one white bird was hovering over the top of the pole. Long ago, this thing must have been thrown overboard to save some poor wretch, who must have been drowned; while even the life-buoy itself had drifted away out of sight.

The forecastle-men fished it up from the bows, and the seamen thronged round it.

'Bad luck! bad luck!' cried the captain of the head; 'we'll number one less before long.'

The ship's cooper strolled by; he, to whose department it belongs to see that the ship's life-buoys are kept in good order.

In men-of-war, night and day, week in and week out, two life-buoys are kept depending from the stern; and two men, with hatchets in their hands, pace up and down, ready at the first cry to cut the cord and drop the buoys overboard. Every two hours they are regularly relieved, like sentinels on guard. No similar precautions are adopted in the merchant- or whaling-service.

Thus deeply solicitous to preserve human life are the regulations of men-of-war; and seldom has there been a better illustration of this solicitude than at the Battle of Trafalgar, when, after 'several thousand' French seamen had been destroyed, according to Lord Collingwood, and, by the official returns, sixteen hundred and ninety Englishmen were killed or wounded, the captains of the surviving ships ordered the life-buoy sentries from their death-dealing guns to their vigilant posts, as officers of the Humane Society.

'There, Bungs!' cried Scrimmage, a sheet-anchor-man,* 'there's a good pattern for you; make us a brace of life-buoys like that; something that will save a man, and not fill and sink under him, as those leaky quarter-casks of yours will the first time there's occasion to drop 'em. I came near pitching off the bowsprit the other day; and, when I scrambled inboard again, I went aft to get a squint at 'em. Why, Bungs, they are all open between the staves. Shame on you! Suppose you yourself should fall overboard, and find yourself going down with buoys under you of your own making— what then?'

* In addition to the *bower-anchors* carried on her bows, a frigate carries large anchors in her fore-chains, called *sheet-anchors*. Hence, the old seamen stationed in that part of a man-of-war are called *sheet-anchor-men*.

'I never go aloft, and don't intend to fall overboard,' replied Bungs.

'Don't believe it!' cried the sheet-anchor-man; 'you lopers that live about the decks here are nearer the bottom of the sea than the light hand that looses the main-royal. Mind your eye, Bungs—mind your eye!'

'I will,' retorted Bungs; 'and you mind yours!'

Next day, just at dawn, I was startled from my hammock by the cry of '*All hands about ship and shorten sail!*' Springing up the ladders, I found that an unknown man had fallen overboard from the chains; and darting a glance toward the poop, perceived, from their gestures, that the life-sentries there had cut away the buoys.

It was blowing a fresh breeze; the frigate was going fast through the water. But the one thousand arms of five hundred men soon tossed her about on the other tack, and checked her further headway.

'Do you see him?' shouted the officer of the watch through his trumpet, hailing the mainmast-head. 'Man or *buoy*, do you see either?'

'See nothing, sir,' was the reply.

'Clear away the cutters!' was the next order. 'Bugler! call away the second, third, and fourth cutters' crews. Hands by the tackles!'

In less than three minutes the three boats were down. More hands were wanted in one of them, and, among others, I jumped in to make up the deficiency.

'Now, men, give way! and each man look out along his oar, and look sharp!' cried the officer of our boat. For a time, in perfect silence, we slid up and down the great seething swells of the sea, but saw nothing.

'There, it's no use,' cried the officer; 'he's gone, whoever he is. Pull away, men—pull away! they'll be recalling us soon.'

'Let him drown!' cried the strokesman; 'he's spoiled my watch below for me.'

'Who the devil is he?' cried another.

'He's one who'll never have a coffin!' replied a third.

'No, no! they'll never sing out, "*All hands bury the dead!*" for him, my hearties!' cried a fourth.

'Silence,' said the officer, 'and look along your oars.' But the sixteen oarsmen still continued their talk; and, after pulling about for two or three hours, we spied the recall-signal at the frigate's fore-t'gallant mast-head, and returned on board, having seen no sign even of the life-buoys.

The boats were hoisted up, the yards braced forward, and away we bowled—one man less.

'Muster all hands!' was now the order; when, upon calling the roll, the cooper was the only man missing.

'I told you so, men,' cried the captain of the head; 'I said we would lose a man before long.'

'Bungs, is it?' cried Scrimmage, the sheet-anchor-man; 'I told him his buoys wouldn't save a drowning man; and now he has proved it!'

XVIII

A Man-of-war full as a Nut

IT was necessary to supply the lost cooper's place; accordingly, word was passed for all who belonged to that calling to muster at the mainmast, in order that one of them might be selected. Thirteen men obeyed the summons—a circumstance illustrative of the fact that many good handicraftsmen are lost to their trades and the world by serving in men-of-war. Indeed, from a frigate's crew might be culled out men of all callings and vocations, from a backslidden parson to a broken-down comedian. The Navy is the asylum for the perverse, the home of the unfortunate. Here the sons of adversity meet the children of calamity, and here the children of calamity meet the offspring of sin. Bankrupt brokers, boot-blacks, blacklegs, and blacksmiths here assemble together; and cast-away tinkers, watchmakers, quill-drivers, cobblers, doctors, farmers, and lawyers compare past experiences and talk of old times. Wrecked on a desert shore, a man-of-war's crew could quickly found an Alexandria by themselves, and fill it with all the things which go to make up a capital.

Frequently, at one and the same time, you see every trade in operation on the gun-deck—coopering, carpentering, tailoring, tinkering, blacksmithing, rope-making, preaching, gambling, and fortune-telling.

In truth, a man-of-war is a city afloat, with long avenues set out with guns instead of trees, and numerous shady lanes, courts, and by-ways. The quarter-deck is a grand square, park, or parade-ground, with a great Pittsfield elm,* in the shape of the mainmast, at one end, and fronted at the other by the palace of the commodore's cabin.

Or, rather, a man-of-war is a lofty, walled, and garrisoned town, like Quebec, where the thoroughfares are mostly ramparts, and peaceable citizens meet armed sentries at every corner.

Or it is like the lodging-houses in Paris, turned upside down; the first floor, or deck, being rented by a lord; the second, by a select club of gentlemen; the third, by crowds of artisans; and the fourth, by a whole rabble of common people.

For even thus is it in a frigate, where the commander has a whole cabin to himself on the spar-deck, the lieutenants their ward-room underneath, and the mass of sailors swing their hammocks under all.

And with its long rows of port-hole casements, each revealing the muzzle of a cannon, a man-of-war resembles a three-story house in a suspicious part of the town, with a basement of indefinite depth, and ugly-looking fellows gazing out at the windows.

77

XIX

The Jacket aloft

AGAIN must I call attention to my white jacket, which about this time came near being the death of me.

I am of a meditative humour, and at sea used often to mount aloft at night, and, seating myself on one of the upper yards, tuck my jacket about me and give loose to reflection. In some ships in which I have done this, the sailors used to fancy that I must be studying astronomy—which, indeed, to some extent, was the case—and that my object in mounting aloft was to get a nearer view of the stars, supposing me, of course, to be short-sighted. A very silly conceit of theirs, some may say, but not so silly after all; for surely the advantage of getting nearer an object by two hundred feet is not to be underrated. Then, to study the stars upon the wide, boundless sea, is divine as it was to the Chaldean Magi,* who observed their revolutions from the plains.

And it is a very fine feeling, and one that fuses us into the universe of things, and makes us a part of the All, to think that, wherever we ocean-wanderers rove, we have still the same glorious old stars to keep us company; that they still shine onward and on, forever beautiful and bright, and luring us, by every ray, to die and be glorified with them.

Ay, ay! we sailors sail not in vain. We expatriate ourselves to nationalize with the universe; and in all our voyages round the world, we are still accompanied by those old circumnavigators, the stars, who are shipmates and fellow-sailors of ours—sailing in heaven's blue, as we on the azure main. Let genteel generations scoff at our hardened hands, and finger-nails tipped with tar—did they ever clasp truer palms than ours? Let them feel of our sturdy hearts, beating like sledge-hammers in those hot smithies, our bosoms; with their amber-headed canes, let them feel of our generous pulses, and swear that they go off like thirty-two-pounders.

Oh, give me again the rover's life—the joy, the thrill, the whirl! Let me feel thee again, old sea! Let me leap into thy saddle once more! I am sick of these terra-firma toils and cares; sick of the dust and reek of towns. Let me hear the clatter of hailstones on icebergs, and not the dull tramp of these plodders, plodding their dull way from their cradles to their graves. Let me snuff thee up, sea-breeze! and whinny in thy spray. Forbid it, sea-gods! intercede for me with Neptune, O sweet Amphitrite,* that no dull clod may fall on my coffin! Be mine the tomb that swallowed up Pharaoh and all his hosts; let me lie down with Drake, where he sleeps in the sea.

But when White-Jacket speaks of the rover's life, he means not life in a man-of-war, which, with its martial formalities and thousand vices, stabs to the heart the soul of all free-and-easy honourable rovers.

I have said that I was wont to mount up aloft and muse; and thus was it with me the night following the loss of the cooper. Ere my watch in the top had expired, high up on the main-royal-yard I reclined, the white jacket folded around me like Sir John Moore in his frosted cloak.*

Eight bells had struck, and my watchmates had hied to their hammocks, and the other watch had gone to their stations, and the *top* below me was full of strangers, and still almost one hundred feet above even *them* I lay entranced; now dozing, now dreaming; now thinking of things past, and anon of the life to come. Well-timed was the latter thought, for the life to come was much nearer overtaking me than I then could imagine. Perhaps I was half-conscious at last of a tremulous voice hailing the main-royal-yard from the *top*. But if so, the consciousness glided away from me, and left me in Lethe.* But when, like lightning, the yard dropped under me, and instinctively I clung with both hands to the *tie*, then I came to myself with a rush, and felt something like a choking hand at my throat. For an instant I thought the Gulf Stream in my head was whirling me away to eternity; but the next moment I found myself standing;

the yard had descended to the *cap*; and shaking myself in my jacket, I felt that I was unharmed and alive.

Who had done this? who had made this attempt on my life? thought I, as I ran down the rigging.

'Here it comes!—Lord! Lord! here it comes! See, see! it is white as a hammock.'

'Who's coming?' I shouted, springing down into the top; 'who's white as a hammock?'

'Bless my soul, Bill, it's only White-Jacket—that infernal White-Jacket again!'

It seems they had spied a moving white spot there aloft, and, sailor-like, had taken me for the ghost of the cooper; and after hailing me, and bidding me descend, to test my corporeality, and getting no answer, they had lowered the halyards in affright.

In a rage I tore off the jacket, and threw it on the deck.

'Jacket,' cried I, 'you must change your complexion! you must hie to the dyer's and be dyed, that I may live. I have but one poor life, white jacket, and that life I cannot spare. I cannot consent to die for *you*, but be dyed you must for me. You can dye many times without injury; but I cannot die without irreparable loss, and running the eternal risk.'

So in the morning, jacket in hand, I repaired to the first lieutenant, and related the narrow escape I had had during the night. I enlarged upon the general perils I ran in being taken for a ghost, and earnestly besought him to relax his commands for once, and give me an order on Brush, the captain of the paint-room, for some black paint, that my jacket might be painted of that colour.

'Just look at it, sir,' I added, holding it up; 'did you ever see anything whiter? Consider how it shines of a night, like a bit of the Milky Way. A little paint, sir:—you cannot refuse.'

'The ship has no paint to spare,' he said; 'you must get along without it.'

'Sir, every rain gives me a soaking;—Cape Horn is at hand—six brushes-full would make it water-proof; and no longer would I be in peril of my life!'

'Can't help it, sir; depart!'

I fear it will not be well with me in the end; for if my own sins are to be forgiven only as I forgive that hard-hearted and unimpressible first lieutenant, then pardon there is none for me.

What! when but one dab of paint would make a man of a ghost, and a mackintosh of a herring-net—to refuse it!

I am full. I can say no more.

XX

How they sleep in a Man-of-war

No more of my luckless jacket for a while; let me speak of my hammock, and the tribulations I endured therefrom.

Give me plenty of room to swing it in; let me swing it between two date-trees on an Arabian plain; or extend it diagonally from Moorish pillar to pillar, in the open marble Court of the Lions in Granada's Alhambra: let me swing it on a high bluff of the Mississippi—one swing in the pure ether for every swing over the green grass; or let me oscillate in it beneath the cool dome of St. Peter's; or drop me in it, as in a balloon, from the zenith, with the whole firmament to rock and expatiate in; and I would not exchange my coarse canvass hammock for the grand state-bed, like a stately coach-and-four, in which they tuck in a king when he passes a night at Blenheim Castle.

When you have the requisite room, you always have 'spreaders' in your hammock; that is, two horizontal sticks, one at each end, which serve to keep the sides apart, and create a wide vacancy between, wherein you can turn over and over—lay on this side or that; on your back, if you please; stretch out your legs; in short, take your ease in your hammock; for of all inns, your bed is the best.

But when, with five hundred other hammocks, yours is crowded and jammed in on all sides, on a frigate berth-deck; the third from above; when *spreaders* are prohibited by an express edict from the captain's cabin; and every man about you is jealously watchful of the rights and privileges of his own proper hammock, as settled by law and usage; *then* your hammock is your Bastille*and canvass jug; into which, or out of which, it is very hard to get; and where sleep is but a mockery and a name.

Eighteen inches a man is all they allow you; eighteen inches in width; in *that* you must swing. Dreadful! they give you more swing than that at the gallows.

During warm nights in the Tropics, your hammock is as a stew-pan; where you stew and stew, till you can almost hear yourself hiss. Vain are all stratagems to widen your accommodations. Let them catch you insinuating your boots or other articles in the head of your hammock, by way of a 'spreader'. Near and far, the whole rank and file of the row to which you belong feel the encroachment in an instant, and are clamorous till the guilty one is found out, and his pallet brought back to its bearings.

In platoons and squadrons, they all lie on a level; their hammock *clews* crossing and recrossing in all directions, so as to present one vast field-bed, midway between the ceiling and the floor; which are about five feet asunder.

One extremely warm night, during a calm, when it was so hot that only a skeleton could keep cool (from the free current of air through its bones), after being drenched in my own perspiration, I managed to wedge myself out of my hammock; and with what little strength I had left, lowered myself gently to the deck. Let me see now, thought I, whether my ingenuity cannot devise some method whereby I can have room to breathe and sleep at the same time. I have it. I will lower my hammock underneath all these others; and then—upon that separate and independent level, at least—I shall have the whole berth-deck to myself. Accordingly, I lowered away my pallet to the desired point— about three inches from the floor—and crawled into it again.

But, alas! this arrangement made such a sweeping semi-circle of my hammock, that, while my head and feet were at par, the small of my back was settling down indefinitely; I felt as if some gigantic archer had hold of me for a bow.

But there was another plan left. I triced up my hammock with all my strength, so as to bring it wholly *above* the tiers of pallets around me. This done, by a last effort I hoisted myself into it; but alas! it was much worse than before. My luckless hammock was stiff and straight as a board; and there I was—laid out in it, with my nose against the ceiling, like a dead man's against the lid of his coffin.

So at last I was fain to return to my old level, and moralize upon the folly, in all arbitrary governments, of striving to get either *below* or *above* those whom legislation has placed upon an equality with yourself.

Speaking of hammocks recalls a circumstance that happened one night in the *Neversink*. It was three or four times repeated, with various but not fatal results.

The watch below was fast asleep on the berth-deck, where perfect silence was reigning, when a sudden shock and a groan roused up all hands; and the hem of a pair of white trowsers vanished up one of the ladders at the fore hatch-way.

We ran toward the groan, and found a man lying on the deck; one end of his hammock having given way, pitching his head close to three twenty-four-pound cannon-shot, which must have been purposely placed in that position. When it was discovered that this man had long been suspected of being an *informer* among the crew, little surprise and less pleasure were evinced at his narrow escape.

XXI

One Reason why Man-of-war's-men are generally short-lived

I CANNOT quit this matter of the hammocks without making mention of a grievance among the sailors that ought to be redressed.

In a man-of-war at sea, the sailors have *watch and watch*; that is, through every twenty-four hours they are on and off duty every four hours. Now, the hammocks are piped down from the nettings (the open space for stowing them, running round the top of the bulwarks) a little after sunset, and piped up again when the forenoon watch is called, at eight o'clock in the morning; so that during the daytime they are inaccessible as pallets. This would be all well enough, did the sailors have a complete night's rest; but every other night at sea, one watch have only four hours in their hammocks. Indeed, deducting the time allowed for the other watch to turn out, for yourself to arrange your hammock, get into it, and fairly get asleep, it may be said that, every other night, you have but three hours' sleep in your hammock. Having then been on deck for twice four hours, at eight o'clock in the morning your *watch below* comes round, and you are not liable to duty until noon. Under like circumstances, a merchant-seaman goes to his *bunk*, and has the benefit of a good long sleep. But in a man-of-war you can do no such thing; your hammock is very neatly stowed in the nettings, and there it must remain till nightfall.

But perhaps there is a corner for you somewhere along the batteries on the gun-deck, where you may enjoy a snug nap. But as no one is allowed to recline on the larboard side of the gun-deck (which is reserved as a corridor for the officers when they go forward to their smoking-room at the *bridle-port*), the starboard side only is left to the seamen. But most of this side, also, is occupied by the carpenters, sail-makers, barbers, and coopers. In short, so few are the corners where you can snatch a nap during daytime in a frigate, that not one in ten of the watch, who have been on deck eight hours, can get a wink of sleep till the following night. Repeatedly, after by good fortune securing a corner, I have been roused from it by some functionary commissioned to keep it clear.

Off Cape Horn, what before had been very uncomfortable became a serious hardship. Drenched through and through by the spray of the sea at night, I have sometimes slept standing on the spar-deck—and shuddered as I slept—for the want of sufficient sleep in my hammock.

During three days of the stormiest weather, we were given

the privilege of the *berth-deck* (at other times strictly interdicted), where we were permitted to spread our jackets, and
take a nap in the morning after the eight hours' night exposure. But this privilege was but a beggarly one, indeed.
Not to speak of our jackets—used for blankets—being soaking wet, the spray, coming down the hatchways, kept the
planks of the berth-deck itself constantly wet; whereas, had
we been permitted our hammocks, we might have swung
dry over all this deluge. But we endeavoured to make ourselves as warm and comfortable as possible, chiefly by close
stowing, so as to generate a little steam, in the absence of any
fireside warmth. You have seen, perhaps, the way in which
they box up subjects intended to illustrate the winter lectures of a professor of surgery. Just so we laid; heel and
point, face to back, dovetailed into each other at every ham
and knee. The wet of our jackets, thus densely packed, would
soon begin to distil. But it was like pouring hot water on you
to keep you from freezing. It was like being 'packed' between
the soaked sheets in a water-cure establishment.

Such a posture could not be preserved for any considerable period without shifting side for side. Three or four
times during the four hours I would be startled from a wet
doze by the hoarse cry of a fellow who did the duty of a
corporal at the after end of my file, '*Sleepers ahoy! stand by
to slew round!*' and, with a double shuffle, we all rolled in
concert, and found ourselves facing the taffrail instead of the
bowsprit. But, however you turned, your nose was sure to
stick to one or other of the steaming backs on your two
flanks. There was some little relief in the change of odour
consequent upon this.

But what is the reason that, after battling out eight stormy
hours on deck at night, man-of-war's-men are not allowed
the poor boon of a dry four hours' nap during the day
following? What is the reason? The commodore, captain,
and first lieutenant, chaplain, purser, and scores of others,
have *all night in*, just as if they were staying at an hotel on
shore. And the junior lieutenants not only have their cots to
go to at any time; but as only one of them is required to head

the watch, and there are so many of them among whom to divide that duty, they are only on deck four hours to twelve hours below. In some cases the proportion is still greater. Whereas, with *the people* it is four hours in and four hours off continually.

What is the reason, then, that the common seamen should fare so hard in this matter? It would seem but a simple thing to let them get down their hammocks during the day for a nap. But no; such a proceeding would mar the uniformity of daily events in a man-of-war. It seems indispensable to the picturesque effect of the spar-deck, that the hammocks should invariably remain stowed in the nettings between sun-rise and sundown. But the chief reason is this—a reason which has sanctioned many an abuse in this world—*precedents are against it*; such a thing as sailors sleeping in their hammocks in the daytime, after being eight hours exposed to a night storm, was hardly ever heard of in the Navy. Though, to the immortal honour of some captains be it said, the fact is upon Navy record that, off Cape Horn, they *have* vouchsafed the morning hammocks to their crew. Heaven bless such tender-hearted officers; and may they and their descendants—ashore or afloat—have sweet and pleasant slumbers while they live, and an undreaming siesta when they die.

It is concerning such things as the subject of this chapter that special enactments of Congress are demanded. Health and comfort—so far as duly attainable under the circumstances—should be legally guaranteed to the man-of-war's-man, and not left to the discretion or caprice of his commander.

XXII

Wash-day and House-cleaning in a Man-of-war

BESIDES the other tribulations connected with your hammock, you must keep it snow-white and clean. Who has not observed the long rows of spotless hammocks exposed in a frigate's nettings, where, through the day, their outsides, at least, are kept airing?

Hence it comes that there are regular mornings appointed for the scrubbing of hammocks; and such mornings are called *scrub-hammock-mornings*, and desperate is the scrubbing that ensues.

Before daylight the operation begins. All hands are called, and at it they go. Every deck is spread with hammocks, fore and aft; and lucky are you, if you can get sufficient superficies* to spread your own hammock in. Down on their knees are five hundred men, scrubbing away with brushes and brooms; jostling, and crowding, and quarrelling about using each other's suds; when all their purser's soap goes to create one indiscriminate yeast.

Sometimes you discover that, in the dark, you have been all the while scrubbing your next neighbour's hammock instead of your own. But it is too late to begin over again; for now the word is passed for every man to advance with his hammock, that it may be tied to a net-like framework of clothes-lines, and hoisted aloft to dry.

That done, without delay you get together your frocks and trowsers, and on the already flooded deck embark in the laundry business. You have no special bucket or basin to yourself—the ship being one vast wash-tub, where all hands wash and rinse out, and rinse out and wash, till at last the word is passed again, to make fast your clothes, that they, also, may be elevated to dry.

Then on all three decks the operation of holy-stoning begins, so called from the queer name bestowed upon the principal instruments employed. These are ponderous flat stones with long ropes at each end, by which the stones are slidden about, to and fro, over the wet and sanded decks; a most wearisome, dog-like, galley-slave employment. For the by-ways and corners about the masts and guns, smaller stones are used, called *prayer-books*; inasmuch as the devout operator has to down with them on his knees.

Finally, a grand flooding takes place, and the decks are

remorselessly thrashed with dry swabs. After which an extraordinary implement—a sort of leathern hoe called a *squilgee*—is used to scrape and squeeze the last dribblings of water from the planks. Concerning this 'squilgee', I think something of drawing up a memoir, and reading it before the Academy of Arts and Sciences. It is a most curious affair.

By the time all these operations are concluded it is *eight bells*, and all hands are piped to breakfast upon the damp and everyway disagreeable decks.

Now, against this invariable daily flooding of the three decks of a frigate, as a man-of-war's-man, White-Jacket most earnestly protests. In sunless weather it keeps the sailor's quarters perpetually damp; so much so, that you can scarce sit down without running the risk of getting the lumbago. One rheumatic old sheet-anchor-man among us was driven to the extremity of sewing a piece of tarred canvass on the seat of his trowsers.

Let those neat and tidy officers who so love to see a ship kept spick and span clean; who institute vigorous search after the man who chances to drop the crumb of a biscuit on deck, when the ship is rolling in a sea-way; let all such swing their hammocks with the sailors, and they would soon get sick of this daily damping of the decks.

Is a ship a wooden platter, that it is to be scrubbed out every morning before breakfast, even if the thermometer be at zero, and every sailor goes barefooted through the flood with the chilblains? And all the while the ship carries a doctor, well aware of Boerhaave's* great maxim, '*Keep the feet dry*.' He has plenty of pills to give you when you are down with a fever, the consequences of these things; but enters no protest at the outset—as it is his duty to do—against the cause that induces the fever.

During the pleasant night-watches, the promenading officers, mounted on their high-heeled boots, pass dry-shod, like the Israelites, over the decks; but by daybreak the roaring tide sets back, and the poor sailors are almost overwhelmed in it, like the Egyptians in the Red Sea.

Oh! the chills, colds, and agues that are caught! No snug

stove, grate, or fireplace to go to; no, your only way to keep warm is to keep in a blazing passion, and anathematize the custom that every morning makes a wash-house of a man-of-war.

Look at it. Say you go on board a line-of-battle ship: you see everything scrupulously neat; you see all the decks clear and unobstructed as the side-walks of Wall Street of a Sunday morning; you see no trace of a sailor's dormitory; you marvel by what magic all this is brought about. And well you may. For consider, that in this unobstructed fabric nearly one thousand mortal men have to sleep, eat, wash, dress, cook, and perform all the ordinary functions of humanity. The same number of men ashore would expand themselves into a township. Is it credible, then, that this extraordinary neatness, and especially this *unobstructedness* of a man-of-war, can be brought about, except by the most rigorous edicts, and a very serious sacrifice, with respect to the sailors, of the domestic comforts of life? To be sure, sailors themselves do not often complain of these things; they are used to them; but man can become used even to the hardest usage. And it is because he *is* used to it, that sometimes he does not complain of it.

Of all men-of-war, the American ships are the most excessively neat, and have the greatest reputation for it. And of all men-of-war the general discipline of the American ships is the most arbitrary.

In the English Navy, the men liberally mess on tables, which, between meals, are triced up out of the way. The American sailors mess on the deck, and peck up their broken biscuit, or *midshipmen's nuts*, like fowls in a barn-yard.

But if this unobstructedness in an American fighting-ship be, at all hazards, so desirable, why not imitate the Turks? In the Turkish Navy they have no mess-chests; the sailors roll their mess-things up in a rug, and thrust them under a gun. Nor do they have any hammocks; they sleep anywhere about the decks in their *gregos*. Indeed, come to look at it, what more does a man-of-war's-man absolutely require to live in than his own skin? That's room enough; and room enough to turn in, if he but knew how to shift his spine, end for end, like a ramrod, without disturbing his next neighbour.

Among all man-of-war's-men, it is a maxim that over-neat vessels are Tartars to the crew; and perhaps it may be safely laid down that, when you see such a ship, some sort of tyranny is not very far off.

In the *Neversink*, as in other national ships, the business of *holy-stoning* the decks was often prolonged, by way of punishment to the men, particularly of a raw, cold morning. This is one of the punishments which a lieutenant of the watch may easily inflict upon the crew, without infringing the statute which places the power of punishment solely in the hands of the captain.

The abhorrence which man-of-war's-men have for this protracted *holy-stoning* in cold, comfortless weather—with their bare feet exposed to the splashing inundations—is shown in a strange story, rife among them, curiously tinctured with their proverbial superstitions.

The first lieutenant of an English sloop of war, a severe disciplinarian, was uncommonly particular concerning the whiteness of the quarter-deck. One bitter winter morning at sea, when the crew had washed that part of the vessel, as usual, and put away their holy-stones, this officer came on deck, and after inspecting it, ordered the holy-stones and prayer-books up again. Once more slipping off the shoes from their frosted feet, and rolling up their trowsers, the crew kneeled down to their task; and in that suppliant posture, silently invoked a curse upon their tyrant; praying, as he went below, that he might never more come out of the ward-room alive. The prayer seemed answered; for being shortly after visited with a paralytic stroke at his breakfast-table, the first lieutenant next morning was carried out of the ward-room feet foremost, dead. As they dropped him over the side—so goes the story—the marine sentry at the gangway turned his back upon the corpse.

To the credit of the humane and sensible portion of the

roll of American Navy captains, be it added, that *they* are not so particular in keeping the decks spotless at all times, and in all weathers; nor do they torment the men with scraping bright-wood* and polishing ring-bolts; but give all such gingerbread-work a hearty coat of black paint, which looks more warlike, is a better preservative, and exempts the sailors from a perpetual annoyance.

XXIII
Theatricals in a Man-of-war

THE *Neversink* had summered out her last Christmas on the Equator; she was now destined to winter out the Fourth of July not very far from the frigid latitudes of Cape Horn.

It is sometimes the custom in the American Navy to celebrate this national holiday by doubling the allowance of spirits to the men; that is, if the ship happen to be lying in harbour. The effects of this patriotic plan may be easily imagined: the whole ship is converted into a dram-shop; and the intoxicated sailors reel about, on all three decks, singing, howling, and fighting. This is the time that, owing to the relaxed discipline of the ship, old and almost forgotten quarrels are revived, under the stimulus of drink; and, fencing themselves up between the guns—so as to be sure of a clear space with at least three walls—the combatants, two and two, fight out their hate, cribbed and cabined like soldiers duelling in a sentry-box. In a word, scenes ensue which would not for a single instant be tolerated by the officers upon any other occasion. This is the time that the most venerable of quarter-gunners and quarter-masters, together with the smallest apprentice boys, and men never known to have been previously intoxicated during the cruise —this is the time that they all roll together in the same muddy trough of drunkenness.

In emulation of the potentates of the Middle Ages, some captains augment the din by authorizing a grand jaildelivery of all the prisoners who, on that auspicious Fourth of the month, may happen to be confined in the ship's prison—*the brig*.

But from scenes like these the *Neversink* was happily delivered. Besides that she was now approaching a most perilous part of the ocean—which would have made it madness to intoxicate the sailors—her complete destitution of *grog*, even for ordinary consumption, was an obstacle altogether insuperable, even had the captain felt disposed to indulge his man-of-war's-men by the most copious libations.

For several days previous to the advent of the holiday, frequent conferences were held on the gun-deck touching the melancholy prospects before the ship.

'Too bad—too bad!' cried a top-man. 'Think of it, ship-mates—a Fourth of July without grog!'

'I'll hoist the commodore's pennant at half-mast that day,' sighed the signal-quarter-master.

'And I'll turn my best uniform jacket wrong side out, to keep company with the pennant, old Ensign,' sympathetically responded an after-guard's-man.

'Ay, do!' cried a forecastle-man. 'I could almost pipe my eye to think on 't.'

'No grog on de day dat tried men's souls!' blubbered Sunshine, the galley-cook.

'Who would be a *Jankee* now?' roared a Hollander of the foretop, more Dutch than sourcrout.*

'Is this the *riglar* fruits of liberty?' touchingly inquired an Irish waister of an old Spanish sheet-anchor-man.

You will generally observe that, of all Americans, your foreign-born citizens are the most patriotic—especially toward the Fourth of July.

But how could Captain Claret, the father of his crew, behold the grief of his ocean children with indifference? He could not. Three days before the anniversary—it still continuing very pleasant weather for these latitudes—it was publicly announced that free permission was given to the sailors to get up any sort of theatricals they desired, wherewith to honour the Fourth.

Now, some weeks prior to the *Neversink*'s sailing from home—nearly three years before the time here spoken of—some of the seamen had clubbed together, and made up a considerable purse, for the purpose of purchasing a theatrical outfit; having in view to diversify the monotony of lying in foreign harbours for weeks together, by an occasional display on the boards—though if ever there was a continual theatre in the world, playing by night and by day, and without intervals between the acts, a man-of-war is that theatre, and her planks are the *boards* indeed.

The sailors who originated this scheme had served in other American frigates, where the privilege of having theatricals was allowed to the crew. What was their chagrin, then, when, upon making an application to the captain, in a Peruvian harbour, for permission to present the much-admired drama of *The Ruffian Boy*, under the captain's personal patronage, that dignitary assured them that there were already enough *ruffian boys* on board, without conjuring up any more from the green-room.

The theatrical outfit, therefore, was stowed down in the bottom of the sailors' bags, who little anticipated *then* that it would ever be dragged out while Captain Claret had the sway.

But immediately upon the announcement that the embargo was removed, vigorous preparations were at once commenced to celebrate the Fourth with unwonted spirit. The half-deck was set apart for the theatre, and the signal-quarter-master was commanded to loan his flags to decorate it in the most patriotic style.

As the stage-struck portion of the crew had frequently during the cruise rehearsed portions of various plays, to while away the tedium of the night-watches, they needed no long time now to perfect themselves in their parts.

Accordingly, on the very next morning after the indulgence had been granted by the captain, the following written placard, presenting a broadside of staring capitals, was found tacked against the mainmast on the gun-deck. It was as if a Drury-Lane* bill had been posted upon the London Monument:

93

CAPE HORN THEATRE.

Grand Celebration of the Fourth of July.

DAY PERFORMANCE.

UNCOMMON ATTRACTION.

THE OLD WAGON PAID OFF!

JACK CHASE. . . . PERCY ROYAL-MAST.

STARS OF THE FIRST MAGNITUDE.

For this time only,

THE TRUE YANKEE SAILOR

The managers of the Cape Horn Theatre beg leave to inform the inhabitants of the Pacific and Southern Oceans that, on the afternoon of the Fourth of July 184—, they will have the honour to present the admired drama of

THE OLD WAGON PAID OFF!

Commodore Bougee	*Tom Brown, of the Foretop.*
Captain Spy-glass	*Ned Brace, of the After-guard.*
Commodore's Cockswain	*Joe Bunk, of the Launch.*
Old Luff	*Quarter-master Coffin.*
Mayor	*Seafull, of the Forecastle.*
PERCY ROYAL-MAST	JACK CHASE.
Mrs. Lovelorn	*Long-locks, of the After-guard.*
Toddy Moll	*Frank Jones.*
Gin and Sugar Sall	*Dick Dash.*

Sailors, Marines, Bar-keepers, Crimps, Aldermen, Police-officers, Soldiers, Landsmen generally.

Long live the Commodore! ‖ Admission Free.

To conclude with the much-admired song by Dibdin, altered to suit all American Tars, entitled

THE TRUE YANKEE SAILOR.

True Yankee Sailor (in costume), Patrick Flinegan, Captain of the Head.

Performance to commence with 'Hail Columbia', by the Brass Band. Ensign rises at three bells P.M. No sailor permitted to enter in his shirt-sleeves. Good order is expected to be maintained. The Master-at-arms and Ship's Corporals to be in attendance to keep the peace.

94

At the earnest entreaties of the seamen, Lemsford, the gun-deck poet, had been prevailed upon to draw up this bill. And upon this one occasion his literary abilities were far from being underrated, even by the least intellectual person on board. Nor must it be omitted that, before the bill was placarded, Captain Claret, enacting the part of censor and grand chamberlain, ran over a manuscript copy of *The Old Wagon Paid Off*, to see whether it contained anything calculated to breed disaffection against lawful authority among the crew. He objected to some parts, but in the end let them all pass.

The morning of The Fourth—most anxiously awaited—dawned clear and fair. The breeze was steady; the air bracing cold; and one and all the sailors anticipated a gleeful afternoon. And thus was falsified the prophecies of certain old growlers averse to theatricals, who had predicted a gale of wind that would quash all the arrangements of the greenroom.

As the men whose regular turns, at the time of the performance, would come round to be stationed in the tops, and at the various halyards and running ropes about the spardeck, could not be permitted to partake in the celebration, there accordingly ensued, during the morning, many amusing scenes of tars who were anxious to procure substitutes at their posts. Through the day, many anxious glances were cast to windward; but the weather still promised fair.

At last *the people* were piped to dinner; two bells struck; and soon after, all who could be spared from their stations hurried to the half-deck. The capstan-bars were placed on shot-boxes, as at prayers on Sundays, furnishing seats for the audience; while a low stage, rigged by the carpenter's gang, was built at one end of the open space. The curtain was composed of a large ensign, and the bulwarks round about were draperied with the flags of all nations. The ten or twelve members of the brass band were ranged in a row at the foot of the stage, their polished instruments in their hands, while the consequential captain of the band himself was elevated upon a gun-carriage.

At three bells precisely a group of ward-room officers emerged from the after hatchway, and seated themselves upon camp-stools, in a central position, with the stars and stripes for a canopy. *That* was the royal box. The sailors looked round for the commodore; but neither commodore nor captain honoured *the people* with their presence.

At the call of a bugle the band struck up *Hail Columbia*, the whole audience keeping time, as at Drury Lane, when *God Save the King* is played after a great national victory.

At the discharge of a marine's musket the curtain rose, and four sailors, in the picturesque garb of Maltese mariners, staggered on the stage in a feigned state of intoxication. The truthfulness of the representation was much heightened by the roll of the ship.

'The Commodore', 'Old Luff', 'The Mayor', and 'Gin and Sugar Sall' were played to admiration, and received great applause. But at the first appearance of that universal favourite, Jack Chase, in the chivalric character of *Percy Royal-Mast*, the whole audience simultaneously rose to their feet, and greeted him with three hearty cheers, that almost took the main-topsail aback.

Matchless Jack, *in full fig*,* bowed again and again, with true quarter-deck grace and self-possession; and when five or six untwisted strands of rope and bunches of oakum were thrown to him, as substitutes for bouquets, he took them one by one, and gallantly hung them from the buttons of his jacket.

'Hurrah! hurrah! hurrah!—go on! go on!—stop hollering—hurrah!—go on!—stop hollering—hurrah!' was now heard on all sides, till at last, seeing no end to the enthusiasm of his ardent admirers, matchless Jack stepped forward, and, with his lips moving in pantomime, plunged into the thick of the part. Silence soon followed, but was fifty times broken by uncontrollable bursts of applause. At length, when that heart-thrilling scene came on, where Percy Royal-Mast rescues fifteen oppressed sailors from the watch-house, in the teeth of a posse of constables, the audience leaped to their feet, overturned the capstan-bars, and to a man hurled their hats on the stage in a delirium of delight. Ah, Jack, that was a ten-stroke*indeed!

The commotion was now terrific; all discipline seemed gone forever; the lieutenants ran in among the men, the captain darted from his cabin, and the commodore nervously questioned the armed sentry at his door as to what the deuce *the people* were about. In the midst of all this, the trumpet of the officer of the deck, commanding the topgallant sails to be taken in, was almost completely drowned. A black squall was coming down on the weather bow, and the boat-swain's mates bellowed themselves hoarse at the main hatchway. There is no knowing what would have ensued, had not the bass drum suddenly been heard, calling all hands to quarters, a summons not to be withstood. The sailors pricked their ears at it, as horses at the sound of a cracking whip, and confusedly stumbled up the ladders to their stations. The next moment all was silent but the wind, howling like a thousand devils in the cordage.

'Stand by to reef all three topsails!—settle away the halyards!—haul out—so: make fast!—aloft, top-men! and reef away!'

Thus, in storm and tempest terminated that day's theatricals. But the sailors never recovered from the disappointment of not having *The True Yankee Sailor* sung by the Irish captain of the head.

And here White-Jacket must moralize a bit. The unwonted spectacle of the row of gun-room officers mingling with *the people* in applauding a mere seaman like Jack Chase, filled me at the time with the most pleasurable emotions. It is a sweet thing, thought I, to see these officers confess a human brotherhood with us, after all; a sweet thing to mark their cordial appreciation of the manly merits of my matchless Jack. Ah! they are noble fellows all round, and I do not know but I have wronged them sometimes in my thoughts.

Nor was it without similar pleasurable feelings that I witnessed the temporary rupture of the ship's stern discipline, consequent upon the tumult of the theatricals. I thought to myself, this now is as it should be. It is good to shake off, now and then, this iron yoke round our necks. And after having once permitted us sailors to be a little noisy, in a harmless way—somewhat merrily turbulent—the officers cannot, with any good grace, be so excessively stern and unyielding as before. I began to think a man-of-war a man-of-peace-and-good-will, after all. But, alas! disappointment came.

Next morning the same old scene was enacted at the gangway. And beholding the row of uncompromising-looking officers there assembled with the captain, to witness punishment—the same officers who had been so cheerfully disposed overnight—an old sailor touched my shoulder, and said, 'See, White-Jacket, all round they have *shipped their quarterdeck faces again*. But this is the way.'

I afterward learned that this was an old man-of-war's-man's phrase, expressive of the facility with which a sea-officer falls back upon all the severity of his dignity, after a temporary suspension of it.

XXIV

Introductory to Cape Horn

AND now, through drizzling fogs and vapours, and under damp, double-reefed topsails, our wet-decked frigate drew nearer and nearer to the squally Cape.

Who has not heard of it? Cape Horn, Cape Horn—a *horn* indeed, that has tossed many a good ship. Was the descent of Orpheus, Ulysses, or Dante into Hell,*one whit more hardy and sublime than the first navigator's weathering of that terrible Cape?

Turned on her heel by a fierce west wind, many an outward-bound ship has been driven across the Southern Ocean to the Cape of Good Hope—*that* way to seek a passage to the Pacific. And that stormy Cape, I doubt not, has sent many a fine craft to the bottom, and told no tales. At those ends of the earth are no chronicles. What signify the broken spars and shrouds that, day after day, are driven before the prows of more fortunate vessels? or the tall masts, imbedded in icebergs, that are found floating by? They but hint the old story—of ships that have sailed from their ports, and never more have been heard of.

Impracticable Cape! You may approach it from this direction or that—in any way you please—from the east, or from the west; with the wind astern, or abeam, or on the quarter; and still Cape Horn is Cape Horn. Cape Horn it is that takes the conceit out of fresh-water sailors, and steeps in a still salter brine the saltest. Woe betide the tyro! the foolhardy, Heaven preserve!

Your Mediterranean captain, who with a cargo of oranges has hitherto made merry runs across the Atlantic, without so much as furling a t'gallant-sail, oftentimes, off Cape Horn, receives a lesson which he carries to the grave; though the grave—as is too often the case—follows so hard on the lesson that no benefit comes from the experience.

Other strangers who draw nigh to this Patagonia termination of our continent, with their souls full of its shipwrecks and disasters—topsails cautiously reefed, and everything guardedly snug—these strangers at first unexpectedly encountering a tolerably smooth sea, rashly conclude that the Cape, after all, is but a bugbear; they have been imposed upon by fables, and founderings and sinkings hereabouts are all cock-and-bull stories.

'Out reefs, my hearties; fore and aft set t'gallant-sails! stand by to give her the fore-topmast stun'-sail!'

But, Captain Rash, those sails of yours were much safer in the sail-maker's loft. For now, while the heedless craft is bounding over the billows, a black cloud rises out of the sea; the sun drops down from the sky; a horrible mist far and wide spreads over the water.

'Hands by the halyards! Let go! Clew up!'

Too late.

For ere the ropes' ends can be cast off from the pins, the tornado is blowing down to the bottom of their throats. The masts are willows, the sails ribbons, the cordage wool; the whole ship is brewed into the yeast of the gale.

And now, if, when the first green sea breaks over him, Captain Rash is not swept overboard, he has his hands full, be sure. In all probability his three masts have gone by the board; and, ravelled into list, his sails are floating in the air. Or, perhaps, the ship *broaches to*, or is *brought by the lee*. In either case, Heaven help the sailors, their wives, and their little ones; and Heaven help the underwriters.

Familiarity with danger makes a brave man braver, but less daring. Thus with seamen: he who goes the oftenest round Cape Horn goes the most circumspectly. A veteran mariner is never deceived by the treacherous breezes which sometimes waft him pleasantly toward the latitude of the Cape. No sooner does he come within a certain distance of it—previously fixed in his own mind—than all hands are turned to setting the ship in storm-trim; and, never mind how light the breeze, down come his t'gallant-yards. He 'bends' his strongest storm-sails, and lashes everything on deck securely. The ship is then ready for the worst; and if, in reeling round the headland, she receives a broadside, it generally goes well with her. If ill, all hands go to the bottom with quiet consciences.

Among sea-captains, there are some who seem to regard the genius of the Cape as a wilful, capricious jade, that must be courted and coaxed into complaisance. First, they come along under easy sail; do not steer boldly for the headland, but tack this way and that—sidling up to it. Now they woo the Jezebel with a t'gallant studding-sail; anon, they deprecate her wrath with double-reefed topsails. When, at length, her unappeasable fury is fairly aroused, and all round the dismantled ship the storm howls and howls for days together, they still persevere in their efforts. First, they try unconditional submission; furling every rag and *heaving to*; laying like a log, for the tempest to toss wheresoever it pleases.

This failing, they set a *spencer* or *trysail*, and shift on the other tack. Equally vain! The gale sings as hoarsely as before. At last, the wind comes round fair; they drop the foresail; square the yards, and scud before it: their implacable foe chasing them with tornadoes, as if to show her insensibility to the last.

Other ships, without encountering these terrible gales, spend week after week endeavouring to turn this boisterous world-corner against a continual head-wind. Tacking hither and thither, in the language of sailors, they *polish* the Cape by beating about its edges so long.

Le Mair and Schouten,* two Dutchmen, were the first navigators who weathered Cape Horn. Previous to this, passages had been made to the Pacific by the Straits of Magellan; nor, indeed, at that period, was it known to a certainty that there was any other route, or that the land now called Terra del Fuego was an island. A few leagues south-ward from Terra del Fuego is a cluster of small islands, the Diegoes; between which and the former island are the Straits of Le Mair, so called in honour of their discoverer, who first sailed through them into the Pacific. Le Mair and Schouten, in their small, clumsy vessels, encountered a series of tremendous gales, the prelude to the long train of similar hardships which most of their followers have experienced. It is a significant fact, that Schouten's vessel, the *Horne*, which gave its name to the Cape, was almost lost in weathering it.

The next navigator round the Cape was Sir Francis Drake,* who, on Raleigh's expedition, beholding for the first time, from the Isthmus of Darien, the 'goodlie South Sea', like a true-born Englishman vowed, please God, to sail an English ship thereon; which the gallant sailor did, to the sore dis-comfiture of the Spaniards on the coasts of Chili and Peru.

But perhaps the greatest hardships on record, in making this celebrated passage, were those experienced by Lord Anson's squadron in 1736. Three remarkable and most interesting narratives record their disasters and sufferings. The first, jointly written by the carpenter and gunner of the *Wager*; the second, by young Byron, a midshipman in the same ship; the third, by the chaplain of the *Centurion*.* White-Jacket has them all; and they are fine reading of a boisterous March night, with the casement rattling in your ear, and the chimney-stacks blowing down upon the pave-ment, bubbling with rain-drops.

But if you want the best idea of Cape Horn, get my friend

Dana's unmatchable *Two Years Before the Mast.** But you can read, and so you must have read it. His chapters describing Cape Horn must have been written with an icicle.

At the present day the horrors of the Cape have somewhat abated. This is owing to a growing familiarity with it; but, more than all, to the improved condition of ships in all respects, and the means now generally in use of preserving the health of the crews in times of severe and prolonged exposure.

XXV

The Dog-days off Cape Horn

COLDER and colder; we are drawing nigh to the Cape. Now gregos, pea-jackets, monkey-jackets, reefing jackets, storm-jackets, oil-jackets, paint-jackets, round jackets, short jackets, long jackets, and all manner of jackets, are the order of the day, not excepting the immortal white jacket, which begins to be sturdily buttoned up to the throat, and pulled down vigorously at the skirts, to bring them well over the loins.

But, alas! those skirts were lamentably scanty; and though, with its quiltings, the jacket was stuffed out about the breasts like a Christmas turkey, and of a dry cold day kept the wearer warm enough in that vicinity, yet about the loins it was shorter than a ballet-dancer's skirts; so that while my chest was in the temperate zone, close adjoining the torrid, my hapless thighs were in Nova Zembla,* hardly an icicle's toss from the Pole.

Then, again, the repeated soakings and dryings it had undergone had by this time made it shrink woefully all over, especially in the arms, so that the wristbands had gradually crawled up near to the elbows; and it required an energetic thrust to push the arm through, in drawing the jacket on.

I endeavoured to amend these misfortunes by sewing a sort of canvass ruffle round the skirts, by way of a continuation or supplement to the original work, and by doing the same with the wristbands.

This is the time for oil-skin suits, dreadnaughts, tarred trowsers and overalls, sea-boots, comforters, mittens, woollen socks, Guernsey frocks, Havre shirts,* buffalo-robe shirts, and moose-skin drawers. Every man's jacket is his wigwam, and every man's hat his caboose.

Perfect licence is now permitted to the men respecting their clothing. Whatever they can rake and scrape together they put on—swaddling themselves in old sails, and drawing old socks over their heads for night-caps. This is the time for smiting your chest with your hand, and talking loud to keep up the circulation.

Colder, and colder, and colder, till at last we spoke a fleet of icebergs bound north. After that, it was one incessant *cold snap*, that almost snapped off our fingers and toes. Cold! It was cold as *Blue Flujin*, where sailors say fire freezes.

And now coming up with the latitude of the Cape, we stood southward to give it a wide berth, and while so doing were becalmed; ay, becalmed off Cape Horn, which is worse, far worse, than being becalmed on the Line.

Here we lay forty-eight hours, during which the cold was intense. I wondered at the liquid sea, which refused to freeze in such a temperature. The clear, cold sky overhead looked like a steel-blue cymbal, that might ring, could you smite it. Our breath came and went like puffs of smoke from pipe-bowls. At first there was a long, gawky swell, that obliged us to furl most of the sails, and even send down t'gallant-yards, for fear of pitching them overboard.

Out of sight of land, at this extremity of both the inhabitable and uninhabitable world, our peopled frigate, echoing with the voices of men, the bleating of lambs, the cackling of fowls, the gruntings of pigs, seemed like Noah's old ark itself, becalmed at the climax of the Deluge.

There was nothing to be done but patiently to await the pleasure of the elements, and 'whistle for a wind', the usual practice of seamen in a calm. No fire was allowed, except for the indispensable purpose of cooking, and heating bottles of water to toast Selvagee's feet. He who possessed the largest stock of vitality stood the best chance to escape freezing. It was horrifying. In such weather any man could have undergone amputation with great ease, and helped take up the arteries himself.

Indeed, this state of affairs had not lasted quite twenty-four hours, when the extreme frigidity of the air, united to our increased tendency to inactivity, would very soon have rendered some of us subjects for the surgeon and his mates, had not a humane proceeding of the captain suddenly impelled us to vigorous exercise.

And here be it said, that the appearance of the boatswain, with his silver whistle to his mouth, at the main hatchway of the gun-deck, is always regarded by the crew with the utmost curiosity, for this betokens that some general order is about to be promulgated through the ship. What now? is the question that runs on from man to man. A short preliminary whistle is then given by 'Old Yarn', as they call him, which whistle serves to collect round him, from their various stations, his four mates. Then Yarn, or Pipes, as leader of the orchestra, begins a peculiar call, in which his assistants join. This over, the order, whatever it may be, is loudly sung out and prolonged, till the remotest corner echoes again. The boatswain and his mates are the town-criers of a man-of-war.

The calm had commenced in the afternoon; and the following morning the ship's company were electrified by a general order, thus set forth and declared: '*D'ye hear there, fore and aft! all hands skylark!*'

This mandate, nowadays never used except upon very rare occasions, produced the same effect upon the men that exhilarating gas* would have done, or an extra allowance of 'grog'. For a time, the wonted discipline of the ship was broken through, and perfect licence allowed. It was a Babel here, a Bedlam there, and a Pandemonium everywhere. The theatricals were nothing compared with it. Then the faint-hearted and timorous crawled to their hiding-places, and the lusty and bold shouted forth their glee. Gangs of men, in all sorts of outlandish habiliments, wild as those worn at some crazy carnival, rushed to and fro, seizing upon whomsoever they pleased—warrant-officers and dangerous pugilists excepted—pulling and hauling the luckless tars about, till fairly baited into a genial warmth. Some were made fast to, and hoisted aloft with a will; others, mounted upon oars, were ridden fore and aft on a rail, to the boisterous mirth of the spectators, any one of whom might be the next victim. Swings were rigged from the tops, or the masts; and the most reluctant wights being purposely selected, spite of all struggles, were swung from east to west, in vast arcs of circles, till almost breathless. Horn-pipes, fandangos, Donnybrook-jigs, reels, and quadrilles were danced under the very nose of the most mighty captain, and upon the very quarter-deck and poop. Sparring and wrestling, too, were all the vogue; *Kentucky bites* were given, and the *Indian hug* exchanged. The din frightened the sea-fowl, that flew by with accelerated wing.

It is worth mentioning that several casualties occurred, of which, however, I will relate but one. While the 'skylarking' was at its height, one of the foretop-men—an ugly-tempered devil of a Portuguese, looking on—swore that he would be the death of any man who laid violent hands upon his inviolable person. This threat being overheard, a band of desperadoes, coming up from behind, tripped him up in an instant, and in the twinkling of an eye the Portuguese was straddling an oar, borne aloft by an uproarious multitude, who rushed him along the deck at a railroad gallop. The living mass of arms all round and beneath him was so dense, that every time he inclined to one side he was instantly pushed upright, but only to fall over again, to receive another push from the contrary direction. Presently, disengaging his hands from those who held them, the enraged seaman drew from his bosom an iron belaying-pin, and recklessly laid about him to right and left. Most of his persecutors fled; but some eight or ten still stood their ground, and, while bearing him aloft, endeavoured to wrest the weapon from his hands. In this attempt one man was struck on the head, and dropped insensible. He was taken up for dead, and carried below to Cuticle, the surgeon, while the Portuguese was put under guard. But the wound did not prove very serious; and in a few days the man was walking about the deck, with his head well bandaged.

This occurrence put an end to the 'skylarking', further

head-breaking being strictly prohibited. In due time the Portuguese paid the penalty of his rashness at the gangway; where once again the officers *shipped their quarter-deck faces*.*

XXVI

The Pitch of the Cape

ERE the calm had yet left us, a sail had been discerned from the fore-topmast-head, at a great distance, probably three leagues or more. At first it was a mere speck, altogether out-of sight from the deck. By the force of attraction, or something else equally inscrutable, two ships in a calm, and equally affected by the currents, will always approximate, more or less. Though there was not a breath of wind, it was not a great while before the strange sail was descried from our bulwarks; gradually, it drew still nearer.

What was she, and whence? There is no object which so excites interest and conjecture, and, at the same time, baffles both, as a sail, seen as a mere speck on these remote seas off Cape Horn.

A breeze! a breeze! for lo! the stranger is now perceptibly nearing the frigate; the officer's spy-glass pronounces her a full-rigged ship, with all sail set, and coming right down to us, though in our own vicinity the calm still reigns.

She is bringing the wind with her. Hurrah! Ay, there it is! Behold how mincingly it creeps over the sea, just ruffling and crisping it.

Our top-men were at once sent aloft to loose the sails, and presently they faintly began to distend. As yet we hardly had steerage-way. Toward sunset the stranger bore down before the wind, a complete pyramid of canvass. Never before, I venture to say, was Cape Horn· so audaciously insulted. Stun'-sails alow and aloft; royals, moonsails, and every-thing else. She glided under our stern, within hailing dis-tance, and the signal-quarter-master ran up our ensign to the gaff.

'Ship ahoy!' cried the lieutenant of the watch, through his trumpet.

'Halloa!' bawled an old fellow in a green jacket, clapping one hand to his mouth, while he held on with the other to the mizzen-shrouds.

'What ship's that?'

'The *Sultan*, Indiaman, from New York, and bound to Callao and Canton, sixty days out, all well. What frigate's that?'

'The United States Ship *Neversink*, homeward bound.'

'Hurrah! hurrah! hurrah!' yelled our enthusiastic country-man, transported with patriotism.

By this time the *Sultan* had swept past, but the lieutenant of the watch could not withhold a parting admonition.

'D'ye hear? You'd better take in some of your flying-kites there. Look out for Cape Horn!'

But the friendly advice was lost in the now increasing wind. With a suddenness by no means unusual in these latitudes, the light breeze soon became a succession of sharp squalls, and our sail-proud braggadocio of an Indiaman was observed to let everything go by the run, his t'gallant stun'-sails and flying-jib taking quick leave of the spars; the flying-jib was swept into the air, rolled together for a few minutes, and tossed about in the squalls like a football. But the wind played no such pranks with the more prudently managed canvass of the *Neversink*, though before many hours it was stirring times with us.

About midnight, when the starboard watch, to which I belonged, was below, the boatswain's whistle was heard, followed by the shrill cry for '*All hands take in sail!* jump, men, and save ship!'

Springing from our hammocks, we found the frigate lean-ing over to it so steeply, that it was with difficulty we could climb the ladders leading to the upper deck.

Here the scene was awful. The vessel seemed to be sailing on her side. The main-deck guns had several days previously been run in and housed, and the port-holes closed, but the lee carronades on the quarter-deck and forecastle were plunging through the sea, which undulated over them in milk-white billows of foam. With every lurch to leeward the yard-arm ends seemed to dip in the sea, while forward the spray dashed over the bows in cataracts, and drenched the men who were on the fore-yard. By this time the deck was alive with the whole strength of the ship's company, five hundred men, officers and all, mostly clinging to the weather bulwarks. The occasional phosphorescence of the yeasting sea cast a glare upon their uplifted faces, as a night fire in a populous city lights up the panic-stricken crowd.

In a sudden gale, or when a large quantity of sail is suddenly to be furled, it is the custom for the first lieutenant to take the trumpet from whoever happens then to be officer of the deck. But Mad Jack had the trumpet that watch; nor did the first lieutenant now seek to wrest it from his hands. Every eye was upon him, as if we had chosen him from among us all, to decide this battle with the elements, by single combat with the spirit of the Cape; for Mad Jack was the saving genius of the ship, and so proved himself that night. I owe this right hand, that is this moment flying over my sheet, and all my present being to Mad Jack. The ship's bows were now butting, battering, ramming, and thundering over and upon the head seas, and with a horrible wallowing sound our whole hull was rolling in the trough of the foam. The gale came athwart the deck, and every sail seemed bursting with its wild breath.

All the quarter-masters, and several of the forecastle-men, were swarming round the double wheel on the quarter-deck. Some jumping up and down, with their hands upon the spokes; for the whole helm and galvanized keel were fiercely feverish with the life imparted to them by the tempest.

'Hard *up* the helm!' shouted Captain Claret, bursting from his cabin like a ghost, in his night-dress.

'Damn you!' raged Mad Jack to the quarter-masters; 'hard *down*—hard *down*, I say, and be damned to you!'

Contrary orders! but Mad Jack's were obeyed. His object was to throw the ship into the wind, so as the better to admit of close-reefing the topsails. But though the halyards were let go, it was impossible to clew down the yards, owing to the enormous horizontal strain on the canvass. It now blew a hurricane. The spray flew over the ship in floods. The gigantic masts seemed about to snap under the world-wide strain of the three entire topsails.

'Clew down! clew down!' shouted Mad Jack, husky with excitement, and in a frenzy, beating his trumpet against one of the shrouds. But, owing to the slant of the ship, the thing could not be done. It was obvious that before many minutes something must go—either sails, rigging, or sticks; perhaps the hull itself, and all hands.

Presently a voice from the top exclaimed that there was a rent in the main-topsail. And instantly we heard a report like two or three muskets discharged together; the vast sail was rent up and down like the Veil of the Temple.* This saved the mainmast; for the yard was now clewed down with comparative ease, and the top-men laid out to stow the shattered canvass. Soon, the two remaining topsails were also clewed down and close-reefed.

Above all the roar of the tempest and the shouts of the crew was heard the dismal tolling of the ship's bell—almost as large as that of a village church—which the violent rolling of the ship was occasioning. Imagination cannot conceive the horror of such a sound in a night tempest at sea.

'Stop that ghost!' roared Mad Jack; 'away, one of you, and wrench off the clapper!'

But no sooner was this ghost gagged, than a still more appalling sound was heard, the rolling to and fro of the heavy shot, which, on the gun-deck, had broken loose from the gun-racks, and converted that part of the ship into an immense bowling-alley. Some hands were sent down to secure them; but it was as much as their lives were worth. Several were maimed; and the midshipmen who were ordered to see the duty performed reported it impossible, until the storm abated.

The most terrific job of all was to furl the mainsail, which, at the commencement of the squalls, had been clewed up, coaxed and quieted as much as possible with the bunt-lines and slab-lines. Mad Jack waited some time for a lull, ere he gave an order so perilous to be executed. For to furl this enormous sail, in such a gale, required at least fifty men on the yard; whose weight, superadded to that of the ponderous stick itself, still further jeopardized their lives. But there was no prospect of a cessation of the gale, and the order was at last given.

At this time a hurricane of slanting sleet and hail was descending upon us; the rigging was coated with a thin glare of ice, formed within the hour.

'Aloft, mainyard-men! and all you maintop-men! and furl the mainsail!' cried Mad Jack.

I dashed down my hat, slipped out of my quilted jacket in an instant, kicked the shoes from my feet, and, with a crowd of others, sprang for the rigging. Above the bulwarks (which in a frigate are so high as to afford much protection to those on deck) the gale was horrible. The sheer force of the wind flattened us to the rigging as we ascended, and every hand seemed congealing to the icy shrouds by which we held.

'Up—up, my brave hearties!' shouted Mad Jack; and up we got, some way or other, all of us, and groped our way out on the yard-arms.

'Hold on, every mother's son!' cried an old quarter-gunner at my side. He was bawling at the top of his compass; but in the gale, he seemed to be whispering; and I only heard him from his being right to windward of me.

But his hint was unnecessary; I dug my nails into the *jack-stays*, and swore that nothing but death should part me and them until I was able to turn round and look to windward. As yet, this was impossible; I could scarcely hear the man to leeward at my elbow; the wind seemed to snatch the words from his mouth and fly away with them to the South Pole.

All this while the sail itself was flying about, sometimes catching over our head, and threatening to tear us from the yard in spite of all our hugging. For about three-quarters of an hour we thus hung suspended right over the rampant billows, which curled their very crests under the feet of some four or five of us clinging to the lee yard-arm, as if to float us from our place.

Presently, the word passed along the yard from windward, that we were ordered to come down and leave the sail to blow, since it could not be furled. A midshipman, it seemed, had been sent up by the officer of the deck to give the order, as no trumpet could be heard where we were.

Those on the weather yard-arm managed to crawl upon the spar and scramble down the rigging; but with us, upon the extreme leeward side, this feat was out of the question; it was, literally, like climbing a precipice, to get to windward in order to reach the shrouds; besides, the entire yard was now encased in ice, and our hands and feet were so numb that we dare not trust our lives to them. Nevertheless, by assisting each other, we contrived to throw ourselves prostrate along the yard, and embrace it with our arms and legs. In this position, the stun'-sail-booms greatly assisted in securing our hold. Strange as it may appear, I do not suppose that, at this moment, the slightest sensation of fear was felt by one man on that yard. We clung to it with might and main; but this was instinct. The truth is, that, in circumstances like these, the sense of fear is annihilated in the unutterable sights that fill all the eye, and the sounds that fill all the ear. You become identified with the tempest; your insignificance is lost in the riot of the stormy universe around.

Below us, our noble frigate seemed thrice its real length—a vast black wedge, opposing its widest end to the combined fury of the sea and wind.

At length the first fury of the gale began to abate, and we at once fell to pounding our hands, as a preliminary operation to going to work; for a gang of men had now ascended to help secure what was left of the sail; we somehow packed it away, at last, and came down.

About noon the next day, the gale so moderated that we shook two reefs out of the topsails, set new courses, and stood due east with the wind astern.

Thus, all the fine weather we encountered after first weighing anchor on the pleasant Spanish coast, was but the prelude to this one terrific night; more especially, that treacherous calm immediately preceding it. But how could we reach our long-promised homes without encountering Cape Horn? by what possibility avoid it? And though some ships have weathered it without these perils, yet by far the greater part must encounter them. Lucky it is that it comes about midway in the homeward-bound passage, so that the sailors have time to prepare for it, and time to recover from it after it is astern.

But, sailor or landsman, there is some sort of a Cape Horn for all. Boys! beware of it; prepare for it in time. Greybeards! thank God it is passed. And ye lucky livers, to whom by some rare fatality your Cape Horns are placid as Lake Lemans, flatter not yourselves that good luck is judgment and discretion; for all the yolk in your eggs, you might have foundered and gone down, had the Spirit of the Cape said the word.

XXVII

Some Thoughts growing out of Mad Jack's countermanding his Superior's Order

IN time of peril, like the needle to the loadstone, obedience, irrespective of rank, generally flies to him who is best fitted to command. The truth of this seemed evinced in the case of Mad Jack, during the gale, and especially at that perilous moment when he countermanded the captain's order at the helm. But every seaman knew, at the time, that the captain's order was an unwise one in the extreme; perhaps worse than unwise.

These two orders, given by the captain and his lieutenant, exactly contrasted their characters. By putting the helm *hard up*, the captain was for *scudding*; that is, for flying away from the gale. Whereas, Mad Jack was for running the ship into its teeth. It is needless to say that, in almost all cases of similar hard squalls and gales, the latter step, though attended with more appalling appearances, is, in reality, the safer of the two, and the most generally adopted.

Scudding makes you a slave to the blast, which drives you headlong before it; but *running up into the wind's eye* enables you, in a degree, to hold it at bay. Scudding exposes to the gale your stern, the weakest part of your hull; the contrary course presents to it your bows, your strongest part. As with ships, so with men; he who turns his back to his foe gives him an advantage. Whereas, our ribbed chests, like the ribbed bows of a frigate, are as bulkheads to dam off an onset.

That night, off the pitch of the Cape, Captain Claret was hurried forth from his disguises, and, at a manhood-testing conjuncture, appeared in his true colours. A thing which every man in the ship had long suspected, that night was proved true. Hitherto, in going about the ship, and casting his glances among the men, the peculiarly lustreless repose of the captain's eye—his slow, even, unnecessarily methodical step, and the forced firmness of his whole demeanour— though, to a casual observer, seemingly expressive of the consciousness of command and a desire to strike subjection among the crew—all this, to some minds, had only been deemed indications of the fact that Captain Claret, while carefully shunning positive excesses, continually kept himself in an uncertain equilibrio between soberness and its reverse; which equilibrio might be destroyed by the first sharp vicissitude of events.

And though this is only a surmise, nevertheless, as having some knowledge of brandy and mankind, White-Jacket will venture to state that, had Captain Claret been an out-and-out temperance man, he would never have given that most imprudent order to *hard up* the helm. He would either have held his peace, and stayed in his cabin, like his gracious majesty the commodore, or else have anticipated Mad Jack's order, and thundered forth 'Hard down the helm!'

To show how little real sway at times have the severest restrictive laws, and how spontaneous is the instinct of discretion in some minds, it must here be added, that though Mad Jack, under a hot impulse, had countermanded an order of his superior officer before his very face, yet that severe Article of War, to which he thus rendered himself obnoxious, was never enforced against him. Nor, so far as any of the crew ever knew, did the captain even venture to reprimand him for his temerity.

It has been said that Mad Jack himself was a lover of strong drink. So he was. But here we only see the virtue of being placed in a station constantly demanding a cool head and steady nerves, and the misfortune of filling a post that does *not* at all times demand these qualities. So exact and methodical in most things was the discipline of the frigate, that, to a certain extent, Captain Claret was exempted from personal interposition in many of its current events, and thereby, perhaps, was he lulled into security, under the enticing lee of his decanter.

But as for Mad Jack, he must stand his regular watches, and pace the quarter-deck at night, and keep a sharp eye to windward. Hence, at sea, Mad Jack tried to make a point of keeping sober, though in very fine weather he was sometimes betrayed into a glass too many. But with Cape Horn before him, he took the temperance pledge outright, till that perilous promontory should be far astern.

The leading incident of the gale irresistibly invites the question, Are there incompetent officers in the American Navy?—that is, incompetent to the due performance of whatever duties may devolve upon them. But in that gallant marine, which, during the late war, gained so much of what is called *glory*, can there possibly be to-day incompetent officers?

As in the camp ashore, so on the quarter-deck at sea—the trumpets of one victory drown the muffled drums of a thousand defeats. And, in degree, this holds true of those events of war which are neuter in their character, neither making renown nor disgrace. Besides, as a long array of ciphers, led by but one solitary numeral, swell, by mere force of aggregation, into an immense arithmetical sum;

even so, in some brilliant actions, do a crowd of officers, each inefficient in himself, aggregate renown when banded together, and led by a numeral Nelson or a Wellington. And the renown of such heroes, by outliving themselves, descends as a heritage to their subordinate survivors. One large brain and one large heart have virtue sufficient to magnetize a whole fleet or an army. And if all the men who, since the beginning of the world, have mainly contributed to the war-like successes or reverses of nations, were now mustered together, we should be amazed to behold but a handful of heroes. For there is no heroism in merely running in and out a gun at a port-hole, enveloped in smoke and vapour, or in firing off muskets in platoons at the word of command. This kind of merely manual valour is often born of trepidation at the heart. There may be men, individually craven, who, united, may display even temerity. Yet it would be false to deny that, in some instances, the lowest privates have acquitted themselves with even more gallantry than their commodores. True heroism is not in the hand, but in the heart and the head.

But are there incompetent officers in the gallant American Navy? For an American, the question is of no grateful cast. White-Jacket must again evade it, by referring to an histori-cal fact in the history of a kindred marine, which, from its long standing and magnitude, furnishes many more examples of all kinds than our own. And this is the only reason why it is ever referred to in this narrative. I thank God I am free from all national invidiousness.

It is indirectly on record in the books of the English Admiralty, that in the year 1808—after the death of Lord Nelson—when Lord Collingwood* commanded on the Mediterranean station, and his broken health induced him to solicit a furlough, that out of a list of upward of one hundred admirals, not a single officer was found who was deemed qualified to relieve the applicant with credit to the country. This fact Collingwood sealed with his life; for, hopeless of being recalled, he shortly after died, worn out, at his post. Now, if this was the case in so renowned a marine as England's, what must be inferred with respect to our own? But herein no special disgrace is involved. For the truth .is, that to be an accomplished and skilful naval generalissimo needs natural capabilities of an uncommon order. Still more, it may safely be asserted, that, worthily to command even a frigate, requires a degree of natural heroism, talent, judgment, and integrity, that is denied to mediocrity. Yet these qualifications are not only required, but demanded; and no one has a right to be a naval captain unless he possesses them.

Regarding lieutenants, there are not a few Selvagees and Paper Jacks* in the American Navy. Many commodores know that they have seldom taken a line-of-battle ship to sea without feeling more or less nervousness when some of the lieutenants have the deck at night.

According to the last *Navy Register* (1849), there are now 68 captains in the American Navy, collectively drawing about $300,000 annually from the public treasury; also, 297 commanders, drawing about $200,000; and 377 lieutenants, drawing about half a million; and 451 midshipmen (including passed-midshipmen), also drawing nearly half a million. Considering the known facts, that some of these officers are seldom or never sent to sea, owing to the Navy Department being well aware of their inefficiency; that others are detailed for pen-and-ink work at observatories, and solvers of logarithms in the Coast Survey; while the really meritorious officers, who are accomplished practical seamen, are known to be sent from ship to ship, with but a small interval of a furlough; considering all this, it is not too much to say, that no small portion of the million and a half of money above mentioned is annually paid to national pensioners in disguise, who live on the Navy without serving it.

Nothing like this can be even insinuated against the *forward officers*—boatswains, gunners, &c.; nor against the *petty officers*—captains of the tops, &c.; nor against the able seamen in the Navy. For if any of *these* are found wanting, they are forthwith disrated or discharged.

True, all experience teaches, that whenever there is a great national establishment, employing large numbers of officials, the public must be reconciled to support many incompetent men; for such is the favouritism and nepotism always prevailing in the purlieus of these establishments, that some incompetent persons are always admitted, to the exclusion of many of the worthy.

Nevertheless, in a country like ours, boasting of the political equality of all social conditions, it is a great reproach that such a thing as a common seaman rising to the rank of a commissioned officer in our Navy is nowadays almost unheard of. Yet, in former times, when officers have so risen to rank, they have generally proved of signal usefulness in the service, and sometimes have reflected solid honour upon the country. Instances in point might be mentioned.

Is it not well to have our institutions of a piece? Any American landsman may hope to become President of the Union—commodore of our squadron of states. And every American sailor should be placed in such a position, that he might freely aspire to command a squadron of frigates.

XXVIII

Edging away

RIGHT before the wind! Ay, blow, blow, ye breezes; so long as *ye* stay fair, and *we* are homeward bound, what care the jolly crew?

It is worth mentioning here that, in nineteen cases out of twenty, a passage from the Pacific round the Cape is almost sure to be much shorter, and attended with less hardship, than a passage undertaken from the Atlantic. The reason is, that the gales are mostly from the westward, also the currents.

But, after all, going before the wind in a frigate, in such a tempest, has its annoyances and drawbacks, as well as many other blessings. The disproportionate weight of metal upon the spar- and gun-decks induces a violent rolling, unknown to merchant-ships. We rolled and rolled on our way, like the world in its orbit, shipping green seas on both sides, until the old frigate dipped and went into it like a diving-bell.

The hatchways of some armed vessels are but poorly secured in bad weather. This was peculiarly the case with those of the *Neversink*. They were merely spread over with an old tarpaulin, cracked and rent in every direction.

In fair weather, the ship's company messed on the gun-deck; but as this was now flooded almost continually, we were obliged to take our meals upon the berth-deck, the next one below. One day, the messes of the starboard watch were seated here at dinner; forming little groups, twelve or fifteen men in each, reclining about the beef-kids and their pots and pans; when all of a sudden the ship was seized with such a paroxysm of rolling that, in a single instant, everything on the berth-deck—pots, kids, sailors, pieces of beef, bread-bags, clothes-bags, and barges—were tossed indiscriminately from side to side. It was impossible to stay one's self; there was nothing but the bare deck to cling to, which was slippery with the contents of the kids, and heaving under us as if there were a volcano in the frigate's hold. While we were yet sliding in uproarious crowds—all seated—the windows of the deck opened, and floods of brine descended, simultaneously with a violent lee roll. The shower was hailed by the reckless tars with a hurricane of yells; although, for an instant, I really imagined we were about being swamped in the sea, such volumes of water came cascading down.

A day or two after, we had made sufficient easting to stand to the northward, which we did, with the wind astern; thus fairly turning the corner without abating our rate of progress. Though we had seen no land since leaving Callao, Cape Horn was said to be somewhere to the west of us; and though there was no positive evidence of the fact, the weather encountered might be accounted pretty good presumptive proof.

The land near Cape Horn, however, is well worth seeing, especially Staten Land. Upon one occasion, the ship in which

I then happened to be sailing drew near this place from the northward, with a fair, free wind, blowing steadily, through a bright translucent day, whose air was almost musical with the clear, glittering cold. On our starboard beam, like a pile of glaciers in Switzerland, lay this Staten Land, gleaming in snow-white barrenness and solitude. Unnumbered white albatross were skimming the sea near by, and clouds of smaller white wings fell through the air like snow-flakes. High, towering in their own turbaned snows, the far inland pinnacles loomed up, like the border of some other world. Flashing walls and crystal battlements, like the diamond watch-towers along heaven's furthest frontier.

After leaving the latitude of the Cape, we had several storms of snow; one night a considerable quantity laid upon the decks, and some of the sailors enjoyed the juvenile diversion of snowballing. Woe unto the 'middy' who that night went forward of the booms. Such a target for snowballs! The throwers could never be known. By some curious sleight in hurling the missiles, they seemed to be thrown on board by some hoydenish sea-nymphs outside the frigate.

At daybreak Midshipman Pert went below to the surgeon with an alarming wound, gallantly received in discharging his perilous duty on the forecastle. The officer of the deck had sent him on an errand, to tell the boatswain that he was wanted in the captain's cabin. While in the very act of performing the exploit of delivering the message, Mr. Pert was struck on the nose with a snowball of wondrous compactness. Upon being informed of the disaster, the rogues expressed the liveliest sympathy. Pert was no favourite.

After one of these storms, it was a curious sight to see the men relieving the uppermost deck of its load of snow. It became the duty of the captain of each gun to keep his own station clean; accordingly, with an old broom, or 'squilgee', he proceeded to business, often quarrelling with his next-door neighbours about their scraping their snow on his premises. It was like Broadway in winter, the morning after a storm, when rival shop-boys are at work cleaning the sidewalk.

Now and then, by way of variety, we had a fall of hail-stones, so big that sometimes we found ourselves dodging them.

The commodore had a Polynesian servant on board, whose services he had engaged at the Society Islands. Unlike his countrymen, Wooloo was of a sedate, earnest, and philo-sophic temperament. Having never been outside of the tropics before, he found many phenomena off Cape Horn which absorbed his attention, and set him, like other philo-sophers, to feign theories corresponding to the marvels he beheld. At the first snow, when he saw the deck covered all over with a white powder, as it were, he expanded his eyes into stew-pans; but upon examining the strange substance, he decided that this must be a species of superfine flour, such as was compounded into his master's *duffs*, and other dainties. In vain did an experienced natural philosopher belonging to the foretop maintain before his face, that in this hypothesis Wooloo was mistaken; Wooloo's opinion remained unchanged for some time.

As for the hailstones, they transported him; he went about with a bucket, making collections, and receiving contribu-tions, for the purpose of carrying them home to his sweet-hearts for glass beads; but having put his bucket away, and returning to it again, and finding nothing but a little water, he accused the bystanders of stealing his precious stones.

This suggests another story concerning him. The first time he was given a piece of 'duff' to eat, he was observed to pick out very carefully every raisin, and throw it away, with a gesture indicative of the highest disgust. It turned out that he had taken the raisins for bugs.

In our man-of-war, this semi-savage, wandering about the gun-deck in his barbaric robe, seemed a being from some other sphere. His tastes were our abominations: ours his. Our creed he rejected: his we. We thought him a loon: he fancied us fools. Had the case been reversed; had we been Polynesians and he an American, our mutual opinion of each other would still have remained the same. A fact proving that neither was wrong, but both right.

XXIX

The Night-watches

THOUGH leaving the Cape behind us, the severe cold still continued, and one of its worst consequences was the almost incurable drowsiness induced thereby during the long night-watches. All along the decks, huddled between the guns, stretched out on the carronade-slides, and in every accessible nook and corner, you would see the sailors wrapped in their monkey-jackets, in a state of half-conscious torpidity, lying still and freezing alive, without the power to rise and shake themselves.

'Up—up, you lazy dogs!' our good-natured third lieutenant, a Virginian, would cry, rapping them with his speaking-trumpet. 'Get up, and stir about.'

But in vain. They would rise for an instant, and as soon as his back was turned, down they would drop, as if shot through the heart.

Often I have lain thus, when the fact, that if I laid much longer I would actually freeze to death, would come over me with such overpowering force as to break the icy spell, and starting to my feet, I would endeavour to go through the combined manual and pedal exercise to restore the circulation. The first fling of my benumbed arm generally struck me in the face, instead of smiting my chest, its true destination. But in these cases one's muscles have their own way.

In exercising my other extremities, I was obliged to hold on to something, and leap with both feet; for my limbs seemed as destitute of joints as a pair of canvass pants spread to dry, and frozen stiff.

When an order was given to haul the braces—which required the strength of the entire watch, some two hundred men—a spectator would have supposed that all hands had received a stroke of the palsy. Roused from their state of enchantment, they came halting and limping across the decks, falling against each other, and, for a few moments, almost unable to handle the ropes. The slightest exertion seemed intolerable; and frequently a body of eighty or a hundred men, summoned to brace the main-yard, would hang over the rope for several minutes, waiting for some active fellow to pick it up and put it into their hands. Even then, it was some time before they were able to do anything. They made all the motions usual in hauling a rope, but it was a long time before the yard budged an inch. It was to no purpose that the officers swore at them, or sent the midshipmen among them to find out who those '*horse marines*' and '*sogers*' were. The sailors were so enveloped in monkey-jackets, that in the dark night there was no telling one from the other.

'Here, *you*, sir!' cries little Mr. Pert, eagerly catching hold of the skirts of an old sea-dog, and trying to turn him round, so as to peer under his tarpaulin. 'Who are *you*, sir? What's your name?'

'Find out, Milk-and-Water,' was the impertinent rejoinder.

'Blast you! you old rascal; I'll have you licked for that! Tell me his name, some of you!' turning round to the bystanders.

'Gammon!' cries a voice at a distance.

'Hang me, but I know *you*, sir! and here's at you!' and, so saying, Mr. Pert drops the impenetrable unknown, and makes into the crowd after the bodiless voice. But the attempt to find an owner for that voice is quite as idle as the effort to discover the contents of the monkey-jacket.

And here sorrowful mention must be made of something which, during this state of affairs, most sorely afflicted me. Most monkey-jackets are of a dark hue; mine, as I have fifty times repeated, and say again, was white. And thus, in those long, dark nights, when it was my quarter-watch on deck, and not in the top, and others went skulking and 'sogering' about the decks, secure from detection—their identity undiscoverable—my own hapless jacket forever proclaimed the name of its wearer. It gave me many a hard job, which otherwise I should have escaped. When an officer wanted a man for any particular duty—running aloft, say, to communicate some slight order to the captains of the tops—how easy, in that mob of incognitos, to individualize '*that white jacket*', and dispatch him on the errand! Then, it would never do for me to hang back when the ropes were being pulled.

Indeed, upon all these occasions, such alacrity and cheerfulness was I obliged to display, that I was frequently held up as an illustrious example of activity, which the rest were called upon to emulate. 'Pull—pull! you lazy lubbers! Look at White-Jacket, there; pull like him!'

Oh! how I execrated my luckless garment! how often I scoured the deck with it, to give it a tawny hue! how often I supplicated the inexorable Brush, captain of the paint-room, for just one brushful of his invaluable pigment! Frequently I meditated giving it a toss overboard; but I had not the resolution. Jacketless at sea! Jacketless so near Cape Horn! The thought was unendurable. And, at least, my garment was a jacket in name, if not in utility.

At length I essayed a 'swap'. 'Here, Bob,' said I, assuming all possible suavity, and accosting a messmate with a sort of diplomatic assumption of superiority, 'suppose I was ready to part with this "grego" of mine, and take yours in exchange —what would you give me to boot?'

'Give you to *boot*?' he exclaimed, with horror; 'I wouldn't take your infernal jacket for a gift!'

How I hailed every snow-squall; for then—blessings on them!—many of the men became *white jackets* along with myself; and, powdered with the flakes, we all looked like millers.

We had six lieutenants, all of whom, with the exception of the first lieutenant, by turns headed the watches. Three of these officers, including Mad Jack, were strict disciplinarians, and never permitted us to lay down on deck during the night. And, to tell the truth, though it caused much growling, it was far better for our health to be thus kept on our feet. So promenading was all the vogue. For some of us, however, it was like pacing in a dungeon; for, as we had to keep at our stations—some at the halyards, some at the braces, and elsewhere—and were not allowed to stroll about indefinitely, and fairly take the measure of the ship's entire keel, we were fain to confine ourselves to the space of a very few feet. But the worst of this was soon over. The suddenness of the change in the temperature consequent on leaving Cape Horn, and steering to the northward with a ten-knot breeze, is a noteworthy thing. To-day, you are assailed by a blast that seems to have edged itself on icebergs; but in a little more than a week, your jacket may be superfluous.

One word more about Cape Horn, and we have done with it.

Years hence, when a ship canal*shall have penetrated the Isthmus of Darien, and the traveller be taking his seat in the cars at Cape Cod for Astoria,* it will be held a thing almost incredible that, for so long a period, vessels bound to the nor'-west coast from New York should, by going round Cape Horn, have lengthened their voyages some thousands of miles. 'In those unenlightened days' (I quote, in advance, the language of some future philosopher), 'entire years were frequently consumed in making the voyage to and from the Spice Islands, the present fashionable watering-place of the beau-monde of Oregon.' Such must be our national progress.

Why, sir, that boy of yours will, one of these days, be sending your grandson to the salubrious city of Jeddo* to spend his summer vacations.

XXX

A Peep through a Port-hole at the subterranean Parts of a Man-of-war

WHILE now running rapidly away from the bitter coast of Patagonia, battling with the night-watches—still cold—as best we may; come under the lee of my white jacket, reader, while I tell of the less painful sights to be seen in a frigate.

A hint has already been conveyed concerning the subterranean depths of the *Neversink*'s hold. But there is no time here to speak of the *spirit-room*, a cellar down in the after hold, where the sailors' 'grog' is kept; nor of the *cable-*

tiers, where the great hawsers and chains are piled, as you see them at a large ship-chandler's on shore; nor of the grocer's vaults, where tierces of sugar, molasses, vinegar, rice, and flour are snugly stowed; nor of the *sail-room*, full as a sail-maker's loft ashore—piled up with great topsails and topgallant-sails, all ready-folded in their places, like so many white vests in a gentleman's wardrobe; nor of the copper and copper-fastened *magazine*, closely packed with kegs of powder, great-gun and small-arm cartridges; nor of the immense *shot-lockers*, or subterranean arsenals, full as a bushel of apples with twenty-four-pound balls; nor of the *bread-room*, a large apartment, tinned all round within, to keep out the mice, where the hard biscuit destined for the consumption of five hundred men on a long voyage is stowed away by the cubic yard; nor of the vast iron *tanks* for fresh water in the hold, like the reservoir lakes at Fairmount, in Philadelphia; nor of the *paint-room*, where the kegs of white lead, and casks of linseed oil, and all sorts of pots and brushes, are kept; nor of the *armourer's smithy*, where the ship's forges and anvils may be heard ringing at times; I say, I have no time to speak of these things, and many more places of note.

But there is one very extensive warehouse among the rest that needs special mention—*the ship's yeoman's store-room*. In the *Neversink* it was down in the ship's basement, beneath the berth-deck, and you went to it by way of the *fore passage*, a very dim, devious corridor, indeed. Entering— say at noonday—you find yourself in a gloomy apartment, lit by a solitary lamp. On one side are shelves, filled with balls of *marline*,* *ratlin-stuff*, *seizing-stuff*, *spun-yarn*, and numerous twines of assorted sizes. In another direction you see large cases containing heaps of articles, reminding one of a shoe-maker's furnishing-store—wooden *serving-mallets*, *fids*, *toggles*, and *heavers*; iron *prickers* and *marling-spikes*;* in a third quarter you see a sort of hardware shop—shelves piled with all manner of hooks, bolts, nails, screws, and *thimbles*; and, in still another direction, you see a block-maker's store, heaped up with lignum-vitae sheaves and wheels.

Through low arches in the bulkhead beyond, you peep in

upon distant vaults and catacombs, obscurely lighted in the far end, and showing immense coils of new ropes, and other bulky articles, stowed in tiers, all savouring of tar.

But by far the most curious department of these mysterious store-rooms is the armoury, where the pikes, cutlasses, pistols, and belts, forming the arms of the boarders in time of action, are hung against the walls, and suspended in thick rows from the beams overhead. Here, too, are to be seen scores of Colt's patent revolvers,* which, though furnished with but one tube, multiply the fatal bullets, as the naval cat-o'-nine-tails, with a cannibal cruelty, in one blow nine times multiplies a culprit's lashes; so that, when a sailor is ordered one dozen lashes, the sentence should read one hundred and eight. All these arms are kept in the brightest order, wearing a fine polish, and may truly be said to *reflect* credit on the yeoman and his mates.

Among the lower grade of officers in a man-of-war, that of yeoman is not the least important. His responsibilities are denoted by his pay. While the *petty officers*, quarter-gunners, captains of the tops, and others, receive but fifteen and eighteen dollars a month—but little more than a mere able seaman— the yeoman in an American line-of-battle ship receives forty dollars, and in a frigate thirty-five dollars per month.

He is accountable for all the articles under his charge, and on no account must deliver a yard of twine or a tenpenny nail to the boatswain or carpenter, unless shown a written requisition and order from the senior lieutenant. The yeoman is to be found burrowing in his underground store-rooms all the day long, in readiness to serve licensed customers. But in the counter, behind which he usually stands, there is no place for a till to drop the shillings in, which takes away not a little from the most agreeable part of a storekeeper's duties. Nor, among the musty, old account-books in his desk, where he registers all expenditures of his stuffs, is there any cash- or cheque-book.

The yeoman of the *Neversink* was a somewhat odd specimen of a troglodite. He was a little old man, round-shouldered, bald-headed, with great goggle-eyes, looking through portentous round spectacles, which he called his *barnacles.* He was imbued with a wonderful zeal for the naval service, and seemed to think that, in keeping his pistols and cutlasses free from rust, he preserved the national honour untarnished.

After *general quarters*, it was amusing to watch his anxious air as the various *petty officers* restored to him the arms used at the martial exercises of the crew. As successive bundles would be deposited on his counter, he would count over the pistols and cutlasses, like an old housekeeper telling over her silver forks and spoons in a pantry before retiring for the night. And often, with a sort of dark lantern in his hand, he might be seen poking into his furthest vaults and cellars, and counting over his great coils of ropes, as if they were all jolly puncheons of old port and Madeira.

By reason of his incessant watchfulness and unaccountable bachelor oddities, it was very difficult for him to retain in his employment the various sailors who, from time to time, were billeted with him to do the duty of subalterns. In particular, he was always desirous of having at least one steady, fault-less young man, of a literary taste, to keep an eye to his account-books, and swab out the armoury every morning. It was an odious business this, to be immured all day in such a bottomless hole, among tarry old ropes and villainous guns and pistols. It was with peculiar dread that I one day noticed the goggle-eyes of *Old Revolver*, as they called him, fastened upon me with a fatal glance of good-will and approbation. He had somehow heard of my being a very learned person, who could both read and write with extraordinary facility; and, moreover, that I was a rather reserved youth, who kept his modest, unassuming merits in the background. But though, from the keen sense of my situation as a man-of-war's-man, all this about my keeping myself in the *back* ground was true enough, yet I had no idea of hiding my diffident merits *under* ground. I became alarmed at the old yeoman's goggling glances, lest he should drag me down into tarry perdition in his hideous store-rooms. But this fate was providentially averted, owing to mysterious causes which I never could fathom.

XXXI

The Gunner under Hatches

AMONG such a crowd of marked characters as were to be met with on board our frigate, many of whom moved in mysterious circles beneath the lowermost deck, and at long intervals flitted into sight like apparitions, and disappeared again for whole weeks together, there were some who inordinately excited my curiosity, and whose names, callings, and precise abodes I industriously sought out, in order to learn something satisfactory concerning them.

While engaged in these inquiries, often fruitless, or but partially gratified, I could not but regret that there was no public printed directory for the *Neversink*, such as they have in large towns, containing an alphabetical list of all the crew, and where they might be found. Also, in losing myself in some remote, dark corner of the bowels of the frigate, in the vicinity of the various store-rooms, shops, and warehouses, I much lamented that no enterprising tar had yet thought of compiling a *Handbook of the Neversink*, so that the tourist might have a reliable guide.

Indeed, there were several parts of the ship under hatches shrouded in mystery, and completely inaccessible to the sailor. Wondrous old doors, barred and bolted in dingy bulkheads, must have opened into regions full of interest to a successful explorer.

They looked like the gloomy entrances to family vaults of buried dead; and when I chanced to see some unknown functionary insert his key, and enter these inexplicable apartments with a battle-lantern, as if on solemn official business, I almost quaked to dive in with him, and satisfy myself whether these vaults indeed contained the mouldering relics of by-gone old commodores and post-captains. But the habitations of the living commodore and captain— their spacious and curtained cabins—were themselves almost as sealed volumes, and I passed them in hopeless wonderment, like a peasant before a prince's palace. Night and day armed sentries guarded their sacred portals, cutlass in hand; and had I dared to cross their path, I would infallibly have been cut down, as if in battle. Thus, though for a period of more than a year I was an inmate of this floating box of live-oak, yet there were numberless things in it that, to the last, remained wrapped in obscurity, or concerning which I could only lose myself in vague speculations. I was as a Roman Jew of the Middle Ages, confined to the Jews' quarter of the town, and forbidden to stray beyond my limits. Or I was as a modern traveller in the same famous city, forced to quit it at last without gaining ingress to the most mysterious haunts—the innermost shrine of the Pope, and the dungeons and cells of the Inquisition.

But among all the persons and things on board that puzzled me, and filled me most with strange emotions of doubt, misgivings, and mystery, was the gunner—a short, square, grim man, his hair and beard grizzled and singed, as if with gunpowder. His skin was of a flecky brown, like the stained barrel of a fowling-piece, and his hollow eyes burned in his head like blue-lights. He it was who had access to many of those mysterious vaults I have spoken of. Often he might be seen groping his way into them, followed by his subalterns, the old quarter-gunners, as if intent upon laying a train of powder to blow up the ship. I remembered Guy Fawkes and the Parliament House, and made earnest inquiry whether this gunner was a Roman Catholic. I felt relieved when informed that he was not.

A little circumstance which one of his *mates* once told me heightened the gloomy interest with which I regarded his chief. He told me that, at periodical intervals, his master the gunner, accompanied by his phalanx, entered into the great magazine under the gun-room, of which he had sole custody and kept the key, nearly as big as the key of the Bastille, and provided with lanterns, something like Sir Humphry Davy's safety-lamp for coal-mines, proceeded to turn, end for end, all the kegs of powder and packages of cartridges stored in this innermost explosive vault, lined throughout with sheets of copper. In the vestibule of the magazine, against the panelling, were several pegs for slippers, and, before penetrating further than that vestibule, every man of the gunner's gang silently removed his shoes, for fear that the nails in their heels might possibly create a spark, by striking against the coppered floor within. Then, with slippered feet, and with hushed whispers, they stole into the heart of the place.

This turning of the powder was to preserve its inflammability. And surely it was a business full of direful interest, to be buried so deep below the sun, handling whole barrels of powder, any one of which, touched by the smallest spark, was powerful enough to blow up a whole street of warehouses.

The gunner went by the name of *Old Combustibles*, though I thought this an undignified name for so momentous a personage, who had all our lives in his hand.

While we lay in Callao, we received from shore several barrels of powder. So soon as the *launch* came alongside with them, orders were given to extinguish all lights and all fires in the ship: and the master-at-arms and his corporals inspected every deck, to see that this order was obeyed: a very prudent precaution, no doubt, but not observed at all in the Turkish Navy. The Turkish sailors will sit on their gun-carriages tranquilly smoking, while kegs of powder are being rolled under their ignited pipe-bowls. This shows the great comfort there is in the doctrine of these Fatalists, and how such a doctrine, in some things at least, relieves men from nervous anxieties. But we are all Fatalists at bottom. Nor need we so much marvel at the heroism of that army officer who challenged his personal foe to bestride a barrel of powder with him—the match to be placed between them —and be blown up in good company, for it is pretty certain that the whole earth itself is a vast hogshead, full of inflammable materials, and which we are always bestriding; at the same time, that all good Christians believe that at any minute the last day may come, and the terrible combustion of the entire planet ensue.

As if impressed with a befitting sense of the awfulness of his calling, our gunner always wore a fixed expression of solemnity, which was heightened by his grizzled hair and beard. But what imparted such a sinister look to him, and what wrought so upon my imagination concerning this man, was a frightful scar crossing his left cheek and forehead. He had been almost mortally wounded, they said, with a sabre-cut, during a frigate engagement in the last war with Britain.

He was the most methodical, exact, and punctual of all the forward officers. Among his other duties, it pertained to him, while in harbour, to see that at a certain hour in the evening one of the great guns was discharged from the forecastle, a ceremony only observed in a flagship. And always at the precise moment you might behold him blowing his match, then applying it; and with that booming thunder in his ear, and the smell of the powder in his hair, he retired to his hammock for the night. What dreams he must have had!

The same precision was observed when ordered to fire a gun to *bring to* some ship at sea; for, true to their name, and preserving its applicability, even in times of peace, all men-of-war are great bullies on the high seas. They domineer over the poor merchantmen, and with a hissing hot ball sent bowling across the ocean, compel them to stop their headway at pleasure.

It was enough to make you a man of method for life, to see the gunner superintending his subalterns, when preparing the main-deck batteries for a great national salute. While lying in harbour, intelligence reached us of the lamentable casualty that befell certain high officers of state, including the acting Secretary of the Navy himself, some other member of the President's cabinet, a commodore, and others, all engaged in experimenting upon a new-fangled engine of war.* At the same time with the receipt of this sad news, orders arrived to fire minute-guns for the deceased head of the naval department. Upon this occasion the gunner was more than usually ceremonious, in seeing that the long twenty-fours were thoroughly loaded and rammed down, and then accurately marked with chalk, so as to be discharged in undeviating rotation, first from the larboard side, and then from the starboard.

But as my ears hummed, and all my bones danced in me

with the reverberating din, and my eyes and nostrils were almost suffocated with the smoke, and when I saw this grim old gunner firing away so solemnly, I thought it a strange mode of honouring a man's memory who had himself been slaughtered by a cannon. Only the smoke, that, after rolling in at the port-holes, rapidly drifted away to leeward, and was lost to view, seemed truly emblematical touching the personage thus honoured, since that great non-combatant, the Bible, assures us that our life is but a vapour*that quickly passeth away.

XXXII

A Dish of Dunderfunk

IN men-of-war, the space on the uppermost deck, round about the mainmast, is the police-office, court-house, and yard of execution, where all charges are lodged, causes tried, and punishment administered. In frigate phrase, to be *brought up to the mast* is equivalent to being presented before the grand jury, to see whether a true bill will be found against you.

From the merciless, inquisitorial *baiting*, which sailors, charged with offences, too often experience *at the mast*, that vicinity is usually known among them as the *bull-ring*.

The mainmast, moreover, is the only place where the sailor can hold formal communication with the captain and officers. If anyone has been robbed; if anyone has been evilly entreated; if anyone's character has been defamed; if anyone has a request to present; if anyone has aught important for the executive of the ship to know—straight to the mainmast he repairs; and stands there—generally with his hat off—waiting the pleasure of the officer of the deck, to advance and communicate with him. Often, the most ludicrous scenes occur, and the most comical complaints are made.

One clear, cold morning, while we were yet running away from the Cape, a raw-boned, crack-pated Down-Easter,* belonging to the waist, made his appearance at the mast, dolefully exhibiting a blackened tin pan, bearing a few crusty traces of some sort of a sea-pie, which had been cooked in it.

'Well, sir, what now?' said the lieutenant of the deck, advancing.

'They stole it, sir; all my nice *dunderfunk*, sir; they did, sir,' whined the Down-Easter, ruefully holding up his pan.

'Stole your *dundlefunk*! what's that?'

'*Dunderfunk*, sir, *dunderfunk*; a cruel nice dish as ever man put into him.'

'Speak out, sir; what's the matter?'

'My *dunderfunk*, sir—as elegant a dish of *dunderfunk* as you ever see, sir—they stole it, sir!'

'Go forward, you rascal!' cried the lieutenant, in a towering rage, 'or else stop your whining. Tell me, what's the matter?'

'Why, sir, them 'ere two fellows, Dobs and Hodnose, stole my *dunderfunk*.'

'Once more, sir, I ask what that *dundledunk* is? Speak!'

'As cruel a nice——'

'Be off, sir! sheer!' and muttering something about *non compos mentis*, the lieutenant stalked away; while the Down-Easter beat a melancholy retreat, holding up his pan like a tambourine, and making dolorous music on it as he went.

'Where are you going with that tear in your eye, like a travelling rat?' cried a top-man.

'Oh! he's going home to Down East,' said another; 'so far eastward, you know, *shippy*, that they have to pry up the sun with a handspike.'

To make this anecdote plainer, be it said that, at sea, the monotonous round of salt beef and pork at the messes of the sailors—where but very few of the varieties of the season are to be found—induces them to adopt many contrivances in order to diversify their meals. Hence the various sea-rolls, made dishes, and Mediterranean pies, well known by man-of-war's-men—*Scouse, Lob-Scouse, Soft-Tack, Soft-Tommy, Skillagalee, Burgoo, Dough-Boys, Lob-Dominion, Dog's-Body,* and lastly, and least known, *Dunderfunk*; all of which come under the general denomination of *Manavalins*.[*]

Dunderfunk is made of hard biscuit, hashed and pounded, mixed with beef fat, molasses, and water, and baked brown in a pan. And to those who are beyond all reach of shore delicacies, this *dunderfunk*, in the feeling language of the Down-Easter, is certainly '*a cruel nice dish*'.

Now the only way that a sailor, after preparing his *dunderfunk*, could get it cooked on board the *Neversink*, was by slily going to *Old Coffee*, the ship's cook, and bribing him to put it into his oven. And as some such dishes or other are well known to be all the time in the oven, a set of unprincipled gourmands are constantly on the look-out for the chance of stealing them. Generally, two or three league together, and while one engages *Old Coffee* in some interesting conversation touching his wife and family at home, another snatches the first thing he can lay hands on in the oven, and rapidly passes it to the third man, who at his earliest leisure disappears with it.

In this manner had the Down-Easter lost his precious pie, and afterward found the empty pan knocking about the forecastle.

XXXIII

A Flogging

I F you begin the day with a laugh, you may, nevertheless, end it with a sob and a sigh.

Among the many who were exceedingly diverted with the scene between the Down-Easter and the lieutenant, none laughed more heartily than John, Peter, Mark, and Antone—four sailors of the starboard watch. The same evening these four found themselves prisoners in the 'brig', with a sentry standing over them. They were charged with violating a well-known law of the ship—having been engaged in one of those tangled, general fights sometimes occurring among sailors. They had nothing to anticipate but a flogging, at the captain's pleasure.

Toward evening of the next day, they were startled by the dread summons of the boatswain and his mates at the principal hatchway—a summons that ever sends a shudder through every manly heart in a frigate:

'*All hands witness punishment, ahoy!*'

The hoarseness of the cry, its unrelenting prolongation, its being caught up at different points, and sent through the lowermost depths of the ship; all this produces a most dismal effect upon every heart not calloused by long habituation to it.

However much you may desire to absent yourself from the scene that ensues, yet behold it you must; or, at least, stand near it you must; for the regulations enjoin the attendance of almost the entire ship's company, from the corpulent captain himself to the smallest boy who strikes the bell.

'*All hands witness punishment, ahoy!*'

To the sensitive seaman that summons sounds like a doom. He knows that the same law which impels it—the same law by which the culprits of the day must suffer; that by that very law he also is liable at any time to be judged and condemned. And the inevitableness of his own presence at the scene; the strong arm that drags him in view of the scourge, and holds him there till all is over; forcing upon his loathing eye and soul the sufferings and groans of men who have familiarly consorted with him, eaten with him, battled out watches with him—men of his own type and badge—all this conveys a terrible hint of the omnipotent authority under which he lives. Indeed, to such a man the naval summons to witness punishment carries a thrill, somewhat akin to what we may impute to the quick and the dead, when they shall hear the Last Trump, that is to bid them all arise in their ranks, and behold the final penalties inflicted upon the sinners of our race.

But it must not be imagined that to all man-of-war's-men this summons conveys such poignant emotions; but it is hard to decide whether one should be glad or sad that this is not the case! whether it is grateful to know that so much pain is avoided, or whether it is far sadder to think that, either from constitutional hard-heartedness or the multiplied searings of habit, hundreds of man-of-war's-men have been made proof against the sense of degradation, pity, and shame.

As if in sympathy with the scene to be enacted, the sun, which the day previous had merrily flashed upon the tin pan of the disconsolate Down-Easter, was now setting over the dreary waters, veiling itself in vapours. The wind blew hoarsely in the cordage; the seas broke heavily against the bows; and the frigate, staggering under whole topsails, strained as in agony on her way.

'*All hands witness punishment, ahoy!*'

At the summons the crew crowded round the mainmast; multitudes eager to obtain a good place on the booms, to overlook the scene; many laughing and chatting, others canvassing the case of the culprits; some maintaining sad, anxious countenances, or carrying a suppressed indignation in their eyes; a few purposely keeping behind to avoid looking on; in short, among five hundred men there was every possible shade of character.

All the officers—midshipmen included—stood together in a group on the starboard side of the mainmast; the first lieutenant in advance, and the surgeon, whose special duty it is to be present at such times, standing close by his side.

Presently the captain came forward from his cabin, and stood in the centre of this solemn group, with a small paper in his hand. That paper was the daily report of offences, regularly laid upon his table every morning or evening, like the day's journal placed by a bachelor's napkin at breakfast.

'Master-at-arms, bring up the prisoners,' he said.

A few moments elapsed, during which the captain, now clothed in his most dreadful attributes, fixed his eyes severely upon the crew, when suddenly a lane formed through the crowd of seamen, and the prisoners advanced—the master-at-arms, rattan in hand, on one side, and an armed marine on the other—and took up their stations at the mast.

'You John, you Peter, you Mark, you Antone,' said the captain, 'were yesterday found fighting on the gun-deck. Have you anything to say?'

Mark and Antone, two steady, middle-aged men, whom I had often admired for their sobriety, replied that they did not strike the first blow; that they had submitted to much before they had yielded to their passions; but as they acknowledged that they had at last defended themselves, their excuse was overruled.

John—a brutal bully, who, it seems, was the real author of the disturbance—was about entering into long extenuation, when he was cut short by being made to confess, irrespective of circumstances, that he had been in the fray.

Peter, a handsome lad about nineteen years old, belonging to the mizzentop, looked pale and tremulous. He was a great favourite in his part of the ship, and especially in his own mess, principally composed of lads of his own age. That morning two of his young messmates had gone to his bag, taken out his best clothes, and, obtaining the permission of the marine sentry at the 'brig', had handed them to him, to be put on against being summoned to the mast. This was done to propitiate the captain, as most captains love to see a tidy sailor. But it would not do. To all his supplications the captain turned a deaf ear. Peter declared that he had been struck twice before he had returned a blow. 'No matter,' said the captain, 'you struck at last, instead of reporting the case to an officer. I allow no man to fight on board here but myself. *I* do the fighting.'

'Now, men,' he added, 'you all admit the charge; you know the penalty. Strip! Quarter-masters, are the gratings rigged?'

The gratings are square frames of barred woodwork, sometimes placed over the hatchways. One of these squares was now laid on the deck, close to the ship's bulwarks, and while the remaining preparations were being made, the master-at-arms assisted the prisoners in removing their jackets and shirts. This done, their shirts were loosely thrown over their shoulders.

At a sign from the captain, John, with a shameless leer,

advanced, and stood passively upon the grating, while the bare-headed old quarter-master, with grey hair streaming in the wind, bound his feet to the crossbars, and, stretching out his arms over his head, secured them to the hammock-nettings above. He then retreated a little space, standing silent.

Meanwhile, the boatswain stood solemnly on the other side, with a green bag in his hand, from which taking four instruments of punishment, he gave one to each of his mates; for a fresh 'cat', applied by a fresh hand, is the ceremonious privilege accorded to every man-of-war culprit.

At another sign from the captain, the master-at-arms, stepping up, removed the shirt from the prisoner. At this juncture a wave broke against the ship's side, and dashed the spray over his exposed back. But though the air was piercing cold, and the water drenched him, John stood still, without a shudder.

The captain's finger was now lifted, and the first boat-swain's mate advanced, combing out the nine tails of his *cat* with his hand, and then, sweeping them round his neck, brought them with the whole force of his body upon the mark. Again, and again, and again; and at every blow, higher and higher rose the long, purple bars on the prisoner's back. But he only bowed over his head, and stood still. Mean-time, some of the crew whispered among themselves in ap-plause of their shipmate's nerve; but the greater part were breathlessly silent as the keen scourge hissed through the wintry air, and fell with a cutting, wiry sound upon the mark. One dozen lashes being applied, the man was taken down, and went among the crew with a smile, saying, 'D——n me! it's nothing when you're used to it! Who wants to fight?'

The next was Antone, the Portuguese. At every blow he surged from side to side, pouring out a torrent of involuntary blasphemies. Never before had he been heard to curse. When cut down, he went among the men, swearing to have the life of the captain. Of course, this was unheard by the officers.

Mark, the third prisoner, only cringed and coughed under his punishment. He had some pulmonary complaint. He was off duty for several days after the flogging; but this was partly to be imputed to his extreme mental misery. It was his first scourging, and he felt the insult more than the injury. He became silent and sullen for the rest of the cruise.

The fourth and last was Peter, the mizzentop lad. He had often boasted that he had never been degraded at the gangway. The day before his cheek had worn its usual red, but now no ghost was whiter. As he was being secured to the gratings, and the shudderings and creepings of his dazzlingly white back were revealed, he turned round his head imploringly; but his weeping entreaties and vows of contrition were of no avail. 'I would not forgive God Almighty!' cried the captain. The fourth boatswain's mate advanced, and at the first blow, the boy, shouting '*My God! Oh! my God!*' writhed and leaped so as to displace the gratings, and scatter the nine tails of the scourge all over his person. At the next blow he howled, leaped, and raged in unendurable torture.

'What are you stopping for, boatswain's mate?' cried the captain. 'Lay on!' and the whole dozen was applied.

'I don't care what happens to me now!' wept Peter, going among the crew, with bloodshot eyes, as he put on his shirt. 'I have been flogged once, and they may do it again if they will. Let them look out for me now!'

'Pipe down!' cried the captain; and the crew slowly dispersed.

Let us have the charity to believe them—as we do—when some captains in the Navy say, that the thing of all others most repulsive to them, in the routine of what they consider their duty, is the administration of corporal punishment upon the crew; for, surely, not to feel scarified to the quick at these scenes would argue a man but a beast.

You see a human being, stripped like a slave; scourged worse than a hound. And for what? For things not essentially criminal, but only made so by arbitrary laws.

XXXIV

Some of the evil Effects of Flogging

THERE are incidental considerations touching this matter of flogging, which exaggerate the evil into a great enormity. Many illustrations might be given, but let us be content with a few.

One of the arguments advanced by officers of the Navy in favour of corporal punishment is this: it can be inflicted in a moment; it consumes no valuable time; and when the prisoner's shirt is put on, *that* is the last of it. Whereas, if another punishment were substituted, it would probably occasion a great waste of time and trouble, besides thereby begetting in the sailor an undue idea of his importance.

Absurd, or worse than absurd, as it may appear, all this is true; and if you start from the same premises with these officers, you must admit that they advance an irresistible argument. But in accordance with this principle, captains in the Navy, to a certain extent, inflict the scourge—which is ever at hand—for nearly all degrees of transgression. In offences not cognizable by a court martial, little, if any, discrimination is shown. It is of a piece with the penal laws that prevailed in England some sixty years ago, when one hundred and sixty different offences were declared by the statute-book to be capital, and the servant-maid who but pilfered a watch was hung beside the murderer of a family.

It is one of the most common punishments for very trivial offences in the Navy, to 'stop' a seaman's *grog* for a day or a week. And as most seamen so cling to their *grog*, the loss of it is generally deemed by them a very serious penalty. You will sometimes hear them say, 'I would rather have my wind *stopped* than my *grog*!'

But there are some sober seamen that would much rather draw the money for it, instead of the grog itself, as provided by law; but they are too often deterred from this by the thought of receiving a scourging for some inconsiderable offence, as a substitute for the stopping of their spirits. This is a most serious obstacle to the cause of temperance in the Navy. But, in many cases, even the reluctant drawing of his grog cannot exempt a prudent seaman from ignominy; for besides the formal administering of the 'cat' at the gangway for petty offences, he is liable to the 'colt', or rope's-end, a bit of *ratlin-stuff*, indiscriminately applied—without stripping the victim—at any time, and in any part of the ship, at the merest wink from the captain. By an express order of that officer, most boatswain's mates carry the 'colt' coiled in their hats, in readiness to be administered at a minute's warning upon any offender. This was the custom in the *Neversink*. And until so recent a period as the administration of President Polk, when the historian Bancroft,* Secretary of the Navy, officially interposed, it was an almost universal thing for the officers of the watch, at their own discretion, to inflict chastisement upon a sailor, and this, too, in the face of the ordinance restricting the power of flogging solely to captains and courts martial. Nor was it a thing unknown for a lieutenant, in a sudden outburst of passion, perhaps inflamed by brandy, or smarting under the sense of being disliked or hated by the seamen, to order a whole watch of two hundred and fifty men, at dead of night, to undergo the indignity of the 'colt'.

It is believed that, even at the present day, there are instances of commanders still violating the law, by delegating the power of the colt to subordinates. At all events, it is certain that, almost to a man, the lieutenants in the Navy bitterly rail against the officiousness of Bancroft, in so materially abridging their usurped functions by snatching the colt from their hands. At the time, they predicted that this rash and most ill-judged interference of the Secretary would end in the breaking up of all discipline in the Navy. But it has not so proved. These officers *now* predict that, if the 'cat' be abolished, the same unfulfilled prediction would be verified.

Concerning the licence with which many captains violate the express laws laid down by Congress for the government of the Navy, a glaring instance may be quoted. For upward of forty years there has been on the American statute-book a law prohibiting a captain from inflicting, on his own authority, more than twelve lashes at one time, and for one offence. If more are to be given, the sentence must be passed by a court martial. Yet, for nearly half a century, this law has been frequently, and with almost perfect impunity, set at naught; though of late, through the exertions of Bancroft and others, it has been much better observed than formerly; indeed, at the present day it is generally respected. Still, while the *Neversink* was lying in a South American port, on the cruise now written of, the seamen belonging to another American frigate informed us that their captain sometimes inflicted, upon his own authority, eighteen and twenty lashes. It is worth while to state that this frigate was vastly admired by the shore ladies for her wonderfully neat appearance. One of her forecastle-men told me that he had used up three jack-knives (charged to him on the books of the purser) in scraping the belaying-pins and the combings of the hatchways.

It is singular that while the lieutenants of the watch in American men-of-war so long usurped the power of inflicting corporal punishment with the colt, few or no similar abuses were known in the English Navy. And though the captain of an English armed ship is authorized to inflict, at his own discretion, *more* than a dozen lashes (I think three dozen), yet it is to be doubted whether, upon the whole, there is as much flogging at present in the English Navy as in the American. The chivalric Virginian, John Randolph of Roanoke, declared, in his place in Congress, that on board of the American man-of-war that carried him out ambassador to Russia he had witnessed more flogging than had taken place on his own plantation of five hundred African slaves in ten years. Certain it is, from what I have personally seen, that the English officers, as a general thing, seem to be less disliked by their crews than the American officers by theirs. The reason probably is, that many of them, from their station in life, have been more accustomed to social command; hence, quarter-deck authority sits more naturally on them. A coarse, vulgar man, who happens to rise to high naval rank by the exhibition of talents not incompatible with vulgarity, invariably proves a tyrant to his crew. It is a thing that American man-of-war's-men have often observed, that the lieutenants from the Southern States, the descendants of the old Virginians, are much less severe, and much more gentle and gentlemanly in command, than the Northern officers, as a class.

According to the present laws and usages of the Navy, a seaman, for the most trivial alleged offences, of which he may be entirely innocent, must, without a trial, undergo a penalty the traces whereof he carries to the grave; for to a man-of-war's-man's experienced eye the marks of a naval scourging with the *cat* are through life discernible. And with these marks on his back, this image of his Creator must rise at the Last Day. Yet so untouchable is true dignity, that there are cases wherein to be flogged at the gangway is no dishonour; though, to abase and hurl down the last pride of some sailor who has piqued him, be sometimes the secret motive, with some malicious officer, in procuring him to be condemned to the lash. But this feeling of the innate dignity remaining untouched, though outwardly the body be scarred for the whole term of the natural life, is one of the hushed things, buried among the holiest privacies of the soul; a thing between a man's God and himself; and forever undiscernible by our fellow-men, who account *that* a degradation which seems so to the corporal eye. But what torments must that seaman undergo, who, while his back bleeds at the gangway, bleeds agonized drops of shame from his soul! Are we not justified in immeasurably denouncing this thing? Join hands with me, then; and, in the name of that Being in whose image the flogged sailor is made, let us demand of legislators, by what right they dare profane what God himself accounts sacred.

Is it lawful for you to scourge a man that is a Roman?*asks the intrepid Apostle, well knowing, as a Roman citizen, that it was not. And now, eighteen hundred years after, is it lawful for you, my countrymen, to scourge a man that is an American?—to scourge him round the world in your frigates?

It is to no purpose that you apologetically appeal to the general depravity of the man-of-war's-man. Depravity in the oppressed is no apology for the oppressor; but rather an additional stigma to him, as being, in a large degree, the effect, and not the cause and justification of oppression.

XXXV

Flogging not lawful

IT is next to idle, at the present day, merely to denounce an iniquity. Be ours, then, a different task.

If there are any three things opposed to the genius of the American Constitution, they are these: irresponsibility in a judge, unlimited discretionary authority in an executive, and the union of an irresponsible judge and an unlimited executive in one person.

Yet by virtue of an enactment of Congress, all the commodores in the American Navy are obnoxious to these three charges, so far as concerns the punishment of the sailor for alleged misdemeanours not particularly set forth in the Articles of War.

Here is the enactment in question.

XXXII. *Of the Articles of War.*—'All crimes committed by persons belonging to the Navy, which are not specified in the foregoing articles, shall be punished according to the laws and customs in such cases at sea.'

This is the article that, above all others, puts the scourge into the hands of the captain, calls him to no account for its exercise, and furnishes him with an ample warrant for inflictions of cruelty upon the common sailor, hardly credible to landsmen.

By this article the captain is made a legislator, as well as a judge and an executive. So far as it goes, it absolutely leaves to his discretion to decide what things shall be considered crimes, and what shall be the penalty; whether an accused person has been guilty of actions by him declared to be crimes; and how, when, and where the penalty shall be inflicted.

In the American Navy there is an everlasting suspension of the Habeas Corpus. Upon the bare allegation of misconduct, there is no law to restrain the captain from imprisoning a seaman, and keeping him confined at his pleasure. While I was in the *Neversink*, the captain of an American sloop of war, from undoubted motives of personal pique, kept a seaman confined in the brig for upward of a month.

Certainly the necessities of navies warrant a code for its government more stringent than the law that governs the land; but that code should conform to the spirit of the political institutions of the country that ordains it. It should not convert into slaves some of the citizens of a nation of freemen. Such objections cannot be urged against the laws of the Russian Navy (not essentially different from our own), because the laws of that Navy, creating the absolute one-man power in the captain, and vesting in him the authority to scourge, conform in spirit to the territorial laws of Russia, which is ruled by an autocrat, and whose courts inflict the *knout* upon the subjects of the land. But with us it is different. Our institutions claim to be based upon broad principles of political liberty and equality. Whereas, it would hardly affect one iota the condition on shipboard of an American man-of-war's-man, were he transferred to the Russian Navy and made a subject of the Czar.

As a sailor, he shares none of our civil immunities; the law of our soil in no respect accompanies the national floating timbers grown thereon, and to which he clings as his home. For him our Revolution was in vain; to him our Declaration of Independence is a lie.

It is not sufficiently borne in mind, perhaps, that though the naval code comes under the head of the martial law, yet, in time of peace, and in the thousand questions arising between man and man on board ship, this code, to a certain extent, may not improperly be deemed municipal. With its crew of 800 or 1,000 men, a three-decker is a city on the sea. But in most of these matters between man and man, the captain, instead of being a magistrate, dispensing what the law promulgates, is an absolute ruler, making and unmaking law as he pleases.

It will be seen that the XXth of the Articles of War provides, that if any person in the Navy negligently perform the duties assigned him, he shall suffer such punishment as a court martial shall adjudge; but if the offender be a private (common sailor), he may, at the discretion of the captain, be put in irons or flogged. It is needless to say, that in cases where an officer commits a trivial violation of this law, a court martial is seldom or never called to sit upon his trial; but in the sailor's case, he is at once condemned to the lash. Thus, one set of sea-citizens is exempted from a law that is hung in terror over others. What would landsmen think, were the state of New York to pass a law against some offence, affixing a fine as a penalty, and then add to that law a section restricting its penal operation to mechanics and day labourers, exempting all gentlemen with an income of one thousand dollars? Yet thus, in the spirit of its practical operation, even thus, stands a good part of the naval laws wherein naval flogging is involved.

But a law should be 'universal', and include in its possible penal operations the very judge himself who gives decisions upon it; nay, the very judge who expounds it. Had Sir William Blackstone violated the laws of England, he would have been brought before the bar over which he had presided, and would there have been tried, with the counsel for the Crown reading to him, perhaps, from a copy of his own *Commentaries*. And should he have been found guilty, he would have suffered like the meanest subject, 'according to law'.

How is it in an American frigate? Let one example suffice. By the Articles of War, and especially by Article I, an American captain may, and frequently does, inflict a severe and degrading punishment upon a sailor, while he himself is forever removed from the possibility of undergoing the like disgrace; and, in all probability, from undergoing any punishment whatever, even if guilty of the same thing—contention with his equals, for instance—for which he punishes another. Yet both sailor and captain are American citizens.

Now, in the language of Blackstone,*again, there is a law, 'coeval with mankind, dictated by God Himself, superior in obligation to any other, and no human laws are of any validity if contrary to this.' That law is the Law of Nature; among the three great principles of which Justinian*includes 'that to every man should be rendered his due.' But we have seen that the laws involving flogging in the Navy do *not* render to every man his due, since in some cases they indirectly exclude the officers from any punishment whatever, and in all cases protect them from the scourge, which is inflicted upon the sailor. Therefore, according to Blackstone and Justinian, those laws have no binding force; and every American man-of-war's-man would be morally justified in resisting the scourge to the uttermost; and, in so resisting, would be religiously justified in what would be judicially styled 'the act of mutiny' itself.

If, then, these scourging laws be for any reason necessary, make them binding upon all who of right come under their sway; and let us see an honest commodore, duly authorized by Congress, condemning to the lash a transgressing captain by the side of a transgressing sailor. And if the commodore himself prove a transgressor, let us see one of his brother commodores take up the lash against *him*, even as the boatswain's mates, the Navy executioners, are often called upon to scourge each other.

Or will you say that a Navy officer is a man, but that an American-born citizen, whose grandsire may have ennobled him by pouring out his blood at Bunker Hill*—will you say that, by entering the service of his country as a common seaman, and standing ready to fight her foes, he thereby loses his manhood at the very time he most asserts it? Will you say that, by so doing, he degrades himself to the liability of the scourge, but if he tarries ashore in time of danger, he is safe from that indignity? All our linked states, all four continents of mankind, unite in denouncing such a thought.

We plant the question, then, on the topmost argument of all. Irrespective of incidental considerations, we assert that flogging in the Navy is opposed to the essential dignity of man, which no legislator has a right to violate; that it is oppressive, and glaringly unequal in its operations; that it is utterly repugnant to the spirit of our democratic institutions; indeed, that it involves a lingering trait of the worst times of a barbarous feudal aristocracy; in a word, we denounce it as religiously, morally, and immutably *wrong*.

No matter, then, what may be the consequences of its abolition; no matter if we have to dismantle our fleets, and our unprotected commerce should fall a prey to the spoiler; the awful admonitions of justice and humanity demand that abolition without procrastination; in a voice that is not to be mistaken, demand that abolition to-day. It is not a dollar-and-cent question of expediency; it is a matter of *right and wrong*. And if any man can lay his hand on his heart, and solemnly say that this scourging is right, let that man but once feel the lash on his own back, and in his agony you will hear the apostate call the seven heavens to witness that it is *wrong*. And, in the name of immortal manhood, would to God that every man who upholds this thing were scourged at the gangway till be recanted!

XXXVI

Flogging not necessary

But White-Jacket is ready to come down from the lofty mast-head of an eternal principle, and fight you—commodores and captains of the Navy—on your own quarter-deck, with your own weapons, at your own paces.

Exempt yourselves from the lash, you take Bible oaths to it that it is indispensable for others; you swear that, without the lash, no armed ship can be kept in suitable discipline. Be it proved to you, officers, and stamped upon your foreheads, that herein you are utterly wrong.

'Send them to Collingwood,' said Lord Nelson, 'and *he* will bring them to order.' This was the language of that renowned admiral, when his officers reported to him certain seamen of the fleet as wholly ungovernable. 'Send them to Collingwood.' And who was Collingwood, that, after these navy rebels had been imprisoned and scourged without being brought to order, Collingwood could convert them to docility?

Who Admiral Collingwood was, as an historical hero, History herself will tell you; nor, in whatever triumphal hall they may be hanging, will the captured flags of Trafalgar fail to rustle at the mention of that name. But what Collingwood was as a disciplinarian on board the ships he commanded perhaps needs to be said. He was an officer, then, who held in abhorrence all corporal punishment; who, though seeing more active service than any sea-officer of his time, yet, for years together, governed his men without inflicting the lash.

But these seamen of his must have been most exemplary saints, to have proved docile under so lenient a sway. Were they saints? Answer, ye jails and alms-houses throughout the length and breadth of Great Britain, which, in Collingwood's time, were swept clean of the last lingering villain and pauper to man His Majesty's fleets.

Still more, *that* was a period when the uttermost resources of England were taxed to the quick; when the masts of her multiplied fleets almost transplanted her forests, all standing, to the sea; when British press-gangs not only boarded foreign ships on the high seas, and boarded foreign pier-heads, but boarded their own merchantmen at the mouth of the Thames, and boarded the very firesides along its banks; when Englishmen were knocked down and dragged into the Navy, like cattle into the slaughter-house, with every mortal provocation to a mad desperation against the service that thus ran their unwilling heads into the muzzles of the enemy's cannon. *This* was the time, and *these* the men that Collingwood governed without the lash.

I know it has been said that Lord Collingwood began by inflicting severe punishments, and afterward ruling his sailors by the mere memory of a by-gone terror, which he could at pleasure revive; and that his sailors knew this, and hence their good behaviour under a lenient sway. But, granting the quoted assertion to be true, how comes it that many American captains, who, after inflicting as severe punishment as ever Collingwood could have authorized—how comes it that *they*, also, have not been able to maintain good order without subsequent floggings, after once showing to the crew with what terrible attributes they were invested? But it is notorious, and a thing that I myself, in several instances, *know* to have been the case, that in the American Navy, where corporal punishment has been most severe, it has also been most frequent.

But it is incredible that, with such crews as Lord Collingwood's—composed, in part, of the most desperate characters, the rakings of the jails—it is incredible that such a set of men could have been governed by the mere *memory* of the lash. Some other influence must have been brought to bear; mainly, no doubt, the influence wrought by a powerful brain, and a determined, intrepid spirit, over a miscellaneous rabble.

It is well known that Lord Nelson himself, in point of policy, was averse to flogging; and that, too, when he had witnessed the mutinous effects of government abuses in the Navy—unknown in our times—and which, to the terror of all England, developed themselves at the great mutiny of the Nore: an outbreak that for several weeks jeopardized the very existence of the British Navy.

But we may press this thing nearly two centuries further back, for it is a matter of historical doubt whether, in Robert Blake's time,* Cromwell's great admiral, such a thing as flogging was known at the gangways of his victorious fleets. And as in this matter we cannot go further back than to Blake, so we cannot advance further than to our own time, which shows Commodore Stockton,* during the recent war with Mexico, governing the American squadron in the Pacific without employing the scourge.

But if of three famous English admirals one has abhorred flogging, another almost governed his ships without it, and to the third it may be supposed to have been unknown, while an American commander has, within the present year almost, been enabled to sustain the good discipline of an entire squadron in time of war without having an instrument of scourging on board, what inevitable inferences must be drawn, and how disastrous to the mental character of all advocates of Navy flogging, who may happen to be Navy officers themselves!

It cannot have escaped the discernment of any observer of mankind, that, in the presence of its conventional inferiors, conscious imbecility in power often seeks to carry off that imbecility by assumptions of lordly severity. The amount of flogging on board an American man-of-war is, in many cases, in exact proportion to the professional and intellectual incapacity of her officers to command. Thus, in these cases, the law that authorizes flogging does but put a scourge into the hand of a fool. In most calamitous instances this has been shown.

It is a matter of record, that some English ships of war have fallen a prey to the enemy through the insubordination of the crew, induced by the witless cruelty of their officers; officers so armed by the law that they could inflict that cruelty without restraint. Nor have there been wanting instances where the seamen have ran away with their ships, as in the case of the *Hermione* and *Danae*,* and forever rid themselves of the outrageous inflictions of their officers by sacrificing their lives to their fury.

Events like these aroused the attention of the British public at the time. But it was a tender theme, the public agitation of which the government was anxious to suppress. Nevertheless, whenever the thing was privately discussed, these terrific mutinies, together with the then prevailing insubordination of the men in the Navy, were almost universally attributed to the exasperating system of flogging. And the necessity for flogging was generally believed to be directly referable to the impressment of such crowds of dissatisfied men. And in high quarters it was held that if, by any mode, the English fleet could be manned without re-course to coercive measures, then the necessity of flogging would cease.

'If we abolish either impressment or flogging, the aboli-tion of the other will follow as a matter of course.' This was the language of the *Edinburgh Review* at a still later period, 1824.

If, then, the necessity of flogging in the British armed marine was solely attributed to the impressment of the sea-men, what faintest shadow of reason is there for the con-tinuance of this barbarity in the American service, which is wholly free from the reproach of impressment?

It is true that, during a long period of non-impressment, and even down to the present day, flogging has been, and still is, the law of the English Navy. But in things of this kind England should be nothing to us, except an example to be shunned. Nor should wise legislators wholly govern them-selves by precedents, and conclude that, since scourging has so long prevailed, some virtue must reside in it. Not so. The world has arrived at a period which renders it the part of Wisdom to pay homage to the prospective precedents of the Future in preference to those of the Past. The Past is dead, and has no resurrection; but the Future is endowed with such a life, that it lives to us even in anticipation. The Past is, in many things, the foe of mankind; the Future is, in all things, our friend. In the Past is no hope; the Future is both hope and fruition. The Past is the text-book of tyrants; the Future the Bible of the Free. Those who are solely governed by the Past stand like Lot's wife, crystallized in the act of looking backward, and forever incapable of looking before.

Let us leave the Past, then, to dictate laws to immovable China; let us abandon it to the Chinese Legitimists of Europe. But for us, we will have another captain to rule over us—that captain who ever marches at the head of his troop, and beckons them forward, not lingering in the rear, and impeding their march with lumbering baggage-wagons of old precedents. *This* is the Past.

But in many things we Americans are driven to a rejection

of the maxims of the Past, seeing that, ere long, the van of the nations must, of right, belong to ourselves. There are occasions when it is for America to make precedents, and not to obey them. We should, if possible, prove a teacher to posterity, instead of being the pupil of by-gone generations. More shall come after us than have gone before; the world is not yet middle-aged.

Escaped from the house of bondage, Israel of old did not follow after the ways of the Egyptians. To her was given an express dispensation; to her were given new things under the sun. And we Americans are the peculiar, chosen people— the Israel of our time;* we bear the ark of the liberties of the world. Seventy years ago we escaped from thrall; and, besides our first birthright—embracing one continent of earth —God has given to us, for a future inheritance, the broad domains of the political pagans, that shall yet come and lie down under the shade of our ark, without bloody hands being lifted. God has predestinated, mankind expects, great things from our race; and great things we feel in our souls. The rest of the nations must soon be in our rear. We are the pioneers of the world; the advance-guard, sent on through the wilderness of untried things, to break a new path in the New World that is ours. In our youth is our strength; in our inexperience our wisdom. At a period when other nations have but lisped, our deep voice is heard afar. Long enough have we been sceptics with regard to ourselves, and doubted whether, indeed, the political Messiah had come. But he has come in *us*, if we would but give utterance to his promptings. And let us always remember, that with ourselves—almost for the first time in the history of earth—national selfishness is unbounded philanthropy; for we cannot do a good to America but we give alms to the world.

XXXVII

Some superior old 'London Dock'*from the Wine-coolers of Neptune

WE had just slid into pleasant weather, drawing near to the tropics, when all hands were thrown into a wonderful excitement by an event that eloquently appealed to many palates.

A man at the fore-topsail-yard sung out that there were eight or ten dark objects floating on the sea, some three points off our lee bow.

'Keep her off three points!' cried Captain Claret, to the quarter-master at the *cun*.

And thus, with all our batteries, store-rooms, and five hundred men, with their baggage, and beds, and provisions, at one move of a round bit of mahogany, our great embattled ark edged away for the strangers, as easily as a boy turns to the right or left in pursuit of insects in the field.

Directly the man on the topsail-yard reported the dark objects to be hogsheads. Instantly all the top-men were straining their eyes, in delirious expectation of having their long *grog-fast* broken at last, and that, too, by what seemed an almost miraculous intervention. It was a curious circumstance that, without knowing the contents of the hogsheads, they yet seemed certain that the staves encompassed the thing they longed for.

Sail was now shortened, our headway was stopped, and a cutter was lowered, with orders to tow the fleet of strangers alongside. The men sprang to their oars with a will, and soon five goodly puncheons lay wallowing in the sea, just under the main-chains. We got overboard the slings, and hoisted them out of the water.

It was a sight that Bacchus and his bacchanals would have gloated over. Each puncheon was of a deep-green colour, so covered with minute barnacles and shell-fish, and streaming with seaweed, that it needed long searching to find out their bung-holes; they looked like venerable old *loggerhead turtles*.* How long they had been tossing about, and making voyages for the benefit of the flavour of their contents, no one could tell. In trying to raft them ashore, or on board of some merchant-ship, they must have drifted off to sea. This we inferred from the ropes that lengthwise united them, and which from one point of view made them resemble a long sea-serpent. They were *struck* into the gun-deck, where the eager crowd being kept off by sentries, the cooper was called with his tools.

'Bung up, and bilge free!' he cried, in an ecstasy, flourishing his driver and hammer.

Upon clearing away the barnacles and moss, a flat sort of shell-fish was found, closely adhering, like a California-shell,* right over one of the bungs. Doubtless this shell-fish had there taken up his quarters, and thrown his own body into the breach, in order the better to preserve the precious contents of the cask. The bystanders were breathless, when at last this puncheon was canted over and a tin pot held to the orifice. What was to come forth? salt water or wine? But a rich purple tide soon settled the question, and the lieutenant assigned to taste it, with a loud and satisfactory smack of his lips, pronounced it port!

'Oporto!' cried Mad Jack, 'and no mistake!'

But, to the surprise, grief, and consternation of the sailors, an order now came from the quarter-deck to 'strike the strangers down into the main-hold!' This proceeding occasioned all sorts of censorious observations upon the captain, who, of course, had authorized it.

It must be related here that, on the passage out from home, the *Neversink* had touched at Madeira; and there, as is often the case with men-of-war, the commodore and captain had laid in a goodly stock of wines for their own private tables, and the benefit of their foreign visitors. And although the commodore was a small, spare man, who evidently emptied but few glasses, yet Captain Claret was a portly gentleman, with a crimson face, whose father had fought at the Battle of the Brandywine,* and whose brother had commanded the well-known frigate named in honour of that engagement. And his whole appearance evinced that Captain Claret himself had fought many Brandywine battles ashore in honour of his sire's memory, and commanded in many bloodless Brandywine actions at sea.

It was therefore with some savour of provocation that the sailors held forth on the ungenerous conduct of Captain Claret, in stepping in between them and Providence, as it were, which by this lucky windfall, they held, seemed bent upon relieving their necessities; while Captain Claret himself, with an inexhaustible cellar, emptied his Madeira decanters at his leisure.

But next day all hands were electrified by the old familiar sound—so long hushed—of the drum rolling to grog.

After that the port was served out twice a day, till all was expended.

XXXVIII

The Chaplain and Chapel in a Man-of-war

THE next day was Sunday; a fact set down in the almanac, spite of merchant-seamen's maxim, that *there are no Sundays off soundings*.

No Sundays off soundings, indeed! No Sundays on shipboard! You may as well say there should be no Sundays in churches; for is not a ship modelled after a church? has it not three spires—three steeples? yea, and on the gun-deck, a bell and a belfry? And does not that bell merrily peal every Sunday morning, to summon the crew to devotions?

At any rate, there were Sundays on board this particular frigate of ours, and a clergyman also. He was a slender, middle-aged man, of an amiable deportment and irreproachable conversation; but I must say, that his sermons were but ill-calculated to benefit the crew. He had drank at the mystic fountain of Plato; his head had been turned by the Germans;

and this I will say, that White-Jacket himself saw him with Coleridge's *Biographia Literaria* in his hand.

Fancy, now, this transcendental divine standing behind a gun-carriage on the main-deck, and addressing five hundred salt-sea sinners upon the psychological phenomena of the soul, and the ontological necessity of every sailor's saving it at all hazards. He enlarged upon the follies of the ancient philosophers; learnedly alluded to the *Phaedon* of Plato; exposed the follies of Simplicius's commentary on Aristotle's *De Caelo*, by arraying against that clever pagan author the admired tract of Tertullian*—*De Praescriptionibus Haereticorum*—and concluded by a Sanscrit invocation. He was particularly hard upon the Gnostics and Marcionites* of the second century of the Christian era; but he never, in the remotest manner, attacked the everyday vices of the nineteenth century, as eminently illustrated in our man-of-war world. Concerning drunkenness, fighting, flogging, and oppression—things expressly or impliedly prohibited by Christianity—he never said aught. But the most mighty commodore and captain sat before him; and in general, if, in a monarchy, the state form the audience of the church, little evangelical piety will be preached. Hence, the harmless, non-committal abstrusities of our chaplain were not to be wondered at. He was no Massillon,* to thunder forth his ecclesiastical rhetoric, even when a Louis le Grand was enthroned among his congregation. Nor did the chaplains who preached on the quarter-deck of Lord Nelson ever allude to the guilty Felix, nor to Delilah,* nor practically reason of righteousness, temperance, and judgment to come, when that renowned admiral sat, sword-belted, before them.

During these Sunday discourses, the officers always sat in a circle round the chaplain, and, with a business-like air, steadily preserved the utmost propriety. In particular, our old commodore himself made a point of looking intensely edified; and not a sailor on board but believed that the commodore, being the greatest man present, must alone comprehend the mystic sentences that fell from our parson's lips.

Of all the noble lords in the ward-room, this lord-spiritual, with the exception of the purser, was in the highest favour with the commodore, who frequently conversed with him in a close and confidential manner. Nor, upon reflection, was this to be marvelled at, seeing how efficacious, in all despotic governments, it is for the throne and altar to go hand in hand.

The accommodations of our chapel were very poor. We had nothing to sit on but the great-gun rammers and capstan-bars, placed horizontally upon shot-boxes. These seats were exceedingly uncomfortable, wearing out our trowsers and our tempers, and, no doubt, impeded the conversion of many valuable souls.

To say the truth, man-of-war's-men, in general, make but poor auditors upon these occasions, and adopt every possible means to elude them. Often the boatswain's mates were obliged to drive the men to service, violently swearing upon these occasions, as upon every other.

'Go to prayers, d—n you! To prayers, you rascals—to prayers!' In this clerical invitation Captain Claret would frequently unite.

At this Jack Chase would sometimes make merry. 'Come, boys, don't hang back,' he would say; 'come, let us go hear the parson talk about his Lord High Admiral Plato, and Commodore Socrates.'

But, in one instance, grave exception was taken to this summons. A remarkably serious, but bigoted seaman, a sheet-anchor-man—whose private devotions may hereafter be alluded to—once touched his hat to the captain, and respectfully said, 'Sir, I am a Baptist; the chaplain is an Episcopalian; his form of worship is not mine; I do not believe with him, and it is against my conscience to be under his ministry. May I be allowed, sir, *not* to attend service on the half-deck?'

'You will be allowed, sir!' said the captain, haughtily, 'to obey the laws of the ship. If you absent yourself from prayers on Sunday mornings, you know the penalty.'

According to the Articles of War, the captain was perfectly

right; but if any law requiring an American to attend divine service against his will be a law respecting the establishment of religion, then the Articles of War are, in this one particular, opposed to the American constitution, which expressly says, 'Congress shall make no law respecting the establishment of religion, or the free exercise thereof.' But this is only one of several things in which the Articles of War are repugnant to that instrument. They will be glanced at in another part of the narrative.

The motive which prompts the introduction of chaplains into the Navy cannot but be warmly responded to by every Christian. But it does not follow, that because chaplains are to be found in men-of-war, that, under the present system, they achieve much good, or that, under any other, they ever will.

How can it be expected that the religion of peace should flourish in an oaken castle of war? How can it be expected that the clergyman, whose pulpit is a forty-two-pounder, should convert sinners to a faith that enjoins them to turn the right cheek when the left is smitten? How is it to be expected that when, according to the XLII nd of the Articles of War, as they now stand unrepealed on the statute book, 'a bounty shall be paid' (to the officers and crew) 'by the United States government of $20 for each person on board any ship of an enemy which shall be sunk or destroyed by any United States ship'; and when, by a subsequent section (vii), it is provided, among other apportionings, that the chaplain shall receive 'two twentieths' of this price paid for sinking and destroying ships full of human beings;—how is it to be expected that a clergyman, thus provided for, should prove efficacious in enlarging upon the criminality of Judas, who, for thirty pieces of silver, betrayed his Master?

Although, by the regulations of the Navy, each seaman's mess on board the *Neversink* was furnished with a Bible, these Bibles were seldom or never to be seen, except on Sunday mornings, when usage demands that they shall be exhibited by the cooks of the messes, when the master-at-arms goes his rounds on the berth-deck. At such times, they usually surmounted a highly polished tin pot placed on the lid of the chest.

Yet, for all this, the Christianity of man-of-war's-men, and their disposition to contribute to pious enterprises, are often relied upon. Several times subscription papers were circulated among the crew of the *Neversink*, while in harbour, under the direct patronage of the chaplain. One was for the purpose of building a seaman's chapel in China; another to pay the salary of a tract-distributor in Greece; a third to raise a fund for the benefit of an African Colonization Society.

Where the captain himself is a moral man, he makes a far better chaplain for his crew than any clergyman can be. This is sometimes illustrated in the case of sloops of war and armed brigs, which are not allowed a regular chaplain. I have known one crew, who were warmly attached to a naval commander worthy of their love, who have mustered even with alacrity to the call to prayer; and when their captain would read the Church of England service to them, would present a congregation not to be surpassed for earnestness and devotion by any Scottish kirk. It seemed like family devotions, where the head of the house is foremost in confessing himself before his Maker. But our own hearts are our best prayer-rooms, and the chaplains who can most help us are ourselves.

XXXIX

The Frigate in Harbour—the Boats—Grand State Reception of the Commodore

IN good time we were up with the parallel of Rio de Janeiro, and, standing in for the land, the mist soon cleared; and high aloft the famed Sugar Loaf pinnacle was seen, our bowsprit pointing for it straight as a die.

As we glided on toward our anchorage, the bands of the various men-of-war in harbour saluted us with national airs, and gallantly lowered their ensigns. Nothing can exceed the courteous etiquette of these ships, of all nations, in greeting their brethren. Of all men, your accomplished duellist is generally the most polite.

We lay in Rio some weeks, lazily taking in stores and otherwise preparing for the passage home. But though Rio is one of the most magnificent bays in the world; though the city itself contains many striking objects; and though much might be said of the Sugar Loaf and Signal Hill heights; and the little islet of Lucia; and the fortified Ilha dos Cobras, or Isle of the Snakes (though the only anacondas and adders now found in the arsenals there are great guns and pistols); and Lord Wood's Nose—a lofty eminence said by seamen to resemble his lordship's conch-shell; and the Praya do Flamingo—a noble tract of beach, so called from its having been the resort, in olden times, of those gorgeous birds; and the charming Bay of Botofogo, which, spite of its name, is fragrant as the neighbouring Larangieros, or Valley of the Oranges; and the green Gloria Hill, surmounted by the belfries of the queenly Church of Nossa Senhora de Gloria; and the iron-grey Benedictine convent near by; and the fine drive and promenade, Passeo Publico; and the massive arch-over-arch aqueduct, Arcos de Carico; and the Emperor's Palace; and the Empress's Gardens; and the fine Church de Candelaria; and the gilded throne on wheels, drawn by eight silken, silver-belled mules, in which, of pleasant evenings, His Imperial Majesty is driven out of town to his Moorish villa of St. Christova—ay, though much might be said of all this, yet must I forbear, if I may, and adhere to my one proper object, *the world in a man-of-war*.

Behold, now, the *Neversink* under a new aspect. With all her batteries, she is tranquilly lying in harbour, surrounded by English, French, Dutch, Portuguese, and Brazilian seventy-fours, moored in the deep-green water, close under the lee of that oblong, castellated mass of rock, Ilha dos Cobras, which, with its port-holes and lofty flagstaffs, looks like another man-of-war, fast anchored in the bay. But what is an insular fortress, indeed, but an embattled land-slide into the sea from the world Gibraltars and Quebecs? And what a mainland fortress but a few decks of a line-of-battle ship transplanted ashore? They are all one—all, as King David, men-of-war from their youth.

Ay, behold now the *Neversink* at her anchors, in many respects presenting a different appearance from what she presented at sea. Nor is the routine of life on board the same.

At sea there is more to employ the sailors, and less temptation to violations of the law. Whereas, in port, unless some particular service engages them, they lead the laziest of lives, beset by all the allurements of the shore, though perhaps that shore they may never touch.

Unless you happen to belong to one of the numerous boats which, in a man-of-war in harbour, are continually plying to and from the land, you are mostly thrown upon your own resources to while away the time. Whole days frequently pass without your being individually called upon to lift a finger; for though, in the merchant-service, they make a point of keeping the men always busy about something or other, yet, to employ five hundred sailors when there is nothing definite to be done, wholly surpasses the ingenuity of any first lieutenant in the Navy.

As mention has just been made of the numerous boats employed in harbour, something more may as well be put down concerning them. Our frigate carried a very large boat —as big as a small sloop—called a *launch*, which was generally used for getting off wood, water, and other bulky articles. Besides this, she carried four boats of an arithmetical progression in point of size—the largest being known as the first cutter, the next largest the second cutter, then the third and fourth cutters. She also carried a commodore's barge, a captain's gig, and a 'dingy', a small yawl, with a crew of apprentice boys. All these boats, except the 'dingy', had their regular crews, who were subordinate to their cockswains—*petty officers*, receiving pay in addition to their seaman's wages.

The *launch* was manned by the old Tritons of the forecastle, who were no ways particular about their dress, while the other boats—commissioned for genteeler duties—were rowed by young fellows, mostly, who had a dandy eye to their personal appearance. Above all, the officers see to it that the commodore's barge and the captain's gig are manned by gentlemanly youths, who may do credit to their country, and form agreeable objects for the eyes of the commodore or captain to repose upon as he tranquilly sits in the stern, when pulled ashore by his barge-men or gig-men, as the case may be. Some sailors are very fond of belonging to the boats, and deem it a great honour to be a *commodore's barge-man*: but others, perceiving no particular distinction in that office, do not court it so much.

On the second day after arriving at Rio, one of the gig-men fell sick, and, to my no small concern, I found myself temporarily appointed to his place.

'Come, White-Jacket, rig yourself in white—that's the gig's uniform to-day; you are a gig-man, my boy—give ye joy!' This was the first announcement of the fact that I heard; but soon after it was officially ratified.

I was about to seek the first lieutenant, and plead the scantiness of my wardrobe, which wholly disqualified me to fill so distinguished a station, when I heard the bugler call away the 'gig'; and, without more ado, I slipped into a clean frock, which a messmate doffed for my benefit, and soon after found myself pulling off his High Mightiness, the Captain, to an English seventy-four.

As we were bounding along, the cockswain suddenly cried 'Oars!' At the word every oar was suspended in the air, while our commodore's barge floated by, bearing that dignitary himself. At the sight, Captain Claret removed his chapeau, and saluted profoundly, our boat laying motionless on the water. But the barge never stopped; and the commodore made but a slight return to the obsequious salute he had received.

We then resumed rowing, and presently I heard 'Oars!' again; but from another boat, the second cutter, which turned out to be carrying a lieutenant ashore. It was now Captain Claret's turn to be honoured. The cutter lay still, and the lieutenant off hat; while the captain only nodded, and we kept on our way.

This naval etiquette is very much like the etiquette at the

Grand Porte of Constantinople,* where, after washing the Sublime Sultan's feet, the Grand Vizier avenges himself on an Emir, who does the same office for him.

When we arrived aboard the English seventy-four, the captain was received with the usual honours, and the gig's crew were conducted below, and hospitably regaled with some spirits, served out by order of the officer of the deck.

Soon after, the English crew went to quarters; and as they stood up at their guns, all along the main-deck, a row of beef-fed Britons, stalwart-looking fellows, I was struck with the contrast they afforded to similar sights on board of the *Never-sink*.

For on board of us, our *quarters* showed an array of rather slender, lean-cheeked chaps. But then I made no doubt, that, in a sea-tussle, these lantern-jawed varlets would have approved themselves as slender Damascus blades, nimble and flexible; whereas these Britons would have been, perhaps, as sturdy broadswords. Yet everyone remembers that story of Saladin and Richard*trying their respective blades; how gallant Richard clove an anvil in twain, or something quite as ponderous, and Saladin elegantly severed a cushion; so that the two monarchs were even—each excelling in his way—though, unfortunately for my simile, in a patriotic point of view, Richard whipped Saladin's armies in the end.

There happened to be a lord on board of this ship—the younger son of an earl, they told me. He was a fine-looking fellow. I chanced to stand by when he put a question to an Irish captain of a gun; upon the seaman's inadvertently saying *sir* to him, his lordship looked daggers at the slight; and the sailor, touching his hat a thousand times, said, 'Pardon, your honour; I meant to say *my lord*, sir!'

I was much pleased with an old white-headed musician, who stood at the main hatchway, with his enormous bass drum full before him, and thumping it sturdily to the tune of *God Save the King!* though small mercy did he have on his drum-heads. Two little boys were clashing cymbals, and another was blowing a fife, with his cheeks puffed out like the plumpest of his country's plum-puddings.

When we returned from this trip, there again took place that ceremonious reception of our captain on board the vessel he commanded, which always had struck me as exceedingly diverting.

In the first place, while in port, one of the quarter-masters is always stationed on the poop with a spy-glass, to look out for all boats approaching, and report the same to the officer of the deck; also, who it is that may be coming in them; so that preparations may be made accordingly. As soon, then, as the gig touched the side, a mightily shrill piping was heard, as if some boys were celebrating the Fourth of July with penny whistles. This proceeded from a boatswain's mate, who, standing at the gangway, was thus honouring the captain's return after his long and perilous absence.

The captain then slowly mounted the ladder, and gravely marching through a lane of *side-boys*, so called—all in their best bibs and tuckers, and who stood making sly faces behind his back—was received by all the lieutenants in a body, their hats in their hands, and making a prodigious scraping and bowing, as if they had just graduated at a French dancing-school. Meanwhile, preserving an erect, inflexible, and ramrod carriage, and slightly touching his chapeau, the captain made his ceremonious way to the cabin, disappearing behind the scenes, like the pasteboard ghost in *Hamlet*.

But these ceremonies are nothing to those in homage of the commodore's arrival, even should he depart and arrive twenty times a day. Upon such occasions, the whole marine guard, except the sentries on duty, are marshalled on the quarter-deck, presenting arms as the commodore passes them; while their commanding officer gives the military salute with his sword, as if making masonic signs. Meanwhile, the boatswain himself—not a *boatswain's mate*—is keeping up a persevering whistling with his silver pipe; for the commodore is never greeted with the rude whistle of a boatswain's subaltern; *that* would be positively insulting.

All the lieutenants and midshipmen, besides the captain himself, are drawn up in a phalanx, and off hat together; and the *side-boys*, whose number is now increased to ten or twelve, make an imposing display at the gangway; while the whole brass band, elevated upon the poop, strike up *See! the Conquering Hero comes!* At least, this was the tune that our captain always hinted, by a gesture, to the captain of the band, whenever the commodore arrived from shore. It conveyed a complimentary appreciation, on the captain's part, of the commodore's heroism during the late war.

To return to the gig. As I did not relish the idea of being a sort of body-servant to Captain Claret—since his gig-men were often called upon to scrub his cabin floor, and perform other duties for him—I made it my particular business to get rid of my appointment in his boat as soon as possible, and the next day after receiving it succeeded in procuring a substitute, who was glad of the chance to fill the position I so much undervalued.

And thus, with our counterlikes and dislikes, most of us man-of-war's-men harmoniously dovetail into each other, and, by our very points of opposition, unite in a clever whole, like the parts of a Chinese puzzle. But as, in a Chinese puzzle, many pieces are hard to place, so there are some unfortunate fellows who can never slip into their proper angles, and thus the whole puzzle becomes a puzzle indeed, which is the precise condition of the greatest puzzle in the world— this man-of-war world itself.

XL

Some of the Ceremonies in a Man-of-war unnecessary and injurious

THE ceremonials of a man-of-war, some of which have been described in the preceding chapter, may merit a reflection or two.

The general usages of the American Navy are founded upon the usages that prevailed in the Navy of monarchical England more than a century ago; nor have they been materially altered since. And while both England and America have become greatly liberalized in the interval; while shore pomp in high places has come to be regarded by the more intelligent masses of men as belonging to the absurd, ridiculous, and mock-heroic; while that most truly august of all the majesties of earth, the President of the United States, may be seen entering his residence with his umbrella under his arm, and no brass band or military guard at his heels, and unostentatiously taking his seat by the side of the meanest citizen in a public conveyance; while this is the case, there still lingers in American men-of-war all the stilted etiquette and childish parade of the old-fashioned Spanish Court of Madrid. Indeed, so far as the things that meet the eye are concerned, an American commodore is by far a greater man than the President of twenty millions of freemen.

But we plain people ashore might very willingly be content to leave these commodores in the unmolested possession of their gilded penny whistles, rattles, and gewgaws, since they seem to take so much pleasure in them, were it not that all this is attended by consequences to their subordinates in the last degree to be deplored.

While hardly anyone will question that a naval officer should be surrounded by circumstances calculated to impart a requisite dignity to his position, it is not the less certain that, by the excessive pomp he at present maintains, there is naturally and unavoidably generated a feeling of servility and debasement in the hearts of most of the seamen who continually behold a fellow-mortal flourishing over their heads like the archangel Michael with a thousand wings. And as, in degree, this same pomp is observed toward their inferiors by all the grades of commissioned officers, even down to a midshipman, the evil is proportionately multiplied.

It would not at all diminish a proper respect for the officers, and subordination to their authority among the seamen, were all this idle parade—only ministering to the arrogance of the officers, without at all benefiting the State—completely done away. But to do so, we voters and lawgivers ourselves must be no respecters of persons.

That saying about *levelling upward, and not downward*, may seem very fine to those who cannot see its self-involved absurdity. But the truth is, that to gain the true level, in some things, we *must* cut downward; for how can you make every sailor a commodore? or how raise the valleys, without filling them up with the superfluous tops of the hills?

Some discreet, but democratic, legislation in this matter is much to be desired. And by bringing down naval officers, in these things at least, without affecting their legitimate dignity and authority, we shall correspondingly elevate the common sailor, without relaxing the subordination in which he should by all means be retained.

XLI

A Man-of-war Library

NOWHERE does time pass more heavily than with most man-of-war's-men on board their craft in harbour.

One of my principal antidotes against *ennui* in Rio was reading. There was a public library on board, paid for by government, and entrusted to the custody of one of the marine corporals, a little, dried-up man, of a somewhat literary turn. He had once been a clerk in a post-office ashore; and, having been long accustomed to hand over letters when called for, he was now just the man to hand over books. He kept them in a large cask on the berth-deck, and, when seeking a particular volume, had to capsize it like a barrel of potatoes. This made him very cross and irritable, as most all librarians are. Who had the selection of these books I do not know, but some of them must have been selected by our chaplain, who so pranced on Coleridge's *High German horse.**

Mason Good's *Book of Nature*—a very good book, to be sure, but not precisely adapted to tarry tastes—was one of these volumes; and Machiavel's *Art of War*—which was very dry fighting; and a folio of Tillotson's *Sermons*—the best of reading for divines, indeed, but with little relish for a maintop-man; and Locke's *Essays*—incomparable essays, everybody knows, but miserable reading at sea; and Plutarch's *Lives*—superexcellent biographies, which pit Greek against Roman in beautiful style, but then, in a sailor's estimation, not to be mentioned with the *Lives of the Admirals*; and Blair's *Lectures,** University Edition—a fine treatise on rhetoric, but having nothing to say about nautical phrases, such as '*splicing the main-brace*', '*passing a gammoning*', '*puddinging the dolphin*', and '*making a carrick bend*'; besides numerous invaluable but unreadable tomes, that might have been purchased cheap at the auction of some college professor's library.

But I found ample entertainment in a few choice old authors, whom I stumbled upon in various parts of the ship, among the inferior officers. One was Morgan's *History of Algiers*, a famous old quarto, abounding in picturesque narratives of corsairs, captives, dungeons, and sea-fights; and making mention of a cruel old Dey, who, toward the latter part of his life, was so filled with remorse for his cruelties and crimes that he could not stay in bed after four o'clock in the morning, but had to rise in great trepidation and walk off his bad feelings till breakfast time. And another venerable octavo, containing a certificate from Sir Christopher Wren to its authenticity, entitled *Knox's Captivity in Ceylon, 1681*—abounding in stories about the Devil, who was superstitiously supposed to tyrannize over that unfortunate land: to mollify him, the priests offered up butter-milk, red cocks, and sausages; and the Devil ran roaring about in the woods, frightening travellers out of their wits; insomuch that the islanders bitterly lamented to Knox that their country was full of devils, and, consequently, there was no hope for their eventual well-being. Knox swears that he himself heard the Devil roar, though he did not see his horns; it was a terrible noise, he says, like the baying of a hungry mastiff.

Then there was Walpole's *Letters*—very witty, pert, and polite—and some odd volumes of plays, each of which was a precious casket of jewels of good things, shaming the trash nowadays passed off for dramas, containing *The Jew of Malta*, *Old Fortunatus*, *The City Madam*, *Volpone*, *The Alchymist*, and other glorious old dramas of the age of Marlow and Jonson, and that literary Damon and Pythias, the magnificent, mellow old Beaumont and Fletcher,* who have sent the long shadow of their reputation, side by side with Shakspeare's, far down the endless vale of posterity. And may that shadow never be less! But as for St. Shak-speare, may his never be more, lest the commentators arise, and settling upon his sacred text, like unto locusts, devour it clean up, leaving never a dot over an i.

I diversified this reading of mine by borrowing Moore's *Loves of the Angels**from Rose-Water, who recommended it as '*de charmingest of wolumes*'; and a negro song-book, containing *Sittin' on a Rail*, *Gumbo Squash*, and *Jim along Josey*, from Broadbit, a sheet-anchor-man. The sad taste of this old tar, in admiring such vulgar stuff, was much denounced by Rose-Water, whose own predilections were of a more elegant nature, as evinced by his exalted opinion of the literary merits of *The Loves of the Angels*.

I was by no means the only reader of books on board the *Neversink*. Several other sailors were diligent readers, though their studies did not lie in the way of belles-lettres. Their favourite authors were such as you may find at the book-stalls around Fulton Market;* they were slightly physiological in their nature. My book experiences on board of the frigate proved an example of a fact which every book-lover must have experienced before me, namely, that though public libraries have an imposing air, and doubtless contain invaluable volumes, yet, somehow, the books that prove most agreeable, grateful, and companionable, are those we pick up by chance here and there; those which seem put into our hands by Providence; those which pretend to little, but abound in much.

XLII

Killing Time in a Man-of-war in Harbour

READING was by no means the only method adopted by
my shipmates in whiling away the long, tedious hours in
harbour. In truth, many of them could not have read, had
they wanted to ever so much; in early youth their primers
had been sadly neglected. Still, they had other pursuits;
some were expert at the needle, and employed their time in
making elaborate shirts, stitching picturesque eagles, and
anchors, and all the stars of the federated states in the collars
thereof; so that when they at last completed and put on these
shirts, they may be said to have hoisted the American
colours.

Others excelled in *tattooing*, or *pricking*, as it is called in a
man-of-war. Of these prickers, two had long been celebrated, in their way, as consummate masters of the art. Each
had a small box full of tools and colouring matter; and they
charged so high for their services, that at the end of the cruise
they were supposed to have cleared upward of four hundred
dollars. They would *prick* you to order a palm-tree, an
anchor, a crucifix, a lady, a lion, an eagle, or anything else
you might want.

The Roman Catholic sailors on board had at least the
crucifix pricked on their arms, and for this reason: if they
chanced to die in a Catholic land, they would be sure of a
decent burial in consecrated ground, as the priest would be
sure to observe the symbol of Mother Church on their persons. They would not fare as Protestant sailors dying in
Callao, who are shoved under the sands of St. Lorenzo, a
solitary, volcanic island in the harbour, overrun with reptiles,
their heretical bodies not being permitted to repose in the
more genial loam of Lima.

And many sailors not Catholics were anxious to have the
crucifix painted on them, owing to a curious superstition of
theirs. They affirm—some of them—·that if you have that

mark tattooed upon all four limbs, you might fall overboard among seven hundred and seventy five thousand white sharks, all dinnerless, and not one of them would so much as dare to smell at your little finger.

We had one foretop-man on board, who, during the entire cruise, was having an endless cable *pricked* round and round his waist, so that, when his frock was off, he looked like a capstan with a hawser coiled round about it. This foretop-man paid eighteen pence per link for the cable, besides being on the smart the whole cruise, suffering the effects of his repeated puncturings; so he paid very dear for his cable.

One other mode of passing time while in port was cleaning and polishing your *bright-work*; for it must be known that, in men-of-war, every sailor has some brass or steel of one kind or other to keep in high order—like housemaids, whose business it is to keep well polished the knobs on the front-door railing and the parlour grates.

Excepting the ring-bolts, eye-bolts, and belaying-pins scattered about the decks, this bright-work, as it is called, is principally about the guns, embracing the *monkey-tails* of the carronades, the screws, *prickers*, little irons, and other things.

The portion that fell to my own share I kept in superior order, quite equal in polish to Rogers's best cutlery. I received the most extravagant encomiums from the officers; one of whom offered to match me against any brasier or brass-polisher in Her British Majesty's Navy. Indeed, I devoted myself to the work body and soul, and thought no pains too painful, and no labour too laborious, to achieve the highest attainable polish possible for us poor lost sons of Adam to reach.

Upon one occasion, even, when woollen rags were scarce, and no burned-brick was to be had from the ship's yeoman, I sacrificed the corners of my woollen shirt, and used some dentifrice I had, as substitutes for the rags and burned-brick. The dentifrice operated delightfully, and made the threading of my carronade-screw shine and grin again, like a set of false teeth in an eager heiress-hunter's mouth.

Still another mode of passing time, was arraying yourself in your best *togs*,* and promenading up and down the gundeck, admiring the shore scenery from the port-holes, which, in an amphitheatrical bay like Rio—belted about by the most varied and charming scenery of hill, dale, moss, meadow, court, castle, tower, grove, vine, vineyard, aqueduct, palace, square, island, fort—is very much like lounging round a circular cosmorama,* and ever and anon lazily peeping through the glasses here and there. Oh! there is something worth living for, even in our man-of-war world; and one glimpse of a bower of grapes, though a cable's length off, is almost satisfaction for dining off a shank-bone salted down.

This promenading was chiefly patronized by the marines, and particularly by Colbrook, a remarkably handsome and very gentlemanly corporal among them. He was a complete lady's man; with fine black eyes, bright red cheeks, glossy jet whiskers, and a refined organization of the whole man. He used to array himself in his regimentals, and saunter about like an officer of the Coldstream Guards, strolling down to his club in St. James's. Every time he passed me he would heave a sentimental sigh, and hum to himself *The Girl I left behind me*. This fine corporal afterward became a representative in the legislature of the state of New Jersey; for I saw his name returned about a year after my return home.

But, after all, there was not much room, while in port, for promenading, at least on the gun-deck, for the whole larboard side is kept clear for the benefit of the officers, who appreciate the advantages of having a clear stroll fore and aft; and they well know that the sailors had much better be crowded together on the other side than that the set of their own coat-tails should be impaired by brushing against their tarry trowsers.

One other way of killing time while in port is playing checkers; that is, when it is permitted; for it is not every Navy captain who will allow such a scandalous proceeding. But, as for Captain Claret, though he *did* like his glass of Madeira uncommonly well, and was an undoubted descen-

dant from the hero of the Battle of the Brandywine, and
though he sometimes showed a suspiciously flushed face
when superintending in person the flogging of a sailor for
getting intoxicated against his particular orders, yet I will
say for Captain Claret that, upon the whole, he was rather
indulgent to his crew, so long as they were perfectly docile.
He allowed them to play checkers as much as they pleased.
More than once I have known him, when going forward to
the forecastle, pick his way carefully among scores of canvass
checker-cloths spread upon the deck, so as not to tread upon
the men—the checker-men and man-of-war's-men included;
but, in a certain sense, they were both one; for, as the sailors
used their checker-men, so, at quarters, their officers used
these man-of-war's-men.

But Captain Claret's leniency in permitting checkers on
board his ship might have arisen from the following little
circumstance, confidentially communicated to me. Soon
after the ship had sailed from home, checkers were prohibited; whereupon the sailors were exasperated against the
captain, and one night, when he was walking round the forecastle, bim! came an iron belaying-pin past his ears; and
while he was dodging that, bim! came another, from the
other side; so that, it being a very dark night, and nobody to
be seen, and it being impossible to find out the trespassers,
he thought it best to get back into his cabin as soon as possible. Some time after—just as if the belaying-pins had
nothing to do with it—it was indirectly rumoured that the
checker-boards might be brought out again, which—as a
philosophical shipmate observed—showed that Captain
Claret was a man of a ready understanding, and could understand a hint as well as any other man, even when conveyed
by several pounds of iron.

Some of the sailors were very precise about their checker-
cloths, and even went so far that they would not let you play
with them unless you first washed your hands, especially if
so be you had just come from tarring down the rigging.

Another way of beguiling the tedious hours, is to get a cosy
seat somewhere, and fall into as snug a little reverie as you

can. Or if a seat is not to be had—which is frequently the case—then get a tolerably comfortable *stand-up* against the bulwarks, and begin to think about home and bread and butter—always inseparably connected to a wanderer—which will very soon bring delicious tears into your eyes; for every one knows what a luxury is grief, when you can get a private closet to enjoy it in, and no Paul Prys intrude. Several of my shore friends, indeed, when suddenly overwhelmed by some disaster, always make a point of flying to the first oyster-cellar, and shutting themselves up in a box, with nothing but a plate of stewed oysters, some crackers, the castor, and a decanter of old port.

Still another way of killing time in harbour, is to lean over the bulwarks, and speculate upon where under the sun you are going to be that day next year, which is a subject full of interest to every living soul; so much so, that there is a particular day of a particular month of the year, which, from my earliest recollections, I have always kept the run of, so that I can even now tell just where I was on that identical day of every year past since I was twelve years old. And when I am all alone, to run over this almanac in my mind is almost as entertaining as to read my diary, and far more interesting than to peruse a table of logarithms on a rainy afternoon. I always keep the anniversary of that day with lamb and peas, and a pint of sherry, for it comes in spring. But when it came round in the *Neversink*, I could get neither lamb, peas, nor sherry.

But perhaps the best way to drive the hours before you four-in-hand,*is to select a soft plank on the gun-deck, and go to sleep. A fine specific, which seldom fails, unless, to be sure, you have been sleeping all the twenty-four hours beforehand.

Whenever employed in killing time in harbour, I have lifted myself up on my elbow and looked around me, and seen so many of my shipmates all employed at the same common business; all under lock and key; all hopeless prisoners like myself; all under martial law; all dieting on salt beef and biscuit; all in one uniform; all yawning, gaping, and stretching in concert, it was then that I used to feel a certain love and affection for them, grounded, doubtless, on a fellow-feeling.

And though, in a previous part of this narrative, I have mentioned that I used to hold myself somewhat aloof from the mass of seamen on board the *Neversink*; and though this was true, and my real acquaintances were comparatively few, and my intimates still fewer, yet, to tell the truth, it is quite impossible to live so long with five hundred of your fellow-beings, even if not of the best families in the land, and with morals that would not be spoiled by further cultivation; it is quite impossible, I say, to live with five hundred of your fellow-beings, be they who they may, without feeling a common sympathy with them at the time, and ever after cherishing some sort of interest in their welfare.

The truth of this was curiously corroborated by a rather equivocal acquaintance of mine, who, among the men, went by the name of *Shakings*. He belonged to the fore hold, whence, of a dark night, he would sometimes emerge to chat with the sailors on deck. I never liked the man's looks; I protest it was a mere accident that gave me the honour of his acquaintance, and generally I did my best to avoid him, when he would come skulking, like a jail-bird, out of his den, into the liberal, open air of the sky. Nevertheless, the anecdote this *holder* told me is well worth preserving, more especially the extraordinary frankness evinced in his narrating such a thing to a comparative stranger.

The substance of his story was as follows: Shakings, it seems, had once been a convict in the New York state's prison at Sing Sing, where he had been for years confined for a crime, which he gave me his solemn word of honour he was wholly innocent of. He told me that, after his term had expired, and he went out into the world again, he never could stumble upon any of his old Sing Sing associates without dropping into a public-house and talking over old times. And when fortune would go hard with him, and he felt out of sorts, and incensed at matters and things in general, he told me that, at such time, he almost wished he was back again in Sing Sing, where he was relieved from all anxieties about what he should eat and drink, and was supported, like the President of the United States and Prince Albert,* at the public charge. He used to have such a snug little cell, he said, all to himself, and never felt afraid of house-breakers, for the walls were uncommonly thick, and his door was securely bolted for him, and a watchman was all the time walking up and down in the passage, while he himself was fast asleep and dreaming. To this, in substance, the *holder* added, that he narrated this anecdote because he thought it applicable to a man-of-war, which he scandalously asserted to be a sort of state prison afloat.

Concerning the curious disposition to fraternize and be sociable, which this Shakings mentioned as characteristic of the convicts liberated from his old homestead at Sing Sing, it may well be asked, whether it may not prove to be some feeling, somehow akin to the reminiscent impulses which influenced them, that shall hereafter fraternally reunite all us mortals, when we shall have exchanged this state's-prison man-of-war world of ours for another and a better.

From the foregoing account of the great difficulty we had in killing time while in port, it must not be inferred that on board of the *Neversink* in Rio there was literally no work to be done. At long intervals the *launch* would come alongside with water-casks, to be emptied into iron tanks in the hold. In this way nearly fifty thousand gallons, as chronicled in the books of the master's mate, were decanted into the ship's bowels—a ninety days' allowance. With this huge Lake Ontario in us, the mighty *Neversink* might be said to resemble the united continent of the eastern hemisphere—floating in a vast ocean herself, and having a Mediterranean floating in her.

XLIII

Smuggling in a Man-of-war

IT is in a good degree owing to the idleness just described, that, while lying in harbour, the man-of-war's-man is exposed to the most temptations, and gets into his saddest scrapes. For though his vessel be anchored a mile from the shore, and her sides are patrolled by sentries night and day, yet these things cannot entirely prevent the seductions of the land from reaching him. The prime agent in working his calamities in port is his old arch-enemy, the ever-devilish god of grog.

Immured as the man-of-war's-man is, serving out his weary three years in a sort of sea-Newgate,* from which he cannot escape, either by the roof or burrowing under ground, he too often flies to the bottle to seek relief from the intolerable *ennui* of nothing to do, and nowhere to go. His ordinary government allowance of spirits, one gill *per diem*, is not enough to give a sufficient fillip to his listless senses; he pronounces his grog basely *watered*; he scouts it, as *thinner than muslin*; he craves a more vigorous *nip at the cable*, a more sturdy *swig at the halyards*; and if opium were to be had, many would steep themselves a thousand fathoms down in the densest fumes of that oblivious drug. Tell him that the delirium tremens and the mania-a-potu* lie in ambush for drunkards, he will say to you, 'Let them bear down upon me, then, before the wind; anything that smacks of life is better than to feel Davy Jones's chest-lid on your nose.'*He is reckless as an avalanche; and though his fall destroy himself and others, yet a ruinous commotion is better than being frozen fast in unendurable solitudes. No wonder, then, that he goes all lengths to procure the thing he craves; no wonder that he pays the most exorbitant prices, breaks through all law, and braves the ignominious lash itself, rather than be deprived of his stimulus.

Now, concerning no one thing in a man-of-war are the

regulations more severe than respecting the smuggling of grog, and being found intoxicated. For either offence there is but one penalty, invariably enforced; and that is, the degradation of the gangway.

All conceivable precautions are taken by most frigate executives to guard against the secret admission of spirits into the vessel. In the first place, no shore boat whatever is allowed to approach a man-of-war in a foreign harbour without permission from the officer of the deck. Even the *bumboats*, the small craft licensed by the officers to bring off fruit for the sailors, to be bought out of their own money—these are invariably inspected before permitted to hold intercourse with the ship's company. And not only this, but every one of the numerous ship's boats—kept almost continually plying to and from the shore—are similarly inspected, sometimes each boat twenty times in the day.

This inspection is thus performed: the boat being descried by the quarter-master from the poop, she is reported to the deck officer, who thereupon summons the master-at-arms, the ship's chief of police. This functionary now stations himself at the gangway, and as the boat's crew, one by one, come up the side, he personally overhauls them, making them take off their hats, and then, placing both hands upon their heads, draws his palms slowly down to their feet, carefully feeling all unusual protuberances. If nothing suspicious is felt, the man is let pass; and so on, till the whole boat's crew, averaging about sixteen men, are examined. The chief of police then descends into the boat, and walks from stem to stern, eyeing it all over, and poking his long rattan into every nook and cranny. This operation concluded, and nothing found, he mounts the ladder, touches his hat to the deck officer, and reports the boat *clean*; whereupon she is hauled out to the booms.

Thus it will be seen that not a man of the ship's company ever enters the vessel from shore without it being rendered next to impossible, apparently, that he should have succeeded in smuggling anything. Those individuals who are permitted to board the ship without undergoing this ordeal are only persons whom it would be preposterous to search—such as the commodore himself, the captain, lieutenants, &c., and gentlemen and ladies coming as visitors.

For anything to be clandestinely thrust through the lower port-holes at night is rendered very difficult, from the watchfulness of the quarter-master in hailing all boats that approach, long before they draw alongside, and the vigilance of the sentries, posted on platforms overhanging the water, whose orders are to fire into a strange boat which, after being warned to withdraw, should still persist in drawing nigh. Moreover, thirty-two-pound shot are slung to ropes, and suspended over the bows, to drop a hole into and sink any small craft which, spite of all precautions, by strategy should succeed in getting under the bows with liquor by night. Indeed, the whole power of martial law is enlisted in this matter; and every one of the numerous officers of the ship, besides his general zeal in enforcing the regulations, adds to that a personal feeling, since the sobriety of the men abridges his own cares and anxieties.

How then, it will be asked, in the face of an argus-eyed police, and in defiance even of bayonets and bullets, do man-of-war's-men contrive to smuggle their spirits? Not to enlarge upon minor stratagems—every few days detected, and rendered naught (such as rolling up, in a neckerchief, a long, slender 'skin' of grog, like a sausage, and in that manner ascending to the deck out of a boat just from shore; or openly bringing on board cocoanuts and melons, procured from a knavish bum-boat, filled with spirits, instead of milk or water)—we will only mention here two or three other modes, coming under my own observation.

While in Rio, a foretop-man, belonging to the second cutter, paid down the money, and made an arrangement with a person encountered at the Palace landing ashore, to the following effect. Of a certain moonless night, he was to bring off three gallons of spirits, *in skins*, and moor them to the frigate's anchor-buoy—some distance from the vessel—attaching something heavy, to sink them out of sight. In the middle watch of the night, the foretop-man slips out of his hammock, and by creeping along in the shadows, eludes the vigilance of the master-at-arms and his mates, gains a port-hole, and softly lowers himself into the water, almost without creating a ripple—the sentries marching to and fro on their overhanging platform above him. He is an expert swimmer, and paddles along under the surface, every now and then rising a little, and lying motionless on his back to breathe—little but his nose exposed. The buoy gained, he cuts the skins adrift, ties them round his body, and in the same adroit manner makes good his return.

This feat is very seldom attempted, for it needs the utmost caution, address, and dexterity; and no one but a super-expert burglar, and faultless Leander*of a swimmer, could achieve it.

From the greater privileges which they enjoy, the *forward officers*, that is, the gunner, boatswain, &c., have much greater opportunities for successful smuggling than the common seamen. Coming alongside one night in a cutter, Yarn, our boatswain, in some inexplicable way contrived to slip several skins of brandy through the air-port of his own state-room. The feat, however, must have been perceived by one of the boat's crew, who immediately, on gaining the deck, sprung down the ladders, stole into the boatswain's room, and made away with the prize, not three minutes before the rightful owner entered to claim it. Though, from certain circumstances, the thief was known to the aggrieved party, yet the latter could say nothing, since he himself had infringed the law. But the next day, in the capacity of captain of the ship's executioners, Yarn had the satisfaction (it was so to him) of standing over the robber at the gangway; for, being found intoxicated with the very liquor the boatswain himself had smuggled, the man had been condemned to a flogging.

This recalls another instance, still more illustrative of the knotted, trebly intertwisted villainy, accumulating at a sort of compound interest in a man-of-war. The cockswain of the commodore's barge takes his crew apart, one by one, and cautiously sounds them as to their fidelity—not to the United States of America, but to himself. Three individuals, whom he deems doubtful—that is, faithful to the United States of America—he procures to be discharged from the barge, and men of his own selection are substituted; for he is always an influential character, this cockswain of the commodore's barge. Previous to this, however, he has seen to it well, that no temperance men—that is, sailors who do not draw their government ration of grog, but take the money for it—he has seen to it, that none of these *balkers* are numbered among his crew. Having now proved his men, he divulges his plan to the assembled body; a solemn oath of secrecy is obtained, and he waits the first fit opportunity to carry into execution his nefarious designs.

At last it comes. One afternoon the barge carries the commodore across the Bay to a fine waterside settlement of noblemen's seats, called Praya Grande. The commodore is visiting a Portuguese marquis, and the pair linger long over their dinner in an arbour in the garden. Meanwhile, the cockswain has liberty to roam about where he pleases. He searches out a place where some choice *red-eye* (brandy) is to be had, purchases six large bottles, and conceals them among the trees. Under the pretence of filling the boat-keg with water, which is always kept in the barge to refresh the crew, he now carries it off into the grove, knocks out the head, puts the bottles inside, reheads the keg, fills it with water, carries it down to the boat, and audaciously restores it to its conspicuous position in the middle, with its bung-hole up. When the commodore comes down to the beach, and they pull off for the ship, the cockswain, in a loud voice, commands the nearest man to take that bung out of the keg—that precious water will spoil. Arrived alongside the frigate, the boat's crew are overhauled, as usual, at the gangway; and nothing being found on them, are passed. The master-at-arms now descending into the barge, and finding nothing suspicious, reports it *clean*, having put his finger into the open bung of the keg and tasted that the water was pure. The barge is ordered out to the booms, and deep night is waited for, ere the cockswain essays to snatch the bottles from the keg.

SMUGGLING IN A MAN-OF-WAR

But, unfortunately for the success of this masterly smuggler, one of his crew is a weak-pated fellow, who, having drank somewhat freely ashore, goes about the gun-deck throwing out profound, tipsy hints concerning some unutterable proceeding on the ship's anvil. A knowing old sheet-anchor-man, an unprincipled fellow, putting this, that, and the other together, ferrets out the mystery; and straightway resolves to reap the goodly harvest which the cockswain has sowed. He seeks him out, takes him to one side, and addresses him thus:

'Cockswain, you have been smuggling off some *red-eye*, which at this moment is in your barge at the booms. Now, cockswain, I have stationed two of my messmates at the portholes, on that side of the ship; and if they report to me that you, or any of your barge-men, offer to enter that barge before morning, I will immediately report you as a smuggler to the officer of the deck.'

The cockswain is astounded; for, to be reported to the deck officer as a smuggler, would inevitably procure him a sound flogging, and be the disgraceful *breaking* of him as a petty officer, receiving four dollars a month beyond his pay as an able seaman. He attempts to bribe the other to secrecy, by promising half the profits of the enterprise; but the sheet-anchor-man's integrity is like a rock; he is no mercenary, to be bought up for a song. The cockswain, therefore, is forced to swear that neither himself, nor any of his crew, shall enter the barge before morning. This done, the sheet-anchor-man goes to his confidants, and arranges his plans. In a word, he succeeds in introducing the six brandy bottles into the ship; five of which he sells at eight dollars a bottle; and then, with the sixth, between two guns, he secretly regales himself and confederates; while the helpless cockswain, stifling his rage, bitterly eyes them from afar.

Thus, though they say that there is honour among thieves, there is little among man-of-war smugglers.

XLIV

A Knave in Office in a Man-of-war

THE last smuggling story now about to be related also occurred while we lay at Rio. It is the more particularly presented, since it furnishes the most curious evidence of the almost incredible corruption pervading nearly all ranks in some men-of-war.

For some days, the number of intoxicated sailors collared and brought up to the mast by the master-at-arms, to be reported to the deck officers—previous to a flogging at the gangway—had in the last degree excited the surprise and vexation of the captain and senior officers. So strict were the captain's regulations concerning the suppression of grog-smuggling, and so particular had he been in charging the matter upon all the lieutenants, and every under-strapper official in the frigate, that he was wholly at a loss how so large a quantity of spirits could have been spirited into the ship, in the face of all these checks, guards, and precautions.

Still additional steps were adopted to detect the smugglers; and Bland, the master-at-arms, together with his corporals, were publicly harangued at the mast by the captain in person, and charged to exert their best powers in suppressing the traffic. Crowds were present at the time, and saw the master-at-arms touch his cap in obsequious homage, as he solemnly assured the captain that he would still continue to do his best; as, indeed, he said, he had always done. He concluded with a pious ejaculation, expressive of his personal abhorrence of smuggling and drunkenness, and his fixed resolution, so help him Heaven, to spend his last wink in sitting up by night, to spy out all deeds of darkness.

'I do not doubt you, master-at-arms,' returned the captain; 'now go to your duty.' This master-at-arms was a favourite of the captain's.

The next morning, before breakfast, when the market-boat came off (that is, one of the ship's boats regularly deputed to bring off the daily fresh provisions for the officers)—when this boat came off, the master-at-arms, as usual, after carefully examining both her and her crew, reported them to the deck officer to be free from suspicion. The provisions were then hoisted out, and among them came a good-sized wooden box, addressed to 'Mr. ——, Purser of the United States Ship *Neversink*.' Of course, any private matter of this sort, destined for a gentleman of the ward-room, was sacred from examination, and the master-at-arms commanded one of his corporals to carry it down into the purser's state-room. But recent occurrences had sharpened the vigilance of the deck officer to an unwonted degree, and seeing the box going down the hatchway, he demanded what that was, and whom it was for.

'All right, sir,' said the master-at-arms, touching his cap; 'stores for the purser, sir.'

'Let it remain on deck,' said the lieutenant. 'Mr. Montgomery!' calling a midshipman, 'ask the purser whether there is any box coming off for him this morning.'

'Ay, ay, sir,' said the middy, touching his cap.

Presently he returned, saying that the purser was ashore.

'Very good, then; Mr. Montgomery, have that box put into the "brig", with strict orders to the sentry not to suffer anyone to touch it.'

'Had I not better take it down into my mess, sir, till the purser comes off?' said the master-at-arms, deferentially.

'I have given my orders, sir!' said the lieutenant, turning away.

When the purser came on board, it turned out that he knew nothing at all about the box. He had never so much as heard of it in his life. So it was again brought up before the deck officer, who immediately summoned the master-at-arms.

'Break open that box!'

'Certainly, sir!' said the master-at-arms; and, wrenching off the cover, twenty-five brown jugs, like a litter of twenty-five brown pigs, were found snugly nestled in a bed of straw.

'The smugglers are at work, sir,' said the master-at-arms, looking up.

'Uncork and taste it,' said the officer.

The master-at-arms did so; and, smacking his lips after a puzzled fashion, was a little doubtful whether it was American whisky or Holland gin; but he said he was not used to liquor.

'Brandy; I know it by the smell,' said the officer; 'return the box to the brig.'

'Ay, ay, sir,' said the master-at-arms, redoubling his activity.

The affair was at once reported to the captain, who, incensed at the audacity of the thing, adopted every plan to detect the guilty parties. Inquiries were made ashore; but by whom the box had been brought down to the market-boat there was no finding out. Here the matter rested for a time.

Some days after, one of the boys of the mizzentop was flogged for drunkenness, and, while suspended in agony at the gratings, was made to reveal from whom he had procured his spirits. The man was called, and turned out to be an old superannuated marine, one Scriggs, who did the cooking for the marine sergeants' and master-at-arms' mess. This marine was one of the most villainous-looking fellows in the ship, with a squinting, pick-lock, grey eye, and hang-dog, gallows gait. How such a most unmartial vagabond had insinuated himself into the honourable marine corps was a perfect mystery. He had always been noted for his personal uncleanliness, and among all hands, fore and aft, had the reputation of being a notorious old miser, who denied himself the few comforts, and many of the common necessaries, of a man-of-war life.

Seeing no escape, Scriggs fell on his knees before the captain, and confessed the charge of the boy. Observing the fellow to be in an agony of fear at the sight of the boatswain's mates and their lashes, and all the striking parade of public punishment, the captain must have thought this a good opportunity for completely pumping him of all his secrets. This terrified marine was at length forced to reveal his having been for some time an accomplice in a complicated system of underhand villainy, the head of which was no less a personage than the indefatigable chief of police, the master-at-arms himself. It appeared that this official had his confidential agents ashore, who supplied him with spirits, and in various boxes, packages, and bundles—addressed to the purser and others—brought them down to the frigate's boats at the landing. Ordinarily, the appearance of these things for the purser and other ward-room gentlemen occasioned no surprise: for almost every day some bundle or other is coming off for them, especially for the purser; and, as the master-at-arms was always present on these occasions, it was an easy matter for him to hurry the smuggled liquor out of sight, and under pretence of carrying the box or bundle down to the purser's room, hide it away upon his own premises.

The miserly marine, Scriggs, with the pick-lock eye, was the man who clandestinely sold the spirits to the sailors, thus completely keeping the master-at-arms in the background. The liquor sold at the most exorbitant prices; at one time reaching twelve dollars the bottle in cash, and thirty dollars a bottle in orders upon the purser, to be honoured upon the frigate's arrival home. It may seem incredible that such prices should have been given by the sailors; but when some man-of-war's-men crave liquor, and it is hard to procure, they would almost barter ten years of their lifetime for but one solitary *tot*, if they could.

The sailors who became intoxicated with the liquor thus smuggled on board by the master-at-arms were, in almost numberless instances, officially seized by that functionary, and scourged at the gangway. In a previous place it has been shown how conspicuous a part the master-at-arms enacts at this scene.

The ample profits of this iniquitous business were divided between all the parties concerned in it; Scriggs, the marine, coming in for one-third. His cook's mess-chest being brought on deck, four canvass bags of silver were found in it, amounting to a sum something short of as many hundred dollars.

The guilty parties were scourged, double-ironed, and for several weeks were confined in the 'brig', under a sentry; all but the master-at-arms, who was merely cashiered, and imprisoned for a time, with bracelets at his wrists. Upon being liberated, he was turned adrift among the ship's company; and, by way of disgracing him still more, was thrust into the *waist*, the most inglorious division of the ship.

Upon going to dinner one day, I found him soberly seated at my own mess; and at first I could not but feel some very serious scruples about dining with him. Nevertheless, he was a man to study and digest; so, upon a little reflection, I was not displeased at his presence. It amazed me, however, that he had wormed himself into the mess, since so many of the other messes had declined the honour; until at last, I ascertained that he had induced a messmate of ours, a distant relation of his, to prevail upon the cook to admit him.

Now it would not have answered for hardly any other mess in the ship to have received this man among them, for it would have torn a huge rent in their reputation; but our mess, A. No. 1—the Forty-two-pounder Club—was composed of so fine a set of fellows; so many captains of tops, and quarter-masters—men of undeniable mark on board ship—of long-established standing and consideration on the gundeck; that with impunity we could do many equivocal things, utterly inadmissible for messes of inferior pretension. Besides, though we all abhorred the monster of Sin itself, yet, from our social superiority, highly rarified education in our lofty top, and large and liberal sweep of the aggregate of things, we were in a good degree free from those useless, personal prejudices, and galling hatreds against conspicuous *sinners*—not *Sin*—which so widely prevail among men of warped understandings, and unchristian and uncharitable hearts. No; the superstitions and dogmas concerning Sin had not laid their withering maxims upon our hearts. We perceived how that evil was but good disguised, and a knave a saint in his way; how that in other planets, perhaps, what we deem wrong, may there be deemed right; even as some substances, without undergoing any mutations in themselves, utterly change their colour, according to the light thrown upon them. We perceived that the anticipated millennium must have begun upon the morning the first worlds were created; and that, taken all in all, our man-of-war world itself was as eligible a round-sterned craft as any to be found in the Milky Way. And we fancied that though some of us, of the gun-deck, were at times condemned to sufferings and slights, and all manner of tribulation and anguish, yet, no doubt, it was only our misapprehension of these things that made us take them for woeful pains instead of the most agreeable pleasures. I have dreamed of a sphere, says Pinzella, where to break a man on the wheel is held the most exquisite of delights you can confer upon him; where for one gentleman in any way to vanquish another, is accounted an everlasting dishonour; where to tumble one into a pit after death, and then throw cold clods upon his up-turned face, is a species of contumely, only inflicted upon the most notorious criminals.

But whatever we messmates thought, in whatever circumstances we found ourselves, we never forgot that our frigate, bad as it was, was homeward bound. Such, at least, were our reveries at times, though sorely jarred, now and then, by events that took our philosophy aback. For after all, philosophy—that is, the best wisdom that has ever in any way been revealed to our man-of-war world—is but a slough and a mire, with a few tufts of good footing here and there.

But there was one man in the mess who would have naught to do with our philosophy—a churlish, ill-tempered, unphilosophical, superstitious old bear of a quarter-gunner; a believer in Tophet,* for which he was accordingly preparing himself. Priming was his name; but methinks I have spoken of him before.

Besides, this Bland, the master-at-arms, was no vulgar, dirty knave. In him—to modify Burke's phrase*—vice *seemed*, but only seemed, to lose half its seeming evil by losing all its apparent grossness. He was a neat and gentlemanly villain, and broke his biscuit with a dainty hand. There was a fine polish about his whole person, and a pliant, insinuating style in his conversation, that was, socially, quite irresistible. Save my noble captain, Jack Chase, he proved himself the most entertaining, I had almost said the most companionable, man in the mess. Nothing but his mouth, that was somewhat small, Moorish-arched, and wickedly delicate, and his snaky, black eye, that at times shone like a dark lantern in a jeweller's shop at midnight, betokened the accomplished scoundrel within. But in his conversation there was no trace of evil; nothing equivocal; he studiously shunned an indelicacy, never swore, and chiefly abounded in passing puns and witticisms, varied with humorous contrasts between ship and shore life, and many agreeable and racy anecdotes, very tastefully narrated. In short—in a merely psychological point of view, at least—he was a charming blackleg. Ashore, such a man might have been an irreproachable mercantile swindler, circulating in polite society.

But he was still more than this. Indeed, I claim for this master-at-arms a lofty and honourable niche in the Newgate Calendar* of history. His intrepidity, coolness, and wonderful self-possession in calmly resigning himself to a fate that thrust him from an office in which he had tyrannized over five hundred mortals, many of whom hated and loathed him, passed all belief; his intrepidity, I say, in now fearlessly gliding among them, like a disarmed swordfish among ferocious white sharks; this, surely, bespoke no ordinary man. While in office, even, his life had often been secretly attempted by the seamen whom he had brought to the gangway. Of dark nights they had dropped shot down the hatchways, destined 'to damage his pepper-box', as they phrased it; they had made ropes with a hangman's noose at the end, and tried to *lasso* him in dark corners. And now he was adrift among them, under notorious circumstances of superlative villainy, at last dragged to light; and yet he blandly smiled, politely offered his cigar-holder to a perfect stranger, and laughed and chatted to right and left, as if springy, buoyant, and elastic, with an angelic conscience, and sure of kind friends wherever he went, both in this life and the life to come.

While he was lying ironed in the 'brig', gangs of the men were sometimes overheard whispering about the terrible reception they would give him when he should be set at large. Nevertheless, when liberated, they seemed confounded by his erect and cordial assurance, his gentlemanly sociability and fearless companionableness. From being an implacable policeman, vigilant, cruel, and remorseless in his office, however polished in his phrases, he was now become a disinterested, sauntering man of leisure, winking at all improprieties, and ready to laugh and make merry with any one. Still, at first, the men gave him a wide berth, and returned scowls for his smiles; but who can forever resist the very Devil himself, when he comes in the guise of a gentleman, free, fine, and frank? Though Goethe's pious Margaret* hates the Devil in his horns and harpooneer's tail, yet she smiles and nods to the engaging fiend in the persuasive, winning, oily, wholly harmless Mephistopheles. But, however it was, I, for one, regarded this master-at-arms with mixed feelings of detestation, pity, admiration, and something opposed to enmity. I could not but abominate him when I thought of his conduct; but I pitied the continual gnawing which, under all his deftly donned disguises, I saw lying at the bottom of his soul. I admired his heroism in sustaining himself so well under such reverses. And when I thought how arbitrary the Articles of War are in defining a man-of-war villain; how much undetected guilt might be sheltered by the aristocratic awning of our quarter-deck; how many florid pursers, ornaments of the ward-room, had been legally protected in defrauding *the people*, I could not but say to myself, Well, after all, though this man is a most wicked one indeed, yet is he even more luckless than depraved.

Besides, a studied observation of Bland convinced me that he was an organic and irreclaimable scoundrel, who did wicked deeds as the cattle browse the herbage, because wicked deeds seemed the legitimate operation of his whole infernal organization. Phrenologically, he was without a soul. Is it to be wondered at, that the devils are irreligious? What, then, thought I, who is to blame in this matter? For one, I will not take the Day of Judgment upon me by authoritatively pronouncing upon the essential criminality of any man-of-war's-man; and Christianity has taught me that, at the Last Day, man-of-war's-men will not be judged by the Articles of War, nor by the United States *Statutes at Large*, but by immutable laws, ineffably beyond the comprehension of the Honourable Board of Commodores and Navy Commissioners.

But though I will stand by even a man-of-war thief, and defend him from being seized up at the gangway, if I can—remembering that my Saviour once hung between two thieves, promising one life eternal—yet I would not, after the plain conviction of a villain, again let him entirely loose to prey upon honest seamen, fore and aft all three decks. But this did Captain Claret; and though the thing may not perhaps be credited, nevertheless, here it shall be recorded.

After the master-at-arms had been adrift among the ship's company for several weeks, and we were within a few days' sail of home, he was summoned to the mast and publicly reinstated in his office as the ship's chief of police. Perhaps Captain Claret had read the *Memoirs* of Vidocq,* and believed in the old saying, *Set a rogue to catch a rogue*. Or, perhaps, he was a man of very tender feelings, highly susceptible to the soft emotions of gratitude, and could not bear to leave in disgrace a person who, out of the generosity of his heart, had, about a year previous, presented him with a rare snuff-box, fabricated from a sperm whale's tooth, with a curious silver hinge, and cunningly wrought in the shape of a whale; also a splendid gold-mounted cane, of a costly Brazilian wood, with a gold plate, bearing the captain's name and rank in the service, the place and time of his birth, and with a vacancy underneath—no doubt providentially left for his heirs to record his decease.

Certain it was that, some months previous to the master-at-arms' disgrace, he had presented these articles to the captain, with his best love and compliments; and the captain had received them, and seldom went ashore without the cane, and never took snuff but out of that box. With some captains, a sense of propriety might have induced them to return these presents, when the generous donor had proved himself unworthy of having them retained; but it was not

Captain Claret who would inflict such a cutting wound upon any officer's sensibilities, though long-established naval customs had habituated him to scourging *the people* upon an emergency.

Now had Captain Claret deemed himself constitutionally bound to decline all presents from his subordinates, the sense of gratitude would not have operated to the prejudice of justice. And, as some of the subordinates of a man-of-war captain are apt to invoke his good wishes and mollify his conscience by making him friendly gifts, it would perhaps have been an excellent thing for him to adopt the plan pursued by the President of the United States, when he received a present of lions and Arabian chargers from the Sultan of Muscat. Being forbidden by his sovereign lords and masters, the imperial people, to accept of any gifts from foreign powers, the President sent them to an auctioneer, and the proceeds were deposited in the Treasury. In the same manner, when Captain Claret received his snuff-box and cane, he might have accepted them very kindly, and then sold them off to the highest bidder, perhaps to the donor himself, who in that case would never have tempted him again.

Upon his return home, Bland was paid off for his full term, not deducting the period of his suspension. He again entered the service in his old capacity.

As no further allusion will be made to this affair, it may as well be stated now, that, for the very brief period elapsing between his restoration and being paid off in port by the purser, the master-at-arms conducted himself with infinite discretion, artfully steering between any relaxation of discipline—which would have awakened the displeasure of the officers—and any unwise severity—which would have revived, in tenfold force, all the old grudges of the seamen under his command.

Never did he show so much talent and tact as when vibrating in this his most delicate predicament; and plenty of cause was there for the exercise of his cunningest abilities; for, upon the discharge of our man-of-war's-men at home, should he *then* be held by them as an enemy, as free and independent citizens they would waylay him in the public streets, and take purple vengeance for all his iniquities, past, present, and possible in the future. More than once a master-at-arms ashore has been seized by night by an exasperated crew and served as Origen served himself, or as his enemies served Abelard.*

But though, under extreme provocation, *the people* of a man-of-war have been guilty of the maddest vengeance, yet, at other times, they are very placable and milky-hearted, even to those who may have outrageously abused them; many things in point might be related, but I forbear.

This account of the master-at-arms cannot better be concluded than by denominating him, in the vivid language of the captain of the foretop, as '*the two ends and middle of the thrice-laid strand of a bloody rascal*,' which was intended for a terse, well-knit, and all-comprehensive assertion, without omission or reservation. It was also asserted that, had Tophet itself been raked with a fine-tooth comb, such another ineffable villain could not by any possibility have been caught.

XLV

Publishing Poetry in a Man-of-war

A DAY or two after our arrival in Rio, a rather amusing incident occurred to a particular acquaintance of mine, young Lemsford, the gun-deck bard.

The great guns of an armed ship have blocks of wood, called *tompions*, painted black, inserted in their muzzles, to keep out the spray of the sea. These tompions slip in and out very handily, like covers to butter firkins.

By advice of a friend, Lemsford, alarmed for the fate of his box of poetry, had latterly made use of a particular gun on the main-deck, in the tube of which he thrust his manuscripts, by simply crawling partly out of the port-hole, removing the tompion, inserting his papers, tightly rolled, and making all snug again.

Breakfast over, he and I were reclining in the maintop—where, by permission of my noble master, Jack Chase, I had invited him—when, of a sudden, we heard a cannonading. It was our own ship.

'Ah!' said a top-man, 'returning the shore salute they gave us yesterday.'

'O Lord!' cried Lemsford, 'my *Songs of the Sirens*!' and he ran down the rigging to the batteries; but just as he touched the gun-deck, gun No. 20—his literary strong-box —went off with a terrific report.

'Well, my after-guard Virgil,' said Jack Chase to him, as he slowly returned up the rigging, 'did you get it? You need not answer; I see you were too late. But never mind, my boy; no printer could do the business for you better. That's the way to publish, White-Jacket,' turning to me—'fire it right into 'em; every canto a twenty-four-pound shot; *hull* the blockheads, whether they will or no. And mind you, Lemsford, when your shot does the most execution, you hear the least from the foe. A killed man cannot even lisp.'

'Glorious Jack!' cried Lemsford, running up and snatching him by the hand, 'Say that again, Jack! look me in the eyes. By all the Homers, Jack, you have made my soul mount like a balloon! Jack, I'm a poor devil of a poet. Not two months before I shipped aboard here, I published a volume of poems, very aggressive on the world, Jack. Heaven knows what it cost me. I published it, Jack, and the cursed publisher sued me for damages; my friends looked sheepish; one or two who liked it were non-committal; and as for the addle-pated mob and rabble, they thought they had found out a fool. Blast them, Jack, what they call the public is a monster, like the idol we saw in Owhyhee, with the head of a jackass, the body of a baboon, and the tail of a scorpion!'

'I don't like that,' said Jack; 'when I'm ashore, I myself am part of the public.'

'Your pardon, Jack; you are not. You are then a part of the people, just as you are aboard the frigate here. The public is one thing, Jack, and the people another.'

'You are right,' said Jack; 'right as this leg. Virgil, you are a trump; you are a jewel, my boy. The public and the people! Ay, ay, my lads, let us hate the one, and cleave to the other.'

XLVI

The Commodore on the Poop, and one of 'the People' under the Hands of the Surgeon

A DAY or two after the publication of Lemsford's *Songs of the Sirens*, a sad accident befell a messmate of mine, one of the captains of the mizzentop. He was a fine little Scot, who, from the premature loss of the hair on the top of his head, always went by the name of *Baldy*. This baldness was no doubt, in great part, attributable to the same cause that early thins the locks of most man-of-war's-men—namely, the hard, unyielding, and ponderous man-of-war and navy-regulation tarpaulin hat which, when new, is stiff enough to sit upon, and indeed, in lieu of his thumb, sometimes serves the common sailor for a bench.

Now, there is nothing upon which the commodore of a squadron more prides himself than upon the celerity with which his men can handle the sails, and go through with all the evolutions pertaining thereto. This is especially manifested in harbour, when other vessels of his squadron are near, and perhaps the armed ships of rival nations.

Upon these occasions, surrounded by his post-captain satraps—each of whom in his own floating island is king—the commodore domineers over all—emperor of the whole oaken archipelago; yea, magisterial and magnificent as the Sultan of the Isles of Sooloo.

But, even as so potent an emperor and Caesar to boot as the great Don of Germany, Charles the Fifth,* was used to divert himself in his dotage by watching the gyrations of the springs and cogs of a long row of clocks, even so does an elderly commodore while away his leisure in harbour, by what is called '*exercising guns*', and also '*exercising yards and* *sails*'; causing the various spars of all the ships under his command to be 'braced', 'topped', and 'cock-billed' in concert, while the commodore himself sits, something like King Canute, on an arm-chest on the poop of his flagship.

But far more regal than any descendant of Charlemagne, more haughty than any Mogul of the East, and almost mysterious and voiceless in his authority as the Great Spirit of the Five Nations,[*] the commodore deigns not to verbalize his commands; they are imparted by signal.

And as for old Charles the Fifth, again, the gay-pranked, coloured suits of cards were invented to while away his dotage, even so, doubtless, must these pretty little signals of blue and red spotted *bunting* have been devised to cheer the old age of all commodores.

By the commodore's side stands the signal-midshipman, with a sea-green bag swung on his shoulder (as a sportsman bears his game-bag), the signal-book in one hand, and the signal-spyglass in the other. As this signal-book contains the masonic signs and tokens of the Navy, and would therefore be invaluable to an enemy, its binding is always bordered with lead, so as to ensure its sinking in case the ship should be captured. Not the only book this that might appropriately be bound in lead, though there be many where the author, and not the bookbinder, furnishes the metal.

As White-Jacket understands it, these signals consist of variously coloured flags, each standing for a certain number. Say there are ten flags, representing the cardinal numbers— the red flag, No. 1; the blue flag, No. 2; the green flag, No. 3, and so forth; then, by mounting the blue flag over the red, that would stand for No. 21; if the green flag were set underneath, it would then stand for 213. How easy, then, by endless transpositions, to multiply the various numbers that may be exhibited at the mizzen-peak, even by only three or four of these flags.

To each number a particular meaning is applied. No. 100, for instance, may mean '*Beat to quarters*.' No. 150, '*All hands to grog*.' No. 2000, '*Strike topgallant-yards*.' No. 2110, '*See anything to windward?*' No. 2800, '*No*.'

And as every man-of-war is furnished with a signal-book, where all these things are set down in order, therefore, though two American frigates—almost perfect strangers to each other—came from the opposite Poles, yet at a distance of more than a mile they could carry on a very liberal conversation in the air.

When several men-of-war of one nation lie at anchor in one port, forming a wide circle round their lord and master, the flagship, it is a very interesting sight to see them all obeying the commodore's orders, who meanwhile never opens his lips.

Thus was it with us in Rio, and hereby hangs the story of my poor messmate Baldy.

One morning, in obedience to a signal from our flagship, the various vessels belonging to the American squadron then in harbour simultaneously loosened their sails to dry. In the evening, the signal was set to furl them. Upon such occasions great rivalry exists between the first lieutenants of the different ships; they vie with each other who shall first have his sails stowed on the yards. And this rivalry is shared between all the officers of each vessel, who are respectively placed over the different top-men; so that the mainmast is all eagerness to vanquish the foremast, and the mizzenmast to vanquish them both. Stimulated by the shouts of their officers, the sailors throughout the squadron exert themselves to the utmost.

'Aloft, top-men! lay out! furl!' cried the first lieutenant of the *Neversink*.

At the word the men sprang into the rigging, and on all three masts were soon climbing about the yards, in reckless haste to execute their orders.

Now, in furling topsails or courses, the point of honour, and the hardest work, is in the *bunt*, or middle of the yard; this post belongs to the first captain of the top.

'What are you 'bout there, mizzentop-men?' roared the first lieutenant, through his trumpet. 'D——n you, you are clumsy as Russian bears! don't you see the maintop-men are nearly off the yard? Bear a hand, bear a hand, or I'll stop your grog all round! You, Baldy! are you going to sleep there in the bunt?'

While this was being said, poor Baldy—his hat off, his face streaming with perspiration—was frantically exerting himself, piling up the ponderous folds of canvass in the middle of the yard; ever and anon glancing at victorious Jack Chase, hard at work at the main-topsail-yard before him.

At last, the sail being well piled up, Baldy jumped with both feet into the bunt, holding on with one hand to the chain *tie*, and in that manner was violently treading down the canvass to pack it close.

'D——n you, Baldy, why don't you move, you crawling caterpillar?' roared the first lieutenant.

Baldy brought his whole weight to bear on the rebellious sail, and in his frenzied heedlessness let go his hold on the tie.

'You, Baldy! are you afraid of falling?' cried the first lieutenant.

At that moment, with all his force, Baldy jumped down upon the sail; the *bunt-gasket* parted; and a dark form dropped through the air. Lighting upon the *top-rim*, it rolled off; and the next instant, with a horrid crash of all his bones, Baldy came, like a thunderbolt, upon the deck.

Aboard of most large men-of-war there is a stout oaken platform, about four feet square, on each side of the quarter-deck. You ascend to it by three or four steps; on top, it is railed in at the sides, with horizontal brass bars. It is called *the horse block*; and there the officer of the deck usually stands, in giving his orders at sea.

It was one of these horse blocks, now unoccupied, that broke poor Baldy's fall. He fell lengthwise across the brass bars, bending them into elbows, and crushing the whole oaken platform, steps and all, right down to the deck in a thousand splinters.

He was picked up for dead, and carried below to the surgeon. His bones seemed like those of a man broken on the wheel, and no one thought he would survive the night. But with the surgeon's skilful treatment he soon promised recovery. Surgeon Cuticle devoted all his science to this case.

A curious framework of wood was made for the maimed man; and placed in this, with all his limbs stretched out, Baldy lay flat on the floor of the sick-bay for many weeks. Upon our arrival home, he was able to hobble ashore on crutches; but from a hale, hearty man, with bronzed cheeks, he was become a mere dislocated skeleton, white as foam; but ere this, perhaps, his broken bones are healed and whole in the last repose of the man-of-war's-man.

Not many days after Baldy's accident in furling sails—in this same frenzied manner, under the stimulus of a shouting officer—a seaman fell from the main-royal-yard of an English line-of-battle ship near us, and buried his ankle-bones in the deck, leaving two indentations there, as if scooped out by a carpenter's gouge.

The royal-yard forms a cross with the mast, and falling from that lofty cross in a line-of-battle ship is almost like falling from the cross of St. Paul's; almost like falling as Lucifer from the well-spring of morning down to the Phlegethon of night.*

In some cases, a man, hurled thus from a yard, has fallen upon his own shipmates in the tops, and dragged them down with him to the same destruction with himself.

Hardly ever will you hear of a man-of-war returning home after a cruise without the loss of some of her crew from aloft, whereas similar accidents in the merchant-service—considering the much greater number of men employed in it—are comparatively few.

Why mince the matter? The death of most of these man-of-war's-men lies at the door of the souls of those officers, who, while safely standing on deck themselves, scruple not to sacrifice an immortal man or two, in order to show off the excelling discipline of the ship. And thus do *the people* of the gun-deck suffer, that the commodore on the poop may be glorified.

XLVII

An Auction in a Man-of-war

SOME allusion has been made to the weariness experienced by the man-of-war's-man while lying at anchor; but there are scenes now and then that serve to relieve it. Chief among these are the purser's auctions, taking place while in harbour. Some weeks, or perhaps months, after a sailor dies in an armed vessel, his bag of clothes is in this manner sold, and the proceeds transferred to the account of his heirs or executors.

One of these auctions came off in Rio, shortly after the sad accident of Baldy.

It was a dreamy, quiet afternoon, and the crew were listlessly lying around, when suddenly the boatswain's whistle was heard, followed by the announcement, 'D'ye hear there, fore and aft! Purser's auction on the spar-deck!'

At the sound, the sailors sprang to their feet and mustered round the mainmast. Presently up came the purser's steward, marshalling before him three or four of his subordinates, carrying several clothes-bags, which were deposited at the base of the mast.

Our purser's steward was a rather gentlemanly man in his way. Like many young Americans of his class, he had at various times assumed the most opposite functions for a livelihood, turning from one to the other with all the facility of a light-hearted, clever adventurer. He had been a clerk in a steamer on the Mississippi River; an auctioneer in Ohio; a stock actor at the Olympic Theatre in New York; and now he was purser's steward in the Navy. In the course of this diversified career his natural wit and waggery had been highly spiced, and every way improved; and he had acquired the last and most difficult art of the joker, the art of lengthening his own face while widening those of his hearers, preserving the utmost solemnity while setting them all in a roar. He was quite a favourite with the sailors, which, in a good degree, was owing to his humour; but likewise to his off-hand, irresistible, romantic, theatrical manner of addressing them.

With a dignified air, he now mounted the pedestal of the main-topsail sheet-bitts, imposing silence by a theatrical wave of his hand; meantime, his subordinates were rummaging the bags, and assorting their contents before him.

'Now, my noble hearties,' he began, 'we will open this auction by offering to your impartial competition a very superior pair of old boots'; and so saying, he dangled aloft one clumsy cowhide cylinder, almost as large as a firebucket, as a specimen of the complete pair.

'What shall I have now, my noble tars, for this superior pair of sea-boots?'

'Where's t'other boot?' cried a suspicious-eyed waister. 'I remember them 'ere boots. They were old Bob's the quarter-gunner's; there was two on 'em, too. I want to see t'other boot.'

'My sweet and pleasant fellow,' said the auctioneer, with his blandest accents, 'the other boot is not just at hand, but I give you my word of honour that it in all respects corresponds to the one you here see—it does, I assure you. Yes: I solemnly guarantee, my noble sea-fencibles,' he added, turning round upon all, 'that the other boot is the exact counterpart of this. Now, then, say the word, my fine fellows. What shall I have? Ten dollars, did you say?' politely bowing toward some indefinite person in the background.

'No; ten cents,' responded a voice.

'Ten cents! ten cents! gallant sailors, for this noble pair of boots,' exclaimed the auctioneer, with affected horror; 'I must close the auction, my tars of Columbia; this will never do. But let's have another bid; now, come,' he added, coaxingly and soothingly. 'What is it? One dollar? One dollar, then—one dollar; going at one dollar; going, going—going. Just see how it vibrates'—swinging the boot to and fro— 'this superior pair of sea-boots vibrating at one dollar; wouldn't pay for the nails in their heels; going, going—*gone*!' And down went the boots.

'Ah, what a sacrifice! what a sacrifice!' he sighed, tearfully eyeing the solitary fire-bucket, and then glancing round the company for sympathy.

'A sacrifice, indeed!' exclaimed Jack Chase, who stood by. 'Purser's steward, you are Mark Antony over the body of Julius Caesar.'

'So I am, so I am,' said the auctioneer, without moving a muscle. 'And look!' he exclaimed, suddenly seizing the boot, and exhibiting it on high, 'look, my noble tars, if you have tears, prepare to shed them now. You all do know this boot. I remember the first time ever old Bob put it on. 'Twas on a winter evening, off Cape Horn, between the starboard carronades—that day his precious grog was stopped. Look! in this place a mouse has nibbled through; see what a rent some envious rat has made; through this another filed, and, as he plucked his cursed rasp away, mark how the boot-leg gaped. This was the unkindest cut of all.—But whose are the boots?' suddenly assuming a business-like air; 'yours? yours? yours?'

But not a friend of the lamented Bob stood by.

'Tars of Columbia,' said the auctioneer, imperatively, 'these boots must be sold; and if I can't sell them one way, I must sell them another. How much *a pound*, now, for this superior pair of old boots? going by *the pound* now, remember, my gallant sailors! what shall I have? one cent, do I hear? going now at one cent a pound—going—going—going—*gone*!'

'Whose are they? Yours, captain of the waist? Well, my sweet and pleasant friend, I will have them weighed out to you when the auction is over.'

In like manner all the contents of the bags were disposed of, embracing old frocks, trowsers, and jackets, the various sums for which they went being charged to the bidders on the books of the purser.

Having been present at this auction, though not a purchaser, and seeing with what facility the most dismantled old garments went off, through the magical cleverness of the accomplished auctioneer, the thought occurred to me, that if ever I calmly and positively decided to dispose of my famous white jacket, this would be the very way to do it. I turned the matter over in my mind a long time.

The weather in Rio was genial and warm, and that I would ever again need such a thing as a heavy quilted jacket—and such a jacket as the white one, too—seemed almost impossible. Yet I remembered the American coast, and that it would probably be autumn when we should arrive there. Yes, I thought of all that, to be sure; nevertheless, the ungovernable whim seized me to sacrifice my jacket and recklessly abide the consequences. Besides, was it not a horrible jacket? To how many annoyances had it subjected me? How many scrapes had it dragged me into? Nay, had it not once jeopardized my very existence? And I had a dreadful presentiment that, if I persisted in retaining it, it would do so again. Enough! I will sell it, I muttered; and so muttering, I thrust my hands further down in my waistband, and walked the maintop in the stern concentration of an inflexible purpose. Next day, hearing that another auction was shortly to take place, I repaired to the office of the purser's steward, with whom I was upon rather friendly terms. After vaguely and delicately hinting at the object of my visit, I came roundly to the point, and asked him whether he could slip my jacket into one of the bags of clothes next to be sold, and so dispose of it by public auction. He kindly acquiesced, and the thing was done.

In due time all hands were again summoned round the mainmast; the purser's steward mounted his post, and the ceremony began. Meantime, I lingered out of sight, but still within hearing, on the gun-deck below, gazing up unperceived at the scene.

As it is now so long ago, I will here frankly make confession that I had privately retained the services of a friend—Williams, the Yankee pedagogue and peddler—whose business it would be to linger near the scene of the auction, and, if the bids on the jacket loitered, to start it roundly himself; and if the bidding then became brisk, he was continually to strike in with the most pertinacious and infatuated bids, and so exasperate competition into the maddest and most extravagant overtures.

A variety of other articles having been put up, the white jacket was slowly produced, and, held high aloft between the auctioneer's thumb and forefinger, was submitted to the inspection of the discriminating public.

Here it behooves me once again to describe my jacket; for, as a portrait taken at one period of life will not answer for a later stage; much more this jacket of mine, undergoing so many changes, needs to be painted again and again, in order truly to present its actual appearance at any given period.

A premature old age had now settled upon it; all over it bore melancholy scars of the masoned-up pockets that had once trenched it in various directions. Some parts of it were slightly mildewed from dampness; on one side several of the buttons were gone, and others were broken or cracked; while, alas! my many mad endeavours to rub it black on the decks had now imparted to the whole garment an exceedingly untidy appearance. Such as it was, with all its faults, the auctioneer displayed it.

'You venerable sheet-anchor-men! and you, gallant fore-top-men! and you, my fine waisters! what do you say now for this superior old jacket? Buttons and sleeves, lining and skirts, it must this day be sold without reservation. How much for it, my gallant tars of Columbia; say the word, and how much?'

'My eyes!' exclaimed a foretop-man, 'don't that 'ere bunch of old swabs belong to Jack Chase's pet? Ar'n't that *the white jacket?*'

'*The white jacket!*' cried fifty voices in response; '*the white jacket!*' The cry ran fore and aft the ship like a slogan, completely overwhelming the solitary voice of my private friend Williams, while all hands gazed at it with straining eyes, wondering how it came among the bags of deceased mariners.

'Ay, noble tars,' said the auctioneer, 'you may well stare at it; you will not find another jacket like this on either side of Cape Horn, I assure you. Why, just look at it! How much, now? Give me a bid—but don't be rash; be prudent, be prudent, men; remember your purser's accounts, and don't be betrayed into extravagant bids.'

'Purser's steward!' cried Grummet, one of the quarter-gunners, slowly shifting his quid from one cheek to the other, like a ballast-stone. 'I won't bid on that 'ere bunch of old swabs, unless you put up ten pounds of soap with it.'

'Don't mind that old fellow,' said the auctioneer. 'How much for the jacket, my noble tars?'

'Jacket!' cried a dandy *bone-polisher** of the gun-room. 'The sail-maker was the tailor, then. How many fathoms of canvass in it, purser's steward?'

'How much for this *jacket*?' reiterated the auctioneer, emphatically.

'*Jacket*, do you call it?' cried a captain of the hold. 'Why not call it a whitewashed man-of-war schooner? Look at the port-holes, to let in the air of cold nights.'

'A reg'lar herring-net,' chimed in Grummet.

'Gives me the *fever-nagur** to look at it,' echoed a mizzen-top-man.

'Silence!' cried the auctioneer. 'Start it now—start it, boys; anything you please, my fine fellows! it *must* be sold. Come, what ought I to have on it, now?'

'Why, purser's steward,' cried a waister, 'you ought to have new sleeves, a new lining, and a new body on it, afore you try to shove it off on a greenhorn.'

'What are you 'busin' that 'ere garment for?' cried an old sheet-anchor-man. 'Don't you see it's a "uniform mustering jacket"—three buttons on one side and none on t' other?'

'Silence!' again cried the auctioneer. 'How much, my sea-fencibles, for this superior old jacket?'

'Well,' said Grummet, 'I'll take it for cleaning-rags at one cent.'

'Oh, come, give us a bid! say something, Columbians.'

'Well, then,' said Grummet, all at once bursting into genuine indignation, 'if you want us to say something, then heave that bunch of old swabs overboard, *say I*, and show us something worth looking at.'

'No one will give me a bid, then? Very good; here, shove it aside. Let's have something else there.'

While this scene was going forward, and my white jacket was thus being abused, how my heart swelled within me! Thrice was I on the point of rushing out of my hiding-place, and bearing it off from derision; but I lingered, still flattering myself that all would be well, and the jacket find a purchaser at last. But no, alas! there was no getting rid of it, except by rolling a forty-two-pound shot in it, and committing it to the deep. But though, in my desperation, I had once contemplated something of that sort, yet I had now become unaccountably averse to it, from certain involuntary superstitious considerations. If I sink my jacket, thought I, it will be sure to spread itself into a bed at the bottom of the sea, upon which I shall sooner or later recline, a dead man. So, unable to conjure it into the possession of another, and withheld from burying it out of sight forever, my jacket stuck to me like the fatal shirt on Nessus.*

XLVIII

Purser, Purser's Steward, and Postmaster in a Man-of-war

As the purser's steward so conspicuously figured at the unsuccessful auction of my jacket, it reminds me of how important a personage that official is on board of all men-of-war. He is the right-hand man, and confidential deputy and clerk, of the purser, who entrusts to him all his accounts with the crew, while, in most cases, he himself, snug and comfortable in his state-room, glances over a file of newspapers instead of overhauling his ledgers.

Of all the non-combatants of a man-of-war, the purser, perhaps, stands foremost in importance. Though he is but a member of the gun-room mess, yet usage seems to assign him a conventional station somewhat above that of his equals in navy rank—the chaplain, surgeon, and professor.

Moreover, he is frequently to be seen in close conversation with the commodore, who, in the *Neversink*, was more than once known to be slightly jocular with our purser. Upon several occasions, also, he was called into the commodore's cabin, and remained closeted there for several minutes together. Nor do I remember that there ever happened a cabinet meeting of the ward-room barons, the lieutenants, in the commodore's cabin, but the purser made one of the party. Doubtless the important fact of the purser having under his charge all the financial affairs of a man-of-war imparts to him the great importance he enjoys. Indeed, we find in every government—monarchies and republics alike—that the personage at the head of the finances invariably occupies a commanding position. Thus, in point of station, the Secretary of the Treasury of the United States is deemed superior to the other heads of departments. Also, in England, the real office held by the great Premier himself is—as everyone knows—that of First Lord of the Treasury.

Now, under this high functionary of state, the official known as the purser's steward was head clerk of the frigate's fiscal affairs. Upon the berth-deck he had a regular counting-room, full of ledgers, journals, and day-books. His desk was as much littered with papers as any Pearl Street merchant's, and much time was devoted to his accounts. For hours together you would see him, through the window of his subterranean office, writing by the light of his perpetual lamp.

Ex-officio, the purser's steward of most ships is a sort of postmaster, and his office the post-office. When the letter bags for the squadron—almost as large as those of the United States mail—arrived on board the *Neversink*, it was the purser's steward that sat at his little window on the berth-deck, and handed you your letter or paper—if any there were to your address. Some disappointed applicants among the sailors would offer to buy the epistles of their more fortunate shipmates, while yet the seal was unbroken—maintaining that the sole and confidential reading of a fond, long, domestic letter from any man's home was far better than no letter at all.

In the vicinity of the office of the purser's steward are the principal store-rooms of the purser, where large quantities of goods of every description are to be found. On board of those ships where goods are permitted to be served out to the crew for the purpose of selling them ashore, to raise money, more business is transacted at the office of a purser's steward in one *liberty-day* morning than all the dry-goods shops in a considerable village would transact in a week.

Once a month, with undeviating regularity, this official has his hands more than usually full. For, once a month, certain printed bills, called mess-bills, are circulated among the crew, and whatever you may want from the purser—be it tobacco, soap, duck, dungeree, needles, thread, knives, belts, calico, ribbon, pipes, paper, pens, hats, ink, shoes, socks, or whatever it may be—down it goes on the mess-bill, which being the next day returned to the office of the steward, the 'slops', as they are called, are served out to the men and charged to their accounts.

Lucky is it for man-of-war's-men that the outrageous impositions to which, but a very few years ago, they were subjected from the abuses in this department of the service, and the unscrupulous cupidity of many of the pursers— lucky is it for them that *now* these things are in a great degree done away. The pursers, instead of being at liberty to make almost what they pleased from the sale of their wares, are now paid by regular stipends laid down by law.

Under the exploded system, the profits of some of these officers were almost incredible. In one cruise up the Mediterranean, the purser of an American line-of-battle ship was, on good authority, said to have cleared the sum of $50,000. Upon that he quitted the service, and retired into the country. Shortly after, his three daughters—not very lovely— married extremely well.

The ideas that sailors entertain of pursers is expressed in a rather inelegant but expressive saying of theirs: 'The purser is a conjurer; he can make a dead man chew tobacco' —insinuating that the accounts of a dead man are sometimes subjected to post-mortem charges. Among sailors, also, pursers commonly go by the name of *nip-cheeses*.

No wonder that on board of the old frigate *Java*, upon her return from a cruise extending over a period of more than four years, one thousand dollars paid off eighty of her crew, though the aggregate wages of the eighty for the voyage must have amounted to about sixty thousand dollars. Even under the present system, the purser of a line-of-battle ship, for instance, is far better paid than any other officer, short of captain or commodore. While the lieutenant commonly receives but eighteen hundred dollars, the surgeon of the fleet but fifteen hundred, the chaplain twelve hundred, the purser of a line-of-battle ship receives thirty-five hundred dollars. In considering his salary, however, his responsibilities are not to be overlooked; they are by no means insignificant.

There are pursers in the Navy whom the sailors exempt from the insinuations above mentioned; nor, as a class, are they so obnoxious to them now as formerly; for one, the florid old purser of the *Neversink*—never coming into disciplinary contact with the seamen, and being withal a jovial and apparently good-hearted gentleman—was something of a favourite with many of the crew.

XLIX

Rumours of a War, and how they were received by the Population of the Neversink

WHILE lying in the harbour of Callao, in Peru, certain rumours had come to us touching a war with England, growing out of the long-vexed north-eastern boundary question.* In Rio these rumours were increased; and the probability of hostilities induced our commodore to authorize proceedings that closely brought home to every man on board the *Neversink* his liability at any time to be killed at his gun.

Among other things, a number of men were detailed to

pass up the rusty cannon-balls from the shot-lockers in the hold, and scrape them clean for service. The commodore was a very neat gentleman, and would not fire a dirty shot into his foe.

It was an interesting occasion for a tranquil observer; nor was it altogether neglected. Not to recite the precise remarks made by the seamen while pitching the shot up the hatchway from hand to hand, like schoolboys playing ball ashore, it will be enough to say that, from the general drift of their discourse—jocular as it was—it was manifest that, almost to a man, they abhorred the idea of going into action.

And why should they desire a war? Would their wages be raised? Not a cent. The prize-money, though, ought to have been an inducement. But of all the 'rewards of virtue', prize-money is the most uncertain; and this the man-of-war's-man knows. What, then, has he to expect from war? What but harder work, and harder usage than in peace; a wooden leg or arm; mortal wounds, and death? Enough, however, that by far the majority of the common sailors of the *Neversink* were plainly concerned at the prospect of war, and were plainly averse to it.

But with the officers of the quarter-deck it was just the reverse. None of them, to be sure, in my hearing at least, verbally expressed their gratification; but it was unavoidably betrayed by the increased cheerfulness of their demeanour toward each other, their frequent fraternal conferences, and their unwonted animation for several days in issuing their orders. The voice of Mad Jack—always a belfry to hear—now resounded like that famous bell of England, Great Tom of Oxford.* As for Selvagee, he wore his sword with a jaunty air, and his servant daily polished the blade.

But why this contrast between the forecastle and the quarter-deck, between the man-of-war's-man and his officer? Because, though war would equally jeopardize the lives of both, yet, while it held out to the sailor no promise of promotion, and what is called *glory*, these things fired the breast of his officers.

It is no pleasing task, nor a thankful one, to dive into the souls of some men; but there are occasions when to bring up the mud from the bottom reveals to us on what soundings we are, on what coast we adjoin.

How were these officers to gain glory? How but by a distinguished slaughtering of their fellow-men? How were they to be promoted? How but over the buried heads of killed comrades and messmates?

This hostile contrast between the feelings with which the common seamen and the officers of the *Neversink* looked forward to this more than possible war, is one of many instances that might be quoted to show the antagonism of their interests, the incurable antagonism in which they dwell. But can men, whose interests are diverse, ever hope to live together in a harmony uncoerced? Can the brotherhood of the race of mankind ever hope to prevail in a man-of-war, where one man's bane is almost another's blessing? By abolishing the scourge, shall we do away tyranny; *that* tyranny which must ever prevail, where of two essentially antagonist classes in perpetual contact, one is immeasurably the stronger? Surely it seems all but impossible. And as the very object of a man-of-war, as its name implies, is to fight the very battles so naturally averse to the seamen; so long as a man-of-war exists, it must ever remain a picture of much that is tyrannical and repelling in human nature.

Being an establishment much more extensive than the American Navy, the English armed marine furnishes a yet more striking example of this thing, especially as the existence of war produces so vast an augmentation of her naval force compared with what it is in time of peace. It is well known what joy the news of Bonaparte's sudden return from Elba created among crowds of British naval officers, who had previously been expecting to be sent ashore on half-pay. Thus, when all the world wailed, these officers found occasion for thanksgiving. I urge it not against them as *men*— their feelings belonged to their profession. Had they not been naval officers, they had not been rejoicers in the midst of despair.

When shall the time come, how much longer will God

postpone it, when the clouds, which at times gather over the horizons of nations, shall not be hailed by any class of humanity, and invoked to burst as a bomb? Standing navies, as well as standing armies, serve to keep alive the spirit of war even in the meek heart of peace. In its very embers and smoulderings they nourish that fatal fire, and half-pay officers, as the priests of Mars, yet guard the temple, though no god be there.

L

The Bay of all Beauties

I HAVE said that I must pass over Rio without a description; but just now such a flood of scented reminiscences steals over me, that I must needs yield and recant, as I inhale that musky air.

More than one hundred and fifty miles' circuit of living green hills embosoms a translucent expanse, so gemmed in by sierras of grass, that among the Indian tribes the place was known as 'The Hidden Water'. On all sides, in the distance, rise high conical peaks, which at sunrise and sunset burn like vast tapers; and down from the interior, through vineyards and forests, flow radiating streams, all emptying into the harbour.

Talk not of Bahia de Todos os Santos—the Bay of All Saints; for though that be a glorious haven, yet Rio is the Bay of all Rivers—the Bay of all Delights—the Bay of all Beauties. From circumjacent hillsides, untiring summer hangs perpetually in terraces of vivid verdure; and, embossed with old mosses, convent and castle nestle in valley and glen.

All round, deep inlets run into the green mountain land, and, overhung with wild Highlands, more resemble Loch Katrines than Lake Lemans. And though Loch Katrine has been sung by the bonneted Scott, and Lake Leman by the coroneted Byron; yet here, in Rio, both the loch and the lake

are but two wild flowers in a prospect that is almost unlimited. For, behold! far away, and away, stretches the broad
blue of the water, to yonder soft-swelling hills of light green,
backed by the purple pinnacles and pipes of the grand Organ
Mountains; fitly so called, for in thunder-time they roll
cannonades down the bay, drowning the blended bass of all
the cathedrals in Rio. Shout amain, exalt your voices, stamp
your feet, jubilate, Organ Mountains! and roll your Te
Deums round the world!

What though, for more than five thousand five hundred
years, this grand harbour of Rio lay hid in the hills, unknown
by the Catholic Portuguese? Centuries ere Haydn performed
before emperors and kings, these Organ Mountains played
his oratorio of the Creation, before the Creator himself. But
nervous Haydn could not have endured that cannonading
choir, since this composer of thunderbolts himself died at
last through the crashing commotion of Napoleon's bom-
bardment of Vienna.

But all mountains are Organ Mountains: the Alps and the
Himmelahs; the Appalachian Chain, the Ural, the Andes,
the Green Hills and the White. All of them play anthems forever: *The Messiah*, and *Samson*, and *Israel in Egypt*, and
Saul, and *Judas Maccabeus*, and *Solomon*.

Archipelago Rio! ere Noah on old Ararat anchored his
ark, there lay anchored in you all these green, rocky isles I
now see. But God did not build on you, isles! those long lines
of batteries; nor did our blessed Saviour stand godfather at
the christening of yon frowning fortress of Santa Cruz,
though named in honour of himself, the divine Prince of
Peace!

Amphitheatrical Rio! in your broad expanse might be held
the Resurrection and the Judgment Day of the whole world's
men-of-war, represented by the flagships of fleets—the flagships of the Phœnician armed galleys of Tyre and Sidon; of
King Solomon's annual squadrons that sailed to Ophir;
whence in after times, perhaps, sailed the Acapulco fleets
of the Spaniards, with golden ingots for ballasting; the flagships of all the Greek and Persian craft that exchanged the

war-hug at Salamis; of all the Roman and Egyptian galleys that, eagle-like, with blood-dripping prows, beaked each other at Actium; of all the Danish keels of the Vikings; of all the mosquito craft of Abba Thule, king of the Pelews, when he went to vanquish Artingall; of all the Venetian, Genoese, and Papal fleets that came to the shock at Lepanto; of both horns of the crescent of the Spanish Armada; of the Portuguese squadron that, under the gallant Gama, chastised the Moors, and discovered the Moluccas; of all the Dutch navies led by Van Tromp, and sunk by Admiral Hawke; of the forty-seven French and Spanish sail-of-the-line that, for three months, essayed to batter down Gibraltar; of all Nelson's seventy-fours that thunderbolted off St. Vincent's, at the Nile, Copenhagen, and Trafalgar; of all the frigate-merchantmen of the East India Company; of Perry's war-brigs, sloops, and schooners that scattered the British armament on Lake Erie;*of all the Barbary corsairs captured by Bainbridge; of the war-canoes of the Polynesian kings, Tammahammaha and Pomare—ay! one and all, with Commodore Noah for their Lord High Admiral—in this abounding Bay of Rio these flagships might all come to anchor, and swing round in concert to the first of the flood.

Rio is a small Mediterranean; and what was fabled of the entrance to that sea, in Rio is partly made true; for here, at the mouth, stands one of Hercules' Pillars, the Sugar Loaf Mountain, one thousand feet high, inclining over a little, like the Leaning Tower of Pisa. At its base crouch, like mastiffs, the batteries of Jose and Theodosia, while opposite, you are menaced by a rock-founded fort.

The channel between—the sole inlet to the bay—seems but a biscuit's toss over; you see naught of the landlocked sea within till fairly in the strait. But, then, what a sight is beheld! Diversified as the harbour of Constantinople, but a thousand-fold grander. When the *Neversink* swept in, word was passed, 'Aloft, top-men! and furl the t'gallant-sails and royals!'

At the sound I sprang into the rigging, and was soon at my perch. How I hung over that main-royal-yard in

a rapture! High in air, poised over that magnificent bay,
a new world to my ravished eyes, I felt like the foremost of
a flight of angels, new-lighted upon earth, from some star
in the Milky Way.

LI

One of 'the People' has an Audience with the Commodore and the Captain on the Quarter-deck

WE had not lain in Rio long, when in the innermost recesses
of the mighty soul of my noble captain of the top—incomparable Jack Chase—the deliberate opinion was formed, and
rock-founded, that our ship's company must have at least
one day's *liberty* to go ashore ere we weighed anchor for
home.

Here it must be mentioned that, concerning anything of
this kind, no sailor in a man-of-war ever presumes to be an
agitator, unless he is of a rank superior to a mere able seaman; and no one short of a petty officer—that is, a captain of
the top, a quarter-gunner, or boatswain's mate—ever
dreams of being a spokesman to the supreme authority of
the vessel in soliciting any kind of favour for himself and
shipmates.

After canvassing the matter thoroughly with several old
quarter-masters and other dignified sea-fencibles, Jack, hat
in hand, made his appearance, one fine evening, at the mast,
and, waiting till Captain Claret drew nigh, bowed, and
addressed him in his own off-hand, polished, and poetical
style. In his intercourse with the quarter-deck, he always presumed upon his being such a universal favourite.

'Sir, this Rio is a charming harbour, and we poor mariners
—your trusty sea-warriors, valiant captain! who, with *you*
at their head, would board the Rock of Gibraltar itself, and
carry it by storm—we poor fellows, valiant captain! have
gazed round upon this ravishing landscape till we can gaze
no more. Will Captain Claret vouchsafe one day's liberty,

and so assure himself of eternal felicity, since, in our flowing cups, he will be ever after freshly remembered?'

As Jack thus rounded off with a snatch from Shakespeare,
he saluted the captain with a gallant flourish of his tarpaulin,
and then, bringing the rim to his mouth, with his head bowed,
and his body thrown into a fine negligent attitude, stood
a picture of eloquent but passive appeal. He seemed to say,
Magnanimous Captain Claret, we fine fellows, and hearts of
oak, throw ourselves upon your unparalleled goodness.

'And what do you want to go ashore for?' asked the captain,
evasively, and trying to conceal his admiration of Jack by
affecting some haughtiness.

'Ah! sir,' sighed Jack, 'why do the thirsty camels of the
desert desire to lap the waters of the fountain and roll in the
green grass of the oasis? Are we not but just from the ocean
Sahara? and is not this Rio a verdant spot, noble captain?
Surely you will not keep us always tethered at anchor, when
a little more cable would admit of our cropping the herbage!
And it is a weary thing, Captain Claret, to be imprisoned
month after month on the gun-deck, without so much as
smelling a citron. Ah! Captain Claret, what sings sweet
Waller?*—

> But who can always on the billows lie?
> The watery wilderness yields no supply.

Compared with such a prisoner, noble captain,

> Happy, thrice happy, who, in battle slain,
> Press'd in Atrides' cause the Trojan plain!

Pope's version,*sir, not the original Greek.'

And so saying, Jack once more brought his hat-rim to his
mouth, and slightly bending forward, stood mute.

At this juncture the Most Serene Commodore himself
happened to emerge from the after gangway, his gilded
buttons, epaulets, and the gold lace on his chapeau glittering
in the flooding sunset. Attracted by the scene between
Captain Claret and so well-known and admired a commoner
as Jack Chase, he approached, and assuming for the moment
an air of pleasant condescension—never shown to his noble

barons the officers of the ward-room—he said, with a smile, 'Well, Jack, you and your shipmates are after some favour, I suppose—a day's liberty, is it not?'

Whether it was the horizontal setting sun, streaming along the deck, that blinded Jack, or whether it was in sun-worshipping homage of the mighty commodore, there is no telling; but just at this juncture noble Jack was standing reverentially holding his hat to his brow, like a man with weak eyes.

'Valiant commodore,' said he, at last, 'this audience is indeed an honour undeserved. I almost sink beneath it. Yes, valiant commodore, your sagacious mind has truly divined our object. Liberty, sir; liberty is, indeed, our humble prayer. I trust your honourable wound, received in glorious battle, valiant commodore, pains you less to-day than common.'

'Ah! cunning Jack!' cried the commodore, by no means blind to the bold sortie of his flattery, but not at all displeased with it. In more respects than one, our commodore's wound was his weak side.

'I think we must give them liberty,' he added, turning to Captain Claret; who thereupon, waving Jack further off, fell into confidential discourse with his superior.

'Well, Jack, we will see about it,' at last cried the commodore, advancing. 'I think we must let you go.'

'To your duty, captain of the maintop!' said the captain rather stiffly. He wished to neutralize somewhat the effect of the commodore's condescension. Besides, he had much rather the commodore had been in his cabin. His presence, for the time, affected his own supremacy in his ship. But Jack was noways cast down by the captain's coldness; he felt safe enough; so he proceeded to offer his acknowledgments.

'"Kind gentlemen,"' he sighed, '"your pains are registered where every day I turn the leaf to read,"—Macbeth, valiant commodore and captain!—what the Thane says to the noble lords, Rosse and Angus.'

And long and lingeringly bowing to the two noble officers, Jack backed away from their presence, still shading his eyes with the broad rim of his hat.

'Jack Chase forever!' cried his shipmates, as he carried the grateful news of liberty to them on the forecastle. 'Who can talk to commodores like our matchless Jack!'

LII

Something concerning Midshipmen

IT was the next morning after matchless Jack's interview with the commodore and captain, that a little incident occurred, soon forgotten by the crew at large, but long remembered by the few seamen who were in the habit of closely scrutinizing everyday proceedings. Upon the face of it, it was but a common event—at least in a man-of-war— the flogging of a man at the gangway. But the under-current of circumstances in the case were of a nature that magnified this particular flogging into a matter of no small importance. The story itself cannot here be related; it would not well bear recital: enough that the person flogged was a middle-aged man of the waist—a forlorn, broken-down, miserable object, truly; one of those wretched landsmen sometimes driven into the Navy by their unfitness for all things else, even as others are driven into the workhouse. He was flogged at the complaint of a midshipman; and hereby hangs the drift of the thing. For though this waister was so ignoble a mortal, yet his being scourged on this one occasion indirectly proceeded from the mere wanton spite and unscrupulousness of the midshipman in question—a youth who was apt to indulge at times in undignified familiarities with some of the men, who, sooner or later, almost always suffered from his capricious preferences.

But the leading principle that was involved in this affair is far too mischievous to be lightly dismissed.

In most cases it would seem to be a cardinal principle with a Navy captain that his subordinates are disintegrated parts of himself, detached from the main body on special service, and that the order of the minutest midshipman must be as deferentially obeyed by the seamen as if proceeding

from the commodore on the poop. This principle was once
emphasized in a remarkable manner by the valiant and handsome Sir Peter Parker,* upon whose death, on a national
arson expedition on the shores of Chesapeake Bay, in 1812
or 1813, Lord Byron wrote his well-known stanzas. 'By the
God of War!' said Sir Peter to his sailors, 'I'll make you touch
your hat to a midshipman's coat, if it's only hung on a
broomstick to dry!'

That the king, in the eye of the law, can do no wrong, is
the well-known fiction of despotic states; but it has remained
for the navies of constitutional monarchies and republics to
magnify this fiction, by indirectly extending it to all the
quarter-deck subordinates of an armed ship's chief magistrate. And though judicially unrecognized, and unacknow-
ledged by the officers themselves, yet this is the principle
that pervades the fleet; this is the principle that is every hour
acted upon, and to sustain which, thousands of seamen have
been flogged at the gangway.

However childish, ignorant, stupid, or idiotic a midshipman, if he but orders a sailor to perform even the most
absurd action, that man is not only bound to render instant
and unanswering obedience, but he would refuse at his peril.
And if, having obeyed, he should then complain to the
captain, and the captain, in his own mind, should be
thoroughly convinced of the impropriety, perhaps of the
illegality of the order, yet, in nine cases out of ten, he would
not publicly reprimand the midshipman, nor by the slightest
token admit before the complainant that, in this particular
thing, the midshipman had done otherwise than perfectly
right.

Upon a midshipman's complaining of a seaman to Lord
Collingwood, when captain of a line-of-battle ship, he
ordered the man for punishment; and, in the interval, calling the midshipman aside, said to him, 'In all probability,
now, the fault is yours—you know; therefore, when the
man is brought to the mast, you had better ask for his
pardon.'

Accordingly, upon the lad's public intercession, Collingwood, turning to the culprit, said, 'This young gentleman has pleaded so humanely for you, that, in the hope you feel a due gratitude to him for his benevolence, I will for this time overlook your offence.' This story is related by the editor of the admiral's *Correspondence*, to show the admiral's kind-heartedness.

Now Collingwood was, in reality, one of the most just, humane, and benevolent admirals that ever hoisted a flag. For a sea-officer, Collingwood was a man in a million. But if a man like him, swayed by old usages, could thus violate the commonest principle of justice—with however good motives at bottom—what must be expected from other captains not so eminently gifted with noble traits as Collingwood?

And if the corps of American midshipmen is mostly replenished from the nursery, the counter, and the lap of unrestrained indulgence at home; and if most of them at least, by their impotency as officers, in all important functions at sea, by their boyish and overweening conceit of their gold lace, by their overbearing manner toward the seamen, and by their peculiar aptitude to construe the merest trivialities of manner into set affronts against their dignity; if by all this they sometimes contract the ill-will of the seamen; and if, in a thousand ways, the seamen cannot but betray it—how easy for any of these midshipmen, who may happen to be unrestrained by moral principle, to resort to spiteful practices in procuring vengeance upon the offenders, in many instances to the extremity of the lash; since, as we have seen, the tacit principle in the Navy seems to be that, in his ordinary intercourse with the sailors, a midshipman can do nothing obnoxious to the public censure of his superiors.

'You fellow, I'll get you *licked* before long,' is often heard from a midshipman to a sailor who, in some way not open to the judicial action of the captain, has chanced to offend him.

At times you will see one of these lads, not five feet high, gazing up with inflamed eye at some venerable six-footer of a forecastle-man, cursing and insulting him by every epithet deemed most scandalous and unendurable among men. Yet that man's indignant tongue is treble-knotted by the law, that suspends death itself over his head should his passion discharge the slightest blow at the boy-worm that spits at his feet.

But since what human nature is, and what it must forever continue to be, is well enough understood for most practical purposes, it needs no special example to prove that, where the merest boys, indiscriminately snatched from the human family, are given such authority over mature men, the results must be proportionable in monstrousness to the custom that authorizes this worse than cruel absurdity.

Nor is it unworthy of remark that, while the noblest-minded and most heroic sea-officers—men of the topmost stature, including Lord Nelson himself—have regarded flogging in the Navy with the deepest concern, and not without weighty scruples touching its general necessity, still, one who has seen much of midshipmen can truly say that he has seen but few midshipmen who were not enthusiastic advocates and admirers of scourging. It would almost seem that they themselves, having so recently escaped the posterior discipline of the nursery and the infant school, are impatient to recover from those smarting reminiscences by mincing the backs of full-grown American freemen.

It should not be omitted here, that the midshipmen in the English Navy are not permitted to be quite so imperious as in the American ships. They are divided into three (I think) probationary classes of 'volunteers', instead of being at once advanced to a warrant. Nor will you fail to remark, when you see an English cutter officered by one of these volunteers, that the boy does not so strut and slap his dirk-hilt with a Bobadil air,* and anticipatingly feel of the place where his warlike whiskers are going to be, and sputter out oaths so at the men, as is too often the case with the little boys wearing best bower-anchors on their lapels in the American Navy.

Yet it must be confessed that at times you see midshipmen who are noble little fellows, and not at all disliked by the crew. Besides three gallant youths, one black-eyed little lad, in particular, in the *Neversink*, was such a one. From his diminutiveness, he went by the name of *Boat-Plug* among the seamen. Without being exactly familiar with them, he had yet become a general favourite, by reason of his kindness of manner, and never cursing them. It was amusing to hear some of the older Tritons invoke blessings upon the youngster, when his kind tones fell on their weather-beaten ears. 'Ah, good luck to you, sir!' touching their hats to the little man; 'you have a soul to be saved, sir!' There was a wonderful deal of meaning involved in the latter sentence. *You have a soul to be saved*, is the phrase which a man-of-war's-man peculiarly applies to a humane and kind-hearted officer. It also implies that the majority of quarter-deck officers are regarded by them in such a light that they deny to them the possession of souls. Ah! but these plebeians sometimes have a sublime vengeance upon patricians. Imagine an outcast old sailor seriously cherishing the purely speculative conceit that some bully in epaulets, who orders him to and fro like a slave, is of an organization immeasurably inferior to himself; must at last perish with the brutes, while he goes to his immortality in heaven!

But from what has been said in this chapter, it must not be inferred that a midshipman leads a lord's life in a man-of-war. Far from it. He lords it over those below him, while lorded over himself by his superiors. It is as if with one hand a schoolboy snapped his fingers at a dog, and at the same time received upon the other the discipline of the usher's ferule.* And though, by the American Articles of War, a Navy captain cannot, of his own authority, legally punish a midshipman, otherwise than by suspension from duty (the same as with respect to the ward-room officers), yet this is one of those sea-statutes which the captain, to a certain extent, observes or disregards at his pleasure. Many instances might be related of the petty mortifications and official insults inflicted by some captains upon their midshipmen; far more severe, in one sense, than the old-fashioned punishment of sending them to the mast-head, though not so arbitrary as sending them before the mast, to do duty with the common sailors— a custom, in former times, pursued by captains in the English Navy.

Captain Claret himself had no special fondness for

midshipmen. A tall, overgrown young midshipman, about sixteen years old, having fallen under his displeasure, he interrupted the humble apologies he was making, by saying, 'Not a word, sir! I'll not hear a word! Mount the netting, sir, and stand there till you are ordered to come down!'

The midshipman obeyed; and, in full sight of the entire ship's company, Captain Claret promenaded to and fro below his lofty perch, reading him a most aggravating lecture upon his alleged misconduct. To a lad of sensibility, such treatment must have been almost as stinging as the lash itself would have been.

In another case a midshipman attempted to carry the day by speaking up to his superior; but in a most unexpected manner he paid the penalty of his indiscretion.

Seeing a reefer's hammock in the quarter-netting, and observing it to be rather equivocally discoloured, the captain demanded to know what particular midshipman was the proprietor of that hammock. When the lad appeared, he said to him, 'What do you call that, sir?' pointing at the discoloration.

'Captain Claret,' said the unabashed reefer, looking him full in the eye, 'you know what that is, sir, as well as I do.'

'So I do, sir. Quarter-master! pitch that hammock overboard.'

The midshipman started, and, hurrying up to it, turned round, and said, 'Captain Claret, I have a purse lashed up here; it's the only safe way I can keep it.'

'Did you hear me, quarter-master?' said the captain; and overboard went the hammock and purse.

The same afternoon, this midshipman reported his *cot-boy* as having neglected to scrub this identical hammock, though repeatedly ordered to do so by his master. Though called a cot-*boy*, the person thus designated happened to be, in fact, a full-grown man. The case being fully laid before the captain at the mast, and the midshipman's charge having been heard, this cot-boy, spite of his protestations, and altogether through the midshipman's instrumentality, was condemned to a flogging.

Thus it will be seen, that though the captain permits himself to domineer over a midshipman, and, in cases of personal contact with him, does not scruple to pronounce him an egregious wrong-doer, and treats him accordingly; yet, in *other* cases, involving the immediate relationship between the midshipman and the sailor, he still sustains the principle that a midshipman can neither say nor do any wrong.

It is to be remembered that, wherever these chapters treat of midshipmen, the officers known as passed-midshipmen are not at all referred to. In the American Navy these officers form a class of young men, who, having seen sufficient service at sea as midshipmen to pass an examination before a Board of Commodores, are promoted to the rank of passed-midshipmen, introductory to that of lieutenant. They are supposed to be qualified to do duty as lieutenants, and in some cases temporarily serve as such. The difference between a passed-midshipman and a midshipman may be also inferred from their respective rates of pay. The former, upon sea-service, receives $750 a year; the latter, $400. There were no passed-midshipmen in the *Neversink*.

LIII

Seafaring Persons peculiarly subject to being under the Weather—the Effects of this upon a Man-of-war Captain

I T has been said that some midshipmen, in certain cases, are guilty of spiteful practices against the man-of-war's-man. But as these midshipmen are presumed to have received the liberal and lofty breeding of gentlemen, it would seem all but incredible that any of their corps could descend to the paltriness of cherishing personal malice against so conventionally degraded a being as a sailor. So, indeed, it would seem. But when all the circumstances are considered, it will not appear extraordinary that some of them should thus cast discredit upon the warrants they wear. Title, and rank, and wealth, and education cannot unmake human nature; the same in cabin-boy and commodore, its only differences lie in the different modes of development.

At sea, a frigate houses and homes five hundred mortals in a space so contracted that they can hardly so much as move but they touch. Cut off from all those outward passing things which ashore employ the eyes, tongues, and thoughts of landsmen, the inmates of a frigate are thrown upon themselves and each other, and all their ponderings are introspective. A morbidness of mind is often the consequence, especially upon long voyages, accompanied by foul weather, calms, or head-winds. Nor does this exempt from its evil influence any rank on board. Indeed, high station only ministers to it the more, since the higher the rank in a man-of-war, the less companionship.

It is an odious, unthankful, repugnant thing to dwell upon a subject like this; nevertheless, be it said, that, through these jaundiced influences, even the captain of a frigate is, in some cases, indirectly induced to the infliction of corporal punishment upon a seaman. Never sail under a Navy captain whom you suspect of being dyspeptic, or constitutionally prone to hypochondria.

The manifestation of these things is sometimes remarkable. In the earlier part of the cruise, while making a long, tedious run from Mazatlan* to Callao on the Main, baffled by light head-winds and frequent intermitting calms, when all hands were heartily wearied by the torrid, monotonous sea, a good-natured foretop-man by the name of Candy— quite a character in his way—standing in the waist among a crowd of seamen, touched me, and said, 'D'ye see the old man there, White-Jacket, walking the poop? Well, don't he look as if he wanted to flog some one? Look at him once.'

But to me, at least, no such indications were visible in the deportment of the captain, though his thrashing the arm-chest with the slack of the spanker out-haul looked a little suspicious. But anyone might have been doing that to pass away a calm.

'Depend on it,' said the top-man, 'he must somehow have

thought I was making sport of *him* a while ago, when I was only taking off old Priming, the gunner's mate. Just look at him once, White-Jacket, while I make believe coil this here rope; if there ar'n't a dozen in that 'ere captain's top-lights, my name is *horse-marine.** If I could only touch my tile to him now, and take my Bible oath on it, that I was only taking off Priming, and not *him*, he wouldn't have such hard thoughts of me. But that can't be done; he'd think I meant to insult him. Well, it can't be helped; I suppose I must look out for a baker's dozen afore long.'

I had an incredulous laugh at this. But two days afterward, when we were hoisting the main-topmast stun'-sail, and the lieutenant of the watch was reprimanding the crowd of seamen at the halyards for their laziness—for the sail was but just crawling up to its place, owing to the languor of the men, induced by the heat—the captain, who had been impatiently walking the deck, suddenly stopped short, and darting his eyes among the seamen, suddenly fixed them, crying out, 'You, Candy, and be damned to you, you don't pull an ounce, you blackguard! Stand up to that gun, sir; I'll teach you to be grinning over a rope that way, without lending your pound of beef to it. Boatswain's mate, where's your *colt*? Give that man a dozen.'

Removing his hat, the boatswain's mate looked into the crown aghast; the coiled rope, usually worn there, was not to be found; but the next instant it slid from the top of his head to the deck. Picking it up, and straightening it out, he advanced toward the sailor.

'Sir,' said Candy, touching and retouching his cap to the captain, 'I was pulling, sir, as much as the rest, sir; I was, indeed, sir.'

'Stand up to that gun,' cried the captain. 'Boatswain's mate, do your duty.'

Three stripes were given, when the captain raised his finger. 'You ——,* do you dare stand up to be flogged with your hat on? Take it off, sir, instantly.'

Candy dropped it on deck.

* The phrase here used I have never seen either written or printed, and should not like to be the first person to introduce it to the public.

'Now go on, boatswain's mate.' And the sailor received his dozen.

With his hand to his back he came up to me, where I stood among the bystanders, saying, 'O Lord, O Lord! that boatswain's mate, too, had a spite agin me; he always thought it was *me* that set afloat that yarn about his wife in Norfolk. O Lord! just run your hand under my shirt, will you, White-Jacket? There! didn't he have a spite agin me, to raise such bars as them? And my shirt all cut to pieces, too—ar'n't it, White-Jacket? Damn me, but these coltings puts the tin in the purser's pocket. O Lord! my back feels as if there was a red-hot gridiron lashed to it. But I told you so—a widow's curse on him, say I—he thought I meant *him*, and not Priming.'

LIV

'The People' are given 'Liberty'

WHENEVER, in intervals of mild benevolence, or yielding to mere politic dictates, kings and commodores relax the yoke of servitude, they should see to it well that the concession seem not too sudden or unqualified; for, in the commoner's estimation, that might argue feebleness or fear.

Hence it was, perhaps, that, though noble Jack had carried the day captive in his audience at the mast, yet more than thirty-six hours elapsed ere anything official was heard of the 'liberty' his shipmates so earnestly coveted. Some of the people began to growl and grumble.

'It's turned out all gammon,*Jack,' said one.

'Blast the commodore!' cried another, 'he bamboozled you, Jack.'

'Lay on your oars awhile,' answered Jack, 'and we shall see; we've struck for liberty, and liberty we'll have! I'm your tribune, boys; I'm your Rienzi.* The commodore must keep his word.'

Next day, about breakfast-time, a mighty whistling and piping was heard at the main hatchway, and presently the boatswain's voice was heard: 'D' ye hear there, fore and aft! all you starboard quarter-watch! get ready to go ashore on liberty!'

In a paroxysm of delight, a young mizzentop-man, standing by at the time, whipped the tarpaulin from his head, and smashed it like a pancake on the deck. 'Liberty!' he shouted, leaping down into the berth-deck after his bag.

At the appointed hour, the quarter-watch mustered round the capstan, at which stood our old First Lord of the Treasury and Paymaster-General, the purser, with several goodly buckskin bags of dollars, piled up on the capstan. He helped us all round to half a handful or so, and then the boats were manned, and, like so many Esterhazys,* we were pulled ashore by our shipmates. All their lives lords may live in listless state; but give the commoners a holiday, and they outlord the commodore himself.

The ship's company were divided into four sections or quarter-watches, only one of which were on shore at a time, the rest remaining to garrison the frigate—the term of liberty for each being twenty-four hours.

With Jack Chase and a few other discreet and gentlemanly top-men, I went ashore on the first day, with the first quarter-watch. Our own little party had a charming time; we saw many fine sights; fell in—as all sailors must—with dashing adventures. But, though not a few good chapters might be written on this head, I must again forbear; for in this book I have nothing to do with the shore further than to glance at it, now and then, from the water; my man-of-war world alone must supply me with the staple of my matter; I have taken an oath to keep afloat to the last letter of my narrative.

Had they all been as punctual as Jack Chase's party, the whole quarter-watch of liberty-men had been safe on board the frigate at the expiration of the twenty-four hours. But this was not the case; and during the entire day succeeding, the midshipmen and others were engaged in ferreting them out of their hiding-places on shore, and bringing them off in scattered detachments to the ship.

They came in all imaginable stages of intoxication; some

with blackened eyes and broken heads; some still more severely injured, having been stabbed in frays with the Portuguese soldiers. Others, unharmed, were immediately dropped on the gun-deck, between the guns, where they lay snoring for the rest of the day. As a considerable degree of licence is invariably permitted to man-of-war's-men just 'off liberty', and as man-of-war's-men well know this to be the case, they occasionally avail themselves of the privilege to talk very frankly to the officers when they first cross the gangway, taking care meanwhile to reel about very industriously, so that there shall be no doubt about their being seriously intoxicated, and altogether *non compos* for the time. And though but few of them have cause to feign intoxication, yet some individuals may be suspected of enacting a studied part upon these occasions. Indeed—judging by certain symptoms—even when really inebriated, some of the sailors must have previously determined upon their conduct; just as some persons who, before taking the exhilarating gas, secretly make up their minds to perform certain mad feats while under its influence, which feats consequently come to pass precisely as if the actors were not accountable for them.

For several days, while the other quarter-watches were given liberty, the *Neversink* presented a sad scene. She was more like a mad-house than a frigate; the gun-deck resounded with frantic fights, shouts, and songs. All visitors from shore were kept at a cable's length.

These scenes, however, are nothing to those which have repeatedly been enacted in American men-of-war upon other stations. But the custom of introducing women on board, in harbour, is now pretty much discontinued, both in the English and American Navy, unless a ship, commanded by some dissolute captain, happens to lie in some far-away, outlandish port, in the Pacific or Indian Ocean.

The British line-of-battle ship, *Royal George*, which in 1782 sunk at her anchors at Spithead, carried down three hundred English women among the one thousand souls that were drowned on that memorable morning.

When, at last, after all the mad tumult and contention of 'liberty', the reaction came, our frigate presented a very different scene. The men looked jaded and wan, lethargic and lazy; and many an old mariner, with hand upon abdomen, called upon the flagstaff to witness that there were more *hot coppers* in the *Neversink* than those in the ship's galley.

Such are the lamentable effects of suddenly and completely releasing *the people* of a man-of-war from arbitrary discipline. It shows that, to such, 'liberty', at first, must be administered in small and moderate quantities, increasing with the patient's capacity to make a good use of it.

Of course, while we lay in Rio, our officers frequently went ashore for pleasure, and, as a general thing, conducted themselves with propriety. But it is a sad thing to say, that, as for Lieutenant Mad Jack, he enjoyed himself so delightfully for three consecutive days in the town that, upon returning to the ship, he sent his card to the surgeon, with his compliments, begging him to drop into his state-room the first time he happened to pass that way in the wardroom.

But one of our surgeon's mates, a young medico of fine family but slender fortune, must have created by far the strongest impression among the hidalgos of Rio. He had read *Don Quixote*, and, instead of curing him of his Quixotism, as it ought to have done, it only made him still more Quixotic. Indeed, there are some natures concerning whose moral maladies the grand maxim of Mr. Similibus Similibus Curantur*Hahneman does not hold true, since, with them, *like cures* not *like*, but only aggravates *like*. Though, on the other hand, so incurable are the moral maladies of such persons, that the antagonist maxim, *contraria contrariis curantur*,* often proves equally false.

Of a warm tropical day, this surgeon's mate must needs go ashore in his blue cloth boat-cloak, wearing it, with a gallant Spanish toss, over his cavalier shoulder. By noon, he perspired very freely; but then his cloak attracted all eyes, and that was huge satisfaction. Nevertheless, his being knock-kneed, and spavined of one leg, sorely impaired the effect of this hidalgo cloak, which, by the way, was somewhat rusty in front, where his chin rubbed against it, and a good deal bedraggled all over, from his having used it as a counterpane off Cape Horn.

As for the midshipmen, there is no knowing what their mammas would have said to their conduct in Rio. Three of them drank a good deal too much; and when they came on board, the captain ordered them to be sewed up in their hammocks, to cut short their obstreperous capers till sober.

This shows how unwise it is to allow children yet in their teens to wander so far from home. It more especially illustrates the folly of giving them long holidays in a foreign land, full of seductive dissipation. Port for men, claret for boys, cried Dr. Johnson. Even so, men only should drink the strong drink of travel; boys should still be kept on milk and water at home. Middies! you may despise your mother's leading-strings, but they are the *man-ropes*, my lads, by which many youngsters have steadied the giddiness of youth, and saved themselves from lamentable falls. And middies! know this, that as infants, being too early put on their feet, grow up bandy-legged, and curtailed of their fair proportions, even so, my dear middies, does it morally prove with some of you, who prematurely are sent off to sea.

These admonitions are solely addressed to the more diminutive class of midshipmen—those under five feet high, and under seven stone in weight.

Truly, the records of the steerages of men-of-war are full of most melancholy examples of early dissipation, disease, disgrace, and death. Answer, ye shades of fine boys, who in the soils of all climes, the round world over, far away sleep from your homes.

Mothers of men! If your hearts have been cast down when your boys have fallen in the way of temptations ashore, how much more bursting your grief, did you know that those boys were, far from your arms, cabined and cribbed in by all manner of iniquities. But this some of you cannot believe. It is, perhaps, well that it is so.

But, hold them fast—all those who have not yet weighed their anchors for the Navy—round and round, hitch over hitch, bind your leading-strings on them, and, clinching a ring-bolt into your chimney-jam, moor your boys fast to that best of harbours, the hearthstone.

But if youth be giddy, old age is staid; even as young saplings, in the litheness of their limbs, toss to their roots in the fresh morning air; but, stiff and unyielding with age, mossy trunks never bend. With pride and pleasure be it said, that, as for our old commodore, though he might treat himself to as many *liberty days* as he pleased, yet throughout our stay in Rio he conducted himself with the utmost discretion.

But he was an old, old man; physically, a very small man; his spine was as an unloaded musket-barrel—not only attenuated, but destitute of a solitary cartridge, and his ribs were as the ribs of a weasel.

Besides, he was commodore of the fleet, supreme lord of the Commons in Blue. It beseemed him, therefore, to erect himself into an ensample of virtue, and show the gun-deck what virtue was. But, alas! when Virtue sits high aloft on a frigate's poop, when Virtue is crowned in the cabin a commodore, when Virtue rules by compulsion, and domineers over Vice as a slave, then Virtue, though her mandates be outwardly observed, bears little interior sway. To be efficacious, Virtue must come down from aloft, even as our blessed Redeemer came down to redeem our whole man-of-war world; to that end, mixing with its sailors and sinners as equals.

LV

Midshipmen entering the Navy early

THE allusion in the preceding chapter to the early age at which some of the midshipmen enter the Navy suggests some thoughts relative to more important considerations.

A very general modern impression seems to be, that, in order to learn the profession of a sea-officer, a boy can hardly be sent to sea too early. To a certain extent, this may be a mistake. Other professions, involving a knowledge of technicalities, and things restricted to one particular field of action, are frequently mastered by men who begin after the age of twenty-one, or even at a later period of life. It was only about the middle of the seventeenth century that the British military and naval services were kept distinct. Previous to that epoch the king's officers commanded indifferently either by sea or by land.

Robert Blake, perhaps one of the most accomplished, and certainly one of the most successful admirals that ever hoisted a flag, was more than half a century old (fifty-one years) before he entered the naval service, or had aught to do, professionally, with a ship. He was of a studious turn, and, after leaving Oxford, resided quietly on his estate, a country gentleman, till his forty-second year, soon after which he became connected with the Parliamentary army.

The historian Clarendon says of him, 'He was the first man that made it manifest that the science (seamanship) might be attained in less time than was imagined.' And doubtless it was to his shore sympathies that the well-known humanity and kindness which Blake evinced in his intercourse with the sailors is in a large degree to be imputed.

Midshipmen sent into the Navy at a very early age are exposed to the passive reception of all the prejudices of the quarter-deck in favour of ancient usages, however useless or pernicious; those prejudices grow up with them, and solidify with their very bones. As they rise in rank, they naturally carry them up; whence the inveterate repugnance of many commodores and captains to the slightest innovations in the service, however salutary they may appear to landsmen.

It is hardly to be doubted that, in matters connected with the general welfare of the Navy, government has paid rather too much deference to the opinions of the officers of the Navy, considering them as men almost born to the service, and therefore far better qualified to judge concerning any and all questions touching it than people on shore. But in a nation under a liberal constitution, it must ever be unwise to make too distinct and peculiar the profession of either branch of its military men. True, in a country like ours, nothing is at present to be apprehended of their gaining political rule; but not a little is to be apprehended concerning their perpetuating or creating abuses among their subordinates, unless civilians have full cognizance of their administrative affairs, and account themselves competent to the complete overlooking and ordering them.

We do wrong when we in any way contribute to the prevailing mystification that has been thrown about the internal affairs of the national sea-service. Hitherto those affairs have been regarded even by some high state functionaries as things beyond their insight—altogether too technical and mysterious to be fully comprehended by landsmen. And this it is that has perpetuated in the Navy many evils that otherwise would have been abolished in the general amelioration of other things. The Army is sometimes remodelled, but the Navy goes down from generation to generation almost untouched and unquestioned, as if its code were infallible, and itself a piece of perfection that no statesman could improve. When a Secretary of the Navy ventures to innovate upon its established customs, you hear some of the Navy officers say, 'What does this landsman know about our affairs? Did he ever head a watch? He does not know starboard from larboard, girt-line from back-stay.'

While we deferentially and cheerfully leave to Navy officers the sole conduct of making and shortening sail, tacking ship, and performing other nautical manœuvres, as may seem to them best; let us beware of abandoning to their discretion those general municipal regulations touching the well-being of the great body of men before the mast; let us beware of being too much influenced by their opinions in matters where it is but natural to suppose that their long-established prejudices are enlisted.

LVI

A Shore Emperor on board a Man-of-war

WHILE we lay in Rio, we sometimes had company from shore; but an unforeseen honour awaited us. One day, the young Emperor, Don Pedro II,* and suite—making a circuit of the harbour, and visiting all the men-of-war in rotation—at last condescendingly visited the *Neversink*.

He came in a splendid barge, rowed by thirty African slaves, who, after the Brazilian manner, in concert rose upright to their oars at every stroke; then sank backward again to their seats with a simultaneous groan.

He reclined under a canopy of yellow silk, looped with tassels of green, the national colours. At the stern waved the Brazilian flag, bearing a large diamond figure in the centre, emblematical, perhaps, of the mines of precious stones in the interior; or, it may be, a magnified portrait of the famous 'Portuguese diamond' itself, which was found in Brazil, in the district of Tejuco, on the banks of the Rio Belmonte.

We gave them a grand salute, which almost made the ship's live-oak *knees* knock together with the tremendous concussions. We manned the yards, and went through a long ceremonial of paying the Emperor homage. Republicans are often more courteous to royalty than royalists themselves. But doubtless this springs from a noble magnanimity.

At the gangway, the Emperor was received by our commodore in person, arrayed in his most resplendent coat and finest French epaulets. His servant had devoted himself to polishing every button that morning with rotten-stone* and rags—your sea air is a sworn foe to metallic glosses; whence it comes that the swords of sea-officers have, of late, so rusted in their scabbards that they are with difficulty drawn.

It was a fine sight to see this Emperor and commodore complimenting each other. Both wore *chapeaux-de-bras*,* and both continually waved them. By instinct, the Emperor knew that the venerable personage before him was as much a monarch afloat as he himself was ashore. Did not our commodore carry the sword of state by his side? For though not borne before him, it must have been a sword of state, since it looked far too lustrous ever to have been his fighting sword. *That* was naught but a limber steel blade, with a plain, serviceable handle, like the handle of a slaughter-house knife.

Who ever saw a star when the noon sun was in sight? But you seldom see a king without satellites. In the suite of the youthful Emperor came a princely train; so brilliant with gems, that they seemed just emerged from the mines of the Rio Belmonte.

You have seen cones of crystallized salt? Just so flashed these Portuguese Barons, Marquises, Viscounts, and Counts. Were it not for their titles, and being seen in the train of their lord, you would have sworn they were eldest sons of jewellers all, who had run away with their fathers' cases on their backs.

Contrasted with these lamp-lustres of Barons of Brazil, how waned the gold lace of our barons of the frigate, the officers of the gun-room! and compared with the long, jewel-hilted rapiers of the Marquises, the little dirks of our cadets of noble houses—the middies—looked like gilded tenpenny nails in their girdles.

But there they stood! Commodore and Emperor, Lieutenants and Marquises, middies and pages! The brazen band on the poop struck up; the marine guard presented arms; and high aloft, looking down on this scene, all *the people* vigorously hurrahed. A top-man next me on the main-royal-yard removed his hat, and diligently manipulated his head in honour of the event; but he was so far out of sight in the clouds, that this ceremony went for nothing.

A great pity it was, that in addition to all these honours, that admirer of Portuguese literature, Viscount Strangford,* of Great Britain—who, I believe, once went out Ambassador Extraordinary to the Brazils—it was a pity that he was not present on this occasion, to yield his tribute of *A Stanza to Braganza*! For our royal visitor was an undoubted Braganza, allied to nearly all the great families of Europe. His grandfather, John VI, had been King of Portugal; his own sister, Maria, was now its Queen. He was, indeed, a distinguished young gentleman, entitled to high consideration, and that consideration was most cheerfully accorded him.

He wore a green dress-coat, with one regal morning-star at the breast, and white pantaloons. In his chapeau was a single, bright, golden-hued feather of the imperial toucan fowl, a magnificent, omnivorous, broad-billed bandit bird of prey, a native of Brazil. Its perch is on the loftiest trees, whence it looks down upon all humbler fowls, and, hawk-like, flies at their throats. The toucan once formed part of the savage regalia of the Indian caciques* of the country, and, upon the establishment of the empire, was symbolically retained by the Portuguese sovereigns.

His Imperial Majesty was yet in his youth; rather corpulent, if anything; with a care-free, pleasant face, and a polite, indifferent, and easy address. His manners, indeed, were entirely unexceptionable.

Now here, thought I, is a very fine lad, with very fine prospects before him. He is supreme Emperor of all these Brazils; he has no stormy night-watches to stand; he can lay abed of mornings just as long as he pleases. Any gentleman in Rio would be proud of his personal acquaintance, and the prettiest girl in all South America would deem herself honoured with the least glance from the acutest angle of his eye.

Yes: this young Emperor will have a fine time of this life, even so long as he condescends to exist. Everyone jumps to obey him; and see, as I live, there is an old nobleman in his suite—the Marquis d'Acarty they call him, old enough to be his grandfather—who, in the hot sun, is standing bare-headed before him, while the Emperor carries his hat on his head.

'I suppose that old gentleman, now,' said a young New-England tar beside me, 'would consider it a great honour to put on his Royal Majesty's boots; and yet, White-Jacket, if yonder Emperor and I were to strip and jump overboard for a bath, it would be hard telling which was of the blood royal when we should once be in the water. Look you, Don Pedro II,' he added, 'how do you come to be Emperor? Tell me that. You cannot pull as many pounds as I on the main-topsail-halyards; you are not as tall as I; your nose is a pug, and mine is a cut-water; and how do you come to be a *brigand*, with that thin pair of spars? A *brigand*, indeed!'

'*Braganza*, you mean,' said I, willing to correct the rhetoric of so fierce a republican, and, by so doing, chastise his censoriousness.

'Braganza! *bragger* it is,' he replied; 'and a bragger, indeed. See that feather in his cap. See how he struts in that coat! He may well wear a green one, top-mates—he's a green-looking swab at the best.'

'Hush, Jonathan,' said I; 'there's the *first luff* looking up. Be still! the Emperor will hear you'; and I put my hand on his mouth.

'Take your hand away, White-Jacket,' he cried; 'there's no law up aloft here. I say, you Emperor—you greenhorn in the green coat, there—look you, you can't raise a pair of whiskers yet; and see what a pair of homeward-bounders I have on my jowls! *Don Pedro*, eh? What's that, after all, but plain Peter—reckoned a shabby name in my country. Damn me, White-Jacket, I wouldn't call my dog Peter!'

'Clap a stopper on your jaw-tackle, will you?' cried Ring-bolt, the sailor on the other side of him. 'You'll be getting us all into darbies*for this.'

'I won't trice up my red rag for nobody,' retorted Jonathan. 'So you had better take a round turn with yours, Ring-bolt, and let me alone, or I'll fetch you such a swat over your figure-head, you'll think a Long Wharf truck-horse kicked you with all four shoes on one hoof! You Emperor—you counter-jumping son of a gun—cock your weather eye up aloft here, and see your betters! I say, top-mates, he ain't any Emperor at all—*I'm* the rightful Emperor. Yes, by the commodore's boots! they stole me out of my cradle here in the palace at Rio, and put that greenhorn in my place. Ay, you timberhead, you, I'm Don Pedro II, and by good rights you ought to be a maintop-man here, with your fist in a tar-bucket! Look you, I say, that crown of yours ought to be on my head; or, if you don't believe *that*, just heave it into the ring once, and see who's the best man.'

'What's this hurrah's nest here aloft?' cried Jack Chase, coming up the t'gallant rigging from the topsail-yard. 'Can't you behave yourself, royal-yard-men, when an emperor's on board?'

'It's this here Jonathan,' answered Ringbolt; 'he's been blackguarding the young nob in the green coat, there. He says Don Pedro stole his hat.'

'How?'

'Crown, he means, noble Jack,' said a top-man.

'Jonathan don't call himself an emperor, does he?' asked Jack.

'Yes,' cried Jonathan; 'that greenhorn standing there by the commodore is sailing under false colours; he's an impostor, I say; he wears my crown.'

'Ha! ha!' laughed Jack, now seeing into the joke, and willing to humour it; 'though I'm born a Briton, boys, yet, by the mast! these Don Pedros are all Perkin Warbecks.* But I say, Jonathan, my lad, don't pipe your eye now about the loss of your crown; for, look you, we all wear crowns, from our cradles to our graves, and though in *double-darbies* in the *brig*, the commodore himself can't unking us.'

'A riddle, noble Jack.'

'Not a bit; every man who has a sole to his foot has a crown to his head. Here's mine'; and so saying, Jack, removing his tarpaulin, exhibited a bald spot, just about the bigness of a crown-piece, on the summit of his curly and classical head.

LVII

The Emperor reviews 'the People' at Quarters

I BEG their Royal Highnesses' pardons all round, but I had almost forgotten to chronicle the fact, that with the Emperor came several other royal princes—kings, for aught we knew —since it was just after the celebration of the nuptials of a younger sister of the Brazilian monarch to some European royalty. Indeed, the Emperor and his suite formed a sort of bridal party, only the bride herself was absent.

The first reception over, the smoke of the cannonading salute having cleared away, and the martial outburst of the brass band having also rolled off to leeward, the people were called down from the yards, and the drum beat to quarters.

To quarters we went; and there we stood up by our iron bulldogs, while our royal and noble visitors promenaded along the batteries, breaking out into frequent exclamations at our warlike array, the extreme neatness of our garments, and, above all, the extraordinary polish of the *bright-work* about the great guns, and the marvellous whiteness of the decks.

'Que gosto!' cried a Marquis, with several dry goods samples of ribbon, tallied with bright buttons, hanging from his breast.

'Que gloria!' cried a crooked, coffee-coloured Viscount, spreading both palms.

'Que alegria!' cried a little Count, mincingly circum-navigating a shot-box.

'Que contentamento he o meu!' cried the Emperor him-self, complacently folding his royal arms, and serenely gazing along our ranks.

Pleasure, *Glory* and *Joy*—this was the burden of the three noble courtiers. *And very pleasing indeed*—was the simple rendering of Don Pedro's imperial remark.

'Ay, ay,' growled a grim rammer-and-sponger behind me; "it's all devilish fine for you nobs to look at; but what would you say if you had to holy-stone the deck yourselves, and wear out your elbows in polishing this cursed old iron, besides getting a dozen at the gangway, if you dropped a grease-spot on deck in your mess? Ay, ay, devilish fine for you, but devilish dull for us!'

In due time the drums beat the retreat, and the ship's company scattered over the decks.

Some of the officers now assumed the part of cicerones, to show the distinguished strangers the bowels of the frigate, concerning which several of them showed a good deal of intelligent curiosity. A guard of honour, detached from the marine corps, accompanied them, and they made the circuit of the berth-deck, where, at a judicious distance, the Emperor peeped down into the cable-tier,* a very subterranean vault.

The captain of the main hold, who there presided, made a .polite bow in the twilight, and respectfully expressed a desire for His Royal Majesty to step down and honour him with a call; but, with his handkerchief to his Imperial nose, His Majesty declined. The party then commenced the ascent to the spar-deck; which, from so great a depth in a frigate, is something like getting up to the top of Bunker Hill Monument from the basement.

While a crowd of the people was gathered about the forward part of the booms, a sudden cry was heard from below; a lieutenant came running forward to learn the cause, when an old sheet-anchor-man, standing by, after touching his hat, hitched up his waistbands, and replied, 'I don't know, sir, but I'm thinking as how one o' them 'ere kings has been tumblin' down the hatchway.'

And something like this it turned out. In ascending one of the narrow ladders leading from the berth-deck to the gun-deck, the Most Noble Marquis of Silva, in the act of elevating the Imperial coat-tails, so as to protect them from rubbing against the newly painted combings of the hatchway, this Noble Marquis's sword, being an uncommonly long one, had caught between his legs, and tripped him head over heels down into the fore-passage.

'Onde ides?' (Where are you going?) said his royal master, tranquilly peeping down toward the falling Marquis; 'and what did you let go of my coat-tails for?' he suddenly added, in a passion, glancing round at the same time, to see if they had suffered from the unfaithfulness of his train-bearer.

'Oh, Lord!' sighed the captain of the foretop, 'who would be a Marquis of Silva?'

Upon being assisted to the spar-deck, the unfortunate Marquis was found to have escaped without serious harm; but, from the marked coolness of his royal master, when the Marquis drew near to apologize for his awkwardness, it was plain that he was condemned to languish for a time under the royal displeasure.

Shortly after, the Imperial party withdrew, under another grand national salute.

LVIII

A Quarter-deck Officer before the Mast

As we were somewhat short-handed while we lay in Rio, we received a small draft of men from a United States sloop of war, whose three years' term of service would expire about the time of our arrival in America.

Under guard of an armed lieutenant and four midshipmen, they came on board in the afternoon. They were immediately mustered in the starboard gangway, that Mr. Bridewell, our first lieutenant, might take down their names, and assign them their stations.

They stood in a mute and solemn row; the officer advanced, with his memorandum-book and pencil.

My casual friend, Shakings, the holder, happened to be by at the time. Touching my arm, he said, 'White-Jacket, this here reminds me of Sing Sing, when a draft of fellows, in darbies, came on from the state prison at Auburn for a change of scene like, you know!'

After taking down four or five names, Mr. Bridewell

accosted the next man, a rather good-looking person, but, from his haggard cheek and sunken eye, he seemed to have been in the sad habit, all his life, of sitting up rather late at night; and though all sailors do certainly keep late hours enough—standing watches at midnight—yet there is no small difference between keeping late hours at sea and keeping late hours ashore.

'What's your name?' asked the officer, of this rather rakish-looking recruit.

'Mandeville, sir,' said the man, courteously touching his cap. 'You must remember me, sir,' he added, in a low, confidential tone, strangely dashed with servility; 'we sailed together once in the old *Macedonian*, sir. I wore an epaulet then; we had the same state-room, you know, sir. I'm your old chum, Mandeville, sir,' and he again touched his cap.

'I remember an *officer* by that name,' said the first lieutenant, emphatically, 'and I know *you*, fellow. But I know you henceforth for a common sailor. I can show no favouritism here. If you ever violate the ship's rules, you shall be flogged like any other seaman. I place you in the foretop; go forward to your duty.'

It seemed this Mandeville had entered the Navy when very young, and had risen to be a lieutenant, as he said. But brandy had been his bane. One night, when he had the deck of a line-of-battle ship, in the Mediterranean, he was seized with a fit of mania-a-potu, and, being out of his senses for the time, went below and turned into his berth, leaving the deck without a commanding officer. For this unpardonable offence he was broken.

Having no fortune, and no other profession than the sea, upon his disgrace he entered the merchant-service as a chief mate; but his love of strong drink still pursuing him, he was again cashiered at sea, and degraded before the mast by the captain. After this, in a state of intoxication, he re-entered the Navy at Pensacola as a common sailor. But all these lessons, so biting-bitter to learn, could not cure him of his sin. He had hardly been a week on board the *Neversink*, when he was found intoxicated with smuggled spirits. They lashed him to the gratings, and ignominiously scourged him under the eye of his old friend and comrade, the first lieutenant.

This took place while we lay in port, which reminds me of the circumstance, that when punishment is about to be inflicted in harbour, all strangers are ordered ashore; and the sentries at the side have it in strict charge to waive off all boats drawing near.

LIX

A Man-of-war Button divides two Brothers

THE conduct of Mandeville, in claiming the acquaintance of the first lieutenant under such disreputable circumstances, was strongly contrasted by the behaviour of another person on board, placed for a time in a somewhat similar situation.

Among the genteel youths of the after-guard was a lad of about sixteen, a very handsome young fellow, with starry eyes, curly hair of a golden colour, and a bright, sunshiny complexion: he must have been the son of some goldsmith. He was one of the few sailors—not in the maintop—whom I used to single out for occasional conversation. After several friendly interviews he became quite frank, and communicated certain portions of his history. There is some charm in the sea, which induces most persons to be very communicative concerning themselves.

We had lain in Rio but a day, when I observed that this lad—whom I shall here call Frank—wore an unwonted expression of sadness, mixed with apprehension. I questioned him as to the cause, but he chose to conceal it. Not three days after, he abruptly accosted me on the gun-deck, where I happened to be taking a promenade.

'I can't keep it to myself any more,' he said; 'I must have a confidant, or I shall go mad!'

'What is the matter?' said I, in alarm.

'Matter enough—look at this!' and he handed me a torn half sheet of an old *New York Herald*, putting his finger upon a particular word in a particular paragraph. It was the announcement of the sailing from the Brooklyn Navy Yard of a United States store-ship, with provisions for the squadron in Rio. It was upon a particular name, in the list of officers and midshipmen, that Frank's finger was placed.

'That is my own brother,' said he; 'he must have got a reefer's warrant since I left home. Now, White-Jacket, what's to be done? I have calculated that the store-ship may be expected here every day; my brother will then see me— he an officer, and I a miserable sailor that any moment may be flogged at the gangway, before his very eyes. Heavens! White-Jacket, what shall I do? Would you run? Do you think there is any chance to desert? I won't see him, by Heaven, with this sailor's frock on, and he with the anchor button!'

'Why, Frank,' said I, 'I do not really see sufficient cause for this fit you are in. Your brother is an officer—very good; and you are nothing but a sailor—but that is no disgrace. If he comes on board here, go up to him, and take him by the hand; believe me, he will be glad enough to see you!'

Frank started from his desponding attitude, and fixing his eyes full upon mine, with clasped hands exclaimed, 'White-Jacket, I have been from home nearly three years; in that time I have never heard one word from my family, and, though God knows how I love them, yet I swear to you, that though my brother can tell me whether my sisters are still alive, yet, rather than accost him in this *lined frock*,* I would go ten centuries without hearing one syllable from home!'

Amazed at his earnestness, and hardly able to account for it altogether, I stood silent a moment; then said, 'Why, Frank, this midshipman is your own brother, you say; now, do you really think that your own flesh and blood is going to give himself airs over you, simply because he sports large brass buttons on his coat? Never believe it. If he does, he can be no brother, and ought to be hanged—that's all!'

'Don't say that again,' said Frank, resentfully; 'my brother is a noble-hearted fellow; I love him as I do myself. You don't understand me, White-Jacket; don't you see, that when my brother arrives, he must consort more or less with our chuckle-headed reefers on board here? There's that namby-pamby Miss Nancy of a white-face, Stribbles, who, the other day, when Mad Jack's back was turned, ordered me to hand him the spyglass, as if he were a commodore. Do you suppose, now, I want my brother to see me a lackey aboard here? By Heaven, it is enough to drive one distracted! What's to be done?' he cried, fiercely.

Much more passed between us, but all my philosophy was in vain, and at last Frank departed, his head hanging down in despondency.

For several days after, whenever the quarter-master reported a sail entering the harbour, Frank was foremost in the rigging to observe it. At length, one afternoon, a vessel drawing near was reported to be the long-expected store-ship. I looked round for Frank on the spar-deck, but he was nowhere to be seen. He must have been below, gazing out of a port-hole. The vessel was hailed from our poop, and came to anchor within a biscuit's toss of our batteries.

That evening I heard that Frank had ineffectually endeavoured to get removed from his place as an oarsman in the first cutter—a boat which, from its size, is generally employed with the *launch* in carrying ship-stores. When I thought that, the very next day, perhaps, this boat would be plying between the store-ship and our frigate, I was at no loss to account for Frank's attempts to get rid of his oar, and felt heartily grieved at their failure.

Next morning the bugler called away the first cutter's crew, and Frank entered the boat with his hat slouched over his eyes. Upon his return, I was all eagerness to learn what had happened, and as the communication of his feelings was a grateful relief, he poured his whole story into my ear.

It seemed that, with his comrades, he mounted the store-ship's side, and hurried forward to the forecastle. Then, turning anxiously toward the quarter-deck, he spied two midshipmen leaning against the bulwarks, conversing. One was the officer of his boat—was the other his brother? No; he was too tall—too large. Thank Heaven! it was *not* him. And perhaps his brother had not sailed from home, after all; there might have been some mistake. But suddenly the strange midshipman laughed aloud, and that laugh Frank had heard a thousand times before. It was a free, hearty laugh—a brother's laugh; but it carried a pang to the heart of poor Frank.

He was now ordered down to the main-deck to assist in removing the stores. The boat being loaded, he was ordered into her, when, looking toward the gangway, he perceived the two midshipmen lounging upon each side of it, so that no one could pass them without brushing their persons. But again pulling his hat over his eyes, Frank, darting between them, gained his oar. 'How my heart thumped,' he said, 'when I actually *felt* him so near me; but I wouldn't look at him—no! I'd have died first!'

To Frank's great relief, the store-ship at last moved further up the bay, and it fortunately happened that he saw no more of his brother while in Rio; and while there, he never in any way made himself known to him.

LX

A Man-of-war's-man shot at

THERE was a seaman belonging to the foretop—a messmate, though not a top-mate of mine, and no favourite of the captain's—who, for certain venial transgressions, had been prohibited from going ashore on liberty when the ship's company went. Enraged at the deprivation—for he had not touched earth in upward of a year—he, some nights after, lowered himself overboard, with the view of gaining a canoe, attached by a rope to a Dutch galiot*some cables'-length distant. In this canoe he proposed paddling himself ashore. Not being a very expert swimmer, the commotion he made in the water attracted the ear of the sentry on that side of the ship, who, turning about in his walk, perceived the faint white spot where the fugitive was swimming in the frigate's shadow. He hailed it; but no reply.

'Give the word, or I fire!'

Not a word was heard.

The next instant there was a red flash, and, before it had completely ceased illuminating the night, the white spot was changed into crimson. Some of the officers, returning from a party at the Beach of the Flamingoes, happened to be drawing near the ship in one of her cutters. They saw the flash, and the bounding body it revealed. In a moment the topman was dragged into the boat, a handkerchief was used for a tourniquet, and the wounded fugitive was soon on board the frigate, when, the surgeon being called, the necessary attentions were rendered.

Now, it appeared, that at the moment the sentry fired, the top-man—in order to elude discovery, by manifesting the completest quietude—was floating on the water, straight and horizontal, as if reposing on a bed. As he was not far from the ship at the time, and the sentry was considerably elevated above him—pacing his platform, on a level with the upper part of the hammock-nettings—the ball struck with great force, with a downward obliquity, entering the right thigh just above the knee, and, penetrating some inches, glanced upward along the bone, burying itself somewhere, so that it could not be felt by outward manipulation. There was no dusky discoloration to mark its internal track, as in the case when a partly spent ball—obliquely hitting—after entering the skin, courses on, just beneath the surface, without penetrating further. Nor was there any mark on the opposite part of the thigh to denote its place, as when a ball forces itself straight through a limb, and lodges, perhaps, close to the skin on the other side. Nothing was visible but a small, ragged puncture, bluish about the edges, as if the rough point of a tenpenny nail had been forced into the flesh, and withdrawn. It seemed almost impossible, that through so small an aperture, a musket bullet could have penetrated.

The extreme misery and general prostration of the man,

caused by the great effusion of blood—though, strange to say, at first he said he felt no pain from the wound itself—induced the surgeon, very reluctantly, to forgo an immediate search for the ball, to extract it, as that would have involved the dilating of the wound by the knife; an operation which, at that juncture, would have been almost certainly attended with fatal results. A day or two, therefore, was permitted to pass, while simple dressings were applied.

The surgeons of the other American ships of war in harbour occasionally visited the *Neversink*, to examine the patient, and incidentally to listen to the expositions of our own surgeon, their senior in rank. But Cadwallader Cuticle, who, as yet, has been but incidentally alluded to, now deserves a chapter by himself.

LXI

The Surgeon of the Fleet

CADWALLADER CUTICLE, M.D., and Honorary Member of the most distinguished Colleges of Surgeons both in Europe and America, was our Surgeon of the Fleet. Nor was he at all blind to the dignity of his position; to which, indeed, he was rendered peculiarly competent, if the reputation he enjoyed was deserved. He had the name of being the foremost surgeon in the Navy, a gentleman of remarkable science and a veteran practitioner.

He was a small, withered man, nearly, perhaps quite, sixty years of age. His chest was shallow, his shoulders bent, his pantaloons hung round skeleton legs, and his face was singularly attenuated. In truth, the corporeal vitality of this man seemed, in a good degree, to have died out of him. He walked abroad, a curious patchwork of life and death, with a wig, one glass eye, and a set of false teeth, while his voice was husky and thick; but his mind seemed undebilitated as in youth; it shone out of his remaining eye with basilisk brilliancy.

Like most old physicians and surgeons who have seen

much service, and have been promoted to high professional place for their scientific attainments, this Cuticle was an enthusiast in his calling. In private, he had once been heard to say, confidentially, that he would rather cut off a man's arm than dismember the wing of the most delicate pheasant. In particular, the department of Morbid Anatomy was his peculiar love; and in his state-room below he had a most unsightly collection of Parisian casts, in plaster and wax, representing all imaginable malformations of the human members, both organic and induced by disease. Chief among these was a cast, often to be met with in the anatomical museums of Europe, and no doubt an unexaggerated copy of a genuine original; it was the head of an elderly woman, with an aspect singularly gentle and meek, but at the same time wonderfully expressive of a gnawing sorrow, never to be relieved. You would almost have thought it the face of some abbess, for some unspeakable crime voluntarily sequestered from human society, and leading a life of agonized penitence without hope, so marvellously sad and tearfully pitiable was this head. But when you first beheld it, no such emotions ever crossed your mind. All your eyes and all your horrified soul were fast fascinated and frozen by the sight of a hideous, crumpled horn, like that of a ram, downward growing out from the forehead, and partly shadowing the face; but as you gazed, the freezing fascination of its horribleness gradually waned, and then your whole heart burst with sorrow, as you contemplated those aged features, ashy, pale and wan. The horn seemed the mark of a curse for some mysterious sin, conceived and committed before the spirit had entered the flesh. Yet that sin seemed something imposed, and not voluntarily sought; some sin growing out of the heartless necessities of the predestination of things; some sin under which the sinner sank in sinless woe.

But no pang of pain, not the slightest touch of concern, ever crossed the bosom of Cuticle when he looked on this cast. It was immovably fixed to a bracket, against the partition of his state-room, so that it was the first object that greeted his eyes when he opened them from his nightly sleep. Nor was it to hide the face, that upon retiring he always hung his Navy cap upon the upward curling extremity of the horn, for that obscured it but little.

The surgeon's cot-boy, the lad who made up his swinging bed and took care of his room, often told us of the horror he sometimes felt when he would find himself alone in his master's retreat. At times he was seized with the idea that Cuticle was a preternatural being; and once entering his room in the middle watch of the night, he started at finding it enveloped in a thick, bluish vapour, and stifling with the odours of brimstone. Upon hearing a low groan from the smoke, with a wild cry he darted from the place, and, rousing the occupants of the neighbouring state-rooms, it was found that the vapour proceeded from smouldering bunches of Lucifer matches, which had become ignited through the carelessness of the surgeon. Cuticle, almost dead, was dragged from the suffocating atmosphere, and it was several days ere he completely recovered from its effects. This accident took place immediately over the powder magazine; but as Cuticle, during his sickness, paid dearly enough for transgressing the laws prohibiting combustibles in the gun-room, the captain contented himself with privately remonstrating with him.

Well knowing the enthusiasm of the surgeon for all specimens of morbid anatomy, some of the ward-room officers used to play upon his credulity, though, in every case, Cuticle was not long in discovering their deceptions. Once, when they had some sago pudding for dinner, and Cuticle chanced to be ashore, they made up a neat parcel of this bluish-white, firm, jelly-like preparation, and placing it in a tin box, carefully sealed with wax, they deposited it on the gun-room table, with a note, purporting to come from an eminent physician in Rio, connected with the Grand National Museum on the Praca d'Acclamacao, begging leave to present the scientific Senhor Cuticle—with the donor's compliments—an uncommonly fine specimen of a cancer.

Descending to the ward-room, Cuticle spied the note, and no sooner read it, than, clutching the case, he opened it, and exclaimed, 'Beautiful! splendid! I have never seen a finer specimen of this most interesting disease.'

'What have you there, Surgeon Cuticle?' said a lieutenant, advancing.

'Why, sir, look at it; did you ever see anything more exquisite?'

'Very exquisite, indeed; let me have a bit of it, will you, Cuticle?'

'Let you have a bit of it!' shrieked the surgeon, starting back. 'Let you have one of my limbs! I wouldn't mar so large a specimen for a hundred dollars; but what can you want of it? You are not making collections!'

'I'm fond of the article,' said the lieutenant; 'it's a fine cold relish to bacon or ham. You know, I was in New Zealand last cruise, Cuticle, and got into sad dissipation there among the cannibals; come, let's have a bit, if it's only a mouthful.'

'Why, you infernal Feejee!' shouted Cuticle, eyeing the other with a confounded expression; 'you don't really mean to eat a piece of this cancer?'

'Hand it to me, and see whether I will not,' was the reply.

'In God's name, take it!' cried the surgeon, putting the case into his hands, and then standing with his own uplifted.

'Steward!' cried the lieutenant, 'the castor—quick! I always use plenty of pepper with this dish, surgeon; it's oystery. Ah! this is really delicious,' he added, smacking his lips over a mouthful. 'Try it now, surgeon, and you'll never keep such a fine dish as this, lying uneaten on your hands, as a mere scientific curiosity.'

Cuticle's whole countenance changed; and, slowly walking up to the table, he put his nose close to the tin case, then touched its contents with his finger and tasted it. Enough. Buttoning up his coat, in all the tremblings of an old man's rage, he burst from the ward-room, and, calling for a boat, was not seen again for twenty-four hours.

But though, like all other mortals, Cuticle was subject at

times to these fits of passion—at least under outrageous provocation—nothing could exceed his coolness when actually
employed in his imminent vocation. Surrounded by moans
and shrieks, by features distorted with anguish inflicted by
himself, he yet maintained a countenance almost super-
naturally calm; and unless the intense interest of the
operation flushed his wan face with a momentary tinge of
professional enthusiasm, he toiled away, untouched by the
keenest misery coming under a fleet-surgeon's eye. Indeed,
long habituation to the dissecting-room and the amputation-
table had made him seemingly impervious to the ordinary
emotions of humanity. Yet you could not say that Cuticle
was essentially a cruel-hearted man. His apparent heartless-
ness must have been of a purely scientific origin. It is not to
be imagined even that Cuticle would have harmed a fly,
unless he could procure a microscope powerful enough to
assist him in experimenting on the minute vitals of the
creature.

But notwithstanding his marvellous indifference to the
sufferings of his patients, and spite even of his enthusiasm
in his vocation—not cooled by frosting old age itself—
Cuticle, on some occasions, would affect a certain disrelish
of his profession, and declaim against the necessity that
forced a man of his humanity to perform a surgical operation.
Especially was it apt to be thus with him, when the case was
one of more than ordinary interest. In discussing it, previous
to setting about it, he would veil his eagerness under an
aspect of great circumspection, curiously marred, however,
by continual sallies of unsuppressible impatience. But the
knife once in his hand, the compassionless surgeon himself, undisguised, stood before you. Such was Cadwallader
Cuticle, our Surgeon of the Fleet.

LXII

A Consultation of Man-of-war Surgeons

IT seems customary for the surgeon of the fleet, when any important operation in his department is on the anvil, and there is nothing to absorb professional attention from it, to invite his brother surgeons, if at hand at the time, to a ceremonious consultation upon it. And this, in courtesy, his brother surgeons expect.

In pursuance of this custom, then, the surgeons of the neighbouring American ships of war were requested to visit the *Neversink* in a body, to advise concerning the case of the top-man, whose situation had now become critical. They assembled on the half-deck, and were soon joined by their respected senior, Cuticle. In a body they bowed as he approached, and accosted him with deferential regard.

'Gentlemen,' said Cuticle, unostentatiously seating himself on a camp-stool, handed him by his cot-boy, 'we have here an extremely interesting case. You have all seen the patient, I believe. At first I had hopes that I should have been able to cut down to the ball, and remove it; but the state of the patient forbade. Since then, the inflammation and sloughing of the part has been attended with a copious suppuration, great loss of substance, extreme debility and emaciation. From this, I am convinced that the ball has shattered and deadened the bone, and now lies impacted in the medullary canal. In fact, there can be no doubt that the wound is incurable, and that amputation is the only resource. But, gentlemen, I find myself placed in a very delicate predicament. I assure you I feel no professional anxiety to perform the operation. I desire your advice, and if you will now again visit the patient with me, we can then return here, and decide what is best to be done. Once more let me say, that I feel no personal anxiety whatever to use the knife.'

The assembled surgeons listened to this address with the most serious attention, and, in accordance with their superior's desire, now descended to the sick-bay, where the patient was languishing. The examination concluded, they returned to the half-deck, and the consultation was renewed.

'Gentlemen,' began Cuticle, again seating himself, 'you have now just inspected the limb; you have seen that there is no resource but amputation; and now, gentlemen, what do you say? Surgeon Bandage, of the *Mohawk*, will you express your opinion?'

'The wound is a very serious one,' said Bandage—a corpulent man, with a high German forehead—shaking his head solemnly.

'Can anything save him but amputation?' demanded Cuticle.

'His constitutional debility is extreme,' observed Bandage, 'but I have seen more dangerous cases.'

'Surgeon Wedge, of the *Malay*,' said Cuticle, in a pet, 'be pleased to give *your* opinion; and let it be definitive, I entreat': this was said with a severe glance toward Bandage.

'If I thought,' began Wedge, a very spare, tall man, elevating himself still higher on his toes, 'that the ball had shattered and divided the whole *femur*, including the *Greater* and *Lesser Trochanter*, the *Linea aspera*, the *Digital fossa*, and the *Intertrochanteric*, I should certainly be in favour of amputation; but that, sir, permit me to observe, is not my opinion.'

'Surgeon Sawyer, of the *Buccaneer*,' said Cuticle, drawing in his thin lower lip with vexation, and turning to a round-faced, florid, frank, sensible-looking man, whose uniform coat very handsomely fitted him, and was adorned with an unusual quantity of gold lace; 'Surgeon Sawyer, of the *Buccaneer*, let us now hear *your* opinion, if you please. Is not amputation the only resource, sir?'

'Excuse me,' said Sawyer, 'I am decidedly opposed to it; for if hitherto the patient has not been strong enough to undergo the extraction of the ball, I do not see how he can be expected to endure a far more severe operation. As there is no immediate danger of mortification, and you say the ball cannot be reached without making large incisions, I should support him, I think, for the present, with tonics, and gentle antiphlogistics,*locally applied. On no account would I proceed to amputation until further symptoms are exhibited.'

'Surgeon Patella, of the *Algerine,*' said Cuticle, in an ill-suppressed passion, abruptly turning round on the person addressed, 'will *you* have the kindness to say whether *you* do not think that amputation is the only resource?'

Now Patella was the youngest of the company, a modest man, filled with a profound reverence for the science of Cuticle, and desirous of gaining his good opinion, yet not wishing to commit himself altogether by a decided reply, though, like Surgeon Sawyer, in his own mind he might have been clearly against the operation.

'What you have remarked, Mr. Surgeon of the Fleet,' said Patella, respectfully hemming, 'concerning the dangerous condition of the limb, seems obvious enough; amputation would certainly be a cure to the wound; but then, as, not-withstanding his present debility, the patient seems to have a strong constitution, he might rally as it is, and by your scientific treatment, Mr. Surgeon of the Fleet'—bowing—'be entirely made whole, without risking amputation. Still, it is a very critical case, and amputation may be indispens-able; and, if it *is* to be performed, there ought to be no delay whatever. That is my view of the case, Mr. Surgeon of the Fleet.'

'Surgeon Patella, then, gentlemen,' said Cuticle, turning round triumphantly, 'is clearly of opinion that amputation should be immediately performed. For my own part—individually, I mean, and without respect to the patient—I am sorry to have it so decided. But this settles the question, gentlemen—in my own mind, however, it was settled before. At ten o'clock to-morrow morning the operation will be per-formed. I shall be happy to see you all on the occasion, and also your juniors' (alluding to the absent assistant surgeons). 'Good morning, gentlemen; at ten o'clock, remember.'

And Cuticle retreated to the ward-room.

LXIII

The Operation

NEXT morning, at the appointed hour, the surgeons arrived in a body. They were accompanied by their juniors, young men ranging in age from nineteen years to thirty. Like the senior surgeons, these young gentlemen were arrayed in their blue navy uniforms, displaying a profusion of bright buttons, and several broad bars of gold lace about the wristbands. As in honour of the occasion, they had put on their best coats; they looked exceedingly brilliant.

The whole party immediately descended to the half-deck, where preparations had been made for the operation. A large garrison-ensign was stretched across the ship by the mainmast, so as completely to screen the space behind. This space included the whole extent aft to the bulkhead of the commodore's cabin, at the door of which the marine orderly paced, in plain sight, cutlass in hand.

Upon two gun-carriages, dragged amidships, the death-board (used for burials at sea) was horizontally placed, covered with an old royal-stun'-sail. Upon this occasion, to do duty as an amputation-table, it was widened by an additional plank. Two match-tubs, near by, placed one upon another, at either end supported another plank, distinct from the table, whereon was exhibited an array of saws and knives of various and peculiar shapes and sizes; also, a sort of steel, something like the dinner-table implement, together with long needles, crooked at the end for taking up the arteries, and large darning-needles, thread, and beeswax, for sewing up a wound.

At the end nearest the larger table was a tin basin of water, surrounded by small sponges, placed at mathematical intervals. From the long horizontal pole of a great-gun rammer—fixed in its usual place overhead—hung a number of towels, with 'U.S.' marked in the corners.

All these arrangements had been made by the 'surgeon's

steward', a person whose important functions in a man-of-war will, in a future chapter, be entered upon at large. Upon the present occasion, he was bustling about, adjusting and readjusting the knives, needles, and carver, like an over-conscientious butler fidgeting over a dinner-table just before the convivialists enter.

But by far the most striking object to be seen behind the ensign was a human skeleton, whose every joint articulated with wires. By a rivet at the apex of the skull, it hung dangling from a hammock-hook fixed in a beam above. Why this object was here will presently be seen; but why it was placed immediately at the foot of the amputation-table, only Surgeon Cuticle can tell.

While the final preparations were being made, Cuticle stood conversing with the assembled surgeons and assistant surgeons, his invited guests.

'Gentlemen,' said he, taking up one of the glittering knives, and artistically drawing the steel across it; 'Gentlemen, though these scenes are very unpleasant, and in some moods, I may say, repulsive to me—yet how much better for our patient to have the contusions and lacerations of his present wound—with all its dangerous symptoms—converted into a clean incision, free from these objections, and occasioning so much less subsequent anxiety to himself and the surgeon! Yes,' he added, tenderly feeling the edge of his knife, 'amputation is our only resource. Is it not so, Surgeon Patella?' turning toward that gentleman, as if relying upon some sort of an assent, however clogged with conditions.

'Certainly,' said Patella, 'amputation is your only resource, Mr. Surgeon of the Fleet; that is, I mean, if you are fully persuaded of its necessity.'

The other surgeons said nothing, maintaining a somewhat reserved air, as if conscious that they had no positive authority in the case, whatever might be their own private opinions; but they seemed willing to behold, and, if called upon, to assist at the operation, since it could not now be averted.

The young men, their assistants, looked very eager, and cast frequent glances of awe upon so distinguished a practitioner as the venerable Cuticle.

'They say he can drop a leg in one minute and ten seconds from the moment the knife touches it,' whispered one of them to another.

'We shall see,' was the reply; and the speaker clapped his hand to his fob, to see if his watch would be forthcoming when wanted.

'Are you all ready here?' demanded Cuticle, now advancing to his steward; 'have not those fellows got through yet?' pointing to three men of the carpenter's gang, who were placing bits of wood under the gun-carriages supporting the central table.

'They are just through, sir,' respectfully answered the steward, touching his hand to his forehead, as if there were a cap-front there.

'Bring up the patient, then,' said Cuticle.

'Young gentlemen,' he added, turning to the row of assistant surgeons, 'seeing you here reminds me of the classes of students once under my instruction at the Philadelphia College of Physicians and Surgeons. Ah, those were happy days!' he sighed, applying the extreme corner of his handkerchief to his glass eye. 'Excuse an old man's emotions, young gentlemen; but when I think of the numerous rare cases that then came under my treatment, I cannot but give way to my feelings. The town, the city, the metropolis, young gentlemen, is the place for you students; at least in these dull times of peace, when the Army and Navy furnish no inducements for a youth ambitious of rising in our honourable profession. Take an old man's advice, and if the war now threatening between the States and Mexico*should break out, exchange your Navy commissions for commissions in the Army. From having no military marine herself, Mexico has always been backward in furnishing subjects for the amputation-tables of foreign navies. The cause of science has languished in her hands. The Army, young gentlemen, is your best school; depend upon it. You will hardly believe it, Surgeon Bandage,' turning to that gentleman, 'but this is my first important case of surgery in a nearly three years' cruise. I have been almost wholly confined in this ship to doctor's practice—prescribing for fevers and fluxes. True, the other day a man fell from the mizzen-topsail-yard; but that was merely an aggravated case of dislocations, and bones splintered and broken. No one, sir, could have made an amputation of it, without severely contusing his conscience. And mine—I may say it, gentlemen, without ostentation—is peculiarly susceptible.'

And so saying, the knife and carver touchingly dropped to his sides, and he stood for a moment fixed in a tender reverie. But a commotion being heard beyond the curtain, he started, and, briskly crossing and recrossing the knife and carver, exclaimed, 'Ah, here comes our patient; surgeons, this side of the table, if you please; young gentlemen, a little further off, I beg. Steward, take off my coat—so; my neckerchief now; I must be perfectly unencumbered, Surgeon Patella, or I can do nothing whatever.'

These articles being removed, he snatched off his wig, placing it on the gun-deck capstan; then took out his set of false teeth, and placed it by the side of the wig; and, lastly, putting his forefinger to the inner angle of his blind eye, spirted out the glass optic with professional dexterity, and deposited that, also, next to the wig and false teeth.

Thus divested of nearly all inorganic appurtenances, what was left of the surgeon slightly shook itself, to see whether anything more could be spared to advantage.

'Carpenter's mates,' he now cried, 'will you never get through with that job?'

'Almost through, sir—just through,' they replied, staring round in search of the strange, unearthly voice that addressed them; for the absence of his teeth had not at all improved the conversational tones of the surgeon of the fleet.

With natural curiosity these men had purposely been lingering, to see all they could; but now, having no further excuse, they snatched up their hammers and chisels, and—like the stage-builders decamping from a public meeting at the eleventh hour, after just completing the rostrum in time for the first speaker—the carpenter's gang withdrew.

The broad ensign now lifted, revealing a glimpse of the crowd of man-of-war's-men outside, and the patient, borne in the arms of two of his messmates, entered the place. He was much emaciated, weak as an infant, and every limb visibly trembled, or rather jarred, like the head of a man with the palsy. As if an organic and involuntary apprehension of death had seized the wounded leg, its nervous motions were so violent that one of the messmates was obliged to keep his hand upon it.

The top-man was immediately stretched upon the table, the attendants steadying his limbs, when, slowly opening his eyes, he glanced about at the glittering knives and saws, the towels and sponges, the armed sentry at the commodore's cabin-door, the row of eager-eyed students, the meagre death's-head of a Cuticle, now with his shirt sleeves rolled up upon his withered arms and knife in hand, and, finally, his eye settled in horror upon the skeleton, slowly vibrating and jingling before him, with the slow, slight roll of the frigate in the water.

'I would advise perfect repose of your every limb, my man,' said Cuticle, addressing him; 'the precision of an operation is often impaired by the inconsiderate restlessness of the patient. But if you consider, my good fellow,' he added, in a patronizing and almost sympathetic tone, and slightly pressing his hand on the limb, 'if you consider how much better it is to live with three limbs than to die with four, and especially if you but knew to what torments both sailors and soldiers were subjected before the time of Celsus,* owing to the lamentable ignorance of surgery then prevailing, you would certainly thank God from the bottom of your heart that *your* operation has been postponed to the period of this enlightened age, blessed with a Bell, a Brodie, and a Lally.* My man, before Celsus's time, such was the general ignorance of our noble science, that, in order to prevent the excessive effusion of blood, it was deemed indispensable to operate with a red-hot knife'—making a professional movement toward the thigh—'and pour scalding oil upon the parts'—elevating his elbow, as if with a teapot in his hand—'still further to sear them, after amputation had been performed.'

'He is fainting!' said one of his messmates; 'quick! some water!' The steward immediately hurried to the top-man with the basin.

Cuticle took the top-man by the wrist, and feeling it awhile, observed, 'Don't be alarmed, men,' addressing the two messmates; 'he'll recover presently; this fainting very generally takes place.' And he stood for a moment, tranquilly eyeing the patient.

Now the surgeon of the fleet and the top-man presented a spectacle which, to a reflecting mind, was better than a churchyard sermon on the mortality of man.

Here was a sailor, who, four days previous, had stood erect —a pillar of life—with an arm like a royal-mast, and a thigh like a windlass. But the slightest conceivable finger-touch of a bit of crooked trigger had eventuated in stretching him out, more helpless than an hour-old babe, with a blasted thigh, utterly drained of its brawn. And who was it that now stood over him like a superior being, and, as if clothed himself with the attributes of immortality, indifferently discoursed of carving up his broken flesh, and thus piecing out his abbreviated days? Who was it, that, in capacity of surgeon, seemed enacting the part of a Regenerator of life? The withered, shrunken, one-eyed, toothless, hairless Cuticle; with a trunk half dead—a *memento mori* to behold!

And while in those soul-sinking and panic-striking premonitions of speedy death which almost invariably accompany a severe gun-shot wound, even with the most intrepid spirits; while thus drooping and dying, this once robust top-man's eye was now waning in his head like a Lapland moon being eclipsed in clouds—Cuticle, who for years had still lived in his withered tabernacle of a body— Cuticle, no doubt sharing in the common self-delusion of old age—Cuticle must have felt his hold of life as secure as the grim hug of a grizzly bear. Verily, life is more awful than death; and let no man, though his live heart beat in him like a cannon—let him not hug his life to himself; for, in the pre-destinated necessities of things, that bounding life of his is not a whit more secure than the life of a man on his death-bed. To-day we inhale the air with expanding lungs, and life runs through us like a thousand Niles; but to-morrow we may collapse in death, and all our veins be dry as the Brook Kedron in a drought.

'And now, young gentlemen,' said Cuticle, turning to the assistant surgeons, 'while the patient is coming to, permit me to describe to you the highly interesting operation I am about to perform.'

'Mr. Surgeon of the Fleet,' said Surgeon Bandage, 'if you are about to lecture, permit me to present you with your teeth; they will make your discourse more readily under-stood.' And so saying, Bandage, with a bow, placed the two semicircles of ivory into Cuticle's hands.

'Thank you, Surgeon Bandage,' said Cuticle, and slipped the ivory into its place.

'In the first place, now, young gentlemen, let me direct your attention to the excellent preparation before you. I have had it unpacked from its case, and set up here from my state-room, where it occupies the spare berth; and all this for your express benefit, young gentlemen. This skeleton I procured in person from the Hunterian Department of the Royal College of Surgeons in London. It is a masterpiece of art. But we have no time to examine it now. Delicacy forbids that I should amplify at a juncture like this'—casting an almost benignant glance toward the patient, now beginning to open his eyes; 'but let me point out to you upon this thigh-bone'—disengaging it from the skeleton, with a gentle twist—'the precise place where I propose to perform the operation. *Here*, young gentlemen, *here* is the place. You perceive it is very near the point of articulation with the trunk.'

'Yes,' interposed Surgeon Wedge, rising on his toes, 'yes, young gentlemen, the point of articulation with the *aceta-bulum* of the *os innominatum*.'

'Where's your *Bell on Bones*, Dick?' whispered one of

the assistants to the student next him. 'Wedge has been spending the whole morning over it, getting out the hard names.'

'Surgeon Wedge,' said Cuticle, looking round severely, 'we will dispense with your commentaries, if you please, at present. Now, young gentlemen, you cannot but perceive, that the point of operation being so near the trunk and the vitals, it becomes an unusually beautiful one, demanding a steady hand and a true eye; and, after all, the patient may die under my hands.'

'Quick, steward! water, water; he's fainting again!' cried the two messmates.

'Don't be alarmed for your comrade, men,' said Cuticle, turning round. 'I tell you it is not an uncommon thing for the patient to betray some emotion upon these occasions—most usually manifested by swooning; it is quite natural it should be so. But we must not delay the operation.—Steward, that knife—no, the next one—there, that's it. He is coming to, I think'—feeling the top-man's wrist. 'Are you all ready, sir?'

This last observation was addressed to one of the *Neversink*'s assistant surgeons, a tall, lank, cadaverous young man, arrayed in a sort of shroud of white canvass, pinned about his throat, and completely enveloping his person. He was seated on a match-tub—the skeleton swinging near his head—at the foot of the table, in readiness to grasp the limb, as when a plank is being severed by a carpenter and his apprentice.

'The sponges, steward,' said Cuticle, for the last time taking out his teeth, and drawing up his shirt sleeve still further. Then, taking the patient by the wrist, 'Stand by, now, you messmates; keep hold of his arms; pin him down. Steward, put your hand on the artery; I shall commence as soon as his pulse begins to—*now, now!*' Letting fall the wrist, feeling the thigh carefully, and bowing over it an instant, he drew the fatal knife unerringly across the flesh. As it first touched the part, the row of surgeons simultaneously dropped their eyes to the watches in their hands, while the patient lay, with eyes horribly distended, in a kind of waking trance. Not a breath was heard; but as the quivering flesh parted in a long, lingering gash, a spring of blood welled up between the living walls of the wound, and two thick streams, in opposite directions, coursed down the thigh. The sponges were instantly dipped in the purple pool; every face present was pinched to a point with suspense; the limb writhed; the man shrieked; his messmates pinioned him; while round and round the leg went the unpitying cut.

'The saw!' said Cuticle.

Instantly it was in his hand.

Full of the operation, he was about to apply it, when, looking up, and turning to the assistant surgeons, he said, 'Would any of you young gentlemen like to apply the saw? A splendid subject!'

Several volunteered; when, selecting one, Cuticle surrendered the instrument to him, saying, 'Don't be hurried, now; be steady.'

While the rest of the assistants looked upon their comrade with glances of envy, he went rather timidly to work; and Cuticle, who was earnestly regarding him, suddenly snatched the saw from his hand. 'Away, butcher! you disgrace the profession. Look at *me*!'

For a few moments the thrilling rasping sound was heard; and then the top-man seemed parted in twain at the hip, as the leg slowly slid into the arms of the pale, gaunt man in the shroud, who at once made away with it, and tucked it out of sight under one of the guns.

'Surgeon Sawyer,' now said Cuticle, courteously turning to the surgeon of the *Mohawk*,* 'would you like to take up the arteries? They are quite at your service, sir.'

'Do, Sawyer; be prevailed upon,' said Surgeon Bandage.

Sawyer complied; and while, with some modesty, he was conducting the operation, Cuticle, turning to the row of assistants, said, 'Young gentlemen, we will now proceed with our illustration. Hand me that bone, steward.' And taking the thigh-bone in his still bloody hands, and holding it conspicuously before his auditors, the surgeon of the fleet began:

'Young gentlemen, you will perceive that precisely at this

spot—*here*—to which I previously directed your attention—
at the corresponding spot precisely—the operation has been
performed. About here, young gentlemen, *here*'—lifting his
hand some inches from the bone—'about *here* the great
artery was. But you noticed that I did not use the tourniquet;
I never do. The forefinger of my steward is far better than
a tourniquet, being so much more manageable, and leaving
the smaller veins uncompressed. But I have been told, young
gentlemen, that a certain Seignior Seignioroni, a surgeon of
Seville, has recently invented an admirable substitute for the
clumsy, old-fashioned tourniquet. As I understand it, it is
something like a pair of *callipers*, working with a small
Archimedes screw—a very clever invention, according to
all accounts. For the padded points at the end of the arches'
—arching his forefinger and thumb—'can be so worked as
to approximate in such a way, as to—but you don't attend
to me, young gentlemen,' he added, all at once starting.

Being more interested in the active proceedings of Surgeon Sawyer, who was now threading a needle to sew up the
overlapping of the stump, the young gentlemen had not
scrupled to turn away their attention altogether from the
lecturer.

A few moments more, and the top-man, in a swoon, was
removed below into the sick-bay. As the curtain settled again
after the patient had disappeared, Cuticle, still holding the
thigh-bone of the skeleton in his ensanguined hands, proceeded with his remarks upon it; and having concluded them,
added, 'Now, young gentlemen, not the least interesting
consequence of this operation will be the finding of the ball,
which, in case of non-amputation, might have long eluded
the most careful search. That ball, young gentlemen, must
have taken a most circuitous route. Nor, in cases where the
direction is oblique, is this at all unusual. Indeed, the learned
Henner[*] gives us a most remarkable—I had almost said an
incredible—case of a soldier's neck, where the bullet, entering at the part called Adam's Apple——'

'Yes,' said Surgeon Wedge, elevating himself, 'the
pomum Adami.'

'Entering the point called *Adam's Apple*,' continued Cuticle, severely emphasizing the last two words, 'ran completely round the neck, and, emerging at the same hole it had entered, shot the next man in the ranks. It was afterward extracted, says Henner, from the second man, and pieces of the other's skin were found adhering to it. But examples of foreign substances being received into the body with a ball, young gentlemen, are frequently observed. Being attached to a United States ship at the time, I happened to be near the spot of the battle of Ayacucho,* in Peru. The day after the action, I saw in the barracks of the wounded a trooper, who having been severely injured in the brain, went crazy, and, with his own holster-pistol, committed suicide in the hospital. The ball drove inward a portion of his woollen night-cap——'

'In the form of a *cul-de-sac*, doubtless,' said the undaunted Wedge.

'For once, Surgeon Wedge, you use the only term that can be employed; and let me avail myself of this opportunity to say to you, young gentlemen, that a man of true science'—expanding his shallow chest a little—'uses but few hard words, and those only when none other will answer his purpose; whereas the smatterer in science'—slightly glancing toward Wedge—'thinks, that by mouthing hard words he proves that he understands hard things. Let this sink deep in your minds, young gentlemen; and, Surgeon Wedge'—with a stiff bow—'permit me to submit the reflection to yourself. Well, young gentlemen, the bullet was afterward extracted by pulling upon the external parts of the *cul-de-sac*—a simple, but exceedingly beautiful operation. There is a fine example, somewhat similar, related in Guthrie;* but, of course, you must have met with it, in so well-known a work as his *Treatise upon Gun-shot Wounds*. When, upward of twenty years ago, I was with Lord Cochrane,* then admiral of the fleets of this very country' —pointing shoreward, out of a port-hole—'a sailor of the vessel to which I was attached, during the blockade of Bahia, had his leg——.' But by this time the fidgets had completely taken possession of his auditors, especially of the senior surgeons; and turning upon them abruptly he added, 'But I will not detain you longer, gentlemen'—turning round upon all the surgeons—'your dinners must be waiting you on board your respective ships. But, Surgeon Sawyer, perhaps you may desire to wash your hands before you go. There is the basin, sir; you will find a clean towel on the rammer. For myself, I seldom use them'—taking out his handkerchief. 'I must leave you now, gentlemen,'—bowing. 'To-morrow, at ten, the limb will be upon the table, and I shall be happy to see you all upon the occasion. Who's there?' turning to the curtain, which then rustled.

'Please, sir,' said the steward, entering, 'the patient is dead.'

'The body, also, gentlemen, at ten precisely,' said Cuticle, once more turning round upon his guests. 'I predicted that the operation might prove fatal; he was very much run down. Good morning'; and Cuticle departed.

'He does not, surely, mean to touch the body?' exclaimed Surgeon Sawyer, with much excitement.

'Oh, no!' said Patella, 'that's only his way; he means, doubtless, that it may be inspected previous to being taken ashore for burial.'

The assemblage of gold-laced surgeons now ascended to the quarter-deck; the second cutter was called away by the bugler, and, one by one, they were dropped aboard of their respective ships.

The following evening the messmates of the top-man rowed his remains ashore, and buried them in the ever-vernal Protestant cemetery, hard by the Beach of the Flamingoes, in plain sight from the bay.

LXIV

Man-of-war Trophies

WHEN the second cutter pulled about among the ships, dropping the surgeons aboard the American men-of-war here and there—as a pilot-boat distributes her pilots at the mouth of a harbour—she passed several foreign frigates, two of which, an Englishman and a Frenchman, had excited not a little remark on board the *Neversink*. These vessels often loosed their sails and exercised yards simultaneously with ourselves, as if desirous of comparing the respective efficiency of the crews.

When we were nearly ready for sea, the English frigate, weighing her anchor, made all sail with the sea-breeze, and began showing off her paces by gliding about among all the men-of-war in harbour, and particularly by running down under the *Neversink*'s stern. Every time she drew near, we complimented her by lowering our ensign a little, and invariably she courteously returned the salute. She was inviting us to a sailing match; and it was rumoured that, when we should leave the bay, our captain would have no objections to gratify her; for, be it known, the *Neversink* was accounted the fleetest keeled craft sailing under the American long pennant. Perhaps this was the reason why the stranger challenged us.

It may have been that a portion of our crew were the more anxious to race with this frigate, from a little circumstance which a few of them deemed rather galling. Not many cables'-length distant from our commodore's cabin lay the frigate *President*, with the red cross of St. George flying from her peak. As its name imported, this fine craft was an American born; but having been captured during the last war with Britain, she now sailed the salt seas as a trophy.

Think of it, my gallant countrymen, one and all, down the sea-coast and along the endless banks of the Ohio and Columbia—think of the twinges we sea-patriots must have felt, to behold the live-oak of the Floridas and the pines of green Maine built into the oaken walls of Old England! But, to some of the sailors, there was a counterbalancing thought, as grateful as the other was galling; and that was, that somewhere, sailing under the Stars and Stripes, was the frigate *Macedonian*, a British-born craft which had once sported the battle-banner of Britain.

It has ever been the custom to spend almost any amount of money in repairing a captured vessel, in order that she may long survive to commemorate the heroism of the conqueror. Thus, in the English Navy, there are many Monsieurs of seventy-fours won from the Gaul. But we Americans can show but few similar trophies, though, no doubt, we would much like to be able so to do.

But I never have beheld any of these floating trophies without being reminded of a scene once witnessed in a pioneer village on the western bank of the Mississippi. Not far from this village, where the stumps of aboriginal trees yet stand in the market-place, some years ago lived a portion of the remnant tribes of the Sioux Indians, who frequently visited the white settlements to purchase trinkets and cloths.

One florid crimson evening in July, when the red-hot sun was going down in a blaze, and I was leaning against a corner in my huntsman's frock, lo! there came stalking out of the crimson west a gigantic red-man, erect as a pine, with his glittering tomahawk, big as a broad-axe, folded in martial repose across his chest. Moodily wrapped in his blanket, and striding like a king on the stage, he promenaded up and down the rustic streets, exhibiting on the back of his blanket a crowd of human hands, rudely delineated in red; one of them seemed recently drawn.

'Who is this warrior?' asked I; 'and why marches he here? and for what are these bloody hands?'

'That warrior is the *Red-Hot Coal*,' said a pioneer in moccasins by my side. 'He marches here to show off his last trophy; every one of those hands attests a foe scalped by his tomahawk; and he has just emerged from Ben Brown's, the painter, who has sketched the last red hand that you see; for last night this *Red-Hot Coal* outburned the *Yellow Torch*, the chief of a band of the Foxes.'

Poor savage! thought I; and is this the cause of your lofty gait? Do you straighten yourself to think that you have committed a murder, when a chance-falling stone has often done the same? Is it a proud thing to topple down six feet perpendicular of immortal manhood, though that lofty living tower needed perhaps thirty good growing summers to bring it to maturity? Poor savage! And you account it so glorious, do you, to mutilate and destroy what God himself was more than a quarter of a century·in building?

And yet, fellow-Christians, what is the American frigate *Macedonian*, or the English frigate *President*, but as two bloody red hands painted on this poor savage's blanket?

Are there no Moravians*in the moon, that not a missionary has yet visited this poor pagan planet of ours, to civilize civilization and christianize Christendom?

LXV
A Man-of-war Race

WE lay in Rio so long—for what reason the commodore only knows—that a saying went abroad among the impatient sailors that our frigate would at last ground on the beef-bones daily thrown overboard by the cooks.

But at last the good tidings came. 'All hands up anchor, ahoy!' And bright and early in the morning up came our old iron, as the sun rose in the east.

The land-breeze at Rio—by which alone vessels may emerge from the bay—is ever languid and faint. It comes from gardens of citrons and cloves, spiced with all the spices of the Tropic of Capricorn. And, like that old exquisite, Mohammed, who so much loved to snuff perfumes and essences, and used to lounge out of the conservatories of Khadija, his wife, to give battle to the robust sons of Koriesh; even so this Rio land-breeze comes jaded with sweet-smelling savours, to wrestle with the wild Tartar breezes of the sea.

Slowly we dropped and dropped down the bay, glided like a stately swan through the outlet, and were gradually rolled by the smooth, sliding billows, broad out upon the deep. Straight in our wake came the tall mainmast of the English fighting frigate, terminating, like a steepled cathedral, in the bannered cross of the religion of peace; and straight after *her* came the rainbow banner of France, sporting God's token that no more would he make war on the earth.

Both Englishman and Frenchman were resolved on a race; and we Yankees swore by our topsails and royals to sink their blazing banners that night among the southern constellations we should daily be extinguishing behind us in our run to the north.

'Ay,' said Mad Jack, 'St. George's banner shall be as the *Southern Cross*, out of sight, leagues down the horizon, while our gallant stars, my brave boys, shall burn all alone in the north, like the Great Bear at the Pole! Come on, Rainbow and Cross!'

But the wind was long languid and faint, not yet recovered from its night's dissipation ashore, and noon advanced, with the Sugar Loaf pinnacle in sight.

Now it is not with ships as with horses; for though, if a horse walk well and fast, it generally furnishes good token that he is not bad at a gallop, yet the ship that in a light breeze is outstripped, may sweep the stakes, so soon as a t'gallant breeze enables her to strike into a canter. Thus fared it with us. First, the Englishman glided ahead, and bluffly passed on; then the Frenchman politely bade us adieu, while the old *Neversink* lingered behind, railing at the effeminate breeze. At one time, all three frigates were irregularly abreast, forming a diagonal line; and so near were all three that the stately officers on the poops stiffly saluted by touching their caps, though refraining from any further civilities. At this juncture, it was a noble sight to behold those fine frigates, with dripping breast-hooks, all rearing and nodding in concert, and to look through their tall spars and wilderness of rigging, that seemed like inextricably entangled, gigantic cobwebs against the sky.

Toward sundown the ocean pawed its white hoofs to the spur of its helter-skelter rider, a strong blast from the eastward, and, giving three cheers from decks, yards, and tops, we crowded all sail on St. George and St. Denis.

But it is harder to overtake than outstrip; night fell upon us, still in the rear—still where the little boat was, which, at the eleventh hour, according to a Rabbinical tradition, pushed after the ark of old Noah.

It was a misty, cloudy night; and though at first our look-outs kept the chase in dim sight, yet at last so thick became the atmosphere, that no sign of a strange spar was to be seen. But the worst of it was, that, when last discerned, the French-man was broad on our weather bow, and the Englishman gallantly leading his van.

The breeze blew fresher and fresher; but, with even our main-royal set, we dashed along through a cream-coloured ocean of illuminated foam. White-Jacket was then in the top, and it was glorious to look down and see our black hull butting the white sea with its broad bows like a ram.

'We must beat them with such a breeze, dear Jack,' said I to our noble captain of the top.

'But the same breeze blows for John Bull, remember,' replied Jack, who, being a Briton, perhaps favoured the Englishman more than the *Neversink*.

'But how we boom through the billows!' cried Jack, gazing over the top-rail; then, flinging forth his arm, recited:

> Aslope, and gliding on the leeward side,
> The bounding vessel cuts the roaring tide.

Camoens! White-Jacket, Camoens!*Did you ever read him? *The Lusiad*, I mean? It's the man-of-war epic of the world, my lad. Give me Gama for a commodore, say I—noble Gama! And Mickle, White-Jacket, did you ever read of him? William Julius Mickle?* Camoens's translator? A dis-appointed man, though, White-Jacket. Besides his version of *The Lusiad*, he wrote many forgotten things. Did you ever see his ballad of *Cumnor Hall*?—No?—Why, it gave Sir Walter Scott the hint of *Kenilworth*. My father knew Mickle when he went to sea on board the old *Romney* man-of-war. How many great men have been sailors, White-Jacket! They say Homer himself was once a tar, even as his hero, Ulysses, was both a sailor and shipwright. I'll swear Shakespeare was once a captain of the forecastle. Do you mind the first scene in *The Tempest*, White-Jacket? And the world-finder, Christopher Columbus, was a sailor! and so was Camoens, who went to sea with Gama, else we had never had the *The Lusiad*, White-Jacket. Yes, I've sailed over the very track that Camoens sailed—round the East Cape into the Indian Ocean. I've been in Don Jose's garden, too, in Macao, and bathed my feet in the blessed dew of the walks where Camoens wandered before me. Yes, White-Jacket, and I have seen and sat in the cave at the end of the flowery, winding way where Camoens, according to tradition, composed certain parts of his *Lusiad*. Ay, Camoens was a sailor once! Then, there's Falconer,* whose *Shipwreck* will never founder, though he himself, poor fellow, was lost at sea in the *Aurora* frigate. Old Noah was the first sailor. And St. Paul, too, knew how to box the compass, my lad! mind you that chapter in *Acts*?* I couldn't spin the yarn better myself. Were you ever in Malta? They called it Melita in the Apostle's day. I have been in Paul's cave there, White-Jacket. They say a piece of it is good for a charm against shipwreck; but I never tried it. There's Shelley, he was quite a sailor. Shelley—poor lad! a Percy, too—but they ought to have let him sleep in his sailor's grave—he was drowned in the Mediterranean, you know, near Leghorn—and not burn his body, as they did, as if he had been a bloody Turk. But many people thought him so, White-Jacket, because he didn't go to mass, and because he wrote *Queen Mab*. Trelawney was by at the burning; and he was an ocean-rover, too!* Ay, and Byron helped put a piece of a keel on the fire; for it was made of bits of a wreck, they say; one wreck burning another! And was not Byron a sailor? an amateur forecastle man, White-Jacket! so he was; else how bid the ocean heave and fall in that grand, majestic way? I say, White-Jacket, d'ye mind me? there never was a very great man yet who spent all his life inland. A snuff of the sea, my boy, is inspiration; and having been once out of sight of land, has been the making of many a true poet and the blasting of many pretenders; for, d'ye see, there's no gammon about the ocean; it knocks the false keel right off a pretender's bows; it tells him just what he is, and makes him feel it, too. A sailor's life, I say, is the thing to bring us mortals out. What does the blessed Bible say? Don't it say that we maintop-men alone see the marvellous sights and wonders? Don't deny the blessed Bible, now! don't do it! How it rocks up here, my boy!' holding on to a shroud; 'but it only proves what I've been saying—the sea is the place to cradle genius! Heave and fall, old sea!'

'And *you*, also, noble Jack,' said I, 'what are you but a sailor?'

'You're merry, my boy,' said Jack, looking up with a glance like that of a sentimental archangel doomed to drag out his eternity in disgrace. 'But mind you, White-Jacket, there are many great men in the world besides commodores and captains. I've that here, White-Jacket'—touching his forehead—'which, under happier skies—perhaps in yon solitary star there, peeping down from those clouds—might have made a Homer of me. But Fate is Fate, White-Jacket; and we Homers who happen to be captains of tops must write our odes in our hearts, and publish them in our heads. But look! the captain's on the poop.'

It was now midnight; but all the officers were on deck.

'Jib-boom, there!' cried the lieutenant of the watch, going forward and hailing the headmost look-out. 'D'ye see anything of those fellows now?'

'See nothing, sir.'

'See nothing, sir,' said the lieutenant, approaching the captain, and touching his cap.

'Call all hands!' roared the captain. 'This keel shan't be beat while I stride it.'

All hands were called, and the hammocks stowed in the nettings for the rest of the night, so that no one could lie between blankets.

Now, in order to explain the means adopted by the captain to ensure us the race, it needs to be said of the *Neversink* that, for some years after being launched, she was accounted one of the slowest vessels in the American Navy. But it chanced upon a time, that, being on a cruise in the Mediterranean, she happened to sail out of Port Mahon in what was then supposed to be very bad trim for the sea. Her bows were rooting in the water, and her stern kicking up its heels in the air. But, wonderful to tell, it was soon discovered that in this comical posture she sailed like a shooting-star; she outstripped every vessel on the station. Thenceforward all her captains, on all cruises, *trimmed her by the head*; and the *Neversink* gained the name of a clipper.

To return. All hands being called, they were now made use of by Captain Claret as make-weights, to trim the ship, scientifically, to her most approved bearings. Some were sent forward on the spar-deck, with twenty-four-pound shot in their hands, and were judiciously scattered about here and there, with strict orders not to budge an inch from their stations, for fear of marring the captain's plans. Others were distributed along the gun- and berth-decks, with similar orders; and, to crown all, several carronade guns were unshipped from their carriages, and swung in their breechings from the beams of the main-deck, so as to impart a sort of vibratory briskness and oscillating buoyancy to the frigate.

And thus we five hundred make-weights stood out that whole night, some of us exposed to a drenching rain, in order that the *Neversink* might not be beaten. But the comfort and consolation of all make-weights is as dust in the balance in the estimation of the rulers of our man-of-war world.

The long, anxious night at last came to an end, and, with the first peep of day, the look-out on the jib-boom was hailed; but nothing was in sight. At last it was broad day; yet still not a bow was to be seen in our rear, nor a stern in our van.

'Where are they?' cried the captain.

'Out of sight, astern, to be sure, sir,' said the officer of the deck.

'Out of sight, *ahead*, to be sure, sir,' muttered Jack Chase, in the top.

Precisely thus stood the question: whether we beat them, or whether they beat us, no mortal can tell to this hour, since we never saw them again; but for one, White-Jacket will lay his two hands on the bow-chasers of the *Neversink*, and take his ship's oath that we Yankees carried the day.

LXVI

Fun in a Man-of-war

AFTER the race (our man-of-war Derby) we had many days fine weather, during which we continued running before the Trades toward the north. Exhilarated by the thought of being homeward bound, many of the seamen became joyous, and the discipline of the ship, if anything, became a little relaxed. Many pastimes served to while away the *dog-watches* in particular. These *dog-watches* (embracing two hours in the early part of the evening) form the only authorized playtime for the crews of most ships at sea.

Among other diversions at present licensed by authority in the *Neversink*, were those of single-stick, sparring, hammer-and-anvil, and head-bumping. All these were under the direct patronage of the captain, otherwise—seeing the consequences they sometimes led to—they would undoubtedly have been strictly prohibited. It is a curious coincidence, that when a navy captain does not happen to be an admirer of the *Fistiana*, his crew seldom amuse themselves in that way.

Single-stick, as everyone knows, is a delightful pastime, which consists in two men standing a few feet apart, and rapping each other over the head with long poles. There is a good deal of fun in it, so long as you are not hit; but a hit— in the judgment of discreet persons—spoils the sport completely. When this pastime is practised by connoisseurs ashore, they wear heavy, wired helmets, to break the force of the blows. But the only helmets of our tars were those with which nature had furnished them. They played with great-gun rammers.

Sparring consists in playing single-stick with bone poles instead of wooden ones. Two men stand apart, and pommel each other with their fists (a hard bunch of knuckles permanently attached to the arms, and made globular, or extended into a palm, at the pleasure of the proprietor), till one of them, finding himself sufficiently thrashed, cries *enough*.

Hammer-and-anvil is thus practised by amateurs: patient No. 1 gets on all-fours, and stays so; while patient No. 2 is taken up by his arms and legs, and his base is swung against the base of patient No. 1, till patient No. 1, with the force of the final blow, is sent flying along the deck.

Head-bumping, as patronized by Captain Claret, consists in two negroes (whites will not answer) butting at each other like rams. This pastime was an especial favourite with the captain. In the dog-watches, Rose-Water and May-Day were repeatedly summoned into the lee waist to tilt at each other, for the benefit of the captain's health.

May-Day was a full-blooded *bull-negro*—so the sailors called him—with a skull like an iron tea-kettle; wherefore May-Day much fancied the sport. But Rose-Water, he was a slender and rather handsome mulatto, and abhorred the pastime. Nevertheless, the captain must be obeyed; so at the word poor Rose-Water was fain to put himself in a posture of defence, else May-Day would incontinently have bumped him out of a port-hole into the sea. I used to pity poor Rose-Water from the bottom of my heart. But my pity was almost aroused into indignation at a sad sequel to one of these gladiatorial scenes.

It seems that, lifted up by the unaffected though verbally unexpressed applause of the captain, May-Day had begun to despise Rose-Water as a poltroon—a fellow all brains and no skull; whereas he himself was a great warrior, all skull and no brains.

Accordingly, after they had been bumping one evening to the captain's content, May-Day confidentially told Rose-Water that he considered him a '*nigger*', which, among some blacks, is held a great term of reproach. Fired at the insult,

Rose-Water gave May-Day to understand that he utterly erred; for his mother, a black slave, had been one of the mistresses of a Virginia planter, belonging to one of the oldest families in that state. Another insulting remark followed this innocent disclosure; retort followed retort; in a word, at last they came together in mortal combat.

The master-at-arms caught them in the act, and brought them up to the mast. The captain advanced.

'Please, sir,' said poor Rose-Water, 'it all come of dat 'ar bumping; May-Day, here, aggrawated me 'bout it.'

'Master-at-arms,' said the captain, 'did you see them fighting?'

'Ay, sir,' said the master-at-arms, touching his cap.

'Rig the gratings,' said the captain. 'I'll teach you two men that, though I now and then permit you to *play*, I will have no *fighting*. Do your duty, boatswain's mate!' And the negroes were flogged.

Justice commands that the fact of the captain's not showing any leniency to May-Day—a decided favourite of his, at least while in the ring—should not be passed over. He flogged both culprits in the most impartial manner.

As in the matter of the scene at the gangway, shortly after the Cape Horn theatricals, when my attention had been directed to the fact that the officers had *shipped their quarterdeck faces*—upon that occasion, I say, it was seen with what facility a sea-officer assumes his wonted severity of demeanour after a casual relaxation of it. This was especially the case with Captain Claret upon the present occasion. For any landsman to have beheld him in the lee waist, of a pleasant dog-watch, with a genial, good-humoured countenance, observing the gladiators in the ring, and now and then indulging in a playful remark—that landsman would have deemed Captain Claret the indulgent father of his crew, perhaps permitting the excess of his kind-heartedness to encroach upon the appropriate dignity of his station. He would have deemed Captain Claret a fine illustration of those two well-known poetical comparisons between a sea-captain and a father, and between a sea-captain and the master of apprentices, instituted by those eminent maritime jurists, the noble Lords Tenterden and Stowell.*

But surely, if there be anything hateful, it is this *shipping of the quarter-deck face* after wearing a merry and good-natured one. How can they have the heart? Methinks, if but once I smiled upon a man—never mind how much beneath me— I could not bring myself to condemn him to the shocking misery of the lash. Oh officers! all round the world, if this quarter-deck face you wear at all, then never unship it for another, to be merely sported for a moment. Of all insults, the temporary condescension of a master to a slave is the most outrageous and galling. That potentate who most condescends, mark him well; for that potentate, if occasion come, will prove your uttermost tyrant.

LXVII

White-Jacket arraigned at the Mast

WHEN with five hundred others I made one of the compelled spectators at the scourging of poor Rose-Water, I little thought what Fate had ordained for myself the next day.

Poor mulatto! thought I, one of an oppressed race, they degrade you like a hound. Thank God! I am a white. Yet I had seen whites also scourged; for, black or white, all my shipmates were liable to that. Still, there is something in us, somehow, that, in the most degraded condition, we snatch at a chance to deceive ourselves into a fancied superiority to others, whom we suppose lower in the scale than ourselves.

Poor Rose-Water! thought I; poor mulatto! Heaven send you a release from your humiliation!

To make plain the thing about to be related, it needs to repeat what has somewhere been previously mentioned, that in *tacking ship* every seaman in a man-of-war has a particular station assigned him. What that station is, should be made known to him by the first lieutenant; and when the word is passed to *tack* or *wear*, it is every seaman's duty to be found at his post. But among the various *numbers* and *stations* given to me by the senior lieutenant, when I first came on board the frigate, he had altogether omitted informing me of my particular place at those times, and, up to the precise period now written of, I had hardly known that I should have had any special place then at all. For the rest of the men, they seemed to me to catch hold of the first rope that offered, as in a merchantman upon similar occasions. Indeed, I subsequently discovered, that such was the state of discipline—in this one particular, at least—that very few of the seamen could tell where their proper stations were, at *tacking* or *wearing*.

'All hands tack ship, ahoy!'—such was the announcement made by the boatswain's mates at the hatchways the morning after the hard fate of Rose-Water. It was just eight bells—noon, and springing from my white jacket, which I had spread between the guns for a bed on the main-deck, I ran up the ladders, and, as usual, seized hold of the main-brace, which fifty hands were streaming along forward. When *main-topsail haul!* was given through the trumpet, I pulled at this brace with such heartiness and good will, that I almost flattered myself that my instrumentality in getting the frigate round on the other tack, deserved a public vote of thanks, and a silver tankard from Congress.

But something happened to be in the way aloft when the yards swung round; a little confusion ensued; and, with anger on his brow, Captain Claret came forward to see what occasioned it.—No one to let go the weather lift of the main-yard! The rope was cast off, however, by a hand, and the yards, unobstructed, came round.

When the last rope was coiled away, the captain desired to know of the first lieutenant who it might be that was stationed at the weather (then the starboard) main-lift. With a vexed expression of countenance the first lieutenant sent a midshipman for the station-bill; when, upon glancing it over, my own name was found put down at the post in question.

At the time I was on the gun-deck below, and did not know

of these proceedings; but a moment after, I heard the boat-swain's mates bawling my name at all the hatchways, and along all three decks. It was the first time I had ever heard it so sent through the furthest recesses of the ship, and well knowing what this generally betokened to other seamen, my heart jumped to my throat, and I hurriedly asked Flute, the boatswain's mate at the fore hatchway, what was wanted of me.

'Captain wants ye at the mast,' he replied. 'Going to flog ye, I guess.'

'What for?'

'My eyes! you've been chalking your face, hain't ye?'

'What am I wanted for?' I repeated.

But at that instant my name was again thundered forth by the other boatswain's mate, and Flute hurried me away, hinting that I would soon find out what the captain desired of me.

I swallowed down my heart in me as I touched the spar-deck, for a single instant balanced myself on my best centre, and then, wholly ignorant of what was going to be alleged against me, advanced to the dread tribunal of the frigate.

As I passed through the gangway, I saw the quarter-masters rigging the gratings; the boatswain with his green bag of scourges; the master-at-arms ready to help off some one's shirt.

Again I made a desperate swallow of my whole soul in me, and found myself standing before Captain Claret. His flushed face obviously showed him in ill humour. Among the group of officers by his side was the first lieutenant, who, as I came aft, eyed me in such a manner that I plainly perceived him to be extremely vexed at me for having been the innocent means of reflecting upon the manner in which he kept up the discipline of the ship.

'Why were you not at your station, sir?' asked the captain.

'What station do you mean, sir?' said I.

It is generally the custom with man-of-war's-men to stand obsequiously touching their hat at every sentence they address to the captain. But as this was not obligatory upon me by the Articles of War, I did not do so upon the present occasion, and previously, I had never had the dangerous honour of a personal interview with Captain Claret.

He quickly noticed my omission of the homage usually rendered him, and instinct told me that, to a certain extent, it set his heart against me.

'What station, sir, do you mean?' said I.

'You pretend ignorance,' he replied; 'it will not help you, sir.'

Glancing at the captain, the first lieutenant now produced the station-bill, and read my name in connection with that of the starboard main-lift.

'Captain Claret,' said I, 'it is the first time I ever heard of my being assigned to that post.'

'How is this, Mr. Bridewell?' he said, turning to the first lieutenant, with a fault-finding expression.

'It is impossible, sir,' said that officer, striving to hide his vexation, 'but this man must have known his station.'

'I have never known it before this moment, Captain Claret,' said I.

'Do you contradict my officer?' he returned. 'I shall flog you!'

I had now been on board the frigate upward of a year, and remained unscourged; the ship was homeward bound, and in a few weeks, at most, I would be a free man. And now, after making a hermit of myself in some things, in order to avoid the possibility of the scourge, here it was hanging over me for a thing utterly unforeseen, for a crime of which I was as utterly innocent. But all that was as naught. I saw that my case was hopeless; my solemn disclaimer was thrown in my teeth, and the boatswain's mate stood curling his fingers through the *cat*.

There are times when wild thoughts enter a man's heart, when he seems almost irresponsible for his act and his deed. The captain stood on the weather side of the deck. Sideways, on an unobstructed line with him, was the opening of the lee gangway, where the side-ladders are suspended in port. Nothing but a slight bit of sinnate-stuff served to rail in this opening, which was cut right down to the level of the captain's feet, showing the far sea beyond. I stood a little to windward of him, and, though he was a large, powerful man, it was certain that a sudden rush against him, along the slanting deck, would infallibly pitch him headforemost into the ocean, though he who so rushed must needs go over with him. My blood seemed clotting in my veins; I felt icy cold at the tips of my fingers, and a dimness was before my eyes. But through that dimness the boatswain's mate, scourge in hand, loomed like a giant, and Captain Claret, and the blue sea seen through the opening at the gangway, showed with an awful vividness. I cannot analyze my heart, though it then stood still within me. But the thing that swayed me to my purpose was not altogether the thought that Captain Claret was about to degrade me, and that I had taken an oath with my soul that he should not. No, I felt my man's manhood so bottomless within me, that no word, no blow, no scourge of Captain Claret could cut me deep enough for that. I but swung to an instinct in me—the instinct diffused through all animated nature, the same that prompts even a worm to turn under the heel. Locking souls with him, I meant to drag Captain Claret from this earthly tribunal of his to that of Jehovah, and let Him decide between us. No other way could I escape the scourge.

Nature has not implanted any power in man that was not meant to be exercised at times, though too often our powers have been abused. The privilege, inborn and inalienable, that every man has, of dying himself, and inflicting death upon another, was not given to us without a purpose. These are the last resources of an insulted and unendurable existence.

'To the gratings, sir!' said Captain Claret; 'do you hear?'

My eye was measuring the distance between him and the sea.

'Captain Claret,' said a voice, advancing from the crowd. I turned to see who this might be, that audaciously interposed at a juncture like this. It was the same remarkably handsome and gentlemanly corporal of marines, Colbrook, who has been previously alluded to, in the chapter describing killing time in a man-of-war.

'I know that man,' said Colbrook, touching his cap, and

speaking in a mild, firm, but extremely deferential manner; 'and I know that he would not be found absent from his station, if he knew where it was.'

This speech was almost unprecedented. Seldom or never before had a marine dared to speak to the captain of a frigate in behalf of a seaman at the mast. But there was something so unostentatiously commanding in the calm manner of the man, that the captain, though astounded, did not in any way reprimand him. The very unusualness of his interference seemed Colbrook's protection.

Taking heart, perhaps, from Colbrook's example, Jack Chase interposed, and in a manly but carefully respectful manner, in substance repeated the corporal's remark, adding that he had never found me wanting in the top.

Captain Claret looked from Chase to Colbrook, and from Colbrook to Chase—one the foremost man among the seamen, the other the foremost man among the soldiers—then all round upon the packed and silent crew, and, as if a slave to Fate, though supreme captain of a frigate, he turned to the first lieutenant, made some indifferent remark, and saying to me, *You may go*, sauntered aft into his cabin; while I, who, in the desperation of my soul, had but just escaped being a murderer and a suicide, almost burst into tears of thanksgiving where I stood.

LXVIII

A Man-of-war Fountain, and other things

LET us forget the scourge and the gangway awhile, and jot down in our memories a few little things pertaining to our man-of-war world. I let nothing slip, however small; and feel myself actuated by the same motive which has prompted many worthy old chroniclers, to set down the merest trifles concerning things that are destined to pass away entirely from the earth, and which, if not preserved in the nick of time, must infallibly perish from the memories of man. Who knows that this humble narrative may not hereafter prove the history of an obsolete barbarism? Who knows that, when men-of-war shall be no more, *White-Jacket* may not be quoted to show to the people in the Millennium what a man-of-war was? God hasten the time! Lo! ye years, escort it hither, and bless our eyes ere we die.

There is no part of a frigate where you will see more going and coming of strangers, and overhear more greetings and gossipings of acquaintances, than in the immediate vicinity of the scuttle-butt, just forward of the main hatchway, on the gun-deck.

The scuttle-butt is a goodly, round, painted cask, standing on end, and with its upper head removed, showing a narrow circular shelf within, where rest a number of tin cups for the accommodation of drinkers. Central, within the scuttle-butt itself, stands an iron pump, which, connecting with the immense water-tanks in the hold, furnishes an unfailing supply of the much-admired Pale Ale, first brewed in the brooks of the Garden of Eden, and stamped with the *brand* of our old father Adam, who never knew what wine was. We are indebted to the old vintner Noah[*]for that. The scuttle-butt is the only fountain in the ship; and here alone can you drink, unless at your meals. Night and day an armed sentry paces before it, bayonet in hand, to see that no water is taken away, except according to law. I wonder that they station no sentries at the port-holes, to see that no air is breathed, except according to Navy regulations.

As five hundred men come to drink at this scuttle-butt; as it is often surrounded by officers' servants drawing water for their masters to wash; by the cooks of the range, who hither come to fill their coffee-pots; and by the cooks of the ship's messes to procure water for their *duffs*; the scuttle-butt may be denominated the town-pump of the ship. And would that my fine countryman, Hawthorne of Salem,[*]had but served on board a man-of-war in his time, that he might give us the reading of a *rill* from the scuttle-butt.

. . . .

As in all extensive establishments—abbeys, arsenals, col-

leges, treasuries, metropolitan post-offices, and monasteries
—there are many snug little niches, wherein are ensconced
certain superannuated old pensioner officials; and, more
especially, as in most ecclesiastical establishments, a few
choice prebendary stalls are to be found, furnished with
well-filled mangers and racks; so, in a man-of-war, there
are a variety of similar snuggeries for the benefit of decrepit
or rheumatic old tars. Chief among these is the office of *mast-
man*.

There is a stout rail on deck, at the base of each mast,
where a number of *braces*, *lifts*, and *bunt-lines* are belayed to
the pins. It is the sole duty of the mast-man to see that these
ropes are always kept clear, to preserve his premises in a
state of the greatest attainable neatness, and every Sunday
morning to dispose his ropes in neat *Flemish coils*.

The *mainmast-man* of the *Neversink* was a very aged seaman, who well deserved his comfortable berth. He had seen
more than half a century of the most active service, and,
through all, had proved himself a good and faithful man. He
furnished one of the very rare examples of a sailor in a green
old age; for, with most sailors, old age comes in youth, and
Hardship and Vice carry them on an early bier to the grave.

As in the evening of life, and at the close of the day, old
Abraham sat at the door of his tent, biding his time to die,
so sits our old mast-man, on the *coat of the mast*, glancing
round him with patriarchal benignity. And that mild expression of his sets off very strangely a face that has been burned
almost black by the torrid suns that shone fifty years ago—
a face that is seamed with three sabre cuts. You would almost
think this old mast-man had been blown out of Vesuvius, to
look alone at his scarred, blackened forehead, chin, and
cheeks. But gaze down into his eye, and though all the snows
of Time have drifted higher and higher upon his brow, yet
deep down in that eye you behold an infantile, sinless look,
the same that answered the glance of this old man's mother
when first she cried for the babe to be laid by her side. That
look is the fadeless, ever infantile immortality within.

. . . .

The Lord Nelsons of the sea, though but barons in the state, yet oftentimes prove more potent than their royal masters; and at such scenes as Trafalgar—dethroning this emperor and reinstating that—enact on the ocean the proud part of mighty Richard Nevil,* the king-making earl of the land. And as Richard Nevil entrenched himself in his moated old man-of-war castle of Warwick, which, underground, was traversed with vaults, hewn out of the solid rock, and intricate as the wards of the old keys of Calais, surrendered to Edward III; even so do these king-commodores house themselves in their water-rimmed, cannon-sentried frigates, oaken-dug, deck under deck, as cell under cell. And as the old Middle-Age warders of Warwick, every night at curfew, patrolled the battlements, and dove down into the vaults to see that all lights were extinguished, even so do the master-at-arms and ship's corporals of a frigate perambulate all the decks of a man-of-war, blowing out all tapers but those burning in the legalized battle-lanterns. Yea, in these things, so potent is the authority of these sea-wardens, that, though almost the lowest subalterns in the ship, yet should they find the senior lieutenant himself sitting up late in his state-room, reading Bowditch's *Navigator*,* or D'Anton *On Gunpowder and Fire-arms*,* they would infallibly blow the light out under his very nose; nor durst that Grand Vizier resent the indignity.

But, unwittingly, I have ennobled, by grand historical comparisons, this prying, pettifogging, Irish informer of a master-at-arms.

You have seen some slim, slip-shod housekeeper, at midnight, ferreting over a rambling old house in the country, starting at fancied witches and ghosts, yet intent on seeing every door bolted, every smouldering ember in the fireplaces smothered, every loitering domestic abed, and every light made dark. This is the master-at-arms taking his night rounds in a frigate.

.   .   .   .   .   .

It may be thought that but little is seen of the commodore in these chapters, and that, since he so seldom appears on the stage, he cannot be so august a personage, after all. But the mightiest potentates keep the most behind the veil. You might tarry in Constantinople a month, and never catch a glimpse of the Sultan. The Grand Lama of Thibet, according to some accounts, is never beheld by the people. But if anyone doubts the majesty of a commodore, let him know that, according to XLII of the Articles of War, he is invested with a prerogative which, according to monarchical jurists, is inseparable from the throne—the plenary pardoning power. He may pardon all offences committed in the squadron under his command.

But this prerogative is only his while at sea, or on a foreign station. A circumstance peculiarly significant of the great difference between the stately absolutism of a commodore enthroned on his poop in a foreign harbour, and an unlaced commodore negligently reclining in an easy-chair in the bosom of his family at home.

LXIX

Prayers at the Guns

THE training-days, or general quarters, now and then taking place in our frigate, have already been described, also the Sunday devotions on the half-deck; but nothing has yet been said concerning the daily morning and evening quarters, when the men silently stand at their guns, and the chaplain simply offers up a prayer.

Let us now enlarge upon this matter. We have plenty of time; the occasion invites; for behold! the homeward-bound *Neversink* bowls along over a jubilant sea.

Shortly after breakfast the drum beats to quarters; and among five hundred men, scattered over all three decks, and engaged in all manner of ways, that sudden rolling march is magical as the monitory sound to which every good Mussulman at sunset drops to the ground whatsoever his hands might have found to do, and, throughout all Turkey, the people in concert kneel toward their holy Mecca.

The sailors run to and fro—some up the deck-ladders, some down—to gain their respective stations in the shortest possible time. In three minutes all is composed. One by one, the various officers stationed over the separate divisions of the ship then approach the first lieutenant on the quarter-deck, and report their respective men at their quarters. It is curious to watch their countenances at this time. A profound silence prevails; and, emerging through the hatchway, from one of the lower decks, a slender young officer appears, hugging his sword to his thigh, and advances through the long lanes of sailors at their guns, his serious eye all the time fixed upon the first lieutenant's—his polar star. Sometimes he essays a stately and graduated step, an erect and martial bearing, and seems full of the vast national importance of what he is about to communicate.

But when at last he gains his destination, you are amazed to perceive that all he has to say is imparted by a freemason touch of his cap, and a bow. He then turns and makes off to his division, perhaps passing several brother lieutenants, all bound on the same errand he himself has just achieved. For about five minutes these officers are coming and going, bringing in thrilling intelligence from all quarters of the frigate; most stoically received, however, by the first lieutenant. With his legs apart, so as to give a broad foundation for the superstructure of his dignity, this gentleman stands stiff as a pike-staff on the quarter-deck. One hand holds his sabre—an appurtenance altogether unnecessary at the time; and which he accordingly tucks, point backward, under his arm, like an umbrella on a sunshiny day. The other hand is continually bobbing up and down to the leather front of his cap, in response to the reports and salutes of his sub-ordinates, to whom he never deigns to vouchsafe a syllable; merely going through the motions of accepting their news, without bestowing thanks for their pains.

This continual touching of caps between officers on board a man-of-war is the reason why you often notice that the glazed fronts of their caps look jaded, lack-lustre, and worn; sometimes slightly oleaginous—though, in other respects, the cap may appear glossy and fresh. But as for the first lieutenant, he ought to have extra pay allowed to him, on account of his extraordinary outlays in cap fronts; for he it is to whom, all day long, reports of various kinds are incessantly being made by the junior lieutenants; and no report is made by them, however trivial, but caps are touched on the occasion. It is obvious that these individual salutes must be greatly multiplied and aggregated upon the senior lieutenant, who must return them all. Indeed, when a subordinate officer is first promoted to that rank, he generally complains of the same exhaustion about the shoulder and elbow that La Fayette*mourned over, when, in visiting America, he did little else but shake the sturdy hands of patriotic farmers from sunrise to sunset.

The various officers of divisions having presented their respects, and made good their return to their stations, the first lieutenant turns round, and, marching aft, endeavours to catch the eye of the captain, in order to touch his own cap to that personage, and thereby, without adding a word of explanation, communicate the fact of all hands being at their guns. He is a sort of retort, or receiver general, to concentrate the whole sum of the information imparted to him, and discharge it upon his superior at one touch of his cap front.

But sometimes the captain feels out of sorts, or in ill humour, or is pleased to be somewhat capricious, or has a fancy to show a touch of his omnipotent supremacy; or, peradventure, it has so happened that the first lieutenant has, in some way, piqued or offended him, and he is not unwilling to show a slight specimen of his dominion over him, even before the eyes of all hands; at all events, only by some one of these suppositions can the singular circumstance be accounted for, that frequently Captain Claret would pertinaciously promenade up and down the poop, purposely averting his eye from the first lieutenant, who would stand below in the most awkward suspense, waiting the first wink from his superior's eye.

'Now I have him!' he must have said to himself, as the captain would turn toward him in his walk; 'now's my time!' and up would go his hand to his cap; but, alas! the captain was off again; and the men at the guns would cast sly winks at each other as the embarrassed lieutenant would bite his lips with suppressed vexation.

Upon some occasions this scene would be repeated several times, till at last Captain Claret, thinking that in the eyes of all hands his dignity must by this time be pretty well bolstered, would stalk toward his subordinate, looking him full in the eyes; whereupon up goes his hand to the cap front, and the captain, nodding his acceptance of the report, descends from his perch to the quarter-deck.

By this time the stately commodore slowly emerges from his cabin, and soon stands leaning alone against the brass rails of the after hatchway. In passing him, the captain makes a profound salutation, which his superior returns, in token that the captain is at perfect liberty to proceed with the ceremonies of the hour.

Marching on, Captain Claret at last halts near the mainmast, at the head of a group of the ward-room officers, and by the side of the chaplain. At a sign from his finger, the brass band strikes up the Portuguese hymn. This over, from commodore to hammock-boy, all hands uncover, and the chaplain reads a prayer. Upon its conclusion, the drum beats the retreat, and the ship's company disappear from the guns. At sea or in harbour, this ceremony is repeated every morning and evening.

By those stationed on the quarter-deck the chaplain is distinctly heard; but the quarter-deck gun division embraces but a tenth part of the ship's company, many of whom are below, on the main-deck, where not one syllable of the prayer can be heard. This seemed a great misfortune; for I well knew myself how blessed and soothing it was to mingle twice every day in these peaceful devotions, and, with the commodore, and captain, and smallest boy, unite in acknowledging Almighty God. There was also a touch of the temporary equality of the Church about it, exceedingly grateful to a man-of-war's-man like me.

My carronade-gun happened to be directly opposite the brass railing against which the commodore invariably leaned at prayers. Brought so close together, twice every day, for more than a year, we could not but become intimately acquainted with each other's faces. To this fortunate circumstance it is to be ascribed, that some time after reaching home, we were able to recognize each other when we chanced to meet in Washington, at a ball given by the Russian Minister, the Baron de Bodisco. And though, while on board the frigate, the commodore never in any manner personally addressed me—nor did I him—yet, at the Minister's social entertainment, we *there* became exceedingly chatty; nor did I fail to observe, among that crowd of foreign dignitaries and magnates from all parts of America, that my worthy friend did not appear so exalted as when leaning, in solitary state, against the brass railing of the *Neversink*'s quarter-deck. Like many other gentlemen, he appeared to the best advantage, and was treated with the most deference, in the bosom of his home, the frigate.

Our morning and evening quarters were agreeably diversified for some weeks by a little circumstance, which, to some of us at least, always seemed very pleasing.

At Callao, half of the commodore's cabin had been hospitably yielded to the family of a certain aristocratic-looking magnate, who was going ambassador from Peru to the Court of the Brazils, at Rio. This dignified diplomatist sported a long, twirling moustache, that almost enveloped his mouth. The sailors said, he looked like a rat with his teeth through a bunch of oakum, or a St. Jago monkey peeping through a prickly-pear bush.

He was accompanied by a very beautiful wife, and a still more beautiful little daughter, about six years old. Between this dark-eyed little gipsy and our chaplain there soon sprung up a cordial love and good feeling, so much so, that they were seldom apart. And whenever the drum beat to quarters, and the sailors were hurrying to their stations, this little signorita would outrun them all to gain her own quarters at the capstan, where she would stand by the chaplain's side, grasping his hand, and looking up archly in his face.

It was a sweet relief from the domineering sternness of our martial discipline—a sternness not relaxed even at our devotions before the altar of the common God of commodore and cabin-boy—to see that lovely little girl standing among the thirty-two-pounders, and now and then casting a wondering, commiserating glance at the array of grim seamen around her.

LXX

Monthly Muster round the Capstan

BESIDES general quarters, and the regular morning and evening quarters for prayers on board the *Neversink*, on the first Sunday of every month we had a grand *muster round the capstan*, when we passed in solemn review before the captain and officers, who closely scanned our frocks and trowsers, to see whether they were according to the Navy cut. In some ships every man is required to bring his bag and hammock along for inspection.

This ceremony acquires its chief solemnity, and, to a novice, is rendered even terrible, by the reading of the Articles of War by the captain's clerk before the assembled ship's company, who, in testimony of their enforced reverence for the code, stand bareheaded till the last sentence is pronounced.

To a mere amateur reader the quiet perusal of these Articles of War would be attended with some nervous emotions. Imagine, then, what *my* feelings must have been, when, with my hat deferentially in my hand, I stood before my lord and master, Captain Claret, and heard these Articles read as the law and gospel, the infallible, unappealable dispensation and code, whereby I lived, and moved, and had my being on board of the United States Ship *Neversink*.

Of some twenty offences—made penal—that a seaman may commit, and which are specified in this code, thirteen are punishable by death.

'*Shall suffer death!*' This was the burden of nearly every Article read by the captain's clerk; for he seemed to have been instructed to omit the longer Articles, and only present those which were brief and to the point.

'*Shall suffer death!*' The repeated announcement falls on your ear like the intermitting discharge of artillery. After it has been repeated again and again, you listen to the reader as he deliberately begins a new paragraph; you hear him reciting the involved, but comprehensive and clear arrangement of the sentence, detailing all possible particulars of the offence described, and you breathlessly await, whether *that* clause also is going to be concluded by the discharge of the terrible minute-gun. When, lo! it again booms on your ear—*shall suffer death!* No reservations, no contingencies; not the remotest promise of pardon or reprieve; not a glimpse of commutation of the sentence; all hope and consolation is shut out—*shall suffer death!* that is the simple fact for you to digest; and it is a tougher morsel, believe White-Jacket when he says it, than a forty-two-pound cannon-ball.

But there is a glimmering of an alternative to the sailor who infringes these Articles. Some of them thus terminate: '*Shall suffer death, or such punishment as a court martial shall adjudge*'. But hints this at a penalty still more serious? Perhaps it means '*death, or worse punishment*'.

Your honours of the Spanish Inquisition, Loyola and Torquemada!* produce, reverend gentlemen, your most secret code, and match these Articles of War, if you can. Jack Ketch,*you* also are experienced in these things! Thou most benevolent of mortals, who standest by us, and hangest round our necks, when all the rest of this world are against us—tell us, hangman, what punishment is this, horribly hinted at as being worse than death? Is it, upon an empty stomach, to read the Articles of War every morning, for the term of one's natural life? Or is it to be imprisoned in a cell, with its walls papered from floor to ceiling with printed copies, in italics, of these Articles of War?

But it needs not to dilate upon the pure, bubbling milk of human kindness, and Christian charity, and forgiveness of injuries which pervade this charming document, so thoroughly imbued, as a Christian code, with the benignant spirit of the Sermon on the Mount. But as it is very nearly alike in the foremost states of Christendom, and as it is nationally set forth by those states, it indirectly becomes an index to the true condition of the present civilization of the world.

As, month after month, I would stand bareheaded among my shipmates, and hear this document read, I have thought to myself, Well, well, White-Jacket, you are in a sad box, indeed. But prick your ears, there goes another minute-gun. It admonishes you to take all bad usage in good part, and never to join in any public meeting that may be held on the gun-deck for a redress of grievances. Listen:

Art. XIII. '*If any person in the Navy shall make, or attempt to make, any mutinous assembly, he shall, on conviction thereof by a court martial, suffer death.*'

Bless me, White-Jacket, are you a great gun yourself, that you so recoil, to the extremity of your breechings, at that discharge?

But give ear again. Here goes another minute-gun. It indirectly admonishes you to receive the grossest insult, and stand still under it:

Art. XIV. '*No private in the Navy shall disobey the lawful orders of his superior officer, or strike him, or draw, or offer to draw, or raise any weapon against him, while in the execution of the duties of his office, on pain of death.*'

Do not hang back there by the bulwarks, White-Jacket; come up to the mark once more; for here goes still another minute-gun, which admonishes you never to be caught napping:

Part of Art. XX. '*If any person in the Navy shall sleep upon his watch, he shall suffer death.*'

Murderous! But then, in time of peace, they do not enforce these bloodthirsty laws? Do they not, indeed? What happened to those three sailors on board an American armed vessel a few years ago, quite within your memory, White-Jacket; yea, while you yourself were yet serving on board this very frigate, the *Neversink*? What happened to those three Americans, White-Jacket—those three sailors, even as you, who once were alive, but now are dead? '*Shall suffer death!*' —those were the three words that hung those three sailors.*

Have a care, then, have a care, lest you come to a sad end, even the end of a rope; lest, with a black-and-blue throat, you turn a dumb diver after pearl-shells; put to bed forever, and tucked in, in your own hammock, at the bottom of the sea. And there you will lie, White-Jacket, while hostile navies are playing cannon-ball billiards over your grave.

By the mainmast! then, in a time of profound peace, I am subject to the cut-throat martial law! And when my own brother, who happens to be dwelling ashore, and does not serve his country as I am doing—when *he* is at liberty to call personally upon the President of the United States, and express his disapprobation of the whole national administration, here am *I*, liable at any time to be run up at the yard-arm, with a necklace, made by no jeweller, round my neck!

A hard case, truly, White-Jacket; but it cannot be helped. Yes; you live under this same martial law. Does not everything around you din the fact in your ears? Twice every day do you not jump to your quarters at the sound of a drum? Every morning, in port, are you not roused from your hammock by the *reveille*, and sent to it again at nightfall by the *tattoo*? Every Sunday are you not commanded in the mere matter of the very dress you shall wear through that blessed day? Can your shipmates so much as drink their 'tot of grog'? nay, can they even drink but a cup of water at the scuttle-butt, without an armed sentry standing over them? Does not every officer wear a sword instead of a cane? You live and move among twenty-four-pounders, White-Jacket; the very cannon-balls are deemed an ornament around you, serving to embellish the hatchways; and should you come to die at sea, White-Jacket, still two cannon-balls would bear you company when you would be committed to the deep. Yea, by all methods, and devices, and inventions, you are momentarily admonished of the fact that you live under the Articles of War. And by virtue of them it is, White-Jacket, that, without a hearing and without a trial, you may, at a wink from the captain, be condemned to the scourge.

Speak you true? Then let me fly!

Nay, White-Jacket, the landless horizon hoops you in.

Some tempest, then, surge all the sea against us! hidden reefs and rocks, arise and dash the ship to chips! I was not born a serf, and will not live a slave! Quick! corkscrew whirlpools, suck us down! world's end whelm us!

Nay, White-Jacket, though this frigate laid her broken bones upon the Antarctic shores of Palmer's Land;* though not two planks adhered; though all her guns were spiked by swordfish blades, and at her yawning hatchways mouth-yawning sharks swam in and out; yet, should you escape the wreck and scramble to the beach, this martial law would meet you still, and snatch you by the throat. Hark!

Art. XLII. Part of Sec. 3. '*In all cases where the crews of the ships or vessels of the United States shall be separated from their vessels by the latter being wrecked, lost, or destroyed, all the command, power, and authority given to the officers of such ships or vessels shall remain, and be in full force, as effectually as if such ship or vessel were not so wrecked, lost, or destroyed.*'

Hear you that, White-Jacket! I tell you there is no escape. Afloat or wrecked, the martial law relaxes not its gripe. And though, by that self-same warrant, for some offence therein set down, you were indeed to 'suffer death', even then the martial law might hunt you straight through the other world, and out again at its other end, following you through all eternity, like an endless thread on the inevitable track of its own point, passing unnumbered needles through.

LXXI

The Genealogy of the Articles of War

As the Articles of War form the ark and constitution of the penal laws of the American Navy, in all sobriety and earnestness it may be well to glance at their origin. Whence came they? And how is it that one arm of the national defences of a republic comes to be ruled by a Turkish code, whose every section almost, like each of the tubes of a revolving pistol, fires nothing short of death into the heart of an offender? How comes it that, by virtue of a law solemnly ratified by a Congress of freemen, the representatives of freemen, thousands of Americans are subjected to the most despotic usages, and, from the dockyards of a republic, absolute monarchies are launched, with the 'glorious Stars and Stripes' for an ensign? By what unparalleled anomaly, by what monstrous grafting of tyranny upon freedom, did these Articles of War ever come to be so much as heard of in the American Navy?

Whence came they? They cannot be the indigenous growth of those political institutions which are based upon that arch-democrat Thomas Jefferson's Declaration of Independence? No; they are an importation from abroad, even from Britain, whose laws we Americans hurled off as tyrannical, and yet retained the most tyrannical of all.

But we stop not here; for these Articles of War had their congenial origin in a period of the history of Britain when the Puritan republic had yielded to a monarchy restored; when a hangman Judge Jeffreys sentenced a world's champion like Algernon Sidney to the block;* when one of a race—by some deemed accursed of God—even a Stuart, was on the throne; and a Stuart, also, was at the head of the Navy, as Lord High Admiral. One, the son of a king beheaded for encroachments upon the rights of his people, and the other, his own brother, afterward a king, James II, who was hurled from the throne for his tyranny. This is the origin of the Articles of War; and it carries with it an unmistakable clue to their despotism.*

Nor is it a dumb thing that the men who, in democratic Cromwell's time, first proved to the nations the toughness of the British oak and the hardihood of the British sailor—

* The first naval Articles of War in the English language were passed in the thirteenth year of the reign of Charles the Second, under the title of 'An Act for establishing Articles and Orders for the regulating and better Government of his Majesty's Navies, Ships-of-War, and Forces by Sea.' This act was repealed, and, so far as concerned the officers, a modification of it

that in Cromwell's time, whose fleets struck terror into the cruisers of France, Spain, Portugal, and Holland, and the corsairs of Algiers and the Levant; in Cromwell's time, when Robert Blake swept the Narrow Seas of all the keels of a Dutch admiral who insultingly carried a broom at his fore-mast;[*] it is not a dumb thing that, at a period deemed so glorious to the British Navy, these Articles of War were unknown.

Nevertheless, it is granted that some laws or other must have governed Blake's sailors at that period; but they must have been far less severe than those laid down in the written code which superseded them; since, according to the father-in-law of James II, the historian of the Rebellion,[*] the English Navy, prior to the enforcement of the new code, was full of officers and sailors who, of all men, were the most republican. Moreover, the same author informs us that the first work undertaken by his respected son-in-law, then Duke of York, upon entering on the duties of Lord High Admiral, was to have a grand re-christening of the men-of-war, which still carried on their sterns names too democratic to suit his High-Tory ears.

substituted, in the twenty-second year of the reign of George the Second, shortly after the Peace of Aix-la-Chapelle, just one century ago [i.e. 1748. Ed.]. This last act, it is believed, comprises, in substance, the Articles of War at this day in force in the British Navy. It is not a little curious, nor without meaning, that neither of these acts explicitly empowers an officer to inflict the lash. It would almost seem as if, in this case, the British law-givers were willing to leave such a stigma out of an organic statute, and bestow the power of the lash in some less solemn, and perhaps less public manner. Indeed, the only broad enactments directly sanctioning naval scourging at sea are to be found in the United States Statute Book and in the 'Sea Laws' of the absolute monarch, Louis le Grand, of France.[†]

Taking for their basis the above-mentioned British Naval Code, and ingrafting upon it the positive scourging laws, which Britain was loth to recognize as organic statutes, our American law-givers, in the year 1800, framed the Articles of War now governing the American Navy. They may be found in the second volume of the *United States Statutes at Large*, under chapter xxxiii.—'An act for the *better* government of the Navy of the United States.'

† For reference to the latter (L'Ord. de la Marine), *vide* Curtis's *Treatise on the Rights and Duties of Merchant-Seamen, according to the General Maritime Law*, part ii. c. 1.

But if these Articles of War were unknown in Blake's time, and also during the most brilliant period of Admiral Benbow's career,* what inference must follow? That such tyrannical ordinances are not indispensable—even during war—to the highest possible efficiency of a military marine.

LXXII

'Herein are the good Ordinances of the Sea, which wise Men, who voyaged round the World, gave to our Ancestors, and which constitute the Books of the Science of good Customs'

—THE CONSULATE OF THE SEA*

THE present usages of the American Navy are such that, though there is no government enactment to that effect, yet, in many respects, its commanders seem virtually invested with the power to observe or violate, as seems to them fit, several of the Articles of War.

According to Article XV, *'No person in the Navy shall quarrel with any other person in the Navy, nor use provoking or reproachful words, gestures, or menaces, on pain of such punishment as a court martial shall adjudge.'*

'Provoking or reproachful words!' Officers of the Navy, answer me! Have you not, many of you, a thousand times violated this law, and addressed to men, whose tongues were tied by this very article, language which no landsman would ever hearken to without flying at the throat of his insulter? I know that worse words than *you* ever used are to be heard addressed by a merchant-captain to his crew; but the merchant-captain does not live under the XVth Article of War.

Not to make an example of him, nor to gratify any personal feeling, but to furnish one certain illustration of what is here asserted, I honestly declare that Captain Claret, of the *Neversink*, repeatedly violated this law in his own proper person.

According to Article III, no officer, or other person in the

Navy, shall be guilty of *'oppression, fraud, profane swearing, drunkenness, or any other scandalous conduct.'*

Again let me ask you, officers of the Navy, whether many of you have not repeatedly, and in more than one particular, violated this law? And here, again, as a certain illustration, I must once more cite Captain Claret as an offender, especially in the matter of profane swearing. I must also cite four of the lieutenants, some eight of the midshipmen, and nearly all the seamen.

Additional articles might be quoted that are habitually violated by the officers, while nearly all those *exclusively* referring to the sailors are unscrupulously enforced. Yet those articles by which the sailor is scourged at the gangway are not one whit more laws than those *other* articles, binding upon the officers, that have become obsolete from immemorial disuse; while still other articles, to which the sailors alone are obnoxious, are observed or violated at the caprice of the captain. Now, if it be not so much the severity as the certainty of punishment that deters from transgression, how fatal to all proper reverence for the enactments of Congress must be this disregard of its statutes.

Still more. This violation of the law, on the part of the officers, in many cases involves oppression to the sailor. But throughout the whole naval code, which so hems in the mariner by law upon law, and which invests the captain with so much judicial and administrative authority over him—in most cases entirely discretionary—not one solitary clause is to be found which in any way provides means for a seaman deeming himself aggrieved to obtain redress. Indeed, both the written and unwritten laws of the American Navy are as destitute of individual guarantees to the mass of seamen as the statute book of the despotic Empire of Russia.

Who put this great gulf between the American captain and the American sailor? Or is the captain a creature of like passions with ourselves? Or is he an infallible archangel, incapable of the shadow of error? Or has a sailor no mark of humanity, no attribute of manhood, that, bound hand and foot, he is cast into an American frigate shorn of all rights and defences, while the notorious lawlessness of the commander has passed into a proverb, familiar to man-of-war's-men, *The law was not made for the captain!* Indeed, he may almost be said to put off the citizen when he touches his quarter-deck; and, almost exempt from the law of the land himself, he comes down upon others with a judicial severity unknown on the national soil. With the Articles of War in one hand, and the cat-o'-nine-tails in the other, he stands an undignified parody upon Mohammed enforcing Moslemism with the sword and the Koran.

The concluding sections of the Articles of War treat of the naval courts martial before which officers are tried for serious offences as well as the seamen. The oath administered to members of these courts—which sometimes sit upon matters of life and death—explicitly enjoins that the members shall not '*at any time divulge the vote or opinion of any particular member of the court, unless required so to do before a court of justice in due course of law.*'

Here, then, is a Council of Ten and a Star Chamber indeed! Remember, also, that though the sailor is sometimes tried for his life before a tribunal like this, in no case do his fellow-sailors, his peers, form part of the court. Yet that a man should be tried by his peers is the fundamental principle of all civilized jurisprudence. And not only tried by his peers, but his peers must be unanimous to render a verdict; whereas, in a court martial, the concurrence of a majority of conventional and social superiors is all that is requisite.

In the English Navy, it is said, they had a law which authorized the sailor to appeal, if he chose, from the decision of the captain—even in a comparatively trivial case—to the higher tribunal of a court martial. It was an English seaman who related this to me. When I said that such a law must be a fatal clog to the exercise of the penal power in the captain, he, in substance, told me the following story.

A top-man guilty of drunkenness being sent to the gratings, and the scourge about to be inflicted, he turned round and demanded a court martial. The captain smiled, and ordered him to be taken down and put into the 'brig'. There he was kept in irons some weeks, when, despairing of being liberated, he offered to compromise at two dozen lashes. 'Sick of your bargain, then, are you?' said the captain. 'No, no! a court martial you demanded, and a court martial you shall have!' Being at last tried before the bar of quarter-deck officers, he was condemned to two hundred lashes. What for? for his having been drunk? No! for his having had the insolence to appeal from an authority in maintaining which the men who tried and condemned him had so strong a sympathetic interest.

Whether this story be wholly true or not, or whether the particular law involved prevails, or ever did prevail, in the English Navy, the thing, nevertheless, illustrates the ideas that man-of-war's-men themselves have touching the tribunals in question.

What can be expected from a court whose deeds are done in the darkness of the recluse courts of the Spanish Inquisition? when that darkness is solemnized by an oath on the Bible? when an oligarchy of epaulets sits upon the bench, and a plebeian top-man, without a jury, stands judicially naked at the bar?

In view of these things, and especially in view of the fact that, in several cases, the degree of punishment inflicted upon a man-of-war's-man is absolutely left to the discretion of the court, what shame should American legislators take to themselves, that with perfect truth we may apply to the entire body of American man-of-war's-men that infallible principle of Sir Edward Coke:*'*It is one of the genuine marks of servitude to have the law either concealed or precarious.*' But still better may we subscribe to the saying of Sir Matthew Hale* in his *History of the Common Law*, that '*the Martial Law, being based upon no settled principles, is, in truth and reality, no law, but something indulged rather than allowed as a law.*'

I know it may be said that the whole nature of this naval code is purposely adapted to the war exigencies of the Navy. But waiving the grave question that might be raised concerning the moral, not judicial, lawfulness of this arbitrary code, even in time of war; be it asked, why is it in force during a time of peace? The United States has now existed as a nation upward of seventy years, and in all that time the alleged necessity for the operation of the naval code—in cases deemed capital—has only existed during a period of two or three years at most.

Some may urge that the severest operations of the code are tacitly made null in time of peace. But though with respect to several of the articles this holds true, yet at any time any and all of them may be legally enforced. Nor have there been wanting recent instances illustrating the spirit of this code, even in cases where the letter of the code was not altogether observed. The well-known case of a United States brig furnishes a memorable example, which at any moment may be repeated. Three men, in a time of peace, were then hung at the yard-arm, merely because, in the captain's judgment, it became necessary to hang them. To this day the question of their complete guilt is socially discussed.[1]

How shall we characterize such a deed? Says Blackstone, 'If anyone that hath commission of martial authority doth, in time of peace, hang, or otherwise execute any man by colour of martial law, this is murder; for it is against Magna Charta.'* *

Magna Charta! We moderns, who may be landsmen, may justly boast of civil immunities not possessed by our fore-fathers; but our remoter forefathers who happened to be mariners may straighten themselves even in their ashes to think that their law-givers were wiser and more humane in their generation than our law-givers in ours. Compare the sea-laws of our Navy with the Roman and Rhodian ocean ordinances; compare them with *The Consulate of the Sea*; compare them with the laws of the Hanse Towns;*compare them with the ancient Wisbury laws.* In the last we find that they were ocean democrats in those days. 'If he strikes, he ought to receive blow for blow.' Thus speak out the Wisbury laws concerning a Gothland sea-captain.

---

* *Commentaries*, b. i. c. xiii.

In final reference to all that has been said in previous chapters touching the severity and unusualness of the laws of the American Navy, and the large authority vested in its commanding officers, be it here observed, that White-Jacket is not unaware of the fact that the responsibility of an officer commanding at sea—whether in the merchant-service or the national marine—is unparalleled by that of any other relation in which man may stand to man. Nor is he unmindful that both wisdom and humanity dictate that, from the peculiarity of his position, a sea-officer in command should be clothed with a degree of authority and discretion inadmissible in any master ashore. But, at the same time, these principles—recognized by all writers on maritime law—have undoubtedly furnished warrant for clothing modern sea-commanders and naval courts martial with powers which exceed the due limits of reason and necessity. Nor is this the only instance where right and salutary principles, in themselves almost self-evident and infallible, have been advanced in justification of things, which in themselves are just as self-evidently wrong and pernicious.

Be it here, once and for all, understood, that no sentimental and theoretic love for the common sailor; no romantic belief in that peculiar noble-heartedness and exaggerated generosity of disposition fictitiously imputed to him in novels; and no prevailing desire to gain the reputation of being his friend, have actuated me in anything I have said, in any part of this work, touching the gross oppression under which I know that the sailor suffers. Indifferent as to who may be the parties concerned, I but desire to see wrong things righted, and equal justice administered to all.

Nor, as has been elsewhere hinted, is the general ignorance or depravity of any race of men to be alleged as an apology for tyranny over them. On the contrary, it cannot admit of a reasonable doubt, in any unbiased mind conversant with the interior life of a man-of-war, that most of the sailor iniquities practised therein are indirectly to be ascribed to the morally debasing effects of the unjust, despotic, and degrading laws under which the man-of-war's-man lives.

LXXIII

Night and Day Gambling in a Man-of-war

MENTION has already been made that the game of draughts, or checkers, was permitted to be played on board the *Neversink*. At the present time, while there was little or no ship-work to be done, and all hands, in high spirits, were sailing homeward over the warm, smooth sea of the Tropics; so numerous became the players, scattered about the decks, that our first lieutenant used ironically to say, that it was a pity they were not tessellated with squares of white and black marble, for the express benefit and convenience of the players. Had this gentleman had his way, our checker-boards would very soon have been pitched out of the ports. But the captain—unusually lenient in some things—permitted them, and so Mr. Bridewell was fain to hold his peace.

But, although this one game was allowable in the frigate, all kinds of gambling were strictly interdicted, under the penalty of the gangway; nor were cards or dice tolerated in any way whatever. This regulation was indispensable, for, of all human beings, man-of-war's-men are perhaps the most inclined to gambling. The reason must be obvious to anyone who reflects upon their condition on shipboard. And gambling—the most mischievous of vices anywhere—in a man-of-war operates still more perniciously than on shore. But quite as often as the law against smuggling spirits is transgressed by the unscrupulous sailors, the statutes against cards and dice are evaded.

Sable night, which, since the beginning of the world, has winked and looked on at so many deeds of iniquity—night is the time usually selected for their operations by man-of-war gamblers. The place pitched upon is generally the berth-deck, where the hammocks are swung, and which is lighted so stintedly as not to disturb the sleeping seamen with any obtruding glare. In so spacious an area the two lanterns swinging from the stanchions diffuse a subdued illumination, like a night-taper in the apartment of some invalid. Owing to their position, also, these lanterns are far from shedding an impartial light, however dim, but fling long angular rays here and there, like burglars' dark lanterns in the fifty-acre vaults of the West India Docks on the Thames.

It may well be imagined, therefore, how well adapted is this mysterious and subterranean Hall of Eblis* to the clandestine proceedings of gamblers, especially as the hammocks not only hang thickly, but many of them swing very low, within two feet of the floor, thus forming innumerable little canvass glens, grottoes, nooks, corners, and crannies, where a good deal of wickedness may be practised by the wary with considerable impunity.

Now the master-at-arms, assisted by his mates, the ship's corporals, reigns supreme in these bowels of the ship. Throughout the night these policemen relieve each other at standing guard over the premises; and, except when the watches are called, they sit in the midst of a profound silence, only invaded by trumpeter's snores, or the ramblings of some old sheet-anchor-man in his sleep.

The two ship's corporals went among the sailors by the names of Leggs and Pounce; Pounce had been a policeman, it was said, in Liverpool; Leggs, a turnkey attached to 'The Tombs',* in New York. Hence their education eminently fitted them for their stations; and Bland, the master-at-arms, ravished with their dexterity in prying out offenders, used to call them his two right hands.

When man-of-war's-men desire to gamble, they appoint the hour, and select some certain corner, in some certain shadow, behind some certain hammock. They then contribute a small sum toward a joint fund to be invested in a bribe for some argus-eyed shipmate, who shall play the part of a spy upon the master-at-arms and corporals while the gaming is in progress. In nine cases out of ten these arrangements are so cunning and comprehensive, that the gamblers, eluding all vigilance, conclude their game unmolested. But now and then, seduced into unwariness, or perhaps, from parsimony, being unwilling to employ the services of a spy, they are suddenly lighted upon by the constables, remorselessly collared, and dragged into the *brig*, there to await a dozen lashes in the morning.

Several times at midnight I have been startled out of a sound sleep by a sudden, violent rush under my hammock, caused by the abrupt breaking up of some nest of gamblers, who have scattered in all directions, brushing under the tiers of swinging pallets, and setting them all in a rocking commotion.

It is, however, while laying in port that gambling most thrives in a man-of-war. Then the men frequently practise their dark deeds in the light of the day, and the additional guards which, at such times, they deem indispensable, are not unworthy of note. More especially, their extra precautions in engaging the services of several spies necessitate a considerable expenditure, so that, in port, the diversion of gambling rises to the dignity of a nabob luxury.

During the day the master-at-arms and his corporals are continually prowling about on all three decks, eager to spy out iniquities. At one time, for example, you see Leggs switching his magisterial rattan, and lurking round the foremast on the spar-deck; the next moment, perhaps, he is three decks down, out of sight, prowling among the cable-tiers. Just so with his master, and Pounce his coadjutor; they are here, there, and everywhere, seemingly gifted with ubiquity.

In order successfully to carry on their proceedings by day, the gamblers must see to it that each of these constables is relentlessly dogged wherever he goes; so that, in case of his approach toward the spot where themselves are engaged, they may be warned of the fact in time to make good their escape. Accordingly, light and active scouts are selected to follow the constable about. From their youthful alertness and activity, the boys of the mizzentop are generally chosen for this purpose.

But this is not all. On board of most men-of-war there is a set of sly, knavish foxes among the crew, destitute of every principle of honour, and on a par with Irish informers. In man-of-war parlance, they come under the denomination of *fancy-men* and *white-mice*. They are called *fancy-men* because, from their zeal in craftily reporting offenders, they are presumed to be regarded with high favour by some of the officers. Though it is seldom that these informers can be certainly individualized, so secret and subtle are they in laying their information, yet certain of the crew, and especially certain of the marines, are invariably suspected to be *fancy-men* and *white-mice*, and are accordingly more or less hated by their comrades.

Now, in addition to having an eye on the master-at-arms and his aids, the day-gamblers must see to it that every person suspected of being a *white-mouse* or *fancy-man* is likewise dogged wherever he goes. Additional scouts are retained constantly to snuff at their trail. But the mysteries of man-of-war vice are wonderful; and it is now to be recorded that, from long habit and observation, and familiarity with the *guardo moves* and *manœuvres* of a frigate, the master-at-arms and his aids can almost invariably tell when any gambling is going on by day; though, in the crowded vessel, abounding in decks, tops, dark places, and outlandish corners of all sorts, they may not be able to pounce upon the identical spot where the gamblers are hidden.

During the period that Bland was suspended from his office as master-at-arms, a person who, among the sailors, went by the name of Sneak, having been long suspected to have been a *white-mouse*, was put in Bland's place. He proved a hang-dog, sidelong catch-thief, but gifted with a marvellous perseverance in ferreting out culprits; following in their track like an inevitable Cuba bloodhound, with his noiseless nose.* When disconcerted, however, you sometimes heard his bay.

'The muffled dice are somewhere around,' Sneak would say to his aids; 'there are them three chaps, there, been dogging me about for the last half-hour. I say, Pounce, has anyone been scouting around *you* this morning?'

'Four on 'em,' says Pounce. 'I know'd it; I know'd the muffled dice was rattlin'!'

'Leggs!' says the master-at-arms to his other aid, 'Leggs, how is it with *you*—any spies?'

'Ten on 'em,' says Leggs. 'There's one on 'em now—that fellow stitching a hat.'

'Halloo, you, sir!' cried the master-at-arms, 'top your boom and sail large, now. If I see you about me again, I'll have you up to the mast.'

'What am I a-doin' now?' says the hat-stitcher, with a face as long as a rope-walk. 'Can't a feller be workin' here, without being 'spected of Tom Coxe's traverse, up one ladder and down t'other?'

'Oh, I know the moves, sir; I have been on board a *guardo*. Top your boom, I say, and be off, or I'll have you hauled up and riveted in a clinch—both fore-tacks over the main-yard, and no bloody knife to cut the seizing. Sheer!*or I'll pitch into you like a shin of beef into a beggar's wallet.'*

It is often observable, that, in vessels of all kinds, the men who talk the most sailor lingo are the least sailor-like in reality. You may sometimes hear even marines jerk out more salt phrases than the captain of the forecastle himself. On the other hand, when not actively engaged in his vocation, you would take the best specimen of a seaman for a landsman. When you see a fellow yawing about the docks like a homeward-bound Indiaman, a long commodore's pennant of black ribbon flying from his mast-head, and fetching up at a grog-shop with a slew of his hull, as if an admiral were coming alongside a three-decker in his barge; you may put that man down for what man-of-war's-men call a *damn-my-eyes tar*, that is, a humbug. And many damn-my-eyes humbugs there are in this man-of-war world of ours.

LXXIV

The Maintop at Night

THE whole of our run from Rio to the Line*was one delightful yachting, so far as fine weather and the ship's sailing were concerned. It was especially pleasant when our quarter-watch lounged in the maintop, diverting ourselves in many agreeable ways. Removed from the immediate presence of the officers, we there harmlessly enjoyed ourselves, more than in any other part of the ship. By day, many of us were very industrious, making hats or mending our clothes. But by night we became more romantically inclined.

Often Jack Chase, an enthusiastic admirer of sea-scenery, would direct our attention to the moonlight on the waves, by fine snatches from his catalogue of poets. I shall never forget the lyric air with which, one morning, at dawn of day, when all the east was flushed with red and gold, he stood leaning against the topmast shrouds, and, stretching his bold hand over the sea, exclaimed, 'Here comes Aurora: top-mates, see!' And, in a liquid, long-lingering tone, he recited the lines,

> With gentle hand, as seeming oft to pause,
> The purple curtains of the morn she draws.*

'Commodore Camoens, White-Jacket.—But bear a hand there; we must rig out that stun'-sail boom—the wind is shifting.'

From our lofty perch, of a moonlight night, the frigate itself was a glorious sight. She was going large before the wind, her stun'-sails set on both sides, so that the canvass on the mainmast and foremast presented the appearance of two majestic, tapering pyramids, more than a hundred feet broad at the base, and terminating in the clouds with the light cope-stone of the royals. That immense area of snow-white canvass sliding along the sea was indeed a magnificent spectacle. The three shrouded masts looked like the apparitions of three gigantic Turkish emirs striding over the ocean.

Nor, at times, was the sound of music wanting, to augment the poetry of the scene. The whole band would be assembled on the poop, regaling the officers, and incidentally ourselves, with their fine old airs. To these, some of us would occasionally dance in the *top*, which was almost as large as an ordinary-sized parlour. When the instrumental melody of the band was not to be had, our nightingales mustered their voices, and gave us a song.

Upon these occasions Jack Chase was often called out, and regaled us, in his own free and noble style, with the *Spanish Ladies*—a favourite thing with British man-of-war's-men—and many other salt-sea ballads and ditties, including,

> Sir Patrick Spens was the best sailor
> That ever sailed the sea.

Also,

> And three times around spun our gallant ship;
> Three times around spun she;
> Three times around spun our gallant ship,
> And she went to the bottom of the sea—
> The sea, the sea, the sea,
> And she went to the bottom of the sea!

These songs would be varied by sundry *yarns* and *twisters* of the top-men. And it was at these times that I always endeavoured to draw out the oldest Tritons into narratives of the war-service they had seen. There were but few of them, it is true, who had been in action; but that only made their narratives the more valuable.

There was an old negro, who went by the name of Tawney, a sheet-anchor-man, whom we often invited into our top of tranquil nights, to hear him discourse. He was a staid and sober seaman, very intelligent, with a fine, frank bearing, one of the best men in the ship, and held in high estimation by everyone.

It seems that, during the last war between England and America, he had, with several others, been 'impressed' upon the high seas, out of a New England merchantman. The ship that impressed him was an English frigate, the *Macedonian*, afterward taken by the *Neversink*, the ship in which we were sailing.

It was the holy Sabbath, according to Tawney, and, as the Briton bore down on the American—her men at their quarters—Tawney and his countrymen, who happened to be stationed at the quarter-deck battery, respectfully accosted the captain—an old man by the name of Cardan—as he passed them, in his rapid promenade, his spy-glass under his arm. Again they assured him that they were not English-men, and that it was a most bitter thing to lift their hands against the flag of that country which harboured the mothers that bore them. They conjured him to release them from their guns, and allow them to remain neutral during the con-flict. But when a ship of any nation is running into action, it is no time for argument, small time for justice, and not much time for humanity. Snatching a pistol from the belt of a boarder standing by, the captain levelled it at the heads of the three sailors, and commanded them instantly to their quarters, under penalty of being shot on the spot. So, side by side with his country's foes, Tawney and his companions toiled at the guns, and fought out the fight to the last; with the exception of one of them, who was killed at his post by one of his own country's balls.

At length, having lost her fore- and main-topmasts, and her mizzenmast having been shot away to the deck, and her fore-yard lying in two pieces on her shattered forecastle, and in a hundred places having been *hulled* with round shot, the English frigate was reduced to the last extremity. Captain Cardan ordered his signal quarter-master to strike the flag.

Tawney was one of those who, at last, helped pull him on board the *Neversink*. As he touched the deck, Cardan saluted Decatur, the hostile commander, and offered his sword; but it was courteously declined. Perhaps the victor remembered the dinner parties that he and the Englishman had enjoyed together in Norfolk,* just previous to the breaking out of hostilities—and while both were in command of the very frigates now crippled on the sea. The *Macedonian*, it seems, had gone into Norfolk with dispatches. *Then* they had laughed and joked over their wine, and a wager of a beaver hat was said to have been made between them upon the event of the hostile meeting of their ships.

Gazing upon the heavy batteries before him, Cardan said to Decatur, 'This is a seventy-four,* not a frigate; no wonder the day is yours!'

This remark was founded upon the *Neversink*'s superiority in guns. The *Neversink*'s main-deck batteries then consisted, as now, of twenty-four-pounders; the *Macedonian*'s of only eighteens. In all, the *Neversink* numbered fifty-four guns and four hundred and fifty men; the *Macedonian*, forty-nine guns and three hundred men; a very great disparity, which, united to the other circumstances of this action, deprives the victory of all claims to glory beyond those that might be set up by a river-horse getting the better of a seal.

But if Tawney spoke truth—and he was a truth-telling man—this fact seemed counterbalanced by a circumstance he related. When the guns of the Englishman were examined, after the engagement, in more than one instance the wad was found rammed against the cartridge, without intercepting the ball. And though, in a frantic sea-fight, such a thing might be imputed to hurry and remissness, yet Tawney, a stickler for his tribe, always ascribed it to quite a different and less honourable cause. But, even granting the cause he assigned to have been the true one, it does not involve anything inimical to the general valour displayed by the British crew. Yet, from all that may be learned from candid persons who have been in sea-fights, there can be but little doubt that on board of all ships, of whatever nation, in time of action, no very small number of the men are exceedingly nervous, to say the least, at the guns; ramming and sponging at a venture. And what special patriotic interest could an impressed man, for instance, take in a fight, into which he had been dragged from the arms of his wife? Or is it to be wondered at that impressed English seamen have not scrupled, in time of war, to cripple the arm that has enslaved them?

During the same general war which prevailed at and previous to the period of the frigate-action here spoken of, a British flag-officer, in writing to the Admiralty, said, 'Everything appears to be quiet in the fleet; but, in preparing for battle last week, several of the guns in the after part of the ship were found to be spiked'; that is to say, rendered useless. Who had spiked them? The dissatisfied seamen. Is it altogether improbable, then, that the guns to which Tawney referred were manned by men who purposely refrained from making them tell on the foe; that, in this one action, the victory America gained was partly won for her by the sulky insubordination of the enemy himself?

During this same period of general war, it was frequently the case that the guns of English armed ships were found in the mornings with their breechings cut overnight. This maiming of the guns, and for the time incapacitating them, was only to be imputed to that secret spirit of hatred to the service which induced the spiking above referred to. But even in cases where no deep-seated dissatisfaction was presumed to prevail among the crew, and where a seaman, in time of action, impelled by pure fear, 'shirked from his gun'; it seems but flying in the face of Him who made such a seaman what he constitutionally was, to sew *coward* upon his back, and degrade and agonize the already trembling wretch in numberless other ways. Nor seems it a practice warranted by the Sermon on the Mount, for the officer of a battery, in time of battle, to stand over the men with his drawn sword (as was done in the *Macedonian*), and run through on the spot the first seaman who showed a semblance of fear. Tawney told me that he distinctly heard this order given by the English captain to his officers of divisions. Were the secret history of all sea-fights written, the laurels of sea-heroes would turn to ashes on their brows.

And how nationally disgraceful, in every conceivable point of view, is the IVth of our American Articles of War: '*If any person in the Navy shall pusillanimously cry for quarter, he shall suffer death.*' Thus, with death before his face from the foe, and death behind his back from his countrymen, the best valour of a man-of-war's-man can never assume the merit of a noble spontaneousness. In this, as in every other case, the Articles of War hold out no reward for good conduct, but only compel the sailor to fight, like a hired murderer, for his pay, by digging his grave before his eyes if he hesitates.

But this Article IV is open to still graver objections.

317

Courage is the most common and vulgar of the virtues; the only one shared with us by the beasts of the field; the one most apt, by excess, to run into viciousness. And since Nature generally takes away with one hand to counterbalance her gifts with the other, excessive animal courage, in many cases, only finds room in a character vacated of loftier things. But in a naval officer, animal courage is exalted to the loftiest merit, and often procures him a distinguished command.

Hence, if some brainless bravo be captain of a frigate in action, he may fight her against invincible odds, and seek to crown himself with the glory of the shambles, by permitting his hopeless crew to be butchered before his eyes, while at the same time that crew must consent to be slaughtered by the foe, under penalty of being murdered by the law. Look at the engagement between the American frigate *Essex* with the two English cruisers, the *Phœbe* and *Cherub*, off the Bay of Valparaiso, during the late war.* It is admitted on all hands that the American captain continued to fight his crippled ship against a greatly superior force; and when, at last, it became physically impossible that he could ever be otherwise than vanquished in the end; and when, from peculiarly unfortunate circumstances, his men merely stood up to their nearly useless batteries to be dismembered and blown to pieces by the incessant fire of the enemy's long guns. Nor, by thus continuing to fight, did this American frigate one iota promote the true interests of her country. I seek not to underrate any reputation which the American captain may have gained by this battle. He was a brave man; *that* no sailor will deny. But the whole world is made up of brave men. Yet I would not be at all understood as impugning his special good name. Nevertheless, it is not to be doubted, that if there were any common-sense sailors at the guns of the *Essex*, however valiant they may have been, those common-sense sailors must have greatly preferred to strike their flag, when they saw the day was fairly lost, than postpone that inevitable act till there were few American arms left to assist in hauling it down. Yet had these men, under these circumstances, 'pusillanimously cried for quarter,' by the IVth Article of War they might have been legally hung.

According to the negro, Tawney, when the captain of the *Macedonian*—seeing that the *Neversink* had his vessel completely in her power—gave the word to strike the flag, one of his officers, a man hated by the seamen for his tyranny, howled out the most terrific remonstrances, swearing that, for his part, he would not give up, but was for sinking the *Macedonian* alongside the enemy. Had he been captain, doubtless he would have done so; thereby gaining the name of a hero in this world;—but what would they have called him in the next?

But as the whole matter of war is a thing that smites common sense and Christianity in the face; so everything connected with it is utterly foolish, unchristian, barbarous, brutal, and savouring of the Feejee Islands, cannibalism, saltpetre, and the devil.

It is generally the case in a man-of-war when she strikes her flag that all discipline is at an end, and the men for a time are ungovernable. This was so on board of the English frigate. The spirit-room was broken open, and buckets of grog were passed along the decks, where many of the wounded were lying between the guns. These mariners seized the buckets, and, spite of all remonstrances, gulped down the burning spirits, till, as Tawney said, the blood suddenly spirted out of their wounds, and they fell dead to the deck.

The negro had many more stories to tell of this fight; and frequently he would escort me along our main-deck batteries —still mounting the same guns used in the battle—pointing out their ineffaceable indentations and scars. Coated over with the accumulated paint of more than thirty years, they were almost invisible to a casual eye; but Tawney knew them all by heart; for he had returned home in the *Neversink*, and had beheld these scars shortly after the engagement.

One afternoon, I was walking with him along the gundeck, when he paused abreast of the mainmast. 'This part of the ship,' said he, 'we called the *slaughter-house* on board the *Macedonian*. Here the men fell, five and six at a time. An enemy always directs its shot here, in order to hurl over the mast, if possible. The beams and carlines overhead in the *Macedonian* slaughter-house were spattered with blood and brains. About the hatchways it looked like a butcher's stall; bits of human flesh sticking in the ring-bolts. A pig that ran about the decks escaped unharmed, but his hide was so clotted with blood, from rooting among the pools of gore, that when the ship struck the sailors hove the animal overboard, swearing that it would be rank cannibalism to eat him.'

Another quadruped, a goat, lost its forelegs in this fight.

The sailors who were killed—according to the usual custom—were ordered to be thrown overboard as soon as they fell; no doubt, as the negro said, that the sight of so many corpses lying around might not appal the survivors at the guns. Among other instances, he related the following. A shot entering one of the port-holes dashed dead two-thirds of a gun's crew. The captain of the next gun, dropping his lock-string, which he had just pulled, turned over the heap of bodies to see who they were; when, perceiving an old messmate who had sailed with him in many cruises, he burst into tears, and, taking the corpse up in his arms, and going with it to the side, held it over the water a moment, and eyeing it, cried, 'Oh God! Tom!'—'D——n your prayers over that thing! overboard with it, and down to your gun!' roared a wounded lieutenant. The order was obeyed, and the heart-stricken sailor returned to his post.

Tawney's recitals were enough to snap this man-of-war world's sword in its scabbard. And thinking of all the cruel carnal glory wrought out by naval heroes in scenes like these, I asked myself whether, indeed, that was a glorious coffin in which Lord Nelson was entombed—a coffin presented to him, during life, by Captain Hallowell; it had been dug out of the mainmast of the French line-of-battle ship *L'Orient*, which, burning up with British fire, destroyed hundreds of Frenchmen at the Battle of the Nile.

Peace to Lord Nelson where he sleeps in his mouldering mast! but rather would I be urned in the trunk of some green tree, and even in death have the vital sap circulating round me, giving of my dead body to the living foliage that shaded my peaceful tomb.

LXXV

'Sink, Burn, and Destroy'

Printed Admiralty orders in time of war.

AMONG innumerable *yarns and twisters* reeled off in our maintop during our pleasant run to the north, none could match those of Jack Chase, our captain.

Never was there better company than ever-glorious Jack. The things which most men only read of, or dream about, he had seen and experienced. He had been a dashing smuggler in his day, and could tell of a long nine-pounder rammed home with wads of French silks; of cartridges stuffed with the finest gunpowder tea; of cannister-shot full of West India sweetmeats; of sailor frocks and trowsers, quilted inside with costly laces; and table-legs, hollow as musket-barrels, compactly stowed with rare drugs and spices. He could tell of a wicked widow, too—a beautiful receiver of smuggled goods upon the English coast—who smiled so sweetly upon the smugglers when they sold her silks and laces, cheap as tape and ginghams. She called them gallant fellows, hearts of game; and bade them bring her more.

He could tell of desperate fights with His British Majesty's cutters, in midnight coves upon a stormy coast; of the capture of a reckless band, and their being drafted on board a man-of-war; of their swearing that their chief was slain; of a writ of habeas corpus sent on board for one of them for a debt—a reserved and handsome man—and his going ashore, strongly suspected of being the slaughtered captain, and this a successful scheme for his escape.

But more than all, Jack could tell of the Battle of Navarino, for he had been a captain of one of the main-deck guns on board Admiral Codrington's flagship, the *Asia*. Were mine the style of stout old Chapman's Homer, even then I would scarce venture to give noble Jack's own version of this fight, wherein, on the 20th of October, A.D. 1827, thirty-two sail of Englishmen, Frenchmen, and Russians, attacked and vanquished in the Levant an Ottoman fleet of three ships-of-the-line, twenty-five frigates, and a swarm of fire-ships and hornet craft.

'We bayed to be at them,' said Jack; 'and when we *did* open fire, we were like dolphin among the flying-fish. "Every man take his bird" was the cry, when we trained our guns. And those guns all smoked like rows of Dutch pipe-bowls, my hearties! My gun's crew carried small flags in their bosoms, to nail to the mast in case the ship's colours were shot away. Stripped to the waistbands, we fought like skinned tigers, and bowled down the Turkish frigates like ninepins. Among their shrouds—swarming thick with small-arm men, like flights of pigeons lighted on pine-trees—our marines sent their leaden peas and gooseberries, like a shower of hailstones in Labrador. It was a stormy time, my hearties! The blasted Turks pitched into the old *Asia*'s hull a whole quarry of marble shot, each ball one hundred and fifty pounds. They knocked three port-holes into one. But we gave them better than they sent. "Up and at them, my bull-dog!" said I, patting my gun on the breech; "tear open hatchways in their Moslem sides!" White-Jacket, my lad, you ought to have been there. The bay was covered with masts and yards, as I have seen a raft of snags in the Arkansas River. Showers of burned rice and olives from the exploding foe fell upon us like manna in the wilderness. "*Allah! Allah! Mohammed! Mohammed!*" split the air; some cried it out from the Turkish port-holes; others shrieked it forth from the drowning waters, their top-knots floating on their shaven skulls like black snakes on half-tide rocks. By those top-knots they believed that their Prophet would drag them up to Paradise, but they sank fifty fathoms, my hearties, to the bottom of the bay. "Ain't the bloody 'Hometons* going to strike yet?" cried my first loader, a Guernsey man, thrusting his neck out of the port-hole, and looking at the Turkish line-of-battle ship near by. That instant his head blew by me like a bursting Paixhan shot, and the flag of Ned Knowles himself was hauled down forever. We dragged his hull to one side, and avenged him with the cooper's anvil, which, endways, we rammed home—a messmate shoved in the dead man's bloody Scotch cap for the wad, and sent it flying into the line-of-battle ship. By the God of War! boys, we hardly left enough of that craft to boil a pot of water with. It was a hard day's work—a sad day's work, my hearties. That night, when all was over, I slept sound enough, with a box of cannister shot for my pillow! But you ought to have seen the boat-load of Turkish flags one of our captains carried home; he swore to dress his father's orchard in colours with them, just as our spars are dressed for a gala day.'

'Though you tormented the Turks at Navarino, noble Jack, yet you came off yourself with only the loss of a splinter, it seems,' said a top-man, glancing at our captain's maimed hand.

'Yes; but I and one of the lieutenants had a narrower escape than that. A shot struck the side of my port-hole, and sent the splinters right and left. One took off my hat rim clean to my brow; another *razeed* the lieutenant's left boot, by slicing off the heel; a third shot killed my powder-monkey, without touching him.'

'How, Jack?'

'It *whizzed* the poor babe dead. He was seated on a *cheese of wads* at the time, and after the dust of the powdered bulwarks had blown away, I noticed he yet sat still, his eyes wide open. "*My little hero!*" cried I, and I clapped him on the back; but he fell on his face at my feet. I touched his heart, and found he was dead. There was not a little-finger mark on him.'

Silence now fell upon the listeners for a time, broken at last by the second captain of the top.

'Noble Jack, I know you never brag, but tell us what you did yourself that day.'

'Why, my hearties, I did not do quite as much as my gun. But I flatter myself it was that gun that brought down the Turkish admiral's mainmast; and the stump left wasn't long enough to make a wooden leg for Lord Nelson.'

'How? but I thought, by the way you pull a lock-string on board here, and look along the sight, that you can steer a shot about right—hey, Jack?'

'It was the Admiral of the Fleet—God Almighty—who directed the shot that dismasted the Turkish admiral,' said Jack; 'I only pointed the gun.'

'But how did you feel, Jack, when the musket-ball carried away one of your hooks there?'

'Feel! only a finger the lighter. I have seven more left, besides thumbs; and they did good service, too, in the torn rigging the day after the fight; for you must know, my hearties, that the hardest work comes after the guns are run in. Three days I helped work, with one hand, in the rigging, in the same trowsers that I wore in the action; the blood had dried and stiffened; they looked like glazed red morocco.'

Now, this Jack Chase had a heart in him like a mastodon's. I have seen him weep when a man has been flogged at the gangway; yet, in relating the story of the Battle of Navarino, he plainly showed that he held the God of the blessed Bible to have been the British Commodore in the Levant, on the bloody 20th of October, A.D. 1827. And thus it would seem that war almost makes blasphemers of the best of men, and brings them all down to the Feejee standard of humanity. Some man-of-war's-men have confessed to me, that as a battle has raged more and more, their hearts have hardened in infernal harmony; and, like their own guns, they have fought without a thought.

Soldier or sailor, the fighting man is but a fiend; and the staff and body-guard of the Devil musters many a baton. But war at times is inevitable. Must the national honour be trampled under foot by an insolent foe?

Say on, say on; but know you this, and lay it to heart, war-voting Bench of Bishops, that He on whom we believe *himself* has enjoined us to turn the left cheek if the right be smitten. Never mind what follows. That passage you cannot expunge from the Bible; that passage is as binding upon us as any other; that passage embodies the soul and substance of the Christian faith; without it, Christianity were like any other faith. And that passage will yet, by the blessing of God, turn the world. But in some things we must turn Quakers first.

But though unlike most scenes of carnage, which have proved useless murders of men, Admiral Codrington's victory undoubtedly achieved the emancipation of Greece, and terminated the Turkish atrocities in that tomahawked state, yet who shall lift his hand and swear that a Divine Providence led the van of the combined fleets of England, France, and Russia at the Battle of Navarino? For if this be so, then it led the van against the Church's own elect—the persecuted Waldenses* in Switzerland—and kindled the Smithfield fires in bloody Mary's time.*

But all events are mixed in a fusion indistinguishable. What we call Fate is even, heartless, and impartial; not a fiend to kindle bigot flames, nor a philanthropist to espouse the cause of Greece. We may fret, fume, and fight; but the thing called Fate everlastingly sustains an armed neutrality.

Yet though all this be so, nevertheless, in our own hearts, we mould the whole world's hereafters; and in our own hearts we fashion our own gods. Each mortal casts his vote for whom he will to rule the worlds; I have a voice that helps to shape eternity; and my volitions stir the orbits of the furthest suns. In two senses, we are precisely what we worship. Ourselves are Fate.

LXXVI
The Chains

WHEN wearied with the tumult and occasional contention of the gun-deck of our frigate, I have often retreated to a port-hole, and calmed myself down by gazing broad off upon a placid sea. After the battle-din of the last two chapters, let us now do the like, and, in the sequestered fore-chains of the *Neversink*, tranquillize ourselves, if we may.

Notwithstanding the domestic communism to which the seamen in a man-of-war are condemned, and the publicity in which actions the most diffident and retiring in their nature must be performed, there is yet an odd corner or two where you may sometimes steal away, and, for a few moments, almost be private.

Chief among these places is the *chains*, to which I would sometimes hie during our pleasant homeward-bound glide over those pensive tropical latitudes. After hearing my fill of the wild yarns of our top, here would I recline—if not disturbed—serenely concocting information into wisdom.

The *chains* designates the small platform outside of the hull, at the base of the large shrouds leading down from the three mast-heads to the bulwarks. At present they seem to be getting out of vogue among merchant-vessels, along with the fine, old-fashioned quarter-galleries, little turret-like appurtenances, which, in the days of the old admirals, set off the angles of an armed ship's stern. Here a naval officer might lounge away an hour after action, smoking a cigar to drive out of his whiskers the villainous smoke of the gunpowder. The picturesque, delightful stern-gallery also, a broad balcony overhanging the sea, and entered from the captain's cabin, much as you might enter a bower from a lady's chamber; this charming balcony, where, sailing over summer seas in the days of the old Peruvian viceroys, the Spanish cavalier, Mendanna of Lima,* made love to the Lady Isabella, as they voyaged in quest of the Solomon Islands, the fabulous Ophir, the Grand Cyclades; and the Lady Isabella, at sunset, blushed like the Orient, and gazed down to the gold-fish and silver-hued flying-fish, that wove the woof and warp of their wakes in bright, scaly tartans and plaids underneath where the lady reclined; this charming balcony—exquisite retreat—has been cut away by Vandalic innovations. Ay, that claw-footed old gallery is no longer in fashion; in commodore's eyes, is no longer genteel.

Out on all furniture fashions but those that are past! Give me my grandfather's old armchair, planted upon four carved frogs, as the Hindoos fabled the world to be supported upon four tortoises; give me his cane, with the gold-loaded top—a cane that, like the musket of General Washington's father and the broadsword of William Wallace,* would break down the back of the switch-carrying dandies of these spindle-shank days; give me his broad-breasted vest, coming bravely down over the hips, and furnished with two strong-boxes of pockets to keep guineas in; toss this toppling cylinder of a beaver overboard, and give me my grandfather's gallant, gable-ended, cocked hat.

But though the quarter-galleries and the stern-gallery of a man-of-war are departed, yet the *chains* still linger; nor can there be imagined a more agreeable retreat. The huge blocks and lanyards forming the pedestals of the shrouds divide the chains into numerous little chapels, alcoves, niches, and altars, where you lazily lounge—outside of the ship, though on board. But there are plenty to divide a good thing with you in this man-of-war world. Often, when snugly seated in one of these little alcoves, gazing off to the horizon, and thinking of Cathay,* I have been startled from my repose by some old quarter-gunner, who, having newly painted a parcel of match-tubs, wanted to set them to dry.

At other times, one of the tattooing artists would crawl over the bulwarks, followed by his sitter; and then a bare arm or leg would be extended, and the disagreeable business of '*pricking*' commence, right under my eyes; or an irruption of tars, with ditty-bags or sea-reticules, and piles of old trowsers to mend, would break in upon my seclusion, and, forming a sewing-circle, drive me off with their chatter.

But once—it was a Sunday afternoon—I was pleasantly reclining in a particularly shady and secluded little niche between two lanyards, when I heard a low, supplicating voice. Peeping through the narrow space between the ropes, I perceived an aged seaman on his knees, his face turned seaward, with closed eyes, buried in prayer. Softly rising, I stole through a port-hole, and left the venerable worshipper alone.

He was a sheet-anchor-man, an earnest Baptist, and was well known, in his own part of the ship, to be constant in his solitary devotions in the *chains*. He reminded me of St. Anthony going out into the wilderness to pray.

This man was captain of the starboard bow-chaser, one of the two long twenty-four-pounders on the forecastle. In time of action, the command of that iron Thalaba the Destroyer* would devolve upon *him*. It would be his business to 'train' it properly; to see it well loaded; the grape and cannister rammed home; also, to 'prick the cartridge', 'take the sight', and give the word for the match-man to apply his wand; bidding a sudden hell to flash forth from the muzzle, in wide combustion and death.

Now, this captain of the bow-chaser was an upright old man, a sincere, humble believer, and he but earned his bread in being captain of that gun; but how, with those hands of his begrimed with powder, could he break that *other* and most peaceful and penitent bread of the Supper? though in that hallowed sacrament, it seemed, he had often partaken ashore. The omission of this rite in a man-of-war—though there is a chaplain to preside over it, and at least a few communicants to partake—must be ascribed to a sense of religious propriety, in the last degree to be commended.

Ah! the best righteousness of our man-of-war world seems but an unrealized ideal, after all; and those maxims which, in the hope of bringing about a millennium, we busily teach to the heathen, we Christians ourselves disregard. In view of the whole present social framework of our world, so ill-adapted to the practical adoption of the meekness of Christianity, there seems almost some ground for the thought, that although our blessed Saviour was full of the wisdom of heaven, yet his gospel seems lacking in the practical wisdom of earth—in a due appreciation of the necessities of nations at times demanding bloody massacres and wars; in a proper estimation of the value of rank, title, and money. But all this only the more crowns the divine consistency of Jesus; since Burnet*and the best theologians demonstrate, that his nature was not merely human—was not that of a mere man of the world.

LXXVII

The Hospital in a Man-of-war

AFTER running with a fine steady breeze up to the Line, it fell calm, and there we lay, three days enchanted on the sea. We were a most puissant man-of-war, no doubt, with our five hundred men, commodore, and captain, backed by our long batteries of thirty-two- and twenty-four-pounders; yet, for all that, there we lay rocking, helpless as an infant in the cradle. Had it only been a gale instead of a calm, gladly would we have charged upon it with our gallant bowsprit, as with a stout lance in rest; but, as with mankind, this serene, passive foe—unresisting and irresistible—lived it out, unconquered to the last.

All these three days the heat was excessive; the sun drew the tar from the seams of the ship; the awnings were spread fore and aft; the decks were kept constantly sprinkled with water. It was during this period that a sad event occurred, though not an unusual one on shipboard. But in order to prepare for its narration, some account of a part of the ship called the *sick-bay* must needs be presented.

The *sick-bay* is that part of a man-of-war where the invalid seamen are placed; in many respects it answers to a public hospital ashore. As with most frigates, the sick-bay of the *Neversink* was on the berth-deck—the third deck from above. It was in the extreme forward part of that deck, embracing the triangular area in the bows of the ship. It was, therefore, a subterranean vault, into which scarce a ray of heaven's glad light ever penetrated, even at noon.

In a sea-going frigate that has all her armament and stores

on board, the floor of the berth-deck is partly below the surface of the water. But in a smooth harbour, some circulation of air is maintained by opening large auger-holes in the upper portion of the sides, called 'air-ports', not much above the water level. Before going to sea, however, these air-ports must be closed, caulked, and the seams hermetically sealed with pitch. These places for ventilation being shut, the sick-bay is entirely barred against the free, natural admission of fresh air. In the *Neversink*, a few lungsful were forced down by artificial means. But as the ordinary *wind-sail* was the only method adopted, the quantity of fresh air sent down was regulated by the force of the wind. In a calm there was none to be had, while in a severe gale the wind-sail had to be hauled up, on account of the violent draught blowing full upon the cots of the sick. An openwork partition divided our sick-bay from the rest of the deck, where the hammocks of the watch were slung; it therefore was exposed to all the uproar that ensued upon the watches being relieved.

An official, called the surgeon's steward, assisted by subordinates, presided over the place. He was the same individual alluded to as officiating at the amputation of the top-man. He was always to be found at his post, by night and by day.

This surgeon's steward deserves a description. He was a small, pale, hollow-eyed young man, with that peculiar Lazarus-like expression so often noticed in hospital attendants. Seldom or never did you see him on deck, and when he *did* emerge into the light of the sun, it was with an abashed look, and an uneasy, winking eye. The sun was not made for *him*. His nervous organization was confounded by the sight of the robust old sea-dogs on the forecastle and the general tumult of the spar-deck, and he mostly buried himself below in an atmosphere which long habit had made congenial.

This young man never indulged in frivolous conversation; he only talked of the surgeon's prescriptions; his every word was a bolus. He never was known to smile; nor did he even look sober in the ordinary way; but his countenance ever wore an aspect of cadaverous resignation to his fate. Strange! that so many of those who would fain minister to our own health should look so much like invalids themselves.

Connected with the sick-bay, over which the surgeon's steward presided—but removed from it in place, being next door to the counting-room of the purser's steward—was a regular apothecary's shop, of which he kept the key. It was fitted up precisely like an apothecary's on shore, displaying tiers of shelves on all four sides, filled with green bottles and gallipots; beneath were multitudinous drawers, bearing incomprehensible gilded inscriptions in abbreviated Latin.

He generally opened his shop for an hour or two every morning and evening. There was a Venetian blind in the upper part of the door, which he threw up when inside, so as to admit a little air. And there you would see him, with a green shade over his eyes, seated on a stool, and pounding his pestle in a great iron mortar that looked like a howitzer, mixing some jalapy compound.* A smoky lamp shed a flickering, yellow-fever tinge upon his pallid face and the closely-packed regiments of gallipots.

Several times when I felt in need of a little medicine, but was not ill enough to report myself to the surgeon at his levees, I would call of a morning upon his steward at the Sign of the Mortar, and beg him to give me what I wanted; when, without speaking a word, this cadaverous young man would mix me my potion in a tin cup, and hand it out through the little opening in his door, like the boxed-up treasurer giving you your change at the ticket-office of a theatre.

But there was a little shelf against the wall of the door, and upon this I would set the tin cup for a while, and survey it; for I never was a Julius Caesar at taking medicine; and to take it in this way, without a single attempt at disguising it; with no counteracting little morsel to hurry down after it; in short, to go to the very apothecary's in person, and there, at the counter, swallow down your dose, as if it were a nice mint-julep taken at the bar of a hotel—*this* was a bitter bolus indeed. But, then, this pallid young apothecary charged nothing for it, and *that* was no small satisfaction; for is it not remarkable, to say the least, that a shore apothecary should actually charge you money—round dollars and cents—for giving you a horrible nausea?

My tin cup would wait a long time on that little shelf; yet 'Pills', as the sailors called him, never heeded my lingering, but in sober, silent sadness continued pounding his mortar or folding up his powders; until at last some other customer would appear, and then, in a sudden frenzy of resolution, I would gulp down my sherry-cobbler, and carry its unspeakable flavour with me far up into the frigate's main-top. I do not know whether it was the wide roll of the ship, as felt in that giddy perch, that occasioned it, but I always got seasick after taking medicine and going aloft with it. Seldom or never did it do me any lasting good.

Now the surgeon's steward was only a subordinate of Surgeon Cuticle himself, who lived in the ward-room among the lieutenants, sailing-master, chaplain, and purser.

The surgeon is, by law, charged with the business of over-looking the general sanitary affairs of the ship. If anything is going on in any of its departments which he judges to be detrimental to the healthfulness of the crew, he has a right to protest against it formally to the captain. When a man is being scourged at the gangway, the surgeon stands by; and if he thinks that the punishment is becoming more than the culprit's constitution can well bear, he has a right to inter-fere and demand its cessation for the time.

But though the Navy regulations nominally vest him with this high discretionary authority over the very commodore himself, how seldom does he exercise it in cases where humanity demands it! Three years is a long time to spend in one ship, and to be at swords' points with its captain and lieutenants during such a period must be very unsocial and every way irksome. No otherwise than thus, at least, can the remissness of some surgeons in remonstrating against cruelty be accounted for.

Not to speak, again, of the continual dampness of the decks consequent upon flooding them with salt water, when we were driving near to Cape Horn, it needs only to be mentioned that, on board of the *Neversink*, men known to be in consumptions gasped under the scourge of the boat-swain's mate, when the surgeon and his two attendants stood by and never interposed. But where the unscrupulousness of martial discipline is maintained, it is in vain to attempt softening its rigour by the ordaining of humanitarian laws. Sooner might you tame the grizzly bear of Missouri than humanize a thing so essentially cruel and heartless.

But the surgeon has yet other duties to perform. Not a sea-man enters the Navy without undergoing a corporal ex-amination, to test his soundness in wind and limb.

One of the first places into which I was introduced when I first entered on board the *Neversink* was the sick-bay, where I found one of the assistant surgeons seated at a green baize table. It was his turn for visiting the apartment. Having been commanded by the deck officer to report my business to the functionary before me, I accordingly hemmed, to attract his attention, and then catching his eye, politely intimated that I called upon him for the purpose of being accurately laid out and surveyed.

'Strip!' was the answer, and, rolling up his gold-laced cuff, he proceeded to manipulate me. He punched me in the ribs, smote me across the chest, commanded me to stand on one leg and hold out the other horizontally. He asked me whether any of my family were consumptive; whether I ever felt a tendency to a rush of blood to the head; whether I was gouty; how often I had been bled during my life; how long I had been ashore; how long I had been afloat; with several other questions which have altogether slipped my memory. He concluded his interrogatories with this extraordinary and unwarranted one—'Are you pious?'

It was a leading question which somewhat staggered me, but I said not a word; when, feeling of my calves, he looked up and incomprehensibly said, 'I am afraid you are not.'

At length he declared me a sound animal, and wrote a certificate to that effect, with which I returned to the deck.

This assistant surgeon turned out to be a very singular

character, and when I became more acquainted with him, I ceased to marvel at the curious question with which he had concluded his examination of my person.

He was a thin, knock-kneed man, with a sour, saturnine expression, rendered the more peculiar from his shaving his beard so remorselessly, that his chin and cheeks always looked blue, as if pinched with cold. His long familiarity with nautical invalids seemed to have filled him full of theological hypoes* concerning the state of their souls. He was at once the physician and priest of the sick, washing down his boluses with ghostly consolation, and among the sailors he went by the name of The Pelican, a fowl whose hanging pouch imparts to it a most chop-fallen, lugubrious expression.

The privilege of going off duty and lying by when you are sick, is one of the few points in which a man-of-war is far better for the sailor than a merchantman. But, as with every other matter in the Navy, the whole thing is subject to the general discipline of the vessel, and is conducted with a severe, unyielding method and regularity, making no allowances for exceptions to rules.

During the half-hour preceding morning quarters, the surgeon of a frigate is to be found in the sick-bay, where, after going his rounds among the invalids, he holds a levee for the benefit of all new candidates for the sick-list. If, after looking at your tongue, and feeling of your pulse, he pronounces you a proper candidate, his secretary puts you down on his books, and you are thenceforth relieved from all duty, and have abundant leisure in which to recover your health. Let the boatswain blow; let the deck officer bellow; let the captain of your gun hunt you up; yet, if it can be answered by your messmates that you are 'down on the list', you ride it all out with impunity. The commodore himself has then no authority over you. But you must not be too much elated, for your immunities are only secure while you are immured in the dark hospital below. Should you venture to get a mouthful of fresh air on the spar-deck, and be there discovered by an officer, you will in vain plead your illness; for it is quite impossible, it seems, that any true man-of-war invalid can be hearty enough to crawl up the ladders. Besides, the raw sea air, as they will tell you, is not good for the sick.

But, notwithstanding all this, notwithstanding the darkness and closeness of the sick-bay, in which an alleged invalid must be content to shut himself up till the surgeon pronounces him cured, many instances occur, especially in protracted bad weather, where pretended invalids will submit to this dismal hospital durance, in order to escape hard work and wet jackets.

There is a story told somewhere of the Devil taking down the confessions of a woman on a strip of parchment, and being obliged to stretch it longer and longer with his teeth, in order to find room for all the lady had to say. Much thus was it with our purser's steward,* who had to lengthen out his manuscript sick-list, in order to accommodate all the names which were presented to him while we were off the pitch of Cape Horn. What sailors call the *Cape Horn Fever* alarmingly prevailed; though it disappeared altogether when we got into fine weather, which, as with many other invalids, was solely to be imputed to the wonder-working effects of an entire change of climate.

It seems very strange, but it is really true, that off Cape Horn some *sogers* of sailors will stand cupping, and bleeding, and blistering, before they will budge. On the other hand, there are cases where a man actually sick and in need of medicine will refuse to go on the sick-list, because in that case his allowance of *grog* must be stopped.

On board of every American man-of-war, bound for sea, there is a goodly supply of wines and various delicacies put on board—according to law—for the benefit of the sick, whether officers or sailors. And one of the chicken-coops is always reserved for the government chickens, destined for a similar purpose. But, on board of the *Neversink*, the only delicacies given to invalid sailors was a little sago or arrowroot, and they did not get *that* unless severely ill; but, so far as I could learn, no wine, in any quantity, was ever prescribed for them, though the government bottles often went into the ward-room, for the benefit of indisposed officers.

And though the government chicken-coop was replenished at every port, yet not four pair of drum-sticks were ever boiled into broth for sick sailors. Where the chickens went someone must have known; but, as I cannot vouch for it myself, I will not here back the hardy assertion of the men, which was that the pious Pelican—true to his name—was extremely fond of poultry. I am still the less disposed to believe this scandal, from the continued leanness of the Pelican, which could hardly have been the case did he nourish himself by so nutritious a dish as the drum-sticks of fowls, a diet prescribed to pugilists in training. But who can avoid being suspicious of a very suspicious person? Pelican! I rather suspect you still.

LXXVIII

Dismal Times in the Mess

I T was on the first day of the long, hot calm which we had on the Equator, that a messmate of mine, by the name of Shenly, who had been for some weeks complaining, at length went on the sick-list.

An old gunner's mate of the mess—Priming, the man with the hare-lip, who, true to his tribe, was charged to the muzzle with bile, and, moreover, rammed home on top of it a wad of sailor superstition—this gunner's mate indulged in some gloomy and savage remarks—strangely tinged with genuine feeling and grief—at the announcement of the sickness of Shenly, coming as it did not long after the almost fatal accident befalling poor Baldy, captain of the mizzentop, another messmate of ours, and the dreadful fate of the amputated foretop-man whom we buried in Rio, also our messmate.

We were cross-legged seated at dinner, between the guns, when the sad news concerning Shenly was first communicated.

'I know'd it, I know'd it,' said Priming, through his nose.

'Blast ye, I told ye so;—poor fellow!—But dam'me, I know'd it. This comes of having *thirteen* in the mess. I hope he ar'n't dangerous, men? Poor Shenly! But, blast it, it warn't till White-Jacket there comed into the mess that these here things began. I don't believe there'll be more nor three of us left by the time we strike soundings, men. But how is he now? Have you been down to see him, any on ye? Damn you, you Jonah! I don't see how you can sleep in your hammock, knowing as you do that by making an odd number in the mess you have been the death of one poor fellow, and ruined Baldy for life, and here's poor Shenly keeled up. Blast you, and your jacket, say I.'

'My dear messmate,' I cried, 'don't blast me any more, for Heaven's sake. Blast my jacket you may, and I'll join you in *that*; but don't blast *me*; for if you do, I shouldn't wonder if I myself was the next man to keel up.'

'Gunner's mate!' said Jack Chase, helping himself to a slice of beef, and sandwiching it between two large biscuits— 'Gunner's mate! White-Jacket there is my particular friend, and I would take it as a particular favour if you would *knock off* blasting him. It's in bad taste, rude, and unworthy a gentleman.'

'Take your back away from that 'ere gun-carriage, will ye now, Jack Chase?' cried Priming, in reply, just then Jack happening to lean up against it. 'Must I be all the time cleaning after you fellows? Blast ye! I spent an hour on that 'ere gun-carriage this very mornin'. But it all comes of White-Jacket there. If it warn't for having one too many, there wouldn't be any crowding and jamming in the mess. I'm blessed if we ar'n't about chock-a-block here! Move further up there, I'm sitting on my leg!'

'For God's sake, gunner's mate,' cried I, 'if it will content you, I and my jacket will leave the mess.'

'I wish you would, and be——to you!' he replied.

'And if he does, you will mess alone, gunner's mate,' said Jack Chase.

'That you will,' cried all.

'And I wish to the Lord you'd let me!' growled Priming,

irritably rubbing his head with the handle of his sheath-knife.

'You are an old bear, gunner's mate,' said Jack Chase.

'I am an old Turk,' he replied, drawing the flat blade of his knife between his teeth, thereby producing a whetting, grating sound.

'Let him alone, let him alone, men,' said Jack Chase. 'Only keep off the tail of a rattlesnake, and he'll not rattle.'

'Look out he don't bite, though,' said Priming, snapping his teeth; and with that he rolled off, growling as he went.

Though I did my best to carry off my vexation with an air of indifference, need I say how I cursed my jacket, that it thus seemed the means of fastening on me the murder of one of my shipmates, and the probable murder of two more. For, had it not been for my jacket, doubtless, I had yet been a member of my old mess, and so have escaped making the luckless odd number among my present companions.

All I could say in private to Priming had no effect; though I often took him aside, to convince him of the philosophical impossibility of my having been accessory to the misfortunes of Baldy, the buried sailor in Rio, and Shenly. But Priming knew better; nothing could move him; and he ever afterward eyed me as virtuous citizens do some notorious underhand villain going unhung of justice.

Jacket! jacket! thou hast much to answer for, jacket!

LXXIX
How Man-of-war's-men die at Sea

SHENLY, my sick messmate, was a middle-aged, handsome, intelligent seaman, whom some hard calamity, or perhaps some unfortunate excess, must have driven into the Navy. He told me he had a wife and two children in Portsmouth, in the state of New Hampshire. Upon being examined by Cuticle, the surgeon, he was, on purely scientific grounds, reprimanded by that functionary for not having previously appeared before him. He was immediately consigned to one of the invalid cots as a serious case. His complaint was of long standing; a pulmonary one, now attended with general prostration.

The same evening he grew so much worse, that, according to man-of-war usage, we, his messmates, were officially notified that we must take turns at sitting up with him through the night. We at once made our arrangements, allotting two hours for a watch. Not till the third night did my own turn come round. During the day preceding, it was stated at the mess that our poor messmate was run down completely; the surgeon had given him up.

At four bells (two o'clock in the morning), I went down to relieve one of my messmates at the sick man's cot. The profound quietude of the calm pervaded the entire frigate through all her decks. The watch on duty were dozing on the carronade-slides, far above the sick-bay; and the watch below were fast asleep in their hammocks, on the same deck with the invalid.

Groping my way under these two hundred sleepers, I entered the hospital. A dim lamp was burning on the table, which was screwed down to the floor. This light shed dreary shadows over the whitewashed walls of the place, making it look like a whited sepulchre under ground. The wind-sail had collapsed, and lay motionless on the deck. The low groans of the sick were the only sounds to be heard; and, as I advanced, some of them rolled upon me their sleepless, silent, tormented eyes.

'Fan him, and keep his forehead wet with this sponge,' whispered my messmate, whom I came to relieve, as I drew near to Shenly's cot, 'and wash the foam from his mouth; nothing more can be done for him. If he dies before your watch is out, call the surgeon's steward; he sleeps in that hammock,' pointing it out. 'Good-bye, good-bye, messmate,' he then whispered, stooping over the sick man; and so saying, he left the place.

Shenly was lying on his back. His eyes were closed, forming two dark-blue pits in his face; his breath was coming and going with a slow, long-drawn, mechanical precision. It was the mere foundering hull of a man that was before me; and though it presented the well-known features of my mess-mate, yet I knew that the living soul of Shenly never more would look out of those eyes.

So warm had it been during the day, that the surgeon himself, when visiting the sick-bay, had entered it in his shirt sleeves; and so warm was now the night, that even in the lofty top I had worn but a loose linen frock and trowsers. But in this subterranean sick-bay, buried in the very bowels of the ship, and at sea cut off from all ventilation, the heat of the night calm was intense. The sweat dripped from me as if I had just emerged from a bath; and stripping myself naked to the waist, I sat by the side of the cot, and with a bit of crumpled paper—put into my hand by the sailor I had relieved—kept fanning the motionless white face before me.

I could not help thinking, as I gazed, whether this man's fate had not been accelerated by his confinement in this heated furnace below; and whether many a sick man round me might not soon improve, if but permitted to swing his hammock in the airy vacancies of the half-deck above, open to the port-holes, but reserved for the promenade of the officers.

At last the heavy breathing grew more and more irregular, and gradually dying away, left forever the unstirring form of Shenly.

Calling the surgeon's steward, he at once told me to rouse the master-at-arms, and four or five of my messmates. The master-at-arms approached, and immediately demanded the dead man's bag, which was accordingly dragged into the bay. Having been laid on the floor, and washed with a bucket of water which I drew from the ocean, the body was then dressed in a white frock, trowsers, and neckerchief, taken out of the bag. While this was going on, the master-at arms—standing over the operation with his rattan, and directing myself and messmates—indulged in much discursive levity, intended to manifest his fearlessness of death.

Pierre, who had been a *chummy* of Shenly's, spent much

time in tying the neckerchief in an elaborate bow, and affectionately adjusting the white frock and trowsers; but the master-at-arms put an end to this by ordering us to carry the body up to the gun-deck. It was placed on the death-board (used for that purpose), and we proceeded with it to-ward the main hatchway, awkwardly crawling under the tiers of hammocks, where the entire watch below was sleep-ing. As, unavoidably, we rocked their pallets, the man-of-war's-men would cry out against us; through the mutterings of curses, the corpse reached the hatchway. Here the board slipped, and some time was spent in readjusting the body. At length we deposited it on the gun-deck, between two guns, and a Union Jack being thrown over it for a pall, I was left again to watch by its side.

I had not been seated on my shot-box three minutes, when the messenger-boy passed me on his way forward; presently the slow, regular stroke of the ship's great bell was heard, proclaiming through the calm the expiration of the watch; it was four o'clock in the morning.

Poor Shenly! thought I, that sounds like your knell! and here you lie becalmed, in the last calm of all!

Hardly had the brazen din died away, when the boatswain and his mates mustered round the hatchway, within a yard or two of the corpse, and the usual thundering call was given for the watch below to turn out.

'All the starboard watch, ahoy! On deck there, below! Wide awake there, sleepers!'

But the dreamless sleeper by my side, who had so often sprung from his hammock at that summons, moved not a limb; the blue sheet over him lay unwrinkled.

A messmate of the other watch now came to relieve me; but I told him I chose to remain where I was till daylight came.

LXXX

The last Stitch

JUST before daybreak, two of the sail-maker's gang drew near, each with a lantern, carrying some canvass, two large shot, needles, and twine. I knew their errand; for in men-of-war the sail-maker is the undertaker.

They laid the body on deck, and, after fitting the canvass to it, seated themselves, cross-legged like tailors, one on each side, and, with their lanterns before them, went to stitching away, as if mending an old sail. Both were old men, with grizzled hair and beard, and shrunken faces. They belonged to that small class of aged seamen who, for their previous long and faithful services, are retained in the Navy more as pensioners upon its merited bounty than anything else. They are set to light and easy duties.

'Ar'n't this the foretop-man, Shenly?' asked the foremost, looking full at the frozen face before him.

'Ay, ay, old Ringrope,' said the other, drawing his hand far back with a long thread, 'I think it's him; and he's further aloft now, I hope, than ever he was at the fore-truck. But I only hopes; I'm afeard this ar'n't the last on him!'

'His hull here will soon be going out of sight below hatches, though, old Thrummings,' replied Ringrope, placing two heavy cannon-balls in the foot of the canvass shroud.

'I don't know that, old man; I never yet sewed up a ship-mate but he spooked me arterward. I tell ye, Ringrope, these 'ere corpses is cunning. You think they sink deep, but they comes up agin as soon as you sails over 'em. They lose the number of their mess, and their messmates sticks their spoons in the rack; but no good—no good, old Ringrope; they ar'n't dead yet. I tell ye, now, ten best bower-anchors wouldn't sink this 'ere top-man. He'll be soon coming in the wake of the thirty-nine spooks what spooks me every night in my hammock—jist afore the mid-watch is called. Small thanks I gets for my pains; and every one on 'em looks so

342

'proachful-like with a sail-maker's needle through his nose. I've been thinkin', old Ringrope, it's all wrong that 'ere last stitch we takes. Depend on 't, they don't like it—none on 'em.'

I was standing leaning over a gun, gazing at the two old men. The last remark reminded me of a superstitious custom generally practised by most sea-undertakers upon these occasions. I resolved that, if I could help it, it should not take place upon the remains of Shenly.

'Thrummings,' said I, advancing to the last speaker, 'you are right. That last thing you do to the canvass is the very reason, be sure of it, that brings the ghosts after you, as you say. So don't do it to this poor fellow, I entreat. Try once, now, how it goes not to do it.'

'What do you say to the youngster, old man?' said Thrummings, holding up his lantern into his comrade's wrinkled face, as if deciphering some ancient parchment.

'I'm agin all innovations,' said Ringrope; 'it's a good old fashion, that last stitch; it keeps 'em snug, d'ye see, youngster. I'm blest if they could sleep sound, if it wa'n't for that. No, no, Thrummings! no innovations; I won't hear on 't. I goes for the last stitch!'

'S'pose you was going to be sewed up yourself, old Ringrope, would you like the last stitch then? You are an old gun, Ringrope; you can't stand looking out at your port-hole much longer,' said Thrummings, as his own palsied hands were quivering over the canvass.

'Better say that to yourself, old man,' replied Ringrope, stooping close to the light to thread his coarse needle, which trembled in his withered hands like the needle in a compass of a Greenland ship near the Pole. 'You ain't long for the sarvice. I wish I could give you some o' the blood in my veins, old man!'

'Ye ain't got ne'er a teaspoonful to spare,' said Thrummings. 'It will go hard, and I wouldn't want to do it; but I'm afeard I'll have the sewing on ye up afore long!'

'Sew *me* up? Me dead and you alive, old man?' shrieked Ringrope. 'Well, I've he'rd the parson of the old *Indepen-*

dence say as how old age was deceitful; but I never seed it so true afore this blessed night. I'm sorry for ye, old man—to see you so innocent-like, and Death all the while turning in and out with you in your hammock, for all the world like a hammock-mate.'

'You lie! old man,' cried Thrummings, shaking with rage. 'It's *you* that have Death for a hammock-mate; it's *you* that will make a hole in the shot-locker soon.'

'Take that back!' cried Ringrope, huskily, leaning far over the corpse, and, needle in hand, menacing his companion with his aguish fist. 'Take that back, or I'll throttle your lean bag of wind for ye!'

'Blast ye! old chaps, ain't ye any more manners than to be fighting over a dead man?' cried one of the sail-maker's mates, coming down from the spar-deck. 'Bear a hand!— bear a hand! and get through with that job!'

'Only one more stitch to take,' muttered Ringrope, creeping near the face.

'Drop your *palm* then, and let Thrummings take it; follow me—the foot of the mainsail wants mending—must do it afore a breeze springs up. D'ye hear, old chap! I say, drop your *palm*, and follow me.'

At the reiterated command of his superior, Ringrope rose, and, turning to his comrade, said, 'I take it all back, Thrummings, and I'm sorry for it, too. But mind ye, take that 'ere last stitch, now; if ye don't, there's no tellin' the consekenses.'

As the mate and his man departed, I stole up to Thrummings. 'Don't do it—don't do it, now, Thrummings— depend on it, it's wrong!'

'Well, youngster, I'll try this here one without it for jist this here once; and if, arter that, he don't spook me, I'll be dead agin the last stitch as long as my name is Thrummings.'

So, without mutilation, the remains were replaced between the guns, the Union Jack again thrown over them, and I reseated myself on the shot-box.

LXXXI

How they bury a Man-of-war's-man at Sea

QUARTERS over in the morning, the boatswain and his four mates stood round the main hatchway, and after giving the usual whistle, made the customary announcement—'*All hands bury the dead, ahoy!*'

In a man-of-war, everything, even to a man's funeral and burial, proceeds with the unrelenting promptitude of the martial code. And whether it is, *All hands bury the dead!* or, *All hands splice the main-brace!* the order is given in the same hoarse tones.

Both officers and men assembled in the lee waist, and through that bareheaded crowd the messmates of Shenly brought his body to the same gangway where it had thrice winced under the scourge. But there is something in death that ennobles even a pauper's corpse; and the captain himself stood bareheaded before the remains of a man whom, with his hat on, he had sentenced to the ignominious gratings when alive.

'*I am the resurrection and the life!*' solemnly began the chaplain, in full canonicals, the prayer-book in his hand.

'Damn you! off those booms!' roared a boatswain's mate to a crowd of top-men, who had elevated themselves to gain a better view of the scene.

'*We commit this body to the deep!*' At the word, Shenly's messmates tilted the board, and the dead sailor sank in the sea.

'Look aloft,' whispered Jack Chase. 'See that bird! it is the spirit of Shenly.'

Gazing upward, all beheld a snow-white, solitary fowl, which—whence coming no one could tell—had been hovering over the mainmast during the service, and was now sailing far up into the depths of the sky.

345

LXXXII

What remains of a Man-of-war's-man after his Burial at Sea

UPON examining Shenly's bag, a will was found, scratched in pencil, upon a blank leaf in the middle of his Bible; or, to use the phrase of one of the seamen, in the midships, atween the Bible and Testament, where the Pothecary (Apocrypha) uses to be.

The will was comprised in one solitary sentence, exclusive of the dates and signatures: '*In case I die on the voyage, the purser will please pay over my wages to my wife, who lives in Portsmouth, New Hampshire.*'

Besides the testator's, there were two signatures of witnesses.

This last will and testament being shown to the purser, who, it seems, had been a notary, or surrogate, or some sort of cosy chamber practitioner in his time, he declared that it must be 'proved'! So the witnesses were called, and after recognizing their hands to the paper, for the purpose of additionally testing their honesty they were interrogated concerning the day on which they had signed—whether it was *Banyan Day*, or *Duff Day*, or *Swamp-seed Day*; for among the sailors on board a man-of-war the land terms, *Monday, Tuesday, Wednesday*, are almost unknown. In place of these they substitute nautical names, some of which are significant of the daily bill of fare at dinner for the week.

The two witnesses were somewhat puzzled by the attorney-like questions of the purser, till a third party came along, one of the ship's barbers, and declared, of his own knowledge, that Shenly executed the instrument on a *Shaving Day*; for the deceased seaman had informed him of the circumstance, when he came to have his beard reaped on the morning of the event.

In the purser's opinion, this settled the question; and it is to be hoped that the widow duly received her husband's death-earned wages.

Shenly was dead and gone; and what was Shenly's epitaph?

—'D. D.'—

opposite his name in the purser's books, in *Black's best Writing Fluid*—funereal name and funereal hue—meaning 'Discharged, Dead.'

LXXXIII
A Man-of-war College

IN our man-of-war world, Life comes in at one gangway and Death goes overboard at the other. Under the man-of-war scourge, curses mix with tears; and the sigh and the sob furnish the bass to the shrill octave of those who laugh to drown buried griefs of their own. Checkers were played in the waist at the time of Shenly's burial; and as the body plunged, a player swept the board. The bubbles had hardly burst, when all hands were *piped down* by the boatswain, and the old jests were heard again, as if Shenly himself were there to hear.

This man-of-war life has not left me unhardened. I cannot stop to weep over Shenly now; that would be false to the life I depict; wearing no mourning weeds, I resume the task of portraying our man-of-war world.

Among the various other vocations, all driven abreast on board of the *Neversink*, was that of the schoolmaster. There were two academies in the frigate. One comprised the apprentice boys, who, upon certain days of the week, were indoctrinated in the mysteries of the primer by an invalid corporal of marines, a slender, wizen-cheeked man, who had received a liberal infant-school education.

The other school was a far more pretentious affair—a sort of Army and Navy seminary combined, where mystical mathematical problems were solved by the midshipmen, and great ships-of-the-line were navigated over imaginary shoals by unimaginable observations of the moon and the stars, and learned lectures were delivered upon great guns, small arms, and the curvilinear lines described by bombs in the air.

The Professor was the title bestowed upon the erudite gentleman who conducted this seminary, and by that title alone was he known throughout the ship. He was domiciled in the ward-room, and circulated there on a social par with the purser, surgeon, and other *non-combatants* and Quakers. By being advanced to the dignity of a peerage in the ward-room, Science and Learning were ennobled in the person of this professor, even as Divinity was honoured in the chaplain enjoying the rank of a spiritual peer.

Every other afternoon, while at sea, the professor assembled his pupils on the half-deck, near the long twenty-four-pounders. A bass drum-head was his desk, his pupils forming a semicircle around him, seated on shot-boxes and match-tubs.

They were in the jelly of youth, and this learned professor poured into their susceptible hearts all the gentle, gunpowder maxims of war. Presidents of Peace Societies and Superintendents of Sabbath Schools, must it not have been a most interesting sight?

But the professor himself was a noteworthy person. A tall, thin, spectacled man, about forty years old, with a student's stoop in his shoulders, and wearing uncommonly scanty pantaloons, exhibiting an undue proportion of his boots. In early life he had been a cadet in the military academy of West Point; but, becoming very weak-sighted, and thereby in a good manner disqualified for active service in the field, he had declined entering the Army, and accepted the office of professor in the Navy.

His studies at West Point had thoroughly grounded him in a knowledge of gunnery; and, as he was not a little of a pedant, it was sometimes amusing, when the sailors were at quarters, to hear him criticise their evolutions at the batteries. He would quote Dr. Hutton's tracts[*] on the subject, also, in the original, *The French Bombardier*, and wind

up by Italian passages from the *Prattica Manuale dell'
Artiglieria*.

Though not required by the Navy regulations to instruct
his scholars in aught but the application of mathematics to
navigation, yet besides this, and besides instructing them in
the theory of gunnery, he also sought to root them in the
theory of frigate and fleet tactics. To be sure, he himself did
not know how to splice a rope or furl a sail; and, owing to his
partiality for strong coffee, he was apt to be nervous when
we fired salutes; yet all this did not prevent him from
delivering lectures on cannonading and 'breaking the
enemy's line'.

He had arrived at his knowledge of tactics by silent, solitary study, and earnest meditation in the sequestered retreat
of his state-room. His case was somewhat parallel to the
Scotchman's—John Clerk, Esq., of Eldin*—who, though he
had never been to sea, composed a quarto treatise on fleet-
fighting, which to this day remains a text-book; and he also
originated a nautical manœuvre, which has given to England
many a victory over her foes.

Now there was a large blackboard, something like a great-
gun target—only it was square—which during the professor's lectures was placed upright on the gun-deck,
supported behind by three boarding-pikes. And here he
would chalk out diagrams of great fleet engagements; making
marks, like the soles of shoes, for the ships, and drawing a
dog-vane in one corner to denote the assumed direction of
the wind. This done, with a cutlass he would point out every
spot of interest.

'Now, young gentlemen, the board before you exhibits
the disposition of the British West Indian squadron under
Rodney,* when, early on the morning of the 9th of April, in
the year of our blessed Lord 1782, he discovered part of the
French fleet, commanded by the Count de Grasse, lying
under the north end of the island of Dominica. It was at
this juncture that the admiral gave the signal for the British
line to prepare for battle, and stand on. D'ye understand,
young gentlemen? Well, the British van having nearly

fetched up with the centre of the enemy—who, be it remembered, were then on the starboard tack—and Rodney's centre and rear being yet becalmed under the lee of the land—the question I ask you is, What should Rodney now do?'

'Blaze away, by all means!' responded a rather confident reefer, who had zealously been observing the diagram.

'But, sir, his centre and rear are still becalmed, and his van has not yet closed with the enemy.'

'Wait till he *does* come in range, and *then* blaze away,' said the reefer.

'Permit me to remark, Mr. Pert, that "*blaze away*" is not a strictly technical term; and also permit me to hint, Mr. Pert, that you should consider the subject rather more deeply before you hurry forward your opinion.'

This rebuke not only abashed Mr. Pert, but for a time intimidated the rest; and the professor was obliged to proceed, and extricate the British fleet by himself. He concluded by awarding Admiral Rodney the victory, which must have been exceedingly gratifying to the family pride of the surviving relatives and connections of that distinguished hero.

'Shall I clean the board, sir?' now asked Mr. Pert, brightening up.

'No, sir; not till you have saved that crippled French ship in the corner. That ship, young gentlemen, is the *Glorieuse*; you perceive she is cut off from her consorts, and the whole British fleet is giving chase to her. Her bowsprit is gone; her rudder is torn away; she has one hundred round-shot in her hull, and two-thirds of her men are dead or dying. What's to be done? the wind being at north-east by north?'

'Well, sir,' said Mr. Dash, a chivalric young gentleman from Virginia, 'I wouldn't strike yet; I'd nail my colours to the main-royal-mast! I would, by Jove!'

'That would not save your ship, sir; besides, your mainmast has gone by the board.'

'I think, sir,' said Mr. Slim, a diffident youth, 'I think, sir, I would haul back the fore-topsail.'

'And why so? of what service would *that* be, I should like to know, Mr. Slim?'

'I can't tell exactly; but I think it would help her a little,' was the timid reply.

'Not a whit, sir—not one particle; besides, you can't haul back your fore-topsail—your foremast is lying across your forecastle.'

'Haul back the main-topsail, then,' suggested another.

'Can't be done; your mainmast, also, has gone by the board!'

'Mizzen-topsail?' meekly suggested little Boat-Plug.

'Your mizzen-topmast, let me inform you, sir, was shot down in the first of the fight!'

'Well, sir,' cried Mr. Dash, 'I'd tack ship, anyway; bid 'em good-bye with a broadside; nail my flag to the keel, if there was no other place; and blow my brains out on the poop!'

'Idle, idle, sir! worse than idle! you are carried away, Mr. Dash, by your ardent Southern temperament! Let me inform you, young gentleman, that this ship,' touching it with his cutlass, 'can *not* be saved.'

Then, throwing down his cutlass, 'Mr. Pert, have the goodness to hand me one of those cannon-balls from the rack.'

Balancing the iron sphere in one hand, the learned professor began fingering it with the other, like Columbus illustrating the rotundity of the globe before the Royal Commission of Castilian Ecclesiastics.

'Young gentlemen, I resume my remarks on the passage of a shot *in vacuo*, which remarks were interrupted yesterday by general quarters. After quoting that admirable passage in Spearman's *British Gunner*,* I then laid it down, you remember, that the path of a shot *in vacuo* describes a parabolic curve. I now add that, agreeably to the method pursued by the illustrious Newton in treating the subject of curvilinear motion, I consider the *trajectory* or curve described by a moving body in space as consisting of a series of right lines, described in successive intervals of time, and constituting the diagonals of parallelograms formed in a vertical plane between the vertical deflections caused by gravity and the production of the line of motion which has been described in each preceding interval of time. This must be obvious; for, if you say that the passage *in vacuo* of this cannon-ball, now held in my hand, would describe otherwise than a series of right lines, &c., then you are brought to the *reductio ad absurdum*,[*] that the diagonals of parallelograms are——'

'All hands reef topsails!' was now thundered forth by the boatswain's mates. The shot fell from the professor's palm; his spectacles dropped on his nose, and the school tumultuously broke up, the pupils scrambling up the ladders with the sailors, who had been overhearing the lecture.

LXXXIV

Man-of-war Barbers

THE allusion to one of the ship's barbers in a previous chapter, together with the recollection of how conspicuous a part they enacted in a tragical drama soon to be related, leads me now to introduce them to the reader.

Among the numerous artists and professors of polite trades in the Navy, none are held in higher estimation or drive a more profitable business than these barbers. And it may well be imagined that the five hundred heads of hair and five hundred beards of a frigate should furnish no small employment for those to whose faithful care they may be entrusted. As everything connected with the domestic affairs of a man-of-war comes under the supervision of the martial executive, so certain barbers are formally licensed by the first lieutenant. The better to attend to the profitable duties of their calling, they are exempted from all ship's duty, except that of standing night-watches at sea, mustering at quarters, and coming on deck when all hands are called. They are rated as *able seamen*, or *ordinary seamen*, and receive their wages as such; but in addition to this, they are liberally recompensed for their professional services. Herein their rate of pay is fixed for every sailor manipulated—so much per quarter, which is charged to the sailor, and credited to his barber on the books of the purser.

It has been seen that while a man-of-war barber is shaving his customers at so much per chin, his wages as a seaman are still running on, which makes him a sort of *sleeping partner* of a sailor; nor are the sailor wages he receives altogether to be reckoned as earnings. Considering the circumstances, however, not much objection can be made to the barbers on this score. But there were instances of men in the *Neversink* receiving government money in part pay for work done for private individuals. Among these were several accomplished tailors, who nearly the whole cruise sat cross-legged on the half-deck, making coats, pantaloons, and vests for the quarter-deck officers. Some of these men, though knowing little or nothing about sailor duties, and seldom or never performing them, stood upon the ship's books as ordinary seamen, entitled to ten dollars a month. Why was this? Previous to shipping they had divulged the fact of their being tailors. True, the officers who employed them upon their wardrobes paid them for their work, but some of them in such a way as to elicit much grumbling from the tailors. At any rate, these makers and menders of clothes did not receive from some of these officers an amount equal to what they could have fairly earned ashore by doing the same work. It was a considerable saving to the officers to have their clothes made on board.

The men belonging to the carpenter's gang furnished another case in point. There were some six or eight allotted to this department. All the cruise they were hard at work. At what? Mostly making chests of drawers, canes, little ships and schooners, swifts,* and other elaborated trifles, chiefly for the captain. What did the captain pay them for their trouble? Nothing. But the United States government paid them; two of them (the mates) at nineteen dollars a month, and the rest receiving the pay of able seamen, twelve dollars.

To return.

The regular days upon which the barbers shall exercise their vocation are set down on the ship's calendar, and known as *shaving days*. On board of the *Neversink* these days are Wednesdays and Saturdays; when, immediately after breakfast, the barbers' shops were opened to customers. They were in different parts of the gun-deck, between the long twenty-four-pounders. Their furniture, however, was not very elaborate, hardly equal to the sumptuous appointments of metropolitan barbers. Indeed, it merely consisted of a match-tub, elevated upon a shot-box, as a barber's chair for the patient. No Psyche glasses;* no hand-mirror; no ewer and basin; no comfortable padded footstool; nothing, in short, that makes a shore 'shave' such a luxury.

Nor are the implements of these man-of-war barbers out of keeping with the rude appearance of their shops. Their razors are of the simplest patterns, and, from their jaggedness, would seem better fitted for the preparing and harrowing of the soil than for the ultimate reaping of the crop. But this is no matter for wonder, since so many chins are to be shaven, and a razor-case holds but two razors. For only two razors does a man-of-war barber have, and, like the marine sentries at the gangways in port, these razors go off and on duty in rotation. One brush, too, brushes every chin, and one lather lathers them all. No private brushes and boxes; no reservations whatever.

As it would be altogether too much trouble for a man-of-war's-man to keep his own shaving tools and shave himself at sea, and since, therefore, nearly the whole ship's company patronize the ship's barbers, and as the seamen must be shaven by evening quarters of the days appointed for the business, it may be readily imagined what a scene of bustle and confusion there is when the razors are being applied. First come, first served, is the motto; and often you have to wait for hours together, sticking to your position (like one of an Indian file of merchants' clerks getting letters out of the post-office), ere you have a chance to occupy the pedestal of the match-tub. Often the crowd of quarrelsome candidates wrangle and fight for precedency, while at all times the interval is employed by the garrulous in every variety of ship gossip.

As the shaving days are unalterable, they often fall upon

days of high seas and tempestuous winds, when the vessel pitches and rolls in a frightful manner. In consequence, many valuable lives are jeopardized from the razor being plied under such untoward circumstances. But these sea-barbers pride themselves upon their sea-legs, and often you will see them standing over their patients, with their feet wide apart, and scientifically swaying their bodies to the motion of the ship, as they flourish their edge-tools about the lips, nostrils, and jugular.

As I looked upon the practitioner and patient at such times, I could not help thinking that, if the sailor had any insurance on his life, it would certainly be deemed forfeited should the president of the company chance to lounge by and behold him in that imminent peril. For myself, I accounted it an excellent preparation for going into a sea-fight, where fortitude in standing up to your gun and running the risk of all splinters comprise part of the practical qualities that make up an efficient man-of-war's-man.

It remains to be related, that these barbers of ours had their labours considerably abridged by a fashion prevailing among many of the crew, of wearing very large whiskers; so that, in most cases, the only parts needing a shave were the upper lip and suburbs of the chin. This had been more or less the custom during the whole three years' cruise; but for some time previous to our weathering Cape Horn, very many of the seamen had redoubled their assiduity in cultivating their beards, preparatory to their return to America. There they anticipated creating no small impression by their immense and magnificent *homeward-bounders*—so they called the long fly-brushes at their chins. In particular, the more aged sailors, embracing the Old Guard of sea-grenadiers on the forecastle, and the begrimed gunner's mates and quarter-gunners, sported most venerable beards of an exceeding length and hoariness, like long, trailing moss hanging from the bough of some aged oak. Above all, the captain of the forecastle, old Ushant—a fine specimen of a sea-sexagenarian—wore a wide, spreading beard, grizzled and grey, that flowed over his breast, and often became tangled and knotted with tar. This Ushant, in all weathers, was ever alert at his duty; intrepidly mounting the fore-yard in a gale, his long beard streaming like Neptune's. Off Cape Horn it looked like a miller's, being all over powdered with frost: sometimes it glittered with minute icicles in the pale, cold, moonlit Patagonian nights. But though he was so active in time of tempest, yet when his duty did not call for exertion, he was a remarkably staid, reserved, silent, and majestic old man, holding himself aloof from noisy revelry, and never participating in the boisterous sports of the crew. He resolutely set his beard against their boyish frolickings, and often held forth like an oracle concerning the vanity thereof. Indeed, at times he was wont to talk philosophy to his ancient companions—the old sheet-anchor-men around him—as well as to the hare-brained tenants of the foretop, and the giddy lads in the mizzen.

Nor was his philosophy to be despised; it abounded in wisdom. For this Ushant was an old man, of strong natural sense, who had seen nearly the whole terraqueous globe, and could reason of civilized and savage, of Gentile and Jew, of Christian and Moslem. The long night-watches of the sailor are eminently adapted to draw out the reflective faculties of any serious-minded man, however humble or uneducated. Judge, then, what half a century of battling out watches on the ocean must have done for this fine old tar. He was a sort of sea-Socrates, in his old age 'pouring out his last philosophy and life,' as sweet Spenser has it;[*] and I never could look at him, and survey his right reverend beard, without bestowing upon him that title which, in one of his satires, Persius[*] gives to the immortal quaffer of the hemlock—*Magister Barbatus*—the bearded master.

Not a few of the ship's company had also bestowed great pains upon their hair, which some of them—especially the genteel young sailor bucks of the after-guard—wore over their shoulders like the ringleted Cavaliers. Many sailors, with naturally tendril locks, prided themselves upon what they call *love-curls*, worn at the side of the head, just before the ear—a custom peculiar to tars, and which seems to have filled the vacated place of the old-fashioned Lord Rodney cue,*which they used to wear some fifty years ago.

But there were others of the crew labouring under the misfortune of long, lank, Winnebago locks,* or carroty bunches of hair, or rebellious bristles of a sandy hue. Ambitious of redundant mops, these still suffered their carrots to grow, spite of all ridicule. They looked like Huns and Scandinavians; and one of them, a young Down-Easter, the unenvied proprietor of a thick crop of inflexible yellow bamboos, went by the name of *Peter the Wild Boy*;*for, like Peter the Wild Boy in France, it was supposed that he must have been caught like a catamount* in the pine woods of Maine. But there were many fine, flowing heads of hair to counterbalance such sorry exhibitions as Peter's.

What with long whiskers and venerable beards, then, of every variety of cut—Charles the Fifth's and Aurelian's*— and endless *goatees* and *imperials*; and what with abounding locks, our crew seemed a company of Merovingians*or Long-haired Kings, mixed with savage Lombards or Longobardi, so called from their lengthy beards.

LXXXV

The great Massacre of the Beards

THE preceding chapter fitly paves the way for the present, wherein it sadly befalls White-Jacket to chronicle a calamitous event, which filled the *Neversink* with long lamentations, that echoed through all her decks and tops. After dwelling upon our redundant locks and thrice-noble beards, fain would I cease, and let the sequel remain undisclosed, but truth and fidelity forbid.

As I now deviously hover and lingeringly skirmish about the frontiers of this melancholy recital, a feeling of sadness comes over me that I cannot withstand. Such a heartless massacre of hair! Such a Bartholomew's Day*and Sicilian

Vespers*of assassinated beards! Ah! who would believe it! With intuitive sympathy I feel of my own brown beard while I write, and thank my kind stars that each precious hair is forever beyond the reach of the ruthless barbers of a man-of-war!

It needs that this sad and most serious matter should be faithfully detailed. Throughout the cruise, many of the officers had expressed their abhorrence of the impunity with which the most extensive plantations of hair were cultivated under their very noses; and they frowned upon every beard with even greater dislike. They said it was unseamanlike; not *ship-shape*; in short, it was disgraceful to the Navy. But as Captain Claret said nothing, and as the officers, of themselves, had no authority to preach a crusade against whisker-andos, the Old Guard on the forecastle still complacently stroked their beards, and the sweet youths of the after-guard still lovingly threaded their fingers through their curls.

Perhaps the captain's generosity in thus far permitting our beards sprung from the fact that he himself wore a small speck of a beard upon his own imperial cheek; which, if rumour said true, was to hide something, as Plutarch relates of the Emperor Adrian.* But, to do him justice—as I always have done—the captain's beard did not exceed the limits prescribed by the Navy Department.

According to a then recent ordinance at Washington, the beards of both officers and seamen were to be accurately laid out and surveyed, and on no account must come lower than the mouth, so as to correspond with the Army standard— a regulation directly opposed to the theocratical law laid down in the nineteenth chapter and twenty-seventh verse of Leviticus, where it is expressly ordained, '*Thou shalt not mar the corners of thy beard.*' But legislators do not always square their statutes by those of the Bible.

At last, when we had crossed the Northern Tropic, and were standing up to our guns at evening quarters, and when the setting sun, streaming in at the port-holes, lit up every hair, till, to an observer on the quarter-deck, the two long, even lines of beards seemed one dense grove; in that evil hour it must have been, that a cruel thought entered into the heart of our captain.

A pretty set of savages, thought he, am I taking home to America; people will think them all catamounts and Turks. Besides, now that I think of it, it's against the law. It will never do. They must be shaven and shorn—that's flat.

There is no knowing, indeed, whether these were the very words in which the captain meditated that night; for it is yet a mooted point among metaphysicians, whether we think in words or whether we think in thoughts. But something like the above must have been the captain's cogitations. At any rate, that very evening the ship's company were astounded by an extraordinary announcement made at the main hatchway of the gun-deck, by the boatswain's mate there stationed. He was afterward discovered to have been tipsy at the time.

'D'ye hear there, fore and aft? All you that have hair on your heads, shave them off; and all you that have beards, trim 'em small!'

Shave off our Christian heads! And then, placing them between our knees, trim small our worshipped beards! The captain was mad.

But directly the boatswain came rushing to the hatchway, and, after soundly rating his tipsy mate, thundered forth a true version of the order that had issued from the quarter-deck. As amended, it ran thus:

'D'ye hear there, fore and aft? All you that have long hair, cut it short; and all you that have large whiskers, trim them down, according to the Navy regulations.'

This was an amendment, to be sure; but what barbarity, after all! What! not thirty days' run from home, and lose our magnificent homeward-bounders? The homeward-bounders we had been cultivating so long? Lose them at one fell swoop? Were the vile barbers of the gun-deck to reap our long, nodding harvests, and expose our innocent chins to the chill air of the Yankee coast? And our viny locks! were they also to be shorn? Was a grand sheep-shearing, such as they annually have at Nantucket, to take place; and our ignoble barbers to carry off the fleece?

Captain Claret! in cutting our beards and our hair, you cut us the unkindest cut of all! Were we going into action, Captain Claret—going to fight the foe with our hearts of flame and our arms of steel, then would we gladly offer up our beards to the terrific God of War, and *that* we would account but a wise precaution against having them tweaked by the foe. *Then*, Captain Claret, you would but be imitating the example of Alexander,* who had his Macedonians all shaven, that in the hour of battle their beards might not be handles to the Persians. But *now*, Captain Claret! when after our long, long cruise, we are returning to our homes, tenderly stroking the fine tassels on our chins, and thinking of father or mother, or sister or brother, or daughter or son; to cut off our beards *now*—the very beards that were frosted white off the pitch of Patagonia—*this* is too bitterly bad, Captain Claret! and, by Heaven, we will not submit. Train your guns inboard, let the marines fix their bayonets, let the officers draw their swords; we *will not* let our beards be reaped—the last insult inflicted upon a vanquished foe in the East!

Where are you, sheet-anchor-men! captains of the tops! gunner's mates! mariners, all! Muster round the capstan your venerable beards, and while you braid them together in token of brotherhood, cross hands and swear that we will enact over again the mutiny of the Nore, and sooner perish than yield up a hair!

The excitement was intense throughout that whole evening. Groups of tens and twenties were scattered about all the decks, discussing the mandate, and inveighing against its barbarous author. The long area of the gun-deck was something like a populous street of brokers, when some terrible commercial tidings have newly arrived. One and all, they resolved not to succumb, and every man swore to stand by his beard and his neighbour.

Twenty-four hours after, at the next evening quarters, the

captain's eye was observed to wander along the men at their guns—not a beard was shaven!

When the drum beat the retreat, the boatswain—now attended by all four of his mates, to give additional solemnity to the announcement—repeated the previous day's order, and concluded by saying, that twenty-four hours would be given for all to acquiesce.

But the second day passed, and at quarters, untouched, every beard bristled on its chin. Forthwith Captain Claret summoned the midshipmen, who, receiving his orders, hurried to the various divisions of the guns, and communicated them to the lieutenants respectively stationed over divisions.

The officer commanding mine turned upon us, and said, 'Men, if to-morrow night I find any of you with long hair, or whiskers of a standard violating the Navy regulations, the names of such offenders shall be put down on the report.'

The affair had now assumed a most serious aspect. The captain was in earnest. The excitement increased tenfold; and a great many of the older seamen, exasperated to the uttermost, talked about *knocking off duty* till the obnoxious mandate was revoked. I thought it impossible that they would seriously think of such a folly; but there is no knowing what man-of-war's-men will sometimes do, under provocation—witness Parker and the Nore.

That same night, when the first watch was set, the men in a body drove the two boatswain's mates from their stations at the fore and main hatchways, and unshipped the ladders; thus cutting off all communication between the gun- and spar-decks, forward of the mainmast.

Mad Jack had the trumpet; and no sooner was this incipient mutiny reported to him, than he jumped right down among the mob, and fearlessly mingling with them, exclaimed, 'What do you mean, men? don't be fools! This is no way to get what you want. Turn to, my lads, turn to! Boatswain's mate, ship that ladder! So! up you tumble, now, my hearties! away you go!'

His gallant, off-handed, confident manner, recognizing no

attempt at mutiny, operated upon the sailors like magic. They *tumbled up*, as commanded; and for the rest of that night contented themselves with privately fulminating their displeasure against the captain, and publicly emblazoning every anchor-button on the coat of admired Mad Jack.

Captain Claret happened to be taking a nap in his cabin at the moment of the disturbance; and it was quelled so soon, that he knew nothing of it till it was officially reported to him. It was afterward rumoured through the ship that he reprimanded Mad Jack for acting as he did. He maintained that he should at once have summoned the marines, and charged upon the 'mutineers'. But if the sayings imputed to the captain were true, he nevertheless refrained from subsequently noticing the disturbance, or attempting to seek out and punish the ringleaders. This was but wise; for there are times when even the most potent governor must wink at transgression, in order to preserve the laws inviolate for the future. And great care is to be taken, by timely management, to avert an incontestable act of mutiny, and so prevent men from being roused, by their own consciousness of transgression, into all the fury of an unbounded insurrection. *Then*, for the time, both soldiers and sailors are irresistible; as even the valour of Caesar was made to know, and the prudence of Germanicus, when their legions rebelled. And not all the concessions of Earl Spencer, as First Lord of the Admiralty, nor the threats and entreaties of Lord Bridport, the Admiral of the Fleet—no, nor His Gracious Majesty's plenary pardon in prospective, could prevail upon the Spithead mutineers (when at last fairly lashed up to the mark) to succumb, until deserted by their own messmates, and a handful was left in the breach.

Therefore, Mad Jack! you did right, and no one else could have acquitted himself better. By your crafty simplicity, good-natured daring, and off-handed air (as if nothing was happening) you perhaps quelled a very serious affair in the bud, and prevented the disgrace to the American Navy of a tragical mutiny, growing out of whiskers, soap-suds, and razors. Think of it, if future historians should devote a long chapter to the great *Rebellion of the Beards* on board the United States Ship *Neversink*. Why, through all time thereafter, barbers would cut down their spiralized poles, and substitute miniature mainmasts for the emblems of their calling.

And here is ample scope for some pregnant instruction, how that events of vast magnitude in our man-of-war world may originate in the pettiest of trifles. But that is an old theme; we waive it, and proceed.

On the morning following, though it was not a regular shaving day, the gun-deck barbers were observed to have their shops open, their match-tub accommodations in readiness, and their razors displayed. With their brushes, raising a mighty lather in their tin pots, they stood eyeing the passing throng of seamen, silently inviting them to walk in and be served. In addition to their usual implements, they now flourished at intervals a huge pair of sheep-shears, by way of more forcibly reminding the men of the edict which that day must be obeyed, or woe betide them.

For some hours the seamen paced to and fro in no very good humour, vowing not to sacrifice a hair. Beforehand, they denounced that man who should abase himself by compliance. But habituation to discipline is magical; and ere long an old forecastle-man was discovered elevated upon a match-tub, while, with a malicious grin, his barber—a fellow who, from his merciless rasping, was called Blue-Skin—seized him by his long beard, and at one fell stroke cut it off and tossed it out of the port-hole behind him. This forecastle-man was ever afterward known by a significant title—in the main equivalent to that name of reproach fastened upon that Athenian* who, in Alexander's time, previous to which all the Greeks sported beards, first submitted to the deprivation of his own. But, spite of all the contempt hurled on our forecastle-man, so prudent an example was soon followed; presently all the barbers were busy.

Sad sight! at which anyone but a barber or a Tartar would have wept! Beards three years old; *goatees* that would have graced a chamois of the Alps; *imperials* that Count D'Orsay would have envied;* and *love-curls* and man-of-war ringlets that would have measured, inch for inch, with the longest tresses of the Fair One with the Golden Locks—all went by the board! Captain Claret! how can you rest in your hammock! By this brown beard which now waves from my chin— the illustrious successor to that first, young, vigorous beard I yielded to your tyranny—by this manly beard, I swear it was barbarous!

My noble captain, Jack Chase, was indignant. Not even all the special favours he had received from Captain Claret, and the plenary pardon extended to him for his desertion into the Peruvian service, could restrain the expression of his feelings. But in his cooler moments, Jack was a wise man; he at last deemed it but wisdom to succumb.

When he went to the barber he almost drew tears from his eyes. Seating himself mournfully on the match-tub, he looked sideways, and said to the barber, who was *slithering* his sheep-shears in readiness to begin: 'My friend, I trust your scissors are consecrated. Let them not touch this beard if they have yet to be dipped in holy water; beards are sacred things, barber. Have you no feeling for beards, my friend? think of it'; and mournfully he laid his deep-dyed, russet cheek upon his hand. 'Two summers have gone by since my chin has been reaped. I was in Coquimbo then, on the Spanish Main; and when the husbandman was sowing his autumnal grain on the Vega,* I started this blessed beard; and when the vine-dressers were trimming their vines in the vineyards, I first trimmed it to the sound of a flute. Ah! barber, have you no heart? This beard has been caressed by the snow-white hand of the lovely Tomasita of Tombez— the Castilian belle of all Lower Peru. Think of *that*, barber! I have worn it as an officer on the quarter-deck of a Peruvian man-of-war. I have sported it at brilliant fandangos in Lima. I have been alow and aloft with it at sea. Yea, barber! it has streamed like an admiral's pennant at the mast-head of this same gallant frigate, the *Neversink*! Oh! barber, barber! it stabs me to the heart! Talk not of hauling down your ensigns and standards when vanquished—what is *that*, barber! to striking the flag that Nature herself has nailed to the mast!'

Here noble Jack's feelings overcame him; he drooped from the animated attitude into which his enthusiasm had momentarily transported him; his proud head sunk upon his chest, and his long, sad beard almost grazed the deck.

'Ay! trail your beards in grief and dishonour, oh crew of the *Neversink*!' sighed Jack. 'Barber, come closer—now, tell me, my friend, have you obtained absolution for this deed you are about to commit? You have not? Then, barber, *I* will absolve you; your hands shall be washed of this sin; it is not you, but another; and though you are about to shear off my manhood, yet, barber, I freely forgive you; kneel, kneel, barber! that I may bless you, in token that I cherish no malice!'

So when this barber, who was the only tender-hearted one of his tribe, had kneeled, been absolved, and then blessed, Jack gave up his beard into his hands, and the barber, clipping it off with a sigh, held it high aloft, and, parodying the style of the boatswain's mates, cried aloud, 'D'ye hear, fore and aft? This is the beard of our matchless Jack Chase, the noble captain of this frigate's maintop!'

LXXXVI

The Rebels brought to the Mast

THOUGH many heads of hair were shorn, and many fine beards reaped that day, yet several still held out, and vowed to defend their sacred hair to the last gasp of their breath. These were chiefly old sailors—some of them petty officers— who, presuming upon their age or rank, doubtless thought that, after so many had complied with the captain's commands, *they*, being but a handful, would be exempted from compliance, and remain a monument of our master's clemency.

That same evening, when the drum beat to quarters, the sailors went sullenly to their guns, and the old tars who still sported their beards stood up, grim, defying, and motionless, as the rows of sculptured Assyrian kings, who, with their magnificent beards, have recently been exhumed by Layard.*

When the proper time arrived, their names were taken down by the officers of divisions, and they were afterward summoned in a body to the mast, where the captain stood ready to receive them. The whole ship's company crowded to the spot, and, amid the breathless multitude, the venerable rebels advanced and unhatted.

It was an imposing display. They were old and venerable mariners; their cheeks had been burned brown in all latitudes, wherever the sun sends a tropical ray. Reverend old tars, one and all; some of them might have been grandsires, with grandchildren in every port round the world. They ought to have commanded the veneration of the most frivolous or magisterial beholder. Even Captain Claret they ought to have humiliated into deference. But a Scythian* is touched with no reverential promptings; and, as the Roman student well knows, the august Senators themselves, seated in the Senate-house, on the majestic hill of the Capitol, had their holy beards tweaked by the insolent chief of the Goths.*

Such an array of beards! spade-shaped, hammer-shaped, dagger-shaped, triangular, square, peaked, round, hemispherical, and forked. But chief among them all was old Ushant's, the ancient captain of the forecastle. Of a Gothic venerableness, it fell upon his breast like a continual iron-grey storm.

Ah! old Ushant, Nestor* of the crew! it promoted my longevity to behold you.

He was a man-of-war's-man of the old Benbow school. He wore a short cue, which the wags of the mizzentop called his *plug of pigtail*. About his waist was a broad boarder's belt, which he wore, he said, to brace his mainmast, meaning his backbone; for at times he complained of rheumatic twinges in the spine, consequent upon sleeping on deck, now and then, during the night-watches of upward of half a century. His sheath-knife was an antique—a sort of old-fashioned pruning-hook; its handle—a sperm whale's tooth —was carved all over with ships, cannon, and anchors. It was attached to his neck by a *lanyard*, elaborately worked into 'rose-knots' and 'Turk's-heads' by his own venerable fingers.

Of all the crew, this Ushant was most beloved by my glorious captain, Jack Chase, who one day pointed him out to me, as the old man was slowly coming down the rigging from the foretop.

'There, White-Jacket! isn't that old Chaucer's shipman?*

> A dagger hanging by a las hadde he,
> About his nekke, under his arm adown;
> The hote sommer hadde made his beard all brown.
> Hardy he is, and wise; I undertake
> With many a tempest has his beard be shake.

From the *Canterbury Tales*, White-Jacket! and must not old Ushant have been living in Chaucer's time, that Chaucer could draw his portrait so well?'

LXXXVII

Old Ushant at the Gangway

THE rebel beards, headed by old Ushant's, streaming like a commodore's *bougee*, now stood in silence at the mast.

'You knew the order!' said the captain, eyeing them severely; 'what does that hair on your chins?'

'Sir,' said the captain of the forecastle, 'did old Ushant ever refuse doing his duty? did he ever yet miss his muster? But, sir, old Ushant's beard is his own!'

'What's that, sir? Master-at-arms, put that man into the brig.'

'Sir,' said the old man, respectfully, 'the three years for which I shipped are expired; and though I am perhaps bound to work the ship home, yet, as matters are, I think my beard might be allowed me. It is but a few days, Captain Claret.'

'Put him into the brig!' cried the captain; 'and now, you old rascals!' he added, turning round upon the rest, 'I give you fifteen minutes to have those beards taken off; if they then remain on your chins, I'll flog you—every mother's son of you—though you were all my own godfathers!'

The band of beards went forward, summoned their barbers, and their glorious pennants were no more. In obedience to orders, they then paraded themselves at the mast, and addressing the captain, said, 'Sir, our *muzzle-lashings* are cast off!'

Nor is it unworthy of being chronicled, that not a single sailor who complied with the general order but refused to sport the vile *regulation-whiskers* prescribed by the Navy Department. No! like heroes they cried, 'Shave me clean! I will not wear a hair, since I cannot wear all!'

On the morrow, after breakfast, Ushant was taken out of irons, and, with the master-at-arms on one side and an armed sentry on the other, was escorted along the gun-deck and up the ladder to the mainmast. There the captain stood, firm as before. They must have guarded the old man thus to prevent his escape to the shore, something less than a thousand miles distant at the time.

'Well, sir, will you have that beard taken off? you have slept over it a whole night now; what do you say? I don't want to flog an old man like you, Ushant!'

'My beard is my own, sir!' said the old man, lowly.

'Will you take it off?'

'It is mine, sir!' said the old man, tremulously.

'Rig the gratings!' roared the captain. 'Master-at-arms, strip him! quarter-masters, seize him up! boatswain's mates, do your duty!'

While these executioners were employed, the captain's excitement had a little time to abate; and when, at last, old Ushant was tied up by the arms and legs, and his venerable back was exposed—that back which had bowed at the guns of the frigate *Constitution* when she captured the *Guérrière* — the captain seemed to relent.

'You are a very old man,' he said, 'and I am sorry to flog

368

you; but my orders must be obeyed. I will give you one more chance; will you have that beard taken off?'

'Captain Claret,' said the old man, turning round painfully in his bonds, 'you may flog me, if you will; but, sir, in this one thing I can *not* obey you.'

'Lay on! I'll see his backbone!' roared the captain, in a sudden fury.

'By Heaven!' thrillingly whispered Jack Chase, who stood by, 'it's only a halter; I'll strike him!'

'Better not,' said a top-mate; 'it's death, or worse punishment, remember.'

'There goes the lash!' cried Jack. 'Look at the old man! By G—d, I can't stand it! Let me go, men!' and with moist eyes Jack forced his way to one side.

'You, boatswain's mate,' cried the captain, 'you are favouring that man! Lay on soundly, sir, or I'll have your own *cat* laid soundly on you.'

One, two, three, four, five, six, seven, eight, nine, ten, eleven, twelve lashes were laid on the back of that heroic old man. He only bowed over his head, and stood as the Dying Gladiator* lies.

'Cut him down,' said the captain.

'And now go and cut your own throat,' hoarsely whispered an old sheet-anchor-man, a messmate of Ushant's.

When the master-at-arms advanced with the prisoner's shirt, Ushant waived him off with the dignified air of a Brahim,* saying, 'Do you think, master-at-arms, that I am hurt? I will put on my own garment. I am never the worse for it, man; and 'tis no dishonour when he who would dishonour you, only dishonours himself.'

'What says he?' cried the captain; 'what says that tarry old philosopher with the smoking back? Tell it to me, sir, if you dare! Sentry, take that man back to the brig. Stop! John Ushant, you have been captain of the forecastle; I break you. And now you go into the brig, there to remain till you consent to have that beard taken off.'

'My beard is my own,' said the old man, quietly. 'Sentry, I am ready.'

369

And back he went into durance between the guns; but after lying some four or five days in irons, an order came to remove them; but he was still kept confined.

Books were allowed him, and he spent much time in reading. But he also spent many hours in braiding his beard, and interweaving with it strips of red bunting, as if he desired to dress out and adorn the thing which had triumphed over all opposition.

He remained a prisoner till we arrived in America; but the very moment he heard the chain rattle out of the hawse-hole, and the ship swing to her anchor, he started to his feet, dashed the sentry aside, and gaining the deck, exclaimed, 'At home, with my beard!'

His term of service having some months previous expired, and the ship being now in harbour, he was beyond the reach of naval law, and the officers durst not molest him. But without unduly availing himself of these circumstances, the old man merely got his bag and hammock together, hired a boat, and throwing himself into the stern, was rowed ashore, amid the unsuppressible cheers of all hands. It was a glorious conquest over the conqueror himself, as well worthy to be celebrated as the Battle of the Nile.

Though, as I afterward learned, Ushant was earnestly entreated to put the case into some lawyer's hands, he firmly declined, saying, 'I have won the battle, my friends, and I do not care for the prize-money.' But even had he complied with these entreaties, from precedents in similar cases it is almost certain that not a sou's worth of satisfaction would have been received.

I know not in what frigate you sail now, old Ushant; but Heaven protect your storied old beard, in whatever typhoon it may blow. And if ever it must be shorn, old man, may it fare like the royal beard of Henry I of England, and be clipped by the right reverend hand of some Archbishop of Sées.*

As for Captain Claret, let it not be supposed that it is here sought to impale him before the world as a cruel, black-hearted man. Such he was not. Nor was he, upon the whole, regarded by his crew with anything like the feelings which man-of-war's-men sometimes cherish toward signally tyrannical commanders. In truth, the majority of the *Neversink*'s crew—in previous cruises habituated to flagrant misusage—deemed Captain Claret a lenient officer. In many things he certainly refrained from oppressing them. It has been related what privileges he accorded to the seamen respecting the free playing of checkers—a thing almost unheard of in most American men-of-war. In the matter of overseeing the men's clothing, also, he was remarkably indulgent, compared with the conduct of other Navy captains, who, by sumptuary regulations, oblige their sailors to run up large bills with the purser for clothes. In a word, of whatever acts Captain Claret might have been guilty in the *Neversink*, perhaps none of them proceeded from any personal, organic hard-heartedness. What he was, the usages of the Navy had made him. Had he been a mere landsman—a merchant, say —he would no doubt have been considered a kind-hearted man.

There may be some who shall read of this Bartholomew Massacre of beards who will yet marvel, perhaps, that the loss of a few hairs, more or less, should provoke such hostility from the sailors, lash them into so frothing a rage; indeed, come near breeding a mutiny.

But these circumstances are not without precedent. Not to speak of the riots, attended with the loss of life, which once occurred in Madrid, in resistance to an arbitrary edict of the king's, seeking to suppress the cloaks of the cavaliers; and not to make mention of other instances that might be quoted, it needs only to point out the rage of the Saxons in the time of William the Conqueror, when that despot commanded the hair on their upper lips to be shaven off—the hereditary moustaches which old generations had sported. The multitude of the dispirited vanquished were obliged to acquiesce; but many Saxon franklins and gentlemen of spirit, choosing rather to lose their castles than their moustaches, voluntarily deserted their firesides, and went into exile. All this is indignantly related by the stout Saxon friar, Matthew Paris,* in his *Historia Major*, beginning with the Norman Conquest.

And that our man-of-war's-men were right in desiring to perpetuate their beards, as martial appurtenances, must seem very plain, when it is considered that, as the beard is the token of manhood, so, in some shape or other, has it ever been held the true badge of a warrior. Bonaparte's grenadiers were stout whiskerandos; and perhaps, in a charge, those fierce whiskers of theirs did as much to appal the foe as the sheen of their bayonets. Most all fighting creatures sport either whiskers or beards; it seems a law of Dame Nature. Witness the boar, the tiger, the cougar, man, the leopard, the ram, the cat—all warriors, and all whiskerandos. Whereas, the peace-loving tribes have mostly enamelled chins.

LXXXVIII

Flogging through the Fleet

THE flogging of an old man like Ushant, most landsmen will probably regard with abhorrence. But though, from peculiar circumstances, his case occasioned a good deal of indignation among the people of the *Neversink*, yet, upon its own proper grounds, they did not denounce it. Man-of-war's-men are so habituated to what landsmen would deem excessive cruelties, that they are almost reconciled to inferior severities.

And here, though the subject of punishment in the Navy has been canvassed in previous chapters, and though the thing is every way a most unpleasant and grievous one to enlarge upon, and though I painfully nerve myself to it while I write, a feeling of duty compels me to enter upon a branch of the subject till now undiscussed. I would not be like the man, who, seeing an outcast perishing by the road-side, turned about to his friend, saying, 'Let us cross the way; my soul so sickens at this sight that I cannot endure it.'

There are certain enormities in this man-of-war world that often secure impunity by their very excessiveness. Some ignorant people will refrain from permanently removing the cause of a deadly malaria, for fear of the temporary spread of its offensiveness. Let us not be of such. The more repugnant and repelling, the greater the evil. Leaving our women and children behind, let us freely enter this Golgotha.

Years ago there was a punishment inflicted in the English, and I believe in the American Navy, called *keel-hauling*—a phrase still employed by man-of-war's-men when they would express some signal vengeance upon a personal foe. The practice still remains in the French national marine, though it is by no means resorted to so frequently as in times past. It consists of attaching tackles to the two extremities of the main-yard, and passing the rope under the ship's bottom. To one end of this rope the culprit is secured; his own shipmates are then made to run him up and down, first on this side, then on that—now scraping the ship's hull under water—anon, hoisted, stunned and breathless, into the air.

But though this barbarity is now abolished from the English and American Navies, there still remains another practice which, if anything, is even worse than *keel-hauling*. This remnant of the Middle Ages is known in the Navy as *flogging through the fleet*. It is never inflicted except by authority of a court martial upon some trespasser deemed guilty of a flagrant offence. Never, that I know of, has it been inflicted by an American man-of-war on the home station. The reason, probably, is, that the officers well know that such a spectacle would raise a mob in any American seaport.

By XLI of the Articles of War, a court martial shall not, 'for any one offence not capital', inflict a punishment beyond one hundred lashes. In cases 'not capital' this law may be, and has been, quoted in judicial justification of the infliction of more than one hundred lashes. Indeed, it would cover a thousand. Thus: one act of a sailor may be construed into the commission of ten different transgressions, for each of which he may be legally condemned to a hundred lashes, to be inflicted without intermission. It will be perceived, that in any case deemed 'capital', a sailor, under the above article, may legally be flogged to the death.

But neither by the Articles of War, nor by any other enactment of Congress, is there any direct warrant for the extraordinary cruelty of the mode in which punishment is inflicted, in cases of flogging through the fleet. But as in numerous other instances, the incidental aggravations of this penalty are indirectly covered by other clauses in the Articles of War; one of which authorizes the authorities of a ship—in certain indefinite cases—to correct the guilty *according to the usages of the sea-service.*

One of these 'usages' is the following:

All hands being called 'to witness punishment' in the ship to which the culprit belongs, the sentence of the court martial condemning him is read, when, with the usual solemnities, a portion of the punishment is inflicted. In order that it shall not lose in severity by the slightest exhaustion in the arm of the executioner, a fresh boatswain's mate is called out at every dozen.

As the leading idea is to strike terror into the beholders, the greatest number of lashes is inflicted on board the culprit's own ship, in order to render him the more shocking spectacle to the crews of the other vessels.

The first infliction being concluded, the culprit's shirt is thrown over him; he is put into a boat—the *Rogue's March* being played meanwhile—and rowed to the next ship of the squadron. All hands of that ship are then called to man the rigging, and another portion of the punishment is inflicted by the boatswain's mates of that ship. The bloody shirt is again thrown over the seaman; and thus he is carried through the fleet or squadron till the whole sentence is inflicted.

In other cases, the launch—the largest of the boats—is rigged with a platform (like a headsman's scaffold), upon which halberds, something like those used in the English Army, are erected. They consist of two stout poles, planted upright. Upon the platform stand a lieutenant, a surgeon, a master-at-arms, and the executioners with their 'cats'.

They are rowed through the fleet, stopping at each ship, till the whole sentence is inflicted, as before.

In some cases the attending surgeon has professionally interfered before the last lash has been given, alleging that immediate death must ensue if the remainder should be administered without a respite. But instead of humanely remitting the remaining lashes, in a case like this, the man is generally consigned to his cot for ten or twelve days; and when the surgeon officially reports him capable of undergoing the rest of the sentence, it is forthwith inflicted. Shylock must have his pound of flesh.

To say, that after being flogged through the fleet, the prisoner's back is sometimes puffed up like a pillow; or to say that in other cases it looks as if burned black before a roasting fire; or to say that you may track him through the squadron by the blood on the bulwarks of every ship, would only be saying what many seamen have seen.

Several weeks, sometimes whole months, elapse before the sailor is sufficiently recovered to resume his duties. During the greater part of that interval he lies in the sick-bay, groaning out his days and nights; and unless he has the hide and constitution of a rhinoceros, he never is the man he was before, but, broken and shattered to the marrow of his bones, sinks into death before his time. Instances have occurred where he has expired the day after the punishment. No wonder that the Englishman, Dr. Granville—himself once a surgeon in the Navy—declares, in his work on Russia,* that the barbarian 'knout' itself is not a greater torture to undergo than the Navy cat-o'-nine-tails.

Some years ago a fire broke out near the powder magazine in an American national ship, one of a squadron at anchor in the Bay of Naples. The utmost alarm prevailed. A cry went fore and aft that the ship was about to blow up. One of the seamen sprang overboard in affright. At length the fire was got under, and the man was picked up. He was tried before a court martial, found guilty of cowardice, and condemned to be flogged through the fleet. In due time the squadron made sail for Algiers, and in that harbour, once haunted by pirates, the punishment was inflicted—the Bay of Naples, though washing the shores of an absolute king, not being deemed a fit place for such an exhibition of American naval law.

While the *Neversink* was in the Pacific, an American sailor, who had deposited a vote for General Harrison*for President of the United States, was flogged through the fleet.

LXXXIX

The social State in a Man-of-war

BUT the floggings at the gangway and the floggings through the fleet, the stealings, highway robberies, swearings, gamblings, blasphemings, thimble-riggings, smugglings, and tipplings of a man-of-war, which throughout this narrative have been here and there sketched from the life, by no means comprise the whole catalogue of evil. One single feature is full of significance.

All large ships of war carry soldiers, called marines. In the *Neversink* there were something less than fifty, two-thirds of whom were Irishmen. They were officered by a lieutenant, an orderly sergeant, two sergeants, and two corporals, with a drummer and fifer. The custom, generally, is to have a marine to each gun; which rule usually furnishes the scale for distributing the soldiers in vessels of different force.

Our marines had no other than martial duty to perform; excepting that, at sea, they stood watches like the sailors, and now and then lazily assisted in pulling the ropes. But they never put foot in rigging or hand in tar-bucket.

On the quarter-bills, these men were stationed at none of the great guns; on the station-bills, they had no posts at the ropes. What, then, were they for? To serve their country in time of battle? Let us see. When a ship is running into action, her marines generally lie flat on their faces behind the bulwarks (the sailors are sometimes ordered to do the same), and when the vessel is fairly engaged, they are usually drawn up in the ship's waist—like a company reviewing in the Park. At close quarters, their muskets may pick off a seaman or two in the rigging, but at long-gun distance they must passively stand in their ranks and be decimated at the enemy's leisure. Only in one case in ten—that is, when their vessel is attempted to be boarded by a large party—are these marines of any essential service as fighting men; with their bayonets they are then called upon to 'repel!'

If comparatively so useless as soldiers, why have marines at all in the Navy? Know, then, that what standing armies are to nations, what turnkeys are to jails, these marines are to the seamen in all large men-of-war. Their muskets are their keys. With those muskets they stand guard over the fresh water; over the grog, when doled; over the provisions, when being served out by the master's mate; over the 'brig' or jail; at the commodore's and captain's cabin doors; and, in port, at both gangways and forecastle.

Surely, the crowd of sailors, who besides having so many sea-officers over them, are thus additionally guarded by soldiers, even when they quench their thirst—surely these man-of-war's-men must be desperadoes indeed; or else the naval service must be so tyrannical that the worst is feared from their possible insubordination. Either reason holds good, or both, according to the character of the officers and crew.

It must be evident that the man-of-war's-man casts but an evil eye on a marine. To call a man a 'horse marine' is, among seamen, one of the greatest terms of contempt.

But the mutual contempt, and even hatred, subsisting between these two bodies of men—both clinging to one keel, both lodged in one household—is held by most Navy officers as the height of the perfection of Navy discipline. It is regarded as the button that caps the uttermost point on their mainmast.

Thus they reason: secure of this antagonism between the marine and the sailor, we can always rely upon it, that if the sailor mutinies, it needs no great incitement for the marine to thrust his bayonet through his heart; if the marine revolts, the pike of the sailor is impatient to charge. Checks and balances, blood against blood, *that* is the cry and the argument.

What applies to the relation in which the marine and sailor stand toward each other—the mutual repulsion implied by a system of checks—will, in degree, apply to nearly the entire interior of a man-of-war's discipline. The whole body of this discipline is emphatically a system of cruel cogs and wheels, systematically grinding up in one common hopper all that might minister to the moral well-being of the crew.

It is the same with both officers and men. If a captain have a grudge against a lieutenant, or a lieutenant against a midshipman, how easy to torture him by official treatment, which shall not lay open the superior officer to legal rebuke. And if a midshipman bears a grudge against a sailor, how easy for him, by cunning practices, born of a boyish spite, to have him degraded at the gangway. Through all the endless ramifications of rank and station, in most men-of-war there runs a sinister vein of bitterness, not exceeded by the fireside hatreds in a family of stepsons ashore. It were sickening to detail all the paltry irritabilities, jealousies, and cabals, the spiteful detractions and animosities, that lurk far down, and cling to the very kelson of the ship. It is unmanning to think of. The immutable ceremonies and iron etiquette of a man-of-war; the spiked barriers separating the various grades of rank; the delegated absolutism of authority on all hands; the impossibility, on the part of the common seaman, of appeal from incidental abuses, and many more things that might be enumerated, all tend to beget in most armed ships a general social condition which is the precise reverse of what any Christian could desire. And though there are vessels that in some measure furnish exceptions to this; and though, in other ships, the thing may be glossed over by a guarded, punctilious exterior, almost completely hiding the truth from casual visitors, while the worst facts touching the common sailor are systematically kept in the background, yet it is certain that what has here been said of the domestic interior of a man-of-war will, in a greater or less degree, apply to most vessels in the Navy. It is not that the officers are so malevolent, nor, altogether, that the man-of-war's-man is so vicious. Some of these evils are un-avoidably generated through the operation of the naval code; others are absolutely organic to a Navy establishment, and, like other organic evils, are incurable, except when they dis-solve with the body they live in.

These things are undoubtedly heightened by the close cribbing and confinement of so many mortals in one oaken box on the sea. Like pears closely packed, the crowded crew mutually decay through close contact, and every plague-spot is contagious. Still more, from this same close confine-ment—so far as it affects the common sailors—arise other evils, so direful that they will hardly bear even so much as an allusion. What too many seamen are when ashore is very well known; but what some of them become when com-pletely cut off from shore indulgences can hardly be imagined by landsmen. The sins for which the cities of the plain were overthrown still linger in some of these wooden-walled Gomorrahs of the deep. More than once complaints were made at the mast in the *Neversink*, from which the deck officer would turn away with loathing, refuse to hear them, and command the complainant out of his sight. There are evils in men-of-war, which, like the suppressed domestic drama of Horace Walpole, will neither bear representing, nor reading, and will hardly bear thinking of. The landsman who has neither read Walpole's *Mysterious Mother*, nor Sophocles's *Œdipus Tyrannus*, nor the Roman story of *Count Cenci*, dramatized by Shelley,* let that landsman guardedly remain in his ignorance of even worse horrors than these, and forever abstain from seeking to draw aside this veil.

XC

The Manning of Navies

'THE gallows and the sea refuse nothing' is a very old sea saying; and, among all the wondrous prints of Hogarth, there is none remaining more true at the present day than that dramatic boat-scene, where, after consorting with harlots, and gambling on tombstones, the Idle Apprentice,* with the villainous low forehead, is at last represented as being pushed off to sea, with a ship and a gallows in the distance. But Hogarth should have converted the ship's masts themselves into Tyburn-trees,* and thus, with the ocean for a background, closed the career of his hero. It would then have had all the dramatic force of the opera of Don Juan,* who, after running his impious courses, is swept from our sight in a tornado of devils.

For the sea is the true Tophet and bottomless pit of many workers of iniquity; and, as the German mystics feign Gehennas within Gehennas,* even so are men-of-war familiarly known among sailors as 'Floating Hells'. And as the sea, according to old Fuller,* is the stable of brute monsters, gliding hither and thither in unspeakable swarms, even so is it the home of many moral monsters, who fitly divide its empire with the snake, the shark, and the worm.

Nor are sailors, and man-of-war's-men especially, at all blind to a true sense of these things. '*Purser rigged and parish damned*' is the sailor saying in the American Navy, when the tyro first mounts the lined frock and blue jacket, aptly manufactured for him in a state prison ashore.

No wonder, that lured by some *crimp**into a service so galling, and, perhaps, persecuted by a vindictive lieutenant, some repentant sailors have actually jumped into the sea to escape from their fate, or set themselves adrift on the wide ocean on the gratings, without compass or rudder.

In one case, a young man, after being nearly cut into dog's meat at the gangway, loaded his pockets with shot and walked overboard.

Some years ago, I was in a whaling ship lying in a harbour of the Pacific, with three French men-of-war alongside. One dark, moody night, a suppressed cry was heard from the face of the waters, and, thinking it was someone drowning, a boat was lowered, when two French sailors were picked up, half dead from exhaustion, and nearly throttled by a bundle of their clothes tied fast to their shoulders. In this manner they had attempted their escape from their vessel. When the French officers came in pursuit, these sailors, rallying from their exhaustion, fought like tigers to resist being captured. Though this story concerns a French armed ship, it is not the less applicable, in degree, to those of other nations.

Mix with the men in an American armed ship; mark how many foreigners there are, though it is against the law to enlist them. Nearly one-third of the petty officers of the *Neversink* were born east of the Atlantic. Why is this? Because the same principle that operates in hindering Americans from hiring themselves out as menial domestics also restrains them, in a great measure, from voluntarily assuming a far worse servitude in the Navy. '*Sailors wanted for the Navy*' is a common announcement along the wharves of our seaports. They are always '*wanted*'. It may have been, in part, owing to this scarcity of man-of-war's-men, that not many years ago black slaves were frequently to be found regularly enlisted with the crew of an American frigate, their masters receiving their pay. This was in the teeth of a law of Congress expressly prohibiting slaves in the Navy. This law, indirectly, means black slaves, nothing being said concerning white ones. But in view of what John Randolph of Roanoke said about the frigate that carried him to Russia, and in view of what most armed vessels actually are at present, the American Navy is not altogether an inappropriate place for hereditary bondmen. Still, the circumstance of their being found in it is of such a nature, that to some it may hardly appear credible. The incredulity of such persons, nevertheless, must yield to the fact, that on board of the United States Ship *Neversink*, during the present cruise, there was a Virginian slave regularly shipped as a seaman, his owner receiving his wages. Guinea*—such was his name among the crew—belonged to the purser, who was a Southern gentleman; he was employed as his body servant. Never did I feel my condition as a man-of-war's-man so keenly as when seeing this Guinea freely circulating about the decks in citizen's clothes, and, through the influence of his master, almost entirely exempted from the disciplinary degradation of the Caucasian crew. Faring sumptuously in the ward-room; sleek and round, his ebon face fairly polished with content; ever gay and hilarious; ever ready to laugh and joke, that African slave was actually envied by many of the sea-men. There were times when I almost envied him myself. Lemsford once envied him outright. 'Ah, Guinea!' he sighed, 'you have peaceful times; you never opened the book I read in.'

One morning, when all hands were called to witness punishment, the purser's slave, as usual, was observed to be hurrying down the ladders toward the ward-room, his face wearing that peculiar, pinched blueness, which, in the negro, answers to the paleness caused by nervous agitation in the white. 'Where are you going, Guinea?' cried the deck officer, a humorous gentleman, who sometimes diverted himself with the purser's slave, and well knew what answer he would now receive from him. 'Where are you going, Guinea?' said this officer; 'turn about; don't you hear the call, sir?' ''Scuse me, massa!' said the slave, with a low salutation; 'I can't 'tand it; I can't, indeed, massa!' and, so saying, he disappeared beyond the hatchway. He was the only person on board, except the hospital steward and the invalids of the sick-bay, who was exempted from being pre-sent at the administering of the scourge. Accustomed to light and easy duties from his birth, and so fortunate as to meet with none but gentle masters, Guinea, though a bond-man, liable to be saddled with a mortgage, like a horse—Guinea, in india-rubber manacles, enjoyed the liberties of the world.

Though his body-and-soul proprietor, the purser, never in any way individualized me while I served on board the frigate, and never did me a good office of any kind (it was hardly in his power), yet, from his pleasant, kind, indulgent manner toward his slave, I always imputed to him a generous heart, and cherished an involuntary friendliness toward him. Upon our arrival home, his treatment of Guinea, under circumstances peculiarly calculated to stir up the resentment of a slave-owner, still more augmented my estimation of the purser's good heart.

Mention has been made of the number of foreigners in the American Navy; but it is not in the American Navy alone that foreigners bear so large a proportion to the rest of the crew, though in no navy, perhaps, have they ever borne so large a proportion as in our own. According to an English estimate, the foreigners serving in the King's ships at one time amounted to one-eighth of the entire body of seamen. How it is in the French Navy, I cannot with certainty say; but I have repeatedly sailed with English seamen who have served in it.

One of the effects of the free introduction of foreigners into any navy cannot be sufficiently deplored. During the period I lived in the *Neversink*, I was repeatedly struck by the lack of patriotism in many of my shipmates. True, they were mostly foreigners, who unblushingly avowed that, were it not for the difference of pay, they would as lief man the guns of an English ship as those of an American or Frenchman. Nevertheless, it was evident that, as for any high-toned patriotic feeling, there was comparatively very little— hardly any of it—evinced by our sailors as a body. Upon reflection, this was not to be wondered at. From their roving career, and the sundering of all domestic ties, many sailors, all the world over, are like the 'Free Companions', who some centuries ago wandered over Europe, ready to fight the battles of any prince who could purchase their swords. The only patriotism is born and nurtured in a stationary home, and upon an immovable hearthstone; but the man-of-war's-man, though in his voyagings he weds the two Poles, and brings both Indies together, yet, let him wander where he will, he carries his one only home along with him: that home is his hammock. '*Born under a gun, and educated on the bowsprit,*' according to a phrase of his own, the man-of-war's-man rolls round the world like a billow, ready to mix with any sea, or be sucked down to death in the maelstrom of any war.

Yet more. The dread of the general discipline of a man-of-

war; the special obnoxiousness of the gangway; the protracted confinement on board ship, with so few 'liberty days';
and the pittance of pay (much less than what can always be
had in the merchant-service)—these things contrive to deter
from the navies of all countries by far the majority of their
best seamen. This will be obvious, when the following
statistical facts, taken from Macpherson's *Annals of Commerce*,* are considered. At one period, upon the peace establishment, the number of men employed in the English
Navy was 25,000; at the same time, the English merchant-
service was employing 118,952. But while the necessities of
a merchantman render it indispensable that the greater part
of her crew be able seamen, the circumstances of a man-of-
war admit of her mustering a crowd of landsmen, soldiers,
and boys in her service. By a statement of Captain Marryat's,*
in his pamphlet (A.D. 1822) *On the Abolition of Impressment*,
it appears that at the close of the Bonaparte wars a full third
of all the crews of His Majesty's fleets consisted of landsmen
and boys.

Far from entering with enthusiasm into the King's ships
when their country was menaced, the great body of English
seamen, appalled at the discipline of the Navy, adopted
unheard-of devices to escape its press-gangs. Some even
hid themselves in caves, and lonely places inland, fearing
to run the risk of seeking a berth in an outward-bound
merchantman, that might have carried them beyond sea. In
the true narrative of *John Nichol, Mariner*, published in 1822
by Blackwood in Edinburgh, and Cadell in London, and
which everywhere bears the spontaneous impress of truth,
the old sailor, in the most artless, touching, and almost un-
complaining manner, tells of his 'skulking like a thief' for
whole years in the country round about Edinburgh, to avoid
the press-gangs, prowling through the land like bandits and
Burkers.* At this time (Bonaparte's wars), according to
Steel's List,* there were forty-five regular press-gang
stations in Great Britain.*

---

* Besides this domestic kidnapping, British frigates, in friendly or neutral
harbours, in some instances pressed into their service foreign sailors of all

In a later instance, a large body of British seamen solemnly assembled upon the eve of an anticipated war, and together determined, that in case of its breaking out, they would at once flee to America, to avoid being pressed into the service of their country—a service which degraded her own guardians at the gangway.

At another time, long previous to this, according to an English Navy officer, Lieutenant Tomlinson,* three thousand seamen, impelled by the same motive, fled ashore in a panic from the colliers between Yarmouth Roads and the Nore. Elsewhere, he says, in speaking of some of the men on board the King's ships, that 'they were most miserable objects.' This remark is perfectly corroborated by other testimony referring to another period. In alluding to the lamented scarcity of good English seamen during the wars of 1808, &c., the author of a pamphlet on *Naval Subjects* says, that all the best seamen, the steadiest and best-behaved men, generally succeeded in avoiding the impress. This writer was, or had been, himself a captain in the British fleet.

Now it may be easily imagined who are the men, and of what moral character they are, who, even at the present day, are willing to enlist as full-grown adults in a service so galling to all shore-manhood as the Navy. Hence it comes that the skulkers and scoundrels of all sorts in a man-of-war are chiefly composed not of regular seamen, but of these 'dock-lopers' of landsmen, men who enter the Navy to draw their grog and murder their time in the notorious idleness of a frigate. But if so idle, why not reduce the number of a man-of-war's crew, and reasonably keep employed the rest? It cannot be done. In the first place, the magnitude of most of

nations from the public wharves. In certain cases, where Americans were concerned, when '*protections*' were found upon their persons, these were destroyed; and to prevent the American consul from claiming his sailor countrymen, the press-gang generally went on shore the night previous to the sailing of the frigate, so that the kidnapped seamen were far out to sea before they could be missed by their friends. These things should be known; for in case the English government again goes to war with its fleets, and should again resort to indiscriminate impressment to man them, it is well that both Englishmen and Americans, that all the world be prepared to put down an iniquity outrageous and insulting to God and man.

these ships requires a large number of hands to brace the heavy yards, hoist the enormous topsails, and weigh the ponderous anchor. And though the occasion for the employment of so many men comes but seldom, it is true, yet when that occasion *does* come—and come it may at any moment—this multitude of men are indispensable.

But besides this, and to crown all, the batteries must be manned. There must be enough men to work all the guns at one time. And thus, in order to have a sufficiency of mortals at hand to 'sink, burn, and destroy', a man-of-war—besides, through her vices, hopelessly depraving the volunteer landsmen and ordinary seamen of good habits, who occasionally enlist—must feed at the public cost a multitude of persons, who, if they did not find a home in the Navy, would probably fall on the parish, or linger out their days in a prison.

Among others, these are the men into whose mouths Dibdin* puts his patriotic verses, full of sea-chivalry and romance. With an exception in the last line, they might be sung with equal propriety by both English and American man-of-war's-men.

> As for me, in all weathers, all times, tides, and ends,
>   Naught's a trouble from duty that springs;
> For my heart is my Poll's, and my rhino's my friend's,
>   And as for my life, it's the king's.
>
> To rancour unknown, to no passion a slave,
>   Nor unmanly, nor mean, nor a railer, &c.

I do not unite with a high critical authority in considering Dibdin's ditties as 'slang songs', for most of them breathe the very poetry of the ocean. But it is remarkable that those songs—which would lead one to think that man-of-war's-men are the most care-free, contented, virtuous, and patriotic of mankind—were composed at a time when the English Navy was principally manned by felons and paupers, as mentioned in a former chapter. Still more, these songs are pervaded by a true Mohammedan sensualism; a reckless acquiescence in fate, and an implicit, unquestioning, dog-like devotion to whoever may be lord and master. Dibdin was a man of genius; but no wonder Dibdin was a government pensioner at £200 per annum.

But notwithstanding the iniquities of a man-of-war, men are to be found in them, at times, so used to a hard life, so drilled and disciplined to servitude, that, with an incomprehensible philosophy, they seem cheerfully to resign themselves to their fate. They have plenty to eat; spirits to drink; clothing to keep them warm; a hammock to sleep in; tobacco to chew; a doctor to medicine them; a parson to pray for them; and, to a penniless castaway, must not all this seem as a luxurious Bill of Fare?

There was on board of the *Neversink* a foretop-man by the name of Landless, who, though his back was cross-barred, and plaided with the ineffaceable scars of all the floggings accumulated by a reckless tar during a ten years' service in the Navy, yet he perpetually wore a hilarious face, and at joke and repartee was a very Joe Miller.*

That man, though a sea-vagabond, was not created in vain. He enjoyed life with the zest of everlasting adolescence; and, though cribbed in an oaken prison, with the turnkey sentries all round him, yet he paced the gun-deck as if it were broad as a prairie, and diversified in landscape as the hills and valleys of the Tyrol. Nothing ever disconcerted him; nothing could transmute his laugh into anything like a sigh. Those glandular secretions, which in other captives sometimes go to the formation of tears, in *him* were expectorated from the mouth, tinged with the golden juice of a weed, wherewith he solaced and comforted his ignominious days.

'Rum and tobacco!' said Landless, 'what more does a sailor want?'

His favourite song was Dibdin's *True English Sailor*, beginning:

> Jack dances and sings, and is always content,
> In his vows to his lass he'll ne'er fail her;
> His anchor's atrip when his money's all spent,
> And this is the life of a sailor.

But poor Landless danced quite as often at the gangway, under the lash, as in the sailor dance-houses ashore.

Another of his songs, also set to the significant tune of *The King, God bless him!* mustered the following lines among many similar ones:

> Oh, when safely landed in Boston or 'York,
> Oh how I will tipple and jig it;
> And toss off my glass while my rhino holds out,
> In drinking success to our frigate!

During the many idle hours when our frigate was lying in harbour, this man was either merrily playing at checkers, or mending his clothes, or snoring like a trumpeter under the lee of the booms. When fast asleep, a national salute from our batteries could hardly move him. Whether ordered to the main-truck in a gale; or rolled by the drum to the grog-tub; or commanded to walk up to the gratings and be lashed, Landless always obeyed with the same invincible indifference.

His advice to a young lad, who shipped with us at Valparaiso, embodies the pith and marrow of that philosophy which enables some man-of-war's-men to wax jolly in the service.

'*Shippy!*' said Landless, taking the pale lad by his neckerchief, as if he had him by the halter; 'Shippy, I've seen sarvice with Uncle Sam—I've sailed in many *Andrew Millers*. Now take my advice, and steer clear of all trouble. D'ye see, touch your tile whenever a swob (officer) speaks to you. And never mind how much they rope's-end you, keep your red-rag belayed; for you must know as how they don't fancy sea-lawyers; and when the sarving out of slops comes round, stand up to it stiffly; it's only an Oh Lord! or two, and a few Oh my Gods!—that's all. And what then? Why, you sleeps it off in a few nights, and turns out at last all ready for your grog.'

This Landless was a favourite with the officers, among whom he went by the name of *Happy Jack*. And it is just such Happy Jacks as Landless that most sea-officers profess to admire; a fellow without shame, without a soul, so dead to the least dignity of manhood that he could hardly be called a man. Whereas, a seaman who exhibits traits of moral sensitiveness, whose demeanour shows some dignity within; this is the man they, in many cases, instinctively dislike. The reason is, they feel such a man to be a continual reproach to them, as being mentally superior to their power. He has no business in a man-of-war; they do not want such men. To them there is an insolence in his manly freedom, contempt in his very carriage. He is unendurable, as an erect, lofty-minded African would be to some slave-driving planter.

Let it not be supposed, however, that the remarks in this and the preceding chapter apply to *all* men-of-war. There are some vessels blessed with patriarchal, intellectual captains, gentlemanly and brotherly officers, and docile and Christianized crews. The peculiar usages of such vessels insensibly soften the tyrannical rigour of the Articles of War; in them, scourging is unknown. To sail in such ships is hardly to realize that you live under the martial law, or that the evils above mentioned can anywhere exist.

And Jack Chase, old Ushant, and several more fine tars that might be added, sufficiently attest, that in the *Neversink* at least, there was more than one noble man-of-war's-man who almost redeemed all the rest.

Wherever, throughout this narrative, the American Navy, in any of its bearings, has formed the theme of a general discussion, hardly one syllable of admiration for what is accounted illustrious in its achievements has been permitted to escape me. The reason is this: I consider, that so far as what is called military renown is concerned, the American Navy needs no eulogist but History. It were superfluous for White-Jacket to tell the world what it knows already. The office imposed upon me is of another cast; and, though I foresee and feel that it may subject me to the pillory in the hard thoughts of some men, yet, supported by what God has given me, I tranquilly abide the event, whatever it may prove.

XCI

Smoking-club in a Man-of-war, with Scenes on the Gun-deck, drawing near Home

THERE is a fable about a painter moved by Jove to the painting of the head of Medusa. Though the picture was true to the life, yet the poor artist sickened at the sight of what his forced pencil had drawn. Thus, borne through my task toward the end, my own soul now sinks at what I myself have portrayed. But let us forget past chapters, if we may, while we paint less repugnant things.

Metropolitan gentlemen have their club; provincial gossipers their news-room; village quidnuncs their barber's shop; the Chinese their opium-houses; American Indians their council-fire; and even cannibals their *Noojona*, or Talkstone, where they assemble at times to discuss the affairs of the day. Nor is there any government, however despotic, that ventures to deny to the least of its subjects the privilege of a sociable chat. Not the Thirty Tyrants*even—the clubbed post-captains of old Athens—could stop the wagging tongues at the street-corners. For chat man must; and by our immortal Bill of Rights, that guarantees to us liberty of speech, chat we Yankees will, whether on board a frigate, or on board our own terra-firma plantations.

In men-of-war, the galley, or cookery, on the gun-deck is the grand centre of gossip and news among the sailors. Here crowds assemble to chat away the half-hour elapsing after every meal. The reason why this place and these hours are selected rather than others is this: in the neighbourhood of the galley alone, and only after meals, is the man-of-war's-man permitted to regale himself with a smoke.

A sumptuary edict, truly, that deprived White-Jacket, for one, of a luxury to which he had long been attached. For how can the mystical motives, the capricious impulses of a luxurious smoker go and come at the beck of a commodore's command? No! when I smoke, be it because of my sovereign

390

good pleasure I choose so to do, though at so unseasonable an hour that I send round the town for a brasier of coals. What! smoke by a sun-dial? smoke on compulsion? make a trade, a business, a vile recurring calling of smoking? and, perhaps, when those sedative fumes have steeped you in the grandest of reveries, and, circle over circle, solemnly rises some immeasurable dome in your soul—far away, swelling and heaving into the vapour you raise—as if from one of Mozart's grandest marches a temple were rising, like Venus from the sea—at such a time, to have your whole Parthenon tumbled about your ears by the knell of the ship's bell announcing the expiration of the half-hour for smoking! Whip me, ye Furies! toast me in saltpetre! smite me, some thunderbolt! charge upon me, endless squadrons of Mamelukes! devour me, Feejees!*but preserve me from a tyranny like this.

No! though I smoked like an Indian summer ere I entered the *Neversink*, so abhorrent was this sumptuary law that I altogether abandoned the luxury rather than enslave it to a time and a place. Herein did I not right, Ancient and Honourable Old Guard of Smokers all round the world?

But there were others of the crew not so fastidious as myself. After every meal, they hied to the galley and solaced their souls with a whiff.

Now, a bunch of cigars, all banded together, is a type and a symbol of the brotherly love between smokers. Likewise, for the time, in a community of pipes is a community of hearts. Nor was it an ill thing for the Indian sachems to circulate their calumet*tobacco-bowl—even as our own forefathers circulated their punch-bowl—in token of peace, charity, and good will, friendly feelings, and sympathizing souls. And this it was that made the gossipers of the galley so loving a club, so long as the vapoury bond united them.

It was a pleasant sight to behold them. Grouped in the recesses between the guns, they chatted and laughed like rows of convivialists in the boxes of some vast dining-saloon. Take a Flemish kitchen-full of good fellows from Teniers; add a fireside group from Wilkie;*throw in a naval sketch from Cruikshank;* and then stick a short pipe into every mother's son's mouth, and you have the smoking scene at the galley of the *Neversink*.

Not a few were politicians; and, as there were some thoughts of a war with England at the time, their discussions waxed warm.

'I tell you what it is, *shippies*!' cried the old captain of gun No. I on the forecastle, 'if that 'ere President of ourn don't luff up into the wind, by the Battle of the Nile! he'll be getting us into a grand fleet engagement afore the Yankee nation has rammed home her cartridges—let alone blowing the match!'

'Who talks of luffing?' roared a roystering foretop-man. 'Keep our Yankee nation large before the wind, say I, till you come plump on the enemy's bows, and then board him in the smoke,' and with that there came forth a mighty blast from his pipe.

'Who says the old man at the helm of the Yankee nation can't steer his *trick* as well as George Washington himself?' cried a sheet-anchor-man.

'But they say he's a cold-water customer, Bill,' cried another; 'and sometimes o' nights I somehow has a presentation that he's goin' to stop our grog.'

'D'ye hear there, fore and aft!' roared the boatswain's mates at the gangway, 'all hands tumble up, and 'bout ship!'

'That's the talk!' cried the captain of gun No. I, as, in obedience to the summons, all hands dropped their pipes and crowded toward the ladders, 'and that's what the President must do—go in stays, my lads, and put the Yankee nation on the other tack.'

But these political discussions by no means supplied the staple of conversation for the gossiping smokers of the galley. The interior affairs of the frigate itself formed their principal theme. Rumours about the private life of the commodore in his cabin; about the captain, in his; about the various officers in the ward-room; about the *reefers* in the steerage, and their madcap frolickings, and about a thousand other matters touching the crew themselves; all these—forming the eternally shifting, domestic by-play of a man-of-war—proved inexhaustible topics for our quidnuncs.*

The animation of these scenes was very much heightened as we drew nearer and nearer our port; it rose to a climax when the frigate was reported to be only twenty-four hours' sail from the land. What they should do when they landed; how they should invest their wages; what they should eat; what they should drink; and what lass they should marry—these were the topics which absorbed them.

'Sink the sea!' cried a forecastle-man. 'Once more ashore, and you'll never again catch old Boombolt afloat. I mean to settle down in a sail-loft.'

'Cable-tier pinches blister all tarpaulin hats!' cried a young after-guard's-man; 'I mean to go back to the counter.'

'Shipmates! take me by the arms, and swab up the lee scuppers with me, but I mean to steer a clam-cart before I go again to a ship's wheel. Let the Navy go by the board—to sea again, I won't.'

'Start my soul-bolts, maties, if any more Blue Peters and sailing signals fly at my fore!' cried the captain of the head. 'My wages will buy a wheelbarrow, if nothing more.'

'I have taken my last dose of salts,' said the captain of the waist, 'and after this mean to stick to fresh water. Ay, maties, ten of us waisters mean to club together, and buy a *serving-mallet boat*,* d'ye see; and if ever we drown, it will be in the "raging canal"!*Blast the sea, shipmates! say I.'

'Profane not the holy element!' said Lemsford, the poet of the gun-deck, leaning over a cannon. 'Know ye not, man-of-war's-men! that by the Parthian magi the ocean was held sacred? Did not Tiridates,* the Eastern monarch, take an immense land circuit to avoid desecrating the Mediterranean, in order to reach his imperial master, Nero, and do homage for his crown?'

'What lingo is that?' cried the captain of the waist.

'Who's Commodore Tiddery-eye?' cried the forecastle-man.

'Hear me out,' resumed Lemsford. 'Like Tiridates, I venerate the sea, and venerate it so highly, shipmates, that evermore I shall abstain from crossing it. In *that* sense, captain of the waist, I echo your cry.'

It was, indeed, a remarkable fact, that nine men out of every ten of the *Neversink*'s crew had formed some plan or other to keep themselves ashore for life, or, at least, on fresh water, after the expiration of the present cruise. With all the experiences of that cruise accumulated in one intense recollection of a moment; with the smell of tar in their nostrils; out of sight of land; with a stout ship under foot, and snuffing the ocean air; with all the things of the sea surrounding them; in their cool, sober moments of reflection; in the silence and solitude of the deep, during the long night-watches, when all their holy home associations were thronging round their hearts; in the spontaneous piety and devotion of the last hours of so long a voyage; in the fullness and the frankness of their souls; when there was naught to jar the well-poised equilibrium of their judgment—under all these circumstances, at least nine-tenths of a crew of five hundred man-of-war's-men resolved forever to turn their backs on the sea. But do men ever hate the thing they love? Do men forswear the hearth and the homestead? What, then, must the Navy be?

But, alas for the man-of-war's-man, who, though he may take a Hannibal oath*against the service; yet, cruise after cruise, and after forswearing it again and again, he is driven back to the spirit-tub and the gun-deck by his old hereditary foe, the ever-devilish god of grog.

On this point, let some of the crew of the *Neversink* be called to the stand.

You, captain of the waist! and you, seamen of the foretop! and you, after-guard's-men and others! how came you here at the guns of the *North Carolina*, after registering your solemn vows at the galley of the *Neversink*?

They all hang their heads. I know the cause; poor fellows! perjure yourselves not again; swear not at all hereafter.

Ay, these very tars—the foremost in denouncing the Navy; who had bound themselves by the most tremendous oaths— these very men, not three days after getting ashore, were rolling round the streets in penniless drunkenness; and next day many of them were to be found on board of the *guardo* or receiving-ship. Thus, in part, is the Navy manned.

But what was still more surprising, and tended to impart a new and strange insight into the character of sailors, and overthrow some long-established ideas concerning them as a class, was this: numbers of men who, during the cruise, had passed for exceedingly prudent, nay, parsimonious persons, who would even refuse you a patch, or a needleful of thread, and, from their stinginess, procured the name of *Ravelings**—no sooner were these men fairly adrift in harbour, and under the influence of frequent quaffings, than their three-years-earned wages flew right and left; they summoned whole boarding-houses of sailors to the bar, and treated them over and over again. Fine fellows! generous-hearted tars! Seeing this sight, I thought to myself, Well, these generous-hearted tars on shore were the greatest curmudgeons afloat! it's the bottle that's generous, not they! Yet the popular conceit concerning a sailor is derived from his behaviour ashore; whereas, ashore he is no longer a sailor, but a landsman for the time. A man-of-war's-man is only a man-of-war's-man at sea; and the sea is the place to learn what he is. But we have seen that a man-of-war is but this old-fashioned world of ours afloat, full of all manner of characters—full of strange contradictions; and though boasting some fine fellows here and there, yet, upon the whole, charged to the combings of her hatchways with the spirit of Belial and all unrighteousness.

XCII
The Last of the Jacket

ALREADY has White-Jacket chronicled the mishaps and inconveniences, troubles and tribulations of all sorts brought upon him by that unfortunate but indispensable garment of his. But now it befalls him to record how this jacket, for the second and last time, came near proving his shroud.

Of a pleasant midnight, our good frigate, now somewhere off the Capes of Virginia, was running on bravely, when the breeze, gradually dying, left us slowly gliding toward our still invisible port.

Headed by Jack Chase, the quarter-watch were reclining in the top, talking about the shore delights into which they intended to plunge, while our captain often broke in with allusions to similar conversations when he was on board the English line-of-battle ship, the *Asia*, drawing nigh to Portsmouth, in England, after the Battle of Navarino.

Suddenly an order was given to set the main-topgallant stun'-sail, and the halyards not being rove, Jack Chase assigned to me that duty. Now this reeving of the halyards of a main-topgallant stun'-sail is a business that eminently demands sharpsightedness, skill, and celerity.

Consider that the end of a line, some two hundred feet long, is to be carried aloft, in your teeth, if you please, and dragged far out on the giddiest of yards, and after being wormed and twisted about through all sorts of intricacies— turning abrupt corners at the abruptest of angles—is to be dropped, clear of all obstructions, in a straight plumb-line right down to the deck. In the course of this business, there is a multitude of sheave-holes and blocks, through which you must pass it; often the rope is a very tight fit, so as to make it like threading a fine cambric needle with rather coarse thread. Indeed, it is a thing only deftly to be done, even by day. Judge, then, what it must be to be threading cambric needles by night, and at sea, upward of a hundred feet aloft in the air.

With the end of the line in one hand, I was mounting the topmast shrouds, when our captain of the top told me that I had better off jacket; but though it was not a very cold night, I had been reclining so long in the top, that I had become somewhat chilly, so I thought best not to comply with the hint.

Having reeved the line through all the inferior blocks, I went out with it to the end of the weather topgallant yard-arm, and was in the act of leaning over and passing it through the suspended jewel-block there, when the ship gave a plunge in the sudden swells of the calm sea, and pitching me still further over the yard, threw the heavy skirts of my jacket right over my head, completely muffling me. Somehow I thought it was the sail that had flapped, and, under that impression, threw up my hands to drag it from my head, relying upon the sail itself to support me meanwhile. Just then the ship gave another sudden jerk, and, head foremost, I pitched from the yard. I knew where I was, from the rush of the air by my ears, but all else was a nightmare. A bloody film was before my eyes, through which, ghost-like, passed and repassed my father, mother, and sisters. An unutterable nausea oppressed me; I was conscious of gasping; there seemed no breath in my body. It was over one hundred feet that I fell—down, down, with lungs collapsed as in death. Ten thousand pounds of shot seemed tied to my head, as the irresistible law of gravitation dragged me, head foremost and straight as a die, toward the infallible centre of this terr-aqueous globe. All I had seen, and read, and heard, and all I had thought and felt in my life, seemed intensified in one fixed idea in my soul. But dense as this idea was, it was made up of atoms. Having fallen from the projecting yard-arm end, I was conscious of a collected satisfaction in feeling, that I should not be dashed on the deck, but would sink into the speechless profound of the sea.

With the bloody, blind film before my eyes, there was a still stranger hum in my head, as if a hornet were there; and I thought to myself, Great God! this is Death! Yet these thoughts were unmixed with alarm. Like frost-work that flashes and shifts its scared hues in the sun, all my braided, blended emotions were in themselves icy cold and calm.

So protracted did my fall seem, that I can even now recall the feeling of wondering how much longer it would be, ere all was over and I struck. Time seemed to stand still, and all the worlds seemed poised on their poles, as I fell, soul-becalmed, through the eddying whirl and swirl of the maelstrom air.

At first, as I have said, I must have been precipitated head foremost; but I was conscious, at length, of a swift, flinging motion of my limbs, which involuntarily threw themselves out, so that at last I must have fallen in a heap. This is more likely, from the circumstance, that when I struck the sea, I felt as if some one had smote me slantingly across the shoulder and along part of my right side.

As I gushed into the sea, a thunder-boom sounded in my ear; my soul seemed flying from my mouth. The feeling of death flooded over me with the billows. The blow from the sea must have turned me, so that I sank almost feet foremost through a soft, seething, foamy lull. Some current seemed hurrying me away; in a trance I yielded, and sank deeper down with a glide. Purple and pathless was the deep calm now around me, flecked by summer lightnings in an azure afar. The horrible nausea was gone; the bloody, blind film turned a pale green; I wondered whether I was yet dead, or still dying. But of a sudden some fashionless form brushed my side—some inert, coiled fish of the sea; the thrill of being alive again tingled in my nerves, and the strong shunning of death shocked me through.

For one instant an agonizing revulsion came over me as I found myself utterly sinking. Next moment the force of my fall was expended; and there I hung, vibrating in the mid-deep. What wild sounds then rang in my ear! One was a soft moaning, as of low waves on the beach; the other wild and heartlessly jubilant, as of the sea in the height of a tempest. Oh soul! thou then heardest life and death: as he who stands upon the Corinthian shore hears both the Ionian and the Ægean waves. The life-and-death poise soon passed; and then I found myself slowly ascending, and caught a dim glimmering of light.

Quicker and quicker I mounted; till at last I bounded up like a buoy, and my whole head was bathed in the blessed air.

I had fallen in a line with the mainmast; I now found myself nearly abreast of the mizzenmast, the frigate slowly gliding by like a black world in the water. Her vast hull loomed out of the night, showing hundreds of seamen in the hammock-nettings, some tossing over ropes, others madly flinging overboard the hammocks; but I was too far out from them immediately to reach what they threw. I essayed to swim toward the ship; but instantly I was conscious of a feeling like being pinioned in a feather-bed, and, moving my hands, felt my jacket puffed out above my tight girdle with water. I strove to tear it off; but it was looped together here and there, and the strings were not then to be sundered by hand. I whipped out my knife, that was tucked at my belt, and ripped my jacket straight up and down, as if I were ripping open myself. With a violent struggle I then burst out of it, and was free. Heavily soaked, it slowly sank before my eyes.

Sink! sink! oh shroud! thought I; sink forever! accursed jacket that thou art!

'See that white shark!' cried a horrified voice from the taffrail; 'he'll have that man down his hatchway! Quick! the *grains*! the *grains*!'*

The next instant that barbed bunch of harpoons pierced through and through the unfortunate jacket, and swiftly sped down with it out of sight.

Being now astern of the frigate, I struck out boldly toward the elevated pole of one of the life-buoys which had been cut away. Soon after, one of the cutters picked me up. As they dragged me out of the water into the air, the sudden transition of elements made my every limb feel like lead, and I helplessly sunk into the bottom of the boat.

Ten minutes after, I was safe on board, and, springing aloft, was ordered to reeve anew the stun'-sail halyards, which, slipping through the blocks when I had let go the end, had unrove and fallen to the deck.

The sail was soon set; and, as if purposely to salute it, a gentle breeze soon came, and the *Neversink* once more glided over the water, a soft ripple at her bows, and leaving a tranquil wake behind.

XCIII

Cable and Anchor all clear

AND now that the white jacket has sunk to the bottom of the sea, and the blessed Capes of Virginia are believed to be broad on our bow—though still out of sight—our five hundred souls are fondly dreaming of home, and the iron throats of the guns round the galley re-echo with their songs and hurrahs—what more remains?

Shall I tell what conflicting and almost crazy surmisings prevailed concerning the precise harbour for which we were bound? For, according to rumour, our commodore had received sealed orders touching that matter, which were not to be broken open till we gained a precise latitude of the coast. Shall I tell how, at last, all this uncertainty departed, and many a foolish prophecy was proved false, when our noble frigate—her longest pennant at her main—wound her stately way into the innermost harbour of Norfolk, like a plumed Spanish grandee threading the corridors of the Escurial*toward the throne-room within? Shall I tell how we kneeled upon the holy soil? how I begged a blessing of old Ushant, and one precious hair of his beard for a keepsake? how Lemsford, the gun-deck bard, offered up a devout ode as a prayer of thanksgiving? how saturnine Nord, the magnifico in disguise, refusing all companionship, stalked off into the woods, like the ghost of an old Calif of Bagdad? how I swayed and swung the hearty hand of Jack Chase, and nipped it to mine with a carrick bend; yea, and kissed that noble hand of my liege lord and captain of my top, my sea-tutor and sire?

Shall I tell how the grand commodore and captain drove off from the pier-head? how the lieutenants, in undress, sat down to their last dinner in the ward-room, and the champagne, packed in ice, spirted and sparkled like the hot springs out of a snow-drift in Iceland? how the chaplain went off in his cassock, without bidding the people adieu? how shrunken Cuticle, the surgeon, stalked over the side, the wired skeleton carried in his wake by his cot-boy? how the lieutenant of marines sheathed his sword on the poop, and, calling for wax and a taper, sealed the end of the scabbard with his family crest and motto—*Denique Caelum?*[*]how the purser in due time mustered his money-bags, and paid us all off on the quarter-deck—good and bad, sick and well, all receiving their wages; though, truth to tell, some reckless, improvident seamen, who had lived too fast during the cruise, had little or nothing now standing on the credit side of their purser's accounts?

Shall I tell of the Retreat of the Five Hundred inland; not, alas! in battle-array, as at quarters, but scattered broadcast over the land?

Shall I tell how the *Neversink* was at last stripped of spars, shrouds, and sails—had her guns hoisted out—her powder-magazine, shot-lockers, and armouries discharged—till not one vestige of a fighting thing was left in her, from furthest stem to uttermost stern?

No! let all this go by; for our anchor still hangs from our bows, though its eager flukes dip their points in the impatient waves. Let us leave the ship on the sea—still with the land out of sight—still with brooding darkness on the face of the deep. I love an indefinite, infinite background—a vast, heaving, rolling, mysterious rear!

It is night. The meagre moon is in her last quarter—that betokens the end of a cruise that is passing. But the stars look forth in their everlasting brightness—and *that* is the everlasting, glorious Future, forever beyond us.

We maintop-men are all aloft in the top; and round our mast we circle, a brother-band, hand in hand, all spliced together. We have reefed the last topsail; trained the last gun; blown the last match; bowed to the last blast; been tranced in the last calm. We have mustered our last round the capstan; been rolled to grog the last time; for the last time swung in our hammocks; for the last time turned out at the sea-gull call of the watch. We have seen our last man scourged at the gangway; our last man gasp out the ghost in the stifling sick-bay; our last man tossed to the sharks. Our last death-denouncing Article of War has been read; and far inland, in that blessed clime whitherward our frigate now glides, the last wrong in our frigate will be remembered no more; when down from our mainmast comes our commodore's pennant, when down sinks its shooting stars from the sky.

'By the mark, nine!' sings the hoary old leadsman, in the chains. And thus, the mid-world Equator passed, our frigate strikes soundings at last.

Hand in hand we top-mates stand, rocked in our Pisgah top.* And over the starry waves, and broad out into the blandly blue and boundless night, spiced with strange sweets from the long-sought land—the whole long cruise predestinated ours, though often in tempest-time we almost refused to believe in that far-distant shore—straight out into that fragrant night, ever-noble Jack Chase, matchless and unmatchable Jack Chase stretches forth his bannered hand, and, pointing shoreward, cries: 'For the last time, hear Camoens, boys!

> How calm the waves, how mild the balmy gale!
> The Halcyons call, ye Lusians spread the sail!
> Appeased, old Ocean now shall rage no more!
> Haste, point our bowsprit for yon shadowy shore.
> Soon shall the transports of your natal soil
> O'erwhelm in bounding joy the thoughts of every toil.'*

The End

A s a man-of-war that sails through the sea, so this earth that sails through the air. We mortals are all on board a fast-sailing, never-sinking, world-frigate, of which God was the shipwright; and she is but one craft in a Milky-Way fleet, of which God is the Lord High Admiral. The port we sail from is forever astern. And though far out of sight of land, for ages and ages we continue to sail with sealed orders, and our last destination remains a secret to ourselves and our officers; yet our final haven was predestinated ere we slipped from the stocks*at Creation.

Thus sailing with sealed orders, we ourselves are the repositories of the secret packet, whose mysterious contents we long to learn. There are no mysteries out of ourselves. But let us not give ear to the superstitious, gun-deck gossip about whither we may be gliding, for, as yet, not a soul on board of us knows—not even the commodore himself; assuredly not the chaplain; even our professor's scientific surmisings are vain. On that point, the smallest cabin-boy is as wise as the captain. And believe not the hypochondriac dwellers below hatches, who will tell you, with a sneer, that our world-frigate is bound to no final harbour whatever; that our voyage will prove an endless circumnavigation of space. Not so. For how can this world-frigate prove our eventual abiding place, when, upon our first embarkation, as infants in arms, her violent rolling—in after life unperceived —makes every soul of us seasick? Does not this show, too, that the very air we here inhale is uncongenial, and only becomes endurable at last through gradual habituation, and that some blessed placid haven, however remote at present, must be in store for us all?

Glance fore and aft our flush decks. What a swarming crew! All told, they muster hard upon eight hundred millions of souls. Over these we have authoritative lieutenants, a sword-belted officer of marines, a chaplain, a professor, a purser, a doctor, a cook, a master-at-arms.

Oppressed by illiberal laws, and partly oppressed by themselves, many of our people are wicked, unhappy, inefficient. We have skulkers and idlers all round, and brow-beaten waisters, who, for a pittance, do our craft's shabby work. Nevertheless, among our people we have gallant fore, main, and mizzen top-men aloft, who, well treated or ill, still trim our craft to the blast.

We have a *brig* for trespassers; a bar by our mainmast, at which they are arraigned; a cat-o'-nine-tails and a gangway, to degrade them in their own eyes and in ours. These are not always employed to convert Sin to Virtue, but to divide them, and protect Virtue and legalized Sin from unlegalized Vice.

We have a sick-bay for the smitten and helpless, whither we hurry them out of sight, and, however they may groan beneath hatches, we hear little of their tribulations on deck; we still sport our gay streamer aloft. Outwardly regarded, our craft is a lie; for all that is outwardly seen of it is the clean-swept deck, and oft-painted planks comprised above the water-line; whereas, the vast mass of our fabric, with all its store-rooms of secrets, forever slides along far under the surface.

When a shipmate dies, straightway we sew him up, and overboard he goes; our world-frigate rushes by, and never more do we behold him again; though, sooner or later, the everlasting undertow sweeps him toward our own destination.

We have both a quarter-deck to our craft and a gun-deck; subterranean shot-lockers and gunpowder magazines; and the Articles of War form our domineering code.

Oh, shipmates and worldmates, all round! we the people suffer many abuses. Our gun-deck is full of complaints. In vain from lieutenants do we appeal to the captain; in vain—while on board our world-frigate—to the indefinite Navy Commissioners, so far out of sight aloft. Yet the worst of our evils we blindly inflict upon ourselves; our officers cannot remove them, even if they would. From the last ills no being can save another; therein each man must be his own saviour. For the rest, whatever befall us, let us never train our murderous guns inboard; let us not mutiny with bloody pikes in our hands. Our Lord High Admiral will yet interpose; and though long ages should elapse, and leave our wrongs unredressed, yet, shipmates and worldmates! let us never forget, that,

> Whoever afflict us, whatever surround,
> Life is a voyage that's homeward bound!

THE END

VARIANT READINGS

This list gives variants between this edition, the London and New York first editions (1850), and Constable's Standard Edition (1922). The readings accepted here are given first. References are to pages and lines of text in this edition. Spelling variations immaterial to variant readings have been ignored; so also have typographical variations (e.g. many words and phrases which the London first edition prints in roman type and the New York first edition in italics). *A* = American Classics edition; *L* = London first edition; *N* = New York first edition; *S* = Constable's Standard Edition (re-issued 1963 by Russell & Russell, Inc.).

'White-Jacket' is hyphenated in *L* except on the title-page, hyphenated in *N* throughout, unhyphenated in *S*.

1. PREFACE 1–28. *L*, *S* / *not in N*.
2. NOTE 1–8. *N*, *S*. / *not in L*.
3. 14. *N*, *S*. laying /*L*. spreading
4. 22. *N*, *S*. *Me? Ah me!* / *not in L*.
7. 25. *L*, *S*. he / *N*. him
11. 11. *N*, *S*. sailor / *L*. merchant-sailor
11. 31. *N*, *S*. London / *L*. London in King James's time
12. 26. *L*. Delphi / *N*, *S*. oracle of Delphi
14. 33. *N*, *S*. neck handkerchiefs / *L*. neckerchiefs
16. 29–30. *L*, *S*. man-of-war's / *N*. men-of-war's
21. 31–2. *N*, *S*. Perhaps . . . real / *L*. Why was this? Why not be companionable with his officers? The
21. 33. *N*, *S*. he / *L*. our Commodore
25. 12–13. *N*, *S*. I . . . then / *L*. The first time I had a look at it,
27. 7. *N*, *S*. perilous / *L*. dignified
27. 30. *L*, *S*. about in / *N*. about with
28. 9. *S*. yeoman / *L*, *N*. yeomen
29. 12. *N*, *S*. equality. / *L*. equality.

For the same reason, the Commodore has his own steward and cook, who wait upon nobody but him; also his own stove, where nothing is cooked but for his meals. So, too, with the Captain. The ward-room officers, also, have their own steward and cook; also, the midshipmen. The cooking for these two classes is done at a distinct part of the great galley—the forward end—a place called 'the range.' This is a wide grate, several feet long.

29. 20. *N*, *S*. *the people* / *L*. *the people*** [*Footnote*] *In the same nomenclature, they are also especially designated as "the men."

29. 21–2. *N*, *S*. old-fashioned, Elizabethan, Franklin-warranted / *L*. old-fashioned

30. 10. *L*, *S*. man-of-war's / *N*. men-of-war's

30. 16–17. *L*, *S*. man-of-war's / *N*. men-of-war's

36. 26. *N*, *S*. a time / *L*. the time

37. 33. *L*, *S*. hands / *N*. their hands

38. 29. *N*, *S*. pockets / *L*. pantries

43. 24. *N*, *S*. their / *L*. the

48. 8. *N*, *S*. a teething child / *L*. teething children

49. 15. *L*. some / *N*, *S*. that some

55. 32. *L*, *S*. his / *N*. this

57. 24. *S*. master-at-arms / *L*, *N*. masters-at-arms

64. 27. *L*, *S*. man-of-war's / *N*. men-of-war's

72. 1. *L*, *S*. man-of-war's / *N*. men-of-war's

79. 25. *L*, *S*. almost / *not in N*.

80. 37. *L*, *N*. brushes-full / *S*. brushfuls

85. 32. *L*. *S*. man-of-war's / *N*. men-of-war's

86. 17. *N*, *S*. was hardly ever heard of / *L*. is not a regular thing

86. 29–30. *L*, *S*. his commander / *N*. their commanders

87. 10–11. *N*, *S*. superficies . . . in / *L*. surface . . . on

89. 26. *N*. the most arbitrary / *L*. *S*. perhaps the most severe

90. 5. *L*, *S*. man-of-war's / *N*. men-of-war's

90. 16. *L*, *S*. man-of-war's / *N*. men-of-war's

92. 26. *N*. *Jankee* / *L*, *S*. *Jankee* (Yankee)

106. 3. *L*, *S*. where / *N*. while

107. 36. *L*, *S*. previously / *N*. previous

108. 8. *N*, *S*. yeasting / *L*. yeasty

111. 14. *L*, *S*. dare / *N*. dared

114. 22. *N*, *S*. many. / *L*. many; and got himself into difficulties, as has been mentioned elsewhere.

114. 37. *N*, *S*. swell / *L*. swells

115. 9. *N*, *S*. or reverses / *not in L*.

115. 12. *L*. smoke and / *N*, *S*. smoke or

117. 20. *N*, *S*. frigates. / *L*. frigates.

But if there is good reason to believe, that there are some incompetent officers in our navy; we have still better, and more abundant reason to know, that there are others, whom both nature and art have united in eminently qualifying for it; and whom the service does not so much honour, as they may be said to honour it.

And the only purpose of this chapter is, to point out as the peculiar desert of individuals, that generalized reputation, which most men, perhaps, are apt to ascribe in the gross, to one and all the members of a popular military establishment.

119. 35. *N, S.* their scraping / *L.* scraping
122. 22. *N, S.* and, so / *L.* so
124. 30. *N.* the less painful / *L, S.* some of the
124. 34. *L, S.* sailors' / *N.* sailor
135. 37. *L, S.* man-of-war's / *N.* men-of-war's
136. 5. *L, S.* man-of-war's / *N.* men-of-war's
136. 13. *N, S.* in agony / *L.* if scourged
139. 29–37. 5. *N, S.* Let . . . laws. / *not in L.*
142. 4–5. *L, S.* time, and for one offence. / *N.* time.
142. 18. *N, S.* used up / *L.* worn out
144. 12. *N, S.* It / *L.* But it
147. 7. *N, S.* Blackstone, again / *L.* a great lawyer
148. 23. *S.* seven / *L, N.* seventh
148. XXXVI *title. N, S. Flogging not necessary / L. Is flogging necessary?*
151. 26. *L, N.* ran / *S.* run
152. 12. *L.* free / *N, S.* freed
153. 19–20. *N, S.* The . . . rear. / *not in L.*
154. 9. *N, S.* at / *L.* of
155. 6. *N, S.* the / *not in L.*
155. 7. *N, S.* long / *L.* section of a
157. 8. *L, N. Phaedon / S. Phaedo*
158. 5–6. *N, S.* in . . . is / *L.* it is, in some governments,
162. 33–4. *N, S.* cockswains / *L.* cockswains, or steersmen
167. 16. *N, S.* Spanish / *not in L.*
175. 22. *L, S.* my / *N.* your own
178. 17. *L.* scouts / *N, S.* scouts at
183. 31. *L, N.* and / *S.* and his
186. 19. *S.* master-at-arms' / *L, N.* masters-at-arms'
187. 26–7. *N, S.* almost numberless / *L.* repeated
188. 18. *L, S.* many / *N.* so many
190. 4. *L.* jeweller's / *N, S.* jeweler
191. 11. *N, S.* Goethe's . . . Margaret / *L.* Clanqui's . . . Zantua
191. 14. *N, S.* Mephistopheles / *L.* Don
191. 20. *N, S.* lying / *not in L.*
194. 32–3. *N, S.* manuscripts / *L.* manuscript
194. 35. *N, S.* again. / *L.* again. Little Quoin, the quarter-gunner, was on the 'sick-list' then.
195. 1. *N, S.* he / *L.* Lemsford

197. 33–4. *N, S.* three or four / *L.* seven or eight
199. 38. *N, S.* soon / *L.* at last
200. 6. *N, S.* hearty / *L.* hearty little
202. 22. *L.* Yes: / *N, S.* And
203. 7–8. *N, S.* without . . . muscle / *not in L.*
214. 26. *N, S.* those / *L.* these
215. 34. *N, S.* grander / *L.* more grand
216. 31. *N, S.* itself / *not in L.*
220. 10. *N, S.* despotic / *L.* certain
230. 10–11. *N, S.* about very industriously / *L.* about [*blank*] industri-ously
237. 14. *L.* ever / *not in N, S.*
238. 31. *N, S.* lay / *L.* lie
238. 34. *N, S.* all / *not in L.*
244. 27. *N, S.* mania-a-potu, / *L.* mania-a-potu, or something like that;
252. 35. *L, N.* present / *S.* present to
256. 38. *N, S.* no / *L.* no more
266. 28. *L, N. Mohawk* / *S. Buccaneer*
268. 33. *L, N. upon* / *S. on*
270. 2. *L, S.* a / *N.* the
280. 22. *N, S.* As . . . of / *L.* During
281. 3. *L.* be / *N, S.* is
283. 22–3. *L.* quarter-masters / *N, S.* quarter-master
284. 28. *N, S.* as / *not in L.*
290. 17. *N, S.* home. / *L.* home.

In the histories of some old states we read of *tasters* being appointed to the court, by way of precaution against poisonings. This taster's business consisted in tasting all dishes previous to his royal master's dining. In modern navies this custom is reversed. Every day, at precisely seven bells of the forenoon watch, (half-past eleven o'clock,) the ship's cook of the *Neversink* would slowly emerge from the main-hatchway, bearing a capacious tin pan, containing a sample of the salt-beef or pork—as the case might be—that day cooked for the people's messes. Inserted uprightly in the steaming meat would be seen a knife and fork. Advancing to the main-mast, the cook deposits the pan on the belaying rail, and solemnly touching his hat, awaits the pleasure of the officer of the deck. It is a ceremony that attracts all eyes; for of all persons in the world, the sailors in a man-of-war are the most keenly anxious for the dinner-time to come; and Old Coffee's inevitable appearance with his pan, at precisely seven bells, was always hailed by them

with delight. To myself, he was better than a clock. Nor was Old
Coffee at all blind to the dignity and importance of the ceremony, in
which he enacted so conspicuous a part. He preserved the utmost
rectitude of carriage; and when it was 'Duff Day,' he would advance
with his tin truncheon borne high aloft, exhibiting a pale, round
duff surmounting the blood-red mass of beef;—he looked something like the figure in the old painting of the executioner presenting
the head of St. John the Baptist in a charger.

In due time, the officer of the deck draws near, spreads his feet
apart at the belaying rails, and squares himself to the inspection.
Drawing out the knife and fork from the beef, he cuts himself a
choice piece; masticates it rapidly, while looking the cook full in the
eye; and if the flavour seems agreeable to him, he sticks the knife
and fork into the beef again, and exclaims, 'Very good: serve it up.'
Thus, in a man-of-war, the lords may be said to be tasters to the
commons.

The ostensible reason of this ceremony is this, that the officer of
the deck may be sure that the ship's cook has faithfully cooked his
meat. But as all the meat is not inspected, and the cook may select
what pieces he pleases for inspection, the test is by no means a
thorough one. A picked and pounded bit of the breast is not a fair
specimen of a radically tough goose.

292. 14. *N, S.* having / *L.* have
297. 36, 298. 2, 4. *N, S.* sailors . . . sailors . . . sailors / *L.* men . . .
men . . . men
330. 14. *L, S.* blowing / *N.* flowing
334. 6. *N, S.* remorsefully / *L.* remorsely
334. 11. *L, S.* he / *not in N.*
335. 15. *L, N.* purser's / *S.* surgeon's
336. 8. *L.* still the / *N, S.* the still
342. 9. *N, S.* hair / *L.* air
349. 34. *N, S.* Grasse / *L.* Grassy
350. 10. *N, S.* reefer, / *L.* reefer,—Mr. Pert,—
352. 6. *L.* topsails / *N, S.* topsail
371. 33. *L, S.* old / *N.* whole
378. 32. glossed / *L.* glosed / *N, S.* glazed
380. 25. *N, S.* lined / *L.* linen
384. 21. *L, S.* was / *N.* were
385. fn.* 6. *N, S.* friends. These / *L.* friends. It is not intended to
revive old feuds. In one sense, let by-gones be by-gones. But these
385. fn.* 10. *N, S.* man. / *L.* man. It is hardly to be anticipated,
however, that in case of war the English government would again

attempt to revive measures, which some of its own statesmen must have deplored from the beginning; and which, as [*sic*] the present day, must surely seem iniquitous to the great body of Englishmen. Indeed, it is perhaps to be doubted, whether Englishmen could again be brought to submit even to domestic impressment.

387. 25. *N*, *S*. glandular / *not in L*.

389. 15. *L*, *S*. soften / *N*. softens

391. 37. *L*. kitchen-full / *N*, *S*. kitchen full

394. 26. *L*, *N*. by / *S*. of

398. 19. *L*, *N*. coiled / *S*. soiled

403. 10. *N*, *S*. surmisings / *L*. surmises

EXPLANATORY NOTES

I WOULD like to acknowledge the debt I owe to Arthur Humphreys, whose edition of *White-Jacket* (Oxford, 1966) has been of enormous help to me in the preparation of these notes. For the explanation of nautical terms, the reader should refer to the separate section (pp. 435–41), prepared by Humphreys for that edition.

3 *Ovid*: Roman poet (43 BC–AD 17); author of *Metamorphoses*, a narrative poem based on Greek and Latin myths and folklore.

scudding under bare poles: running before a gale with minimum sail.

4 *Lambert or Edson*: Lambert was a 52-stone Leicester man who died in 1809; Edson was a 'living skeleton' on display at P. T. Barnum's American Museum in the 1840s.

5 *the White Lady of Avenel*: ghostly apparition in Scott's *The Monastery* (1820).

Orpheus: musician in Greek myth whose playing had the power to charm men and animals; he made use of this skill in his journey into the underworld in an attempt to rescue his wife Eurydice.

middies: midshipmen; see Ch. 6.

Dodona: like Delphi, a site of the oracle of Zeus (Jupiter).

6 *nipper-men*: responsible for nipping rope or cable.

7 *Lord George Gordon . . . Lord Mansfield*: Gordon was an agitator against Roman Catholics who in 1780 led a mob in London, in protest against recent legislation that alleviated some of the hardships they suffered. A week of rioting ensued, during which the house of Lord Chief Justice Mansfield was burnt. The Gordon Riots provide the background to Dickens's novel *Barnaby Rudge* (1841).

8 *the fore, main, and mizzentop*: the three masts of the ship (in order from bows to stern) are the foremast, mainmast, and mizzenmast; the platforms at the head of the lower part of the mast are thus called the foretop, maintop, and mizzentop.

a bowl of tar: possibly coffee, or rum.

8 *Decatur, Hull, and Bainbridge*: American naval commanders famous for their exploits in the Tripolitan War against the Barbary pirates in the Mediterranean (1803–5) and in the War of 1812 against the British. Stephen Decatur (1779–1820) captured the *Macedonian* in the latter conflict in an action described in Ch. 74 of *White-Jacket*. Isaac Hull (1773–1843) commanded the frigate *Constitution*, known as 'Old Ironsides', which defeated the British vessel *Guerrière*. William Bainbridge (1774–1833) captured the frigate *Java* off Brazil during the War of 1812.

main-brace: tackle controlling the yard (horizontal spar for sail) on the mainmast.

9 *ratlin*: also ratline; one of the small lines forming the steps in the ship's rigging.

troglodites: cave-dwellers.

10 *the massacre of the Three Days of September*: in 1792, during the French Revolution, when the Paris Commune eliminated many of its enemies. Carlyle's *French Revolution* (1837) is Melville's likely source.

11 *Jedediah Buxton*: a man of the previous century famous for feats of rapid calculation.

Hatteras: Cape Hatteras, on the American Atlantic seaboard; the easternmost point in North Carolina.

Sawney: foolish; old derogatory nickname for a Scotsman.

12 *the great Battle of Navarino*: a victory over the Turks in 1827 for a combined British, French, and Russian fleet, in support of Greek independence. See the description in Ch. 75.

13 *Rob Roy, Don Juan, and Pelham*: eponymous heroes, respectively, of a novel by Scott (1817), a narrative poem by Byron (1819–24), and a society novel by Bulwer Lytton (1828).

Camoens: Luis de Camoens (1524–80), the great Portuguese poet, who published his national epic *Os Lusíadas*, translated as *The Lusiads*, in 1572.

14 *dungeree*: made of a cheap calico cloth.

15 *Vineyarder*: man from Martha's Vineyard in Massachusetts.

16 *Mahon*: the Minorca headquarters of the American Mediterranean squadron.

puncheons: casks.

17 *the Rights of Man*: the title of an influential work by the British radical Thomas Paine. Published 1791–2, it was inspired by the French Revolution.

the civil commotions of Peru: Peru won its independence between 1821 and 1824, with the assistance of Bolívar and San Martín, but two decades of civil strife followed before the Presidency of Ramón Castilla began in 1845.

18 *Vattel*: Eméric de Vattel (1714–67), Swiss jurist specializing in the Law of Nations.

21 *the late war with England*: the War of 1812, resulting from territorial and commercial tensions. The Americans achieved some naval successes, but the British were able to blockade the coast and raid at will. The Treaty of Ghent (1814) largely restored the pre-war situation.

Golcondas: Golconda, in India, was famed for its wealth.

Wandering Jew: legendary figure cursed to wander, unable to die, until the Day of Judgement.

22 *flageolets*: form of flute.

25 *Lady Hamilton*: Emma Hamilton (1765–1815), the wife of Sir William Hamilton; mistress of Nelson from 1798 to his death.

the siege of Gibraltar: the British colony was successfully defended between 1779 and 1783 by General Sir George Elliott.

27 *castor*: vessel for sprinkling (usually sugar).

japanned: covered in black lacquer.

28 *rattan*: cane.

Vidocq in vigilance: François Eugène Vidocq (1775–1857), a former criminal who became a police spy, and then rose to command a department of the Paris police which was immensely successful in crime detection.

29 *Franklin-warranted*: by Benjamin Franklin (1706–90) in his *Autobiography*.

33 *Stultz*: the most fashionable tailor in early and mid-nineteenth century London.

Byron and Bligh: John Byron (1723–86), the grandfather of the poet, was called 'foul-weather Jack'. Later an admiral, he suffered shipwreck on the coast of Patagonia during Anson's circumnavigation in 1740, and described the experience in his *Narrative*.

The 'narrative' of William Bligh (1754–1817) deals with the mutiny which occurred when he commanded the *Bounty* on an expedition to Tahiti in 1789.

33 *Alceste . . . Medusa*: the *Alceste* was lost in the Java Sea in 1817; the *Medusa* went down off the west coast of Africa in 1816. As depicted in Géricault's famous painting, the survivors drifted on a raft until they were rescued.

35 *Ferdinand, Count Fathom*: villainous eponymous hero of a novel by Tobias Smollett (1753); the son of a seller of gin.

36 *manufactory*: factory.

38 *right-and-left kids*: kid gloves.

39 *masoned up my lockers and pantries*: sewing up the pockets of the jacket is compared figuratively to sealing up these storage spaces with stone.

41 *Rydal Mount*: Wordsworth's home in the Lake District from 1814 to his death in 1850.

'*in a fine frenzy rolling*': Theseus in *A Midsummer Night's Dream*, v. i. 12, describing the eye of the poet and comparing him to the lunatic and the lover.

42 *Parnassus and the Nine*: Parnassus, a mountain in Greece, was held sacred to Apollo and the Nine Muses, each responsible for a different art.

Maecenas: the famous patron of the Roman poet Virgil.

Quarterly Review: influential British literary periodical founded in 1809.

47 *Aeolian harp*: instrument which produces sound when stirred by the wind.

demijohn: bottle enclosed in wickerwork basket.

Peregrine Pickle . . . Gil Blas . . . Goldsmith: *The Adventures of Peregrine Pickle* (1751) is another novel by Smollett; *Gil Blas* (4 vols., 1715–35), also a picaresque romance, was written by the Frenchman Alain-René Lesage, although it is set in Spain. It was the model for Smollett's sea novel *Roderick Random* (1748), which was in turn an important influence on *White-Jacket*. The work by Oliver Goldsmith, a friend of Smollett, is probably *The Vicar of Wakefield* (1766).

49 *blue-light*: sanctimonious.

52 *Montaigne*: Michel Eyquem de Montaigne (1533–92), the philosophical French writer whose self-questioning *Essais* were admired by Melville.

Coleridge . . . enlisted: the poet enlisted in the army in 1793, while a student at Cambridge, under the name Silas Comberbache; but his manner of speech led him to be detected as an outsider.

54 *Tokay*: sweet Hungarian wine.

56 *the Black Prince*: Edward, Prince of Wales (1330–76), son of Edward III, and father of Richard II.

57 *Sabaean odours*: evoking the lands occupied by the Saba or Sheba, an ancient Yemenite people.

old Ocean smiled: Milton, *Paradise Lost*, iv. 164–5.

Salt-Junk: salt beef.

58 *Coleman and Stetson*: owners of the Astor House hotel, New York, at this time.

59 *St. Domingo*: island near to Cuba.

61 *objurgations*: chidings.

62 *Peter told a lie*: Mark 14: 71–2.

64 *Seminole campaigns*: the brutal wars of 1817–18 and 1835–42 which eventually enabled the US Government to remove the Seminole Indians from Florida to beyond the Mississippi.

66 *again and again*: celebrated song written in 1759 to mark a naval victory by Hawke which defeated a French invasion plan.

68 *the Battle of Trafalgar*: the victory over the Franco-Spanish fleet in 1805 in which Nelson lost his life.

the king of Macedon: Philip II, king of Macedonia (382–336 BC), the father of Alexander the Great, who conquered the whole of Greece.

69 *the Battle of the Nile*: Nelson's victory over the French at the mouth of the Nile in 1798.

70 *woollen*: probably a misprint for 'wooden'.

71 *Seneca*: Lucius Annaeus Seneca (*c*.5 BC–AD 65), Roman philosopher and statesman. He died by opening his veins after taking part in an unsuccessful conspiracy against Nero, whose education he had overseen.

77 *Pittsfield elm*: Melville lived near Pittsfield, Massachusetts, throughout the 1850s.

78 *the Chaldean Magi*: a priestly caste in Persia and other parts of the Middle East with occult powers founded on astrology; exemplified by the wise men from the East who visit the infant Jesus in Matthew 2: 1–12.

79 *Amphitrite*: sea goddess and consort of Neptune.

Sir John Moore in his frosted cloak: British general who died in 1809 after defeating the French at Corunna in Spain during the Napoleonic campaign; Charles Wolfe's popular poem 'Lines on the Burial of Sir John Moore at Corunna' was published in 1817.

Lethe: one of the rivers of the classical underworld; when tasted by the souls of the dead, it caused them to forget all they had said or done while living.

82 *Bastille*: prison.

87 *superficies*: surface area.

88 *Boerhaave's*: Herman Boerhaave (1668–1738), famous Dutch physician and author of works on medicine.

91 *bright-wood*: probably a misprint for 'bright-work'.

92 *sourcrout*: German, from the cabbage dish sauerkraut.

93 *Drury-Lane*: famous London theatre from the seventeenth century onwards.

96 *in full fig*: in full dress.

97 *a ten-stroke*: a triumph; in bowling, a shot which knocks down all ten pins, later called a strike.

98 *the descent of Orpheus, Ulysses, or Dante into Hell*: Orpheus in Greek myth, and Ulysses in Homer's *Odyssey*, descended into the underworld; Dante describes his own journey into Hell in the *Inferno* of the *Divina Commedia*.

101 *Le Mair and Schouten*: two Dutch navigators who achieved the feats described by Melville in an expedition of 1614–16.

Sir Francis Drake: the famous English sailor (1540–96) never weathered Cape Horn and had been dead for twenty years when Le Mair and Schouten did so. The voyage of 1572–3 during which he saw the Pacific from the Isthmus of Darien was not 'Raleigh's expedition' to South America, which took place in 1595–6. He passed through the Straits of Magellan when circumnavigating the world in 1577–80.

Lord Anson's squadron . . . chaplain of the Centurion: in 1740–4, during the war with Spain and France, Lord George Anson circumnavigated the world in a voyage regarded as the most triumphant achievement of its kind since Drake. 'Young Byron' is the future admiral mentioned in Ch. 8. The best-known account of Anson's circumnavigation was the one compiled by Richard Walter, the chaplain of the *Centurion*, with the title *A Voyage Round the World* (1748).

102 *Dana's unmatchable Two Years Before the Mast*: Richard Henry Dana Jr. (1815–82), later a lawyer and diplomat, interrupted his studies at Harvard to serve as a common sailor in a ship travelling round Cape Horn to California and back. The realism of the celebrated account of his experiences which he published in 1840 undoubtedly had an influence on *White-Jacket*. For the influence of this novel on *White-Jacket*, see Introduction.

Nova Zembla: large archipelago east of the Barents Sea, between Russia and the Arctic.

103 *Guernsey frocks, Havre shirts*: types of woollen jersey.

104 *exhilarating gas*: 'laughing gas' nitrous oxide.

106 *shipped their quarter-deck faces*: looked serious and official.

109 *like the Veil of the Temple*: Matthew 27: 51–4.

115 *Lord Collingwood*: British admiral (1750–1810), second in command to Nelson at Trafalgar, and in command of the Mediterranean squadron after the latter's death.

116 *Paper Jacks*: lacking the appropriate practical experience.

124 *a ship canal*: there were plans for such a canal throughout the century, but a French project foundered between 1879 and 1889. The Panama Canal did not open until 1914.

the cars at Cape Cod for Astoria: Cape Cod is in Massachusetts, Astoria on the Pacific coast in Oregon; there were several schemes for a transcontinental railroad at the time when Melville was writing, and the first was completed in 1869.

Jeddo: former name of Tokyo.

125 *marline*: small rope for winding round a larger one to prevent wearing.

fids: wooden pins used to separate the strands of rope.

toggles: small pieces of wood used for attaching rope.

125 *prickers*: spikes used in making holes in canvas and splicing rope.

marling-spikes: also used in separating strands of rope.

126 *Colt's patent revolvers*: patented in 1835, and first employed by the USA in the war with Mexico.

131 *the lamentable casualty . . . engine of war*: a party including the Secretary for the Navy, Abel Upshur, were killed by an explosion in February 1844 when inspecting the *Princeton*, the first screw-driven warship.

132 *our life is but a vapour*: James 4: 14.

Down-Easter: from the north-eastern USA; Yankee.

134 *Scouse . . . Manavalins*: Scouse and Lob-Scouse were forms of stew, incorporating meat, potatoes, and ship's biscuits; Soft-Tack was bread baked at sea; Burgoo was boiled oatmeal porridge; Manavalins were odds and ends, usually left over from the officers' table.

141 *the historian Bancroft*: George Bancroft (1800–91), one of the leading historians of the period, became Secretary for the Navy in 1845 and established the Annapolis Naval Academy. As acting Secretary for War, he took decisions which precipitated war with Mexico over Texas and California.

143 *to scourge a man that is a Roman*: the words of St Paul in Acts 22: 25, when arrested in Jerusalem.

147 *Blackstone*: Sir William Blackstone, English jurist (1723–80), whose *Commentaries on the Laws of England* (1765–9) was the definitive work on the subject. It formed the basis of the legal system of the American states.

Justinian: Justinian I (*c*.482–565), Emperor of the Eastern Roman Empire from 527, famous for his codification of the laws.

Bunker Hill: Boston site of the first battle of the War of American Independence (Revolutionary War) in June 1775; a British victory, but American morale was strengthened by the courage of their smaller force. Melville's paternal grandfather fought there.

150 *the great mutiny of the Nore*: the most serious instance of such unrest in the history of the British Navy. After the sailors at Spithead had mutinied in April 1797, those at the Nore, at the mouth of the Thames, followed suit in May, causing panic in London. Eventually the mutineers' control was broken, and twenty-five men were hanged. See the passage at the start of Ch. 3

of Melville's *Billy Budd, Sailor*, which is set on a British warship in the summer of the same year.

Robert Blake's time: Blake (1599–1657) was an admiral under Cromwell, best known for his battles with Van Tromp in the Dutch War of 1652–3, and his victories over the Spanish. He was responsible for the Articles of War and the Fighting Instructions, and is credited with creating the modern navy.

Commodore Stockton: Robert Stockton (1795–1866), served in the War of 1812 and commanded the Pacific fleet during the 1846–7 war with Mexico which led to the American acquisition of Texas and California. As a Senator 1851–3, after Melville published *White-Jacket*, he introduced a bill to abolish flogging in the Navy.

151 *the Hermione and Danae*: the mutiny on HMS *Hermione* took place in 1797 in the West Indies, when members of the crew killed a tyrannical captain and his officers. The mutineers handed the ship over to the Spanish, but they were eventually captured and hanged. The mutiny of the crew of HMS *Danae* occurred in 1800.

153 *we Americans are the peculiar, chosen people—the Israel of our time*: an analogy often found in American writing of the 1840s and 1850s.

154 *'London Dock'*: wine from the great cellars of the London docks.

155 *loggerhead turtles*: particularly large species of turtle.

California-shell: molluscs resembling barnacles.

the Battle of the Brandywine: an engagement in 1777 during the War of American Independence in which Washington suffered severe losses.

157 *Biographia Literaria*: an important work by Coleridge (1817) combining autobiography, philosophy, and his theory of poetry.

the Phaedon of Plato: a dialogue on immortality admired by Melville.

Simplicius's commentary: sixth century philosopher who wrote commentaries on Aristotle and Epictetus.

Tertullian: Carthaginian theologian (*c.*160–220), vigorous in polemics on behalf of the early Christian Church. *De Praescriptionibus Haereticorum* (Concerning the Writings of the Heretics) is a typical controversial work.

157 *Gnostics and Marcionites*: Gnosticism was a religious movement of many different forms which flourished before and during the early Christian era. Initiates believed that spiritual knowledge (gnosis) was to be achieved through mystical experience and access to a secret tradition. Marcion (*c*.100–*c*.165) founded a Gnostic sect in 140, and was denounced by Tertullian.

Massillon: Jean Baptiste Massillon (1663–1742), French bishop who preached before both Louis XIV (presumably Melville's 'le Grand') and Louis XV.

Felix: Antoninus Felix, the Roman governor of Judea, induced his wife Drusilla to desert her previous husband. St Paul, summoned before him to defend himself against the charges of the Jewish leaders, made him tremble by referring to 'righteousness, temperance, and judgement to come' (Acts 24: 1–25).

Delilah: the wife of Samson who betrayed him to the Philistines (Judges 16: 4–21).

164 *Grand Porte of Constantinople*: the Court of the Turkish Sultan, and the centre of imperial government.

Saladin and Richard: the sultan of Egypt and Syria (1137–93), whose last years were occupied by wars with Christian armies for control of the Holy Land; and Richard I 'Cœur de Lion' (1157–99), who led a force of crusaders which defeated him.

168 *Coleridge's High German horse*: a reference to the influence of German philosophy on Coleridge's thought, as reflected in works like *Biographia Literaria*.

169 *Machiavel's Art of War*: *Seven Books on the Art of War* by the Florentine statesman and political philosopher Niccolo Machiavelli (1469–1527), best known for the treatise *The Prince*.

Tillotson's Sermons: John Tillotson (1630–94), Archbishop of Canterbury at the end of his life, was regarded as the greatest preacher of his era.

Locke's Essays: either a collection of works by the English philosopher (1632–1704), or the important *Essay Concerning Human Understanding*.

Plutarch's Lives: a book in which the Greek historian (AD 46–120) provided portraits of the leading figures of the ages before his own.

Blair's Lectures: Hugh Blair (1718–1800), a preacher and Professor of Rhetoric at Edinburgh University.

170 *Walpole's Letters*: Hugh Walpole (1717–97), novelist and essayist, whose literary reputation owes much to his talents as a letter writer.

The Jew of Malta . . . The Alchymist: of the plays in the list, *The Jew of Malta* (*c*.1590) is by Marlowe, and both *Volpone* (1606) and *The Alchemist* (1610) are by Jonson. *Old Fortunatus* (*c*.1598) is an allegorical work by Thomas Dekker; *The City Madam* (1632) is a social comedy from the Caroline era by Philip Massinger.

Damon and Pythias: models of devoted friendship.

Beaumont and Fletcher: two early seventeenth-century playwrights who both produced plays on their own, but are best known for the works they wrote in collaboration in the six or seven years before Beaumont's death in 1616.

Moore's Loves of the Angels: a poem, derived from an oriental original, by the Irish born poet Thomas Moore (1779–1852), which achieved a great success in 1823.

Fulton Market: adjacent to the port of New York.

173 *togs*: clothes.

cosmorama: display offering a series of views of different parts of the world, using lenses and mirrors.

175 *drive the hours before you four-in-hand*: as if in a coach drawn by four horses.

177 *Prince Albert*: German nobleman who married Queen Victoria in 1840, becoming Consort in 1842 and Prince Consort in 1857.

178 *sea-Newgate*: Newgate was an ancient and famous London prison, finally closed in 1880.

mania-a-potu: delirium tremens.

to feel Davy Jones's chest-lid on your nose: to be in Davy Jones's locker, i.e. dead. The name was used by sailors to signify the evil spirit of the sea.

181 *faultless Leander*: youth who in a Greek tale (and Marlowe's narrative poem) swam the Hellespont each night to reach his lover Hero.

189 *Tophet*: Hell; in the Old Testament, a land associated with suffering.

Burke's phrase: Edmund Burke wrote of the moral condition of the *ancien régime* in *Reflections on the Revolution in France* (1790): 'Vice itself lost half its evil, by losing all its grossness.'

190 *Newgate Calendar*: a publication which first appeared around 1773, describing the major crimes and criminals of the eighteenth century. Another series was issued in the 1820s.

191 *Goethe's pious Margaret*: the heroine of his *Faust, Part One* (1808), a village girl seduced by the hero with the assistance of the devil Mephistopheles.

192 *Memoirs of Vidocq*: published in 1828; see note to p. 28.

194 *Origen . . . Abelard*: both men were castrated, the early church father Origen (185–254) by his own hand, the theologian Peter Abelard (1079–1142) on the orders of the uncle of his lover Heloise.

196 *Charles the Fifth*: King of Spain, and Holy Roman Emperor from 1519 to 1555, when he renounced his powers and retreated to a monastery in Estremadura. In the novella *Benito Cereno* (1856) many of the traits Melville ascribes to the eponymous hero are derived from Charles V in this period of seclusion.

197 *the Five Nations*: the Iroquois Indians, a confederacy of five tribes in western New York. One of the chiefs who supposedly effected this league during the seventeenth century was immortalized by Longfellow as Hiawatha. The Iroquois also figure regularly in the novels of Cooper.

200 *Phlegethon*: one of the three rivers of the classical underworld. The passage perhaps recalls the account of the fall of Mulciber (Vulcan) in *Paradise Lost*, I, 742–6.

206 *bone-polisher*: Humphreys suggests this may mean 'servant'.

fever-nagur: fever-and-ague, a malarial illness.

207 *Nessus*: killed by Hercules, the centaur Nessus gave the latter's wife Deianira some of his poisoned blood as a charm. She smeared it on the robe of Hercules, with fatal results.

210 *the long-vexed north-eastern boundary question*: disagreement between Britain and the USA over the boundary between Maine and New Brunswick in (British-ruled) Canada led to local hostilities 1839–42. However, Melville may have in mind a slightly later dispute over the north-western boundary.

211 *Great Tom*: in the gate tower of Christ Church, Oxford.

215 *Salamis*: battle of 480 BC in which the Greeks defeated the Persians.

Actium: battle of 31 BC in which the Roman navy under Octavian defeated the combined forces of Cleopatra and Mark Antony.

Lepanto: battle of 1571 in which the combined navies of several Christian countries under Don John of Austria defeated the Turks.

the gallant Gama: presumably a reference to the Portuguese navigator Vasco da Gama's first expedition of 1497–9, although this did not include the Moluccas.

Van Tromp . . . Admiral Hawke: Melville apparently confuses Admiral Blake, the seventeenth-century opponent of Van Tromp, with Admiral Edward Hawke (1705–81).

Perry's war-brigs . . . on Lake Erie: the American Oliver Perry secured the surrender of an entire English squadron on Lake Erie in 1813, during the War of 1812.

217 *what sings sweet Waller*: 'Instructions to a Painter', ll.77–8, by Edmund Waller (1606–87).

Pope's version: from his translation of the *Odyssey*, v. 393–4.

220 *Sir Peter Parker*: young naval captain killed by an enemy shot in the War of 1812, and commemorated in Byron's 'Elegiac Stanzas' (1814).

222 *Bobadil air*: Captain Bobadill in Jonson's *Every Man in His Humour* (1598), a boastful but cowardly old soldier.

223 *the usher's ferule*: the teacher's rod, used for punishment.

226 *Mazatlan*: port on the Pacific coast of Mexico.

227 *horse-marine*: a poor sailor; someone not fit to be on board ship.

228 *gammon*: nonsense, a hoax.

Rienzi: Cola de Rienzi (1313–54), who in 1347 led a rising against the noble rulers of Rome, and held power himself for seven months. The subject of a novel by Bulwer Lytton (1835), which inspired a Wagner opera (1842).

229 *Esterhazys*: a powerful family of Hungarian aristocrats.

231 *Similia Similibus Curantur*: likes are cured by likes; the theory underlying the homoeopathic system of medical treatment first proposed and practised by the German doctor Christian Hahnemann in 1796.

contraria contrariis curantur: opposites are cured by opposites.

236 *the young Emperor, Don Pedro II*: Brazil was declared independent in 1822, and Pedro I proclaimed Emperor. Rebellion in 1831 obliged him to abdicate in favour of his son Pedro II, then aged 5, who ruled in his own right 1840–89, introducing liberal reforms.

237 *rotten-stone*: decomposed limestone powder used for polishing.

chapeaux-de-bras: silk three-cornered hats, which could be carried under the arm.

238 *Viscount Strangford*: British diplomat (1780–1855), who published translations of poems by Camoens in 1803, and was envoy-extraordinary to the Portuguese Court in Brazil, 1808–15.

caciques: native chiefs.

239 *darbies*: handcuffs.

240 *Perkin Warbecks*: impostors; from the pretender to the English throne (*c.*1474–99) who claimed to be one of the princes murdered in the Tower.

242 *cable-tier*: racks used for stowing cable.

246 *lined frock*: a quilted coat the sailor would make for himself.

248 *galiot*: cargo boat.

257 *antiphlogistics*: the phlogiston theory, widely accepted throughout the 18th century, asserted that combustible material contained a common substance which was given that name. The theory became obsolete when Lavoisier (1743–94) discovered oxygen.

260 *the war now threatening between the States and Mexico*: Melville's voyage on the SS *United States* was in 1843–4; the war in which the USA acquired Texas and California from Mexico occurred in 1846–7.

262 *Celsus*: a Roman physician of the 1st century AD who published the treatise *De Medicina*.

a Bell, a Brodie, and a Lally: Bell was a surgeon at the Battle of Waterloo, and later a professor of anatomy; Brodie served as physician to both William IV and Victoria; Larrey, rather than Lally or Lalley, was surgeon-in-chief to the Grande Armée of Napoleon.

266 *Mohawk*: Melville's error for 'Buccaneer'.

267 *Henner*: a misprint for John Hennen, another military surgeon during the Napoleonic Wars.

268 *the battle of Ayacucho*: the final defeat of the Spanish forces in the Peruvian War of Independence, 1821–4.

Guthrie: also a surgeon during the Napoleonic Wars.

Lord Cochrane: Thomas Cochrane, 10th Earl of Dundonald (1775–1860) served with great distinction in the British navy during the war against France; after imprisonment on a fraud charge, he took command of the navies of Chile (1817–20) and Brazil (1823–5) in their struggles for independence.

272 *Moravians*: a Protestant sect known for their zealous missionary work.

274 *Camoens!*: see note to p. 13. The quotation is from *The Lusiads*: I, 763–4. As he was born in 1524, the year before Vasco da Gama died, Camoens could not have taken part in any of the latter's expeditions. He did, however, sail to Goa and Macao, and experienced shipwreck.

Mickle: William Mickle (1734–88), a Scottish poet whose translation of *The Lusiads* was published in 1775.

275 *Falconer*: William Falconer (1732–69), another Scottish poet, author of 'The Shipwreck' (1762).

St. Paul . . . Acts: Acts 27 describes a stormy voyage in which the vessel carrying Paul is finally cast ashore on the island of Malta.

Shelley . . . ocean-rover, too: Byron and the sailor-adventurer Trelawney had the body of the poet cremated on the shore when he was drowned in 1822, while sailing near Spezia on the Italian coast.

281 *the noble Lords Tenterden and Stowell*: Charles Abbott, Baron Tenterden (1762–1836) wrote the treatise *Law Relative to Merchant Ships and Seamen*; William Scott, Baron Stowell (1745–1836), an authority on the law of nations, also contributed to maritime law.

287 *the old vintner Noah*: Genesis 9: 20 describes Noah as planting a vineyard.

Hawthorne of Salem: the novelist and short story writer Nathaniel Hawthorne (1804–64), a friend and neighbour of Melville's at the time when *White-Jacket* was written; the reference is to his story 'A Rill from the Town Pump', published in *Twice-Told Tales* (1837).

289 *Richard Nevil*: Richard Neville, Earl of Warwick (1428–71), known as The Kingmaker; as a leading Yorkist in the Wars of the Roses, he installed Edward IV in 1461, and then reinstated Henry VI in 1470 when driven to revolt. He was defeated by Edward at Barnet and killed in 1471.

Bowditch's Navigator: The New American Practical Navigator, a standard work by Nathaniel Bowditch (1773–1838).

D'Anton On Gunpowder and Fire-arms: J. V. P. D. D'Antoni, whose *Treatise on Gunpowder* was translated in 1789.

292 *La Fayette*: the Marquis de Lafayette (1757–1834), who gave the American colonists important military assistance during the War of Independence. In 1824 he was fêted when he returned to the USA at the invitation of Congress.

296 *Loyola and Torquemada*: the Spanish Inquisition was an ecclesiastical tribunal established by the Pope at the request of the Spanish monarchy in 1478 to deal with Jews, Moslems, and Christian heretics. Tomas de Torquemada (1420–98) was made its first Inquisitor General in 1483, and displayed pitiless cruelty towards his victims. Ignatius de Loyola (1491–1556), who founded the Jesuits in 1534, was never party to the activities of the Inquisition, and indeed was himself twice arrested on suspicion of heresy.

Jack Ketch: a seventeenth-century hangman, famous for his incompetence.

298 *those three sailors*: three American seamen serving on the *Somers were executed without trial on suspicion of mutiny in 1842, on the orders of Captain Alexander Mackenzie. Melville's cousin Guert Gansevoort was involved in the case.*

299 *Palmer's Land*: a whaling and sealing base in the South Shetland Isles.

300 *Algernon Sidney to the block*: English politician with republican views (1622–83), arrested after the Rye House Plot in 1683, and found guilty and beheaded, after a trial before the notorious Judge Jeffreys.

301 *broom at his fore-mast*: some accounts of the Anglo-Dutch naval war of 1652–3 mention the story that the Dutch commander carried a broom on his mast, indicating his intention to sweep the English from the Channel.

the historian of the Rebellion: Edward Hyde, Earl of Clarendon (1609–74), who transferred his allegiance from the Parliamentarians to the Royalists during the 1640s; his three-volume *History of the Rebellion in England* was published posthumously, 1704–7.

302 *Admiral Benbow's career*: John Benbow (1650–1702), English admiral, joined the Navy in 1678 and commanded the fleet in the battles of the 1690s.

THE CONSULATE OF THE SEA: the *Consolat de mar*, a code of maritime law based on the practices of Mediterranean ports in the Middle Ages. The first known edition was published in Catalan in Barcelona in 1494; Melville quotes a translation of the opening words.

305 *Sir Edward Coke*: English jurist (1552–1634) who served as Speaker of the House of Commons, Attorney General and Chief Justice of the King's Bench, and vigorously defended British liberties against the encroachments of Crown and Church.

Sir Matthew Hale: another famous judge (1606–76) who became Chief Justice of the King's Bench; *History of the Common Law* was published posthumously in 1713.

306 *Magna Charta*: the 'Great Charter' signed by King John in 1215 to stave off baronial revolt, consisting of a broad statement of legal principles. It contained a clause affirming the right of freemen to be tried by their equals. In the seventeenth century figures like Sir Edward Coke invoked Magna Carta in opposing the absolutist tendencies of James I and Charles I. It is still regarded as the cornerstone of English and American law.

the Hanse Towns: the Hanseatic League, a loose federation of nearly a hundred towns, largely in Germany, including Lübeck, Bremen, and Hamburg. It dominated trade in the North Sea and the Baltic in the fourteenth and fifteenth centuries.

Wisbury laws: Visby, a port on the Baltic island of Gottland and member of the Hanseatic League, which gave its name to a thirteenth-century code of maritime law.

309 *Eblis*: in the Koran, the leader of the fallen angels, called Azazel before his rebellion. Humphreys notes that Beckford's novel *Vathek* (1786) ends with the hero being tortured in the subterranean palace of Eblis.

'The Tombs': the so-called Hall of Justice in downtown Manhattan, used mainly as a prison; the hero of Melville's story 'Bartleby' (1853) is taken there.

311 *Cuba bloodhound, with his noiseless nose*: a particularly savage breed used in Cuba for tracking criminals as well as for driving cattle.

312 *Sheer*: move away.

like a shin of beef into a beggar's wallet: as quickly as a beggar would thrust a piece of meat into his bag.

the Line: the Equator.

313 *she draws*: *The Lusiads*, I. 433–4.

315 *Norfolk*: major naval base in Virginia.

seventy-four: ship with seventy-four guns; a frigate would only have thirty-two to thirty-eight guns.

318 *during the late war*: the engagement described took place in 1814, when the *Essex* was commanded by Captain David Porter.

322 *'Hometons*: Muhammedans.

325 *the persecuted Waldenses*: a movement which began around 1170, led by Peter Waldo of Lyons, believing in austere morality and devotion to the simplicity of the Gospels. Their centre was in the Alps. Declared heretical, they came to reject the authority of the Pope, and were persecuted until the late seventeenth century.

bloody Mary's time: Mary I (1516–58), Queen of England 1553–8; a Catholic whose reign saw the burning of 300 Protestants, hence the epithet.

326 *the Spanish cavalier, Mendanna of Lima*: Alvaro de Mandana de Neyra (*c.*1542–96), a Spanish navigator, discovered the Solomon Islands in a voyage from Lima, 1567–8. His wife accompanied him on a later voyage in 1595. Ophir was a legendary land which was the supposed source of the gold of Solomon's temple; the Cyclades are in the Aegean rather than the Pacific.

327 *William Wallace*: Scottish patriot (*c.*1274–1305) who led a rising against the English.

Cathay: China.

328 *Thalaba the Destroyer*: hero of a poem by Southey, with the task of vanquishing a race of magicians.

329 *Burnet*: probably Gilbert Burnet (1643–1715), a proponent of a broad Church who was made royal chaplain and Bishop of Salisbury by William III. His most important theological work is the *Exposition of the Thirty-Nine Articles* (1699).

331 *jalapy compound*: a jalap is a purgative root, originally from Mexico.

334 *hypoes*: normally, attacks of hypochondria; here, as in the opening paragraphs of *Moby-Dick*, it seems also to connote melancholia, pessimism.

335 *purser's steward*: error for 'surgeon's steward'.

348 *Dr. Hutton's tracts*: Charles Hutton (1737–1823), a mathematician who became Professor at the Woolwich Naval Academy; the French and Italian books mentioned date from 1731 and 1586, respectively, and had presumably ceased to be of practical value.

349 *John Clerk, Esq., of Eldin*: author of an *Essay on Naval Tactics* (1782).

Rodney: George Rodney (1719–92), English admiral with an outstanding record of success. He retired and was raised to the peerage after his victory in the engagement described.

351 *Spearman's British Gunner*: a standard work published in 1828.

352 *reductio ad absurdum*: reduction to absurdity; a method of disproving an argument by following its logic to reach a clearly false conclusion.

353 *swifts*: reels for thread.

354 *Psyche glasses*: (full-length) cheval-glasses.

356 *as sweet Spenser has it*: slightly misquoting the description of the death of Socrates in *The Faerie Queene*, II. vii. 52, line 8.

Persius: Roman satirist (34–62); the phrase occurs in *Satires* IV. 1.

357 *cue*: twist of hair at the back of the head.

Winnebago locks: resembling the hair of a Red Indian.

Peter the Wild Boy: child found near Hanover in 1725. He behaved like an animal, and was never taught to pronounce more than a few syllables. He was brought to England by George I, and died there in 1785.

catamount: puma or lynx.

Aurelian's: presumably, in the style of that of the philosophical Roman Emperor Marcus Aurelius (AD 121–80).

Merovingians: dynasty which ruled the Franks from the fifth century to the eighth.

Bartholomew's Day: the occasion of the massacre of thousands of French Huguenots (Protestants) in 1572.

358 *Sicilian Vespers*: the massacre of the French occupying Sicily on Easter Monday 1282, which began on the stroke of the bell announcing Vespers.

Emperor Adrian: Hadrian, Roman Emperor AD 117–38. Humphreys suggests that Melville's source was the article on 'Beards' in William Smith, *Dictionary of Greek and Roman Antiquities* (1840–2). The story does not appear to occur in Plutarch's works.

360 *the example of Alexander*: a story related of Alexander in the *Life of Theseus* in Plutarch's *Lives*.

363 *that Athenian*: Melville's likely source is again Smith's *Dictionary of Greek and Roman Antiquities*.

364 *Count D'Orsay would have envied*: Alfred Guillaume Gabriel, Count D'Orsay (1801–52), 'the last of the dandies', came to England from France in 1822 and became a leader of fashion.

the Vega: a region of the island of Hispaniola, which is now divided between Haiti and the Dominican Republic.

366 *the rows of sculptured Assyrian kings . . . Layard*: in the British Museum, visited by Melville in 1849. They were recovered from the site of Nineveh by Sir Austin Layard (1817–94) in 1845–7.

Scythian: from Scythia, a large area of European and Asiatic Russia.

chief of the Goths: Melville's inaccurate recollection of Livy's description (*History*, V. xli) of the entry of the Gauls into Rome in 385, when the catalyst for a massacre was an incident in which an invader stroked the beard of one of the dignitaries.

Nestor: the oldest of the Greeks at the siege of Troy; hence used for the oldest man in any company.

367 *old Chaucer's shipman*: from the description of the shipman in the 'General Prologue' to the *Canterbury Tales*, ll. 392–4, 405–6.

369 *the Dying Gladiator*: famous Roman statue which in fact depicts a dying Gaul.

Brahim: Brahmin, the highest caste in India.

370 *Henry I . . . Archbishop of Sées*: in 1105 the king attended a Mass in Normandy during which the Bishop of Sées denounced the luxury of his court, citing the length of their hair. Henry set an example by allowing the Bishop to cut his own locks.

372 *Matthew Paris*: English chronicler (c.1200–59), whose great work was the *Historia Major*, covering the period from the Creation to the year of his death. It was eventually published in 1571.

375 *his work on Russia*: Augustus Granville, *St. Petersburg: a Journal of Travel* (1828).

376 *General Harrison*: William Harrison (1773–1841), who died a month after his inauguration as President of the United States in 1841. No evidence has been found for Melville's allegation.

379 *Walpole's Mysterious Mother . . . Shelley*: a tragedy of 1768 in which a man unwittingly has intercourse with his mother, and marries the daughter who results from the union. Sophocles' *Oedipus Tyrannus* and Shelley's *The Cenci* (1819) both also involve incest, but Melville presumably intends to hint at a different form of perverse sexuality.

330 *the Idle Apprentice*: in the 'Industry and Idleness' series of 1747.

Tyburn-trees: gallows.

the opera of Don Juan: Mozart's *Don Giovanni* (1787).

Gehennas: places of eternal torment; like Tophet, Gehenna came to be used as another name for Hell.

old Fuller: Thomas Fuller (1608–61), a prolific author who wrote the book of essays and character portraits *The Holy State and The Profane State* (1642–8). Melville refers to a passage in the portrait of 'The Good Sea-Captain'.

crimp: man who tricks or forces others into serving on ships which are short of sailors.

381 *Guinea*: the negro mute in the opening chapter of Melville's novel *The Confidence-Man* (1857) is called Black Guinea.

384 *Macpherson's Annals of Commerce*: published in 1805.

a statement of Captain Marryat's: Frederick Marryat (1792–1848), who in 1830 retired from the Navy in order to write novels. Impressment ceased to be employed systematically in England after the Napoleonic Wars, and finally disappeared with the creation of a career Navy in 1853.

Burkers: body-snatchers; the term derives from William Burke, executed in Edinburgh in 1829 for committing several murders in order to sell the bodies as dissection subjects.

384 *Steel's List*: superseded by the Navy List after the Napoleonic Wars.

385 *Lieutenant Tomlinson*: Robert Tomlinson, who published a proposal for recruitment by other means in 1774.

386 *Dibdin*: Charles Dibdin (1745–1814), an actor and writer best known for his sea songs, which include 'Tom Bowling' and 'Poor Jack'.

387 *Joe Miller*: an English comic actor (1684–1738). After his death a certain John Mottley produced a compilation called *Joe Miller's Jest-Book*, without having received his permission, which proved to be very successful. Byron was to complain of critics who 'take hackney'd jokes from Miller'.

390 *the Thirty Tyrants*: the thirty oligarchs appointed by Sparta to rule Athens after the Peloponnesian War. Their reign lasted only a year, 405–404 BC.

Mamelukes: the bodyguard of the Sultan in the Middle Ages.

391 *Feejees*: cannibals from Fiji.

calumet: peace-pipe.

Teniers: both David Teniers the elder (1582–1649) and the younger (1610–90) were Flemish genre painters; the elder is more associated with tavern scenes.

Wilkie: Sir David Wilkie, Scottish painter (1785–1841), also specializing in genre pictures.

392 *Cruikshank*: George Cruikshank, English graphic artist, illustrator and caricaturist (1792–1878).

393 *quidnuncs*: newsmongers.

serving-mallet boat: canal boat.

"raging canal": the Erie Canal, from Buffalo to Lake Erie, which Melville had travelled on when going out west to Illinois in 1840. Jokes about the frequency of storms were common.

Tiridates: according to Pliny, *Natural History*, XXX. vi, King Tiridates was a Magus (member of a priestly caste) and this made him concerned to avoid 'wronging' the sea when crossing it.

394 *a Hannibal oath*: the Carthaginian general (247–182 BC) was required by his father to take an oath of eternal enmity to Rome while still a boy.

395 *Ravelings*: users of scraps of thread or material.

399 *grains*: harpoons.

400 *Escurial*: the Escorial, the palace, mausoleum, and monastery erected by Philip II between 1563 and 1584.

401 *Denique Coelum*: 'at last heaven'; the Melville family motto.

402 *Pisgah top*: Moses sees the Promised Land from Mount Pisgah in Deuteronomy 34.

the thoughts of every toil: *The Lusiads*, x. 1078–83.

403 *the stocks*: framework on which a ship is built.

SAILS

Reproduced from *The Oxford Companion to Ships and the Sea*, edited by Peter Kemp (Oxford Paperbacks, 1988), p. 738.

SOME NAUTICAL TERMS

This list deals only with such terms as are not self-evident, explained in the text, or insignificant.

admiral of the blue	admiral commanding one of the divisions—red (centre), white (van), and blue (rear)—into which the British Navy was divided. The context suggests that Melville puns on 'blue blood' also.
Andrew Miller	sailors' slang for man-of-war.
back-stay	long rope, part of the standing rigging slanting abaft, from upper mast-head to the ship's side.
ballyhoo (or ballahoo, ballahou)	two-masted vessel formerly used in West Indies with masts raking in opposite directions—therefore, an awkward-looking, slovenly craft; also known, for obscure reasons, as a 'ballyhoo of blazes', a term Melville doubtless thinks apt for the blazing fires of blubber kept going as a whaler was rendering down the whale-fat.
beat to quarters	summon ship's company by drum-beat to assemble for drill, emergency, &c.
belay	make fast (rope) round cleat, belaying-pin, &c.; also a command to desist, or cancel an order (i.e. = 'stop pulling and make fast').
best bower-anchor	the larger of the two main anchors, in the bows, or a badge of this design.
Billy-tackle	portable tackle, the smallest tackle, two single blocks, or a single and a double, useful for tightening braces, &c.
blue-light	pyrotechnic light with a blue flame, used as a night-signal to summon a pilot.
boom	swinging yard or spar, for extending the foot of a sail; see also 'top your boom'.

435

booms	spars extending over ship's side for making smaller vessels fast.
braces	tackle for controlling the yards (spars) on which sails are set.
breast-hook	V-shaped wood or metal construction connecting timbers at vessel's stem.
bridle-port	aperture in the bulwarks aft, for running out cable or hawser.
bunt	middle part of the head of a sail.
bunt-gasket, bunt-line	small ropes attached to yard, for hauling and securing sail after furling.
Burton	simple kind of hoisting tackle (cf. Billy-tackle).
cable-tier pinch	pinchbar, crowbar, for manipulating lengths of cable in the stowage tiers or racks.
carlins, carlines	short fore-and-aft timbers between transverse beams.
carrick bend	knot for joining hawsers.
chains, fore-chains	see Chapter LXXVI.
clews	fastenings for suspending hammocks.
clew up	truss sails up to yards.
cock-billed	cocked, tilted towards the vertical.
combings, coamings	sill or rim round hatchways to keep water out.
cun (con, conn)	action or post of conning, navigating a vessel by eye.
darbies	handcuffs.
dead-eye	perforated block used in setting up shrouds or stays.
duck	cloth used for light sails or working suits.
fishing a mast, yard, &c.	strengthening or joining with a fish-shaped splicing timber.
Flemish coil	an artistic coiling down of a rope with each coil lying tight against the preceding.

flying-jib	light sail set beyond the jib, the foremost sail of all.
forecastle	the foremost deck-house on a sailing ship; a term used for the seamen's quarters wherever they may be.
fore-peak	foremost compartment under the deck, in the angle of the bows, for storing ropes and gear.
fore-tack ('both fore-tacks over the main-yard')	fore-tacks were ropes for hauling the lower edge of the sail up to the yard at the top: the phrase = 'properly hauled up and fastened'.
fore-truck	circular boss of wood on the foremast, usually fitted with sheaves for flag-halyards.
gaff	spar angled to a mast, on which gaff sails may be set and flags flown.
gammoning	lashing securing a bowsprit in place.
gasket	small rope for securing furled sail to yard.
girt-line	rope on head of lower mast to hoist up the rigging.
guardo	receiving-ship for temporary quartering of enlisted men; 'guardo move'—trick played upon a novice in a receiving-ship.
half-deck	section of deck below the spar- or main-deck, between mainmast and cabins.
halyard	rope for hauling sails, yards, flags, &c.
hawse-hole	hole for cable. 'To come in at the hawse-hole' or 'come up through the hawse-pipe' is to be promoted to officer rank from the crew.
heave and pall (or pawl)	take in cable by heaving the capstan, preventing the latter from running back by engaging a pawl (a metal piece fitting into a toothed rack). A capstan shanty goes 'Heave around the capstan, gain a pawl'.
holder	man working in the hold.

hurrah's nest	scene of confusion; 'a complete "hurrah's nest", as sailors say "everything on top and nothing at hand" ' (Dana, *Two Years Before the Mast*, ch. II).
in stays	going about from one tack to another.
jack-stay	rod or rope along a yard, to which a sail may be fixed.
Jimmy Dux	nickname for a butcher's assistant or galley boy—originally a rating in charge of poultry; more correctly Jimmy Ducks.
kelson	longitudinal timbers strengthening keel and distributing stress.
kid	(1) glove; (2) metal dish for carrying food from the galley.
knees	pieces of wood which have grown with a natural angle, used to connect a ship's beams and timbers.
loblolly-boy	surgeon's mate.
lock-string	string to the lock, the mechanism for exploding the charge of a gun.
luff	bring the ship up into the wind by putting the helm down.
main-royal	royal (light sail above the topgallant sail) on the mainmast, set only in fine weather.
match-tub	tub with perforated cover through which hung the slow-matches for firing cannon.
messenger	rope, wire, or chain for attaching to the anchor-cable in heaving up the anchor: see page 32.
mizzentop	the 'top' (see below) on the mizzenmast, the after mast of a three-masted ship.
moonsail	moon-raker sail carried above the sky-sail (which in a square-rigged ship was usually the highest sail), carried in only a few ships and set only in fine weather.
orlop	lowest deck.

438

Paixhan shot	highly destructive shot, from a particularly formidable piece of naval ordnance named after its French inventor.
palm	leather protecting pad worn on the hand, with a metal plate on it for pushing the head of the needle in sewing canvas.
passing a gammoning	passing the coil of rope used in lashing a bowsprit.
pea-jacket	short coarse cloth coat.
puddinging (or puddening) the dolphin	putting the 'pudding' (fender) against the 'dolphin' (wooden structure in harbour for securing a ship); or, safe-guarding the 'dolphin' with a 'pudding'.
quarter-deck	upper deck between stern and after-mast, where officers have quarters.
reef	one of three or four strips across the top of a square sail that can be fastened up to reduce sail's surface, which is single-, double-, or treble-reefed according to the number of reefs taken in.
reefer	slang for midshipman.
ring-bolt	bolt with ring for fastening rope.
riveted in a clinch	fastened tight (a clinch being the joining of two overlapping strakes [boat's planks] by passing through and clenching a rivet).
royal	square sail, the topmost unless a skysail is carried.
seizing	binding for fastening two ropes securely together.
shakings	odd scraps of yarn, sackings, and canvas, traditionally the mate's perquisites for selling.
sheet-anchor	the largest anchor, the best for holding the ship in an emergency.
sheet-bitts	strong posts to which ropes from sails are secured.
shrouds	set of ropes forming part of standing rigging and securing the mast or topmast.

sinnate (sennit, sennet)	braided or plaited yarn.
slab-line	small rope for trussing sail.
spanker	fore-and-aft sail set on mizzenmast.
spanker outhaul	rope used in hauling out the spanker.
spar-deck	upper deck from bow to stern, in certain types of vessel.
spencer	see 'trysail'.
spinnaker	see 'spanker'.
splice the main-brace	issue a tot of rum to all hands. This was done, supposedly, as rarely as the actual splicing of the main-brace (the tackle for controlling the main-yard)—the main-brace being so important that when needing attention it was renewed rather than spliced.
stay	rope supporting mast or spar; see also 'in stays'.
steady-spit-box-musterer	? regular spittoon orderly. Sailors chewed tobacco, and on vessels which prized their clean decks spittoons were doubtless necessary equipment. Melville may be jocular, however, in ranking their custodians as a regular navy trade.
studding-sail, stun'-sail	narrow sail set in light winds on a small extra yard beyond the outer edges of square sails, to extend the sail area.
tack	make ship go about from one board (side) to another through, i.e. facing, the wind; opposite of 'wear'.
taffrail	rail above bulwarks round the stern of a ship.
thrumming	matting made of small rope yarns.
tierer	man who stows the cable in the tier (the rack for holding anchor-gear, hawsers, &c.).
Tom Coxe's traverse	naval term for antics of a dodger, of the kind mentioned in the text.

top	platform round the head of the lower mast.
topgallant-mast, -sail	mast, sail, next above the topmast or top-sail, which was itself above the lowest mast or sail; the third stage upwards of masts or sails.
topmast, -sail	the second stage upwards of masts or sails.
top-rim (i.e. top-brim)	middle of the foot of a sail.
top your boom	nautical slang; = 'get to work!' 'get moving!'
truck	wooden cap on flagstaff or mast-head.
trysail	small fore-and-aft sail set with a gaff in heavy weather, instead of mainsail or foresail, for steadying the vessel.
Turk's head	ornamental knot resembling a turban.
veerer	man who pays out cable; 'to veer' is the opposite of 'to haul'.
waister	man working in the waist or midships.
wear	make ship go about from one tack to another, stern to wind.
weather lift	lift (rope from mast to suspend the yard-arm end) on the weather side.
yard	horizontal spar across mast.

THE WORLD'S CLASSICS

A Select List

SERGEI AKSAKOV: A Russian Gentleman
Translated by J. D. Duff
Edited by Edward Crankshaw

HANS ANDERSEN: Fairy Tales
Translated by L. W. Kingsland
Introduction by Naomi Lewis
Illustrated by Vilhelm Pedersen and Lorenz Frølich

JANE AUSTEN: Emma
Edited by James Kinsley and David Lodge

Mansfield Park
Edited by James Kinsley and John Lucas

ROBERT BAGE: Hermsprong
Edited by Peter Faulkner

WILLIAM BECKFORD: Vathek
Edited by Roger Lonsdale

CHARLOTTE BRONTË: Jane Eyre
Edited by Margaret Smith

THOMAS CARLYLE: The French Revolution
Edited by K. J. Fielding and David Sorensen

LEWIS CARROLL: Alice's Adventures in Wonderland
and Through the Looking Glass
Edited by Roger Lancelyn Green
Illustrated by John Tenniel

GEOFFREY CHAUCER: The Canterbury Tales
Translated by David Wright

ANTON CHEKHOV: The Russian Master and Other Stories
Translated by Ronald Hingley

JOSEPH CONRAD: Victory
Edited by John Batchelor
Introduction by Tony Tanner

CHARLES DICKENS: Christmas Books
Edited by Ruth Glancy

Dr. Wortle's School
Edited by John Halperin

Orley Farm
Edited by David Skilton

VILLIERS DE L'ISLE-ADAM: Cruel Tales
Translated by Robert Baldick
Edited by A. W. Raitt

VIRGIL: The Aeneid
Translated by C. Day Lewis
Edited by Jasper Griffin

HORACE WALPOLE: The Castle of Otranto
Edited by W. S. Lewis

IZAAK WALTON and CHARLES COTTON:
The Compleat Angler
Edited by John Buxton
Introduction by John Buchan

OSCAR WILDE: Complete Shorter Fiction
Edited by Isobel Murray

The Picture of Dorian Gray
Edited by Isobel Murray

ÉMILE ZOLA:
The Attack on the Mill and other stories
Translated by Douglas Parmeé

A complete list of Oxford Paperbacks, including The World's Classics, OPUS, Past Masters, Oxford Authors, Oxford Shakespeare, and Oxford Paperback Reference, is available in the UK from the Arts and Reference Publicity Department (RS), Oxford University Press, Walton Street, Oxford OX2 6DP.

In the USA, complete lists are available from the Paperbacks Marketing Manager, Oxford University Press, 200 Madison Avenue, New York, NY 10016.

Oxford Paperbacks are available from all good bookshops. In case of difficulty, customers in the UK can order direct from Oxford University Press Bookshop, Freepost, 116 High Street, Oxford, OX1 4BR, enclosing full payment. Please add 10 per cent of published price for postage and packing.